Praise for Jamie Brenner's
Summer Longing

"Jamie Brenner's latest glittering read is her best summer book yet, a combination of page-turning plot and heartfelt human connection that will stay with readers long after the last sunset of the season. With *Summer Longing,* Brenner draws a world of hope and second chances that will leave readers wondering, with newfound optimism, what the next chapter might hold for their own lives."

—Kristy Woodson Harvey, author of *Slightly South of Simple*

"Lots of summer sun warms this light, charming beach read."

—*Kirkus Reviews*

"A baby left on a doorstep begins *Summer Longing,* and the mystery pulls us along by the heartstrings to find out what happens to the endearing, maddening, fascinating families in a dreamy coastal town."

—Nancy Thayer, bestselling author of *Girls of Summer*

"Jamie Brenner's *Summer Longing* is a satisfying beach read. It touches on more serious issues but doesn't dwell and reminds us that this is a summer read best enjoyed in the sunshine with a cool drink and a warm breeze."

—*Confessions of a Book Addict*

Summer
Longing

Summer Longing

Jamie Brenner

BACK BAY BOOKS
Little, Brown and Company
New York   Boston   London

Back Bay Books / Little, Brown and Company
Hachette Book Group
1290 Avenue of the Americas, New York, NY 10104
littlebrown.com

Originally published in hardcover by Little, Brown and Company, May 2020
First Back Bay paperback edition, May 2021

Back Bay Books is an imprint of Little, Brown and Company, a division of Hachette Book Group, Inc. The Back Bay Books name and logo are trademarks of Hachette Book Group, Inc.

The publisher is not responsible for websites (or their content) that are not owned by the publisher.

The Hachette Speakers Bureau provides a wide range of authors for speaking events. To find out more, go to hachettespeakersbureau.com or call (866) 376-6591.

ISBN 978-0-316-47685-0 (hc) / 978-0-316-47684-3 (pb)
LCCN 2019943543

Printing 1, 2021

LSC-C

Printed in the United States of America

Dedicated to my friends in Provincetown. Thank you for sharing your homes and hearts with me.

Summer Longing

Chapter One

She hadn't been on a summer vacation in thirty years. Although, if she really thought about it, a trip didn't count as a vacation if you weren't coming back. Either way, there would be no more meetings, no more deadlines, no more fires to put out. Ruth was free.

She was also anxious. The ferry ride from Boston to Cape Cod was choppier than she'd anticipated. Ruth had planned to pass the hour-and-a-half journey on the upper deck, out in the fresh air. She'd lasted about five minutes; the sun was strong and the speed of the ferry created a lot of wind and, well, she wasn't used to traveling by boat. For the past few months she'd been driving back and forth from Philadelphia while she searched for her summer rental. But now, with everything either packed up and sent to town or already in storage, she didn't need her car. She wanted to experience the journey to Provincetown like a native—by water.

She'd told only a few friends about her decision to sell her business and her house and retire in Provincetown. Her announcement was met with "Isn't there a closer beach?" and "But the winters!" To the latter, she replied, "But the *summers.*" Really, though, why should she have to explain herself at all?

Ruth sensed the ferry was approaching Cape Cod before the shore became visible. The line for the snack bar disappeared, laptops were closed, and suitcases were retrieved from the metal racks. She checked the time; within the hour, she would walk in the front door of the most perfect beach cottage, and her new life would begin.

Ruth closed the novel she had been reading and peered out the water-streaked window of the cabin. The Pilgrim Monument, a two-hundred-and-fifty-foot tower in the center of Provincetown, came into view. The sight of it made her feel almost giddy, like a teenager. This was what she could not fully convey to her friends. The feeling she got in Provincetown was not definable by geography or weather or logic; it was like falling in love.

Next to her, a couple strapped their baby into a stroller. The baby fussed and fussed. Rattles and pacifiers were produced, to no avail. Oh, Ruth was so happy that that high-maintenance phase of life was behind her.

Ahead, she could vaguely make out the small shops lining MacMillan Wharf and, in the far distance, the steeple of the town library. To her right, the long breakwater was covered end to end with double-crested cormorants, standing with their wings spread to dry. Yes, she knew the name of the black birds now. She learned something new every time she visited. Unlike so many small towns, closed and unknowable, Province-town was a place that offered itself to you, unfurling like a beach blanket shaken out in the sun.

How many summers had she been too busy working to enjoy the beautiful weather? She'd spent long weekends in windowless rooms testing products or fixing packaging errors or filling out spreadsheets. For decades, her complexion had been as pale in August as it was in February. Not anymore.

Beside her, the baby began to wail. Okay, perhaps it was time for the deck.

Ruth picked up her suitcase and climbed the stairs to the upper level, gripping the wet, slippery handrail all the way. Outside, she was met with a light spray of water against her cheeks; it was startling at first, but the intake of breath gave her a burst of adrenaline. She leaned over the side railing and took in the vista of sailboats and the bustling seaport, the pier already filled with art merchants and vacationers lined up for whale-watching tours. To her left, twelve-foot black-and-white photos of the town's Portuguese matriarchs greeted her from the sides of boathouses.

The motor quieted as the ferry pulled up to the dock. A crowd gathered on the wharf, and people waved at the boat, eager to greet friends and family.

She had arrived.

Ruth followed the line of people down the metal gangplank to the dock, rolling her suitcase behind her. As her fellow passengers were welcomed with hugs or excitedly shouted names, Ruth turned left and headed toward Commercial Street alone.

The wheels of her suitcase bumped against the uneven wooden boards of the pier walkway. She passed the small buildings that housed crafts shops and offices for whale-watching tours and sunset cruises, maintaining a steady pace. A traffic cop directed the flow of pedestrians and cars heading west. A Cape Cab idled near the curb, and Ruth slid into the back seat.

The taxi driver turned left down one-way Commercial, heading in the opposite direction of her house in the East End. He would have to turn around on Bradford, but she didn't mind the circuitous route. She rolled down the window and looked to her right at Cabot's Candy. On the opposite side of the street was the quirky Marine Specialties store, then the stately red-brick post office. Sights that were becoming more and more familiar with each visit.

Except she was no longer visiting. Today was her first official day as a Provincetown resident. She had hoped, when she originally set her plan in motion, that by the time she had her Philadelphia life packed up, she'd have a permanent new home in Provincetown. But finding a house for sale on the peninsula—just three miles long and two streets wide— had proved to be a challenge.

"Your best bet is to be patient and rent," said Clifford Henry, the real estate agent.

Patience was a skill that Ruth, at age fifty-eight, had yet to master. She was a firm believer in the full-speed-ahead approach. That's how she'd met all of life's challenges, and for the most part, it had paid off. But for now, Provincetown was forcing her to slow down. She would rent for the summer while looking for her forever home.

Although it was difficult to imagine finding anything as perfect as Shell Haven.

The three-story white-shingled Georgian cottage had major curb appeal. It had a wraparound open porch, a pediment roof with a widow's walk, and a front lawn blooming with blue and white hydrangea bushes. Inside, the kitchen had a beautiful built-in hutch, and the master bedroom had a view of the bay. For Ruth, it was love at first sight.

"I'll take it," she'd told Clifford Henry the day he gave her a tour of the rental property. "And for the record, this is exactly the type of house I'm looking to buy."

"You and everyone else, sweetheart," he'd replied.

The cabbie made a right off Bradford onto narrow Bangs Street, then got back onto Commercial. Ruth buzzed with anticipation. One block, and there on the right, the house came into view.

Ruth paid the driver and took a minute on the sidewalk to adjust her handbag and get a good grip on her suitcase before following the red-brick path framed by blue hydrangeas to the porch steps. *You're almost home,* she told herself.

One of the owners of the house, Fern Douglas, had told her she'd leave the house keys in the mailbox. This seemed to Ruth an odd and not entirely safe system, but she realized she needed to learn to go with things a little more. What was the point of moving to a place like Provincetown if she couldn't relax there?

The narrow black metal mailbox was affixed to the side of the house. Ruth rested her bag on a bench and reached inside. Her hand met only empty space.

She bent down and peered inside. No key.

You've got to be kidding me. Suddenly exhausted, she walked up to the front door to see if Fern had simply left it unlocked. No.

Ruth rang the bell. Had she somehow mixed things up? But no, of course not. She was right on time on the date they'd agreed she would move in. She rummaged through her bag, dug out her phone, and dialed Fern Douglas. The call went straight to voice mail.

So unprofessional!

She hesitated only a few seconds before knocking on the doorframe. The door behind the screen cracked open.

"Ms. Cooperman?" a woman asked. She looked to be in her late thirties and had green eyes and strawberry-blond hair that skimmed her shoulders. She was not Fern Douglas.

"Yes," Ruth said, striking a note somewhere between cheery and extremely put out. "Is Fern Douglas here? The keys were supposed to be in the mailbox—"

"Yes, apologies. The move-in date has been delayed a night. You have a reservation at the Beach Rose Inn," the woman said.

What? "I need to speak to Fern. Is she here?"

"No," the woman said.

"Can you reach her for me? Or tell me where to find her?"

"No," the woman repeated. "But I can give you directions to the inn."

Chapter Two

Elise Douglas liked to think of herself as a team player. She knew that in marriage, this was an essential trait. And if anyone had asked her on that late-spring morning what the most important thing in her life was, she would have said, without hesitation, her marriage.

The problem was that if someone had asked what the second most important thing in her life was, she might have said her home. It had taken a lot of time and luck to find Shell Haven, a glorious eighteenth-century house. Three years into their life in Provincetown, the two of them had moved in and devoted themselves to lovingly restoring it. It had been intended as the place to start their family. Now, two summers later, they were moving out.

"It's temporary," Fern had reminded her.

"It's for the entire season."

"A minor inconvenience, considering how much our tenant is paying."

Fern was right, of course. She had a way of being maddeningly practical no matter the situation. For Elise, renting out the house felt like a personal loss, like they were giving away a piece of their lives for the summer. For Fern, it was just business.

When Fern had her mind set on something, it was very difficult to argue with her. And that's why, for the past few months, ever since the house-renting plan had been put in motion, Elise had simply pushed it to the back of her mind. She didn't think about it at all, pretended it was not happening.

But now it was move-out day.

They were supposed to have left the previous day, ensuring that the house was in pristine condition for their summer tenant. But Elise had begged Fern for one more night under their own roof, and Fern acquiesced. They slept in the guest room and woke up early to change the sheets and pack any last-minute things they might have forgotten. It had been, Elise had to admit, a true indulgence on Fern's part. It was, Elise had to admit, *Fern* being a team player.

Elise knew she had to let go. But earlier that morning, watching Fern retrieve their spare set of house keys and leave them in the mailbox for their tenant, something in her snapped. In the past year, she'd given up so much. Too much. She did not want to give up her house too.

And so, after Fern left for work, Elise opened the door and walked out onto the porch. She blinked for a moment in the sunlight, hesitated for just a few seconds, and then reached inside the black metal mailbox just outside the door. She felt around until her fingers touched the house keys, pulled them out, and dropped them into the pocket of her robe.

What she'd done next, well—she wasn't proud of it. She realized, as she walked to the tea shop to join Fern, that she had perhaps crossed a line by displacing their tenant. But there was nothing she could do about it now, and she was already late for work.

She climbed the front steps of the two-story Colonial in the middle of Commercial Street that housed Tea by the Sea. Their shop had been open for business for exactly one week.

Elise had dreamed about owning a tea shop for over a decade. In her twenties she'd waited tables at Boston Seaport restaurants, one of which offered a small selection of specialty teas. It was the first time Elise understood that Lipton didn't define tea any more than Folger's defined coffee. She broke up the long hours on her feet with tea breaks between shifts. Tea forced her to slow down, be mindful. She learned about velvety white tea, the earthiness of green teas, the complex flavors of oolong.

The dream of owning her own shop was fanciful, and she'd never imagined it would become a reality. And then Fern made it happen.

The shop was all white walls with ceiling fans, tin ceiling tiles, rows of shelves with the shop's own brand of artisanal tea, and, in the back of the store, a long white counter. On one side, two big chairs were arranged in front of the large picture windows with unobstructed views of the bay. And everywhere, the aroma of fruity tea leaves.

Looking at the beautiful space they'd created, she realized how badly she'd behaved with the house. She could practically feel the keys burning in her pocket.

She had been impulsive and now she had to fix it. She had to confess to Fern.

But Fern was busy. She was sitting across the room in front of the window with a notepad, interviewing yet another applicant for their part-time position. The young woman was very dressed up for an afternoon in P'town, even for a job interview. She wore a pastel print skirt and matching ballerina flats.

It was that time of year; a tide of young people swept into town for the summer, and enough of them were looking for jobs that small businesses and restaurants could staff up after the long, DIY winter. Fern had interviewed almost a dozen late-teen or twenty-something women in the past two weeks. She'd offered the position to a few but lost them to restaurants, where they would earn higher tips.

Fern stood up and shook the applicant's hand; the young woman left with a shy smile at Elise.

"How did that go?" Elise said. "She looks familiar."

"We met her last summer when we were selling at the farmers' market. Her name's Cynthia. Family lives in Chatham but she wants to spend the summer here. She seemed unconcerned about tips as long as we can give her enough hours." She looked up at Elise and smiled. "We'll see."

Fern climbed on a chair and reached above the front counter to write the iced tea of the day on the chalkboard: *Chai Tide.* It was a blend of black tea and spices like cardamom, cinnamon, fennel, ginger, black pepper, and cloves.

"I thought we were going to do the ginger peach for the iced today," Elise said.

"We're low on that," said Fern.

"Listen, I need to tell you something," she said, walking to the counter. She climbed up to stand on it so she was level with Fern perched on the chair. She took the chalk from her hand and drew a big heart on the chalkboard. "I love you."

Fern smiled. "I love you too. Now erase that so I have space for the menu."

"Look, I really tried to be ready to hand over the house today. But I still feel like I need more time. It's a big adjustment. So I did something that—"

"Elise, I know it's been a rough year. But try to be positive. Look at this beautiful place we have. Please—let this be enough."

Elise nodded, swallowing hard. She turned back to the chalkboard and, with one sweep of her palm, erased the heart. Before she could say another word, the front door's bells tinkled, announcing the arrival of their real estate agent, Clifford Henry. Clifford was a youthful forty-something with bright blue eyes and heavily highlighted brown hair that he wore slicked back.

Clifford Henry, who'd brokered the rental to Ruth Cooperman.

Elise began to perspire.

"My tea divas! What is that divine smell?"

"That's our Strawberry Meadows, a green sencha tea with bits of dried strawberry in it," Fern said. "Would you like a cup?"

"Of course! Iced, please. But ladies, we have a problem, do we not?"

"What problem?" Fern said, stepping down from the chair.

"I just got an earful from Ruth Cooperman," Clifford said. "She's at the inn waiting for me to straighten things out. So let's do that, shall we?"

Fern turned to Elise. Clifford looked at Elise.

Elise climbed down from the counter, removed the keys from her pocket, and slid them over to Clifford.

Ruth carried her suitcase up yet another set of front steps to yet another porch, aware on some level that the Beach Rose Inn—a three-story gray-shingled house with wide steps leading to a wraparound veranda—was quite charming. But *she was in no mood.*

Her real estate agent had not, by her estimation, been sufficiently outraged by this turn of events.

"I'm sure this is just a misunderstanding," he'd said when she'd shown up at his office. "It's the start of the season and things can be…glitchy. It's nothing to be upset about. I'll take care of it."

Considering what she was paying for the house, she certainly hoped so.

She opened the front door of the inn and almost tripped over a sleeping chocolate Lab. Across the room, a barefoot young woman stood on a step stool, hanging a mosaic-framed mirror on the wall.

"Rach, that's too high," said a man standing near her.

The woman turned around with a toss of her long, golden-brown hair. She reached her hand down to the man, and he passed her a nail.

"No, it's not. It's eye level," she said.

"In what universe is that eye level? You're standing on a stool."

The woman noticed Ruth. "Oh, hello there. Can I help you?" she asked, stepping off the stool.

Ruth, completely worn out, let go of her suitcase and sank onto a cushioned ottoman. The lobby was warm and welcoming, with white walls and woodwork, framed black-and-white prints of historical Provincetown, pale gray couches flanking a white wicker table. Ruth appreciated the decorative accents of antique copper candlesticks, glass bowls filled with seashells, a wide bookshelf with well-worn hardcovers and warped paperbacks. But the most arresting aspect of the space were the mosaics, some made of tile, others made of stone and shells. One wall featured a large stained-glass starfish. Spectacular. "I was told to ask for Amelia," she said.

The woman and man exchanged a look.

"I'm Rachel Duncan," the woman said. "Amelia's granddaughter. She didn't tell me we had a guest checking in today, but come on in. This is my husband, Luke."

The man had taken her place hanging the mosaic. He climbed down, smiling warmly at Ruth. He looked to be in his midthirties and had sandy-brown hair and bright green-blue eyes.

"Luke Duncan," he said, shaking her hand. "Nice to meet you."

"Yes, well, I'm not staying here," Ruth said. "There was just a misunderstanding at my house."

Again, the woman and her husband exchanged a look.

"You should probably talk to—" Rachel said.

"I'm here, I'm here," a voice called from somewhere. And then an old woman entered—a very old woman. She walked briskly toward Ruth. She had long white hair and creased skin and wore a green-and-purple-batik sundress. She smiled at Ruth; her eyes were dark with a twinkle of mischief. "You must be Ruth. I'm Amelia."

"I was just explaining this is a misunderstanding."

"Yes, yes, it will all be straightened out," Amelia said. "In the meantime, I was just putting out a bite to eat."

Ruth, accepting the fact that she had completely lost control of the day, followed Amelia to the backyard. Really, she shouldn't have been surprised by the odd turn of events. Provincetown was nothing if not quirky. Yes, it was the place where the Pilgrims had first landed. But it was also a haven for the artistic and the downright eccentric. Over the decades, Provincetown had developed its own unique rhythm, its own code. It was peaceful and welcoming, and at the same time, there was always the sense that anything could happen.

The bay stretched out before them, sun-dappled, dotted with distant sailboats. The backyard, with a long wooden table in the center, extended to the edge of the beach. The table was set with a pitcher of iced tea, a coffeepot, several small tins, a few coffee mugs, an assortment of glasses in pale translucent colors, and a bread basket.

Ruth, too hungry to politely hesitate, sat facing the water and poured herself coffee. Amelia passed her the bread basket, its contents enclosed in a folded cloth napkin. Ruth unwrapped it to find a round yellow loaf, half of it sliced into thick pieces.

"Broa," Amelia said. "Portuguese corn bread. There's butter and jam in those tins but I honestly don't think it needs a thing."

Ruth reached for the bread and took a bite. It was rich and buttery but not too sweet. "I appreciate your hospitality, but I'm not staying," Ruth said. "I'm supposed to move into my summer rental today. Well, technically I already moved in. I sent my things and I was going to get the keys this morning, but there was a delay. I'm just waiting for my real estate agent to sort it out."

"Fern and Elise's place. I heard. It's a lovely home."

"There you are," a man called from the back porch. He walked toward them holding a large blue cooler. Ruth found herself straightening in her seat. He had thick dark hair, chiseled features, and dramatic dark eyes. He looked to be about thirty. "As requested, two dozen oysters fresh off the water."

"Marco, you're a lifesaver," Amelia said.

"Anytime." The man kissed Amelia on the cheek and set down the cooler. "Marco Barros," he said, holding out his hand.

Ruth shook it, trying not to beam like a teenager. "Ruth Cooperman."

"She's renting Fern and Elise's place for the summer," Amelia said.

"Nice to meet you. I have to run, Amelia. My father just helped me pull a bunch of cages and you wouldn't believe the condition they're in."

"Rough spring?"

"Not ideal. But I'm managing."

"I'm sure you're more than managing. Tell your mother I said hi."

When he was gone, Amelia said, "Marco's family runs the boatyard. A few years ago he started an oyster farm. His sister just finished her first year at Princeton. Good kids."

Ruth nodded.

"Do you have children?"

Momentarily thrown by the question, Ruth looked down at her coffee mug, turned it in her hands. "I do. A daughter. Olivia."

"Will she be visiting this summer?"

"No, she will not." She didn't have the heart to tell the woman that the last time she had spoken to her daughter was months ago, and that had been just a perfunctory conversation. Her daughter did not even know she'd moved to Provincetown.

Ruth's phone buzzed with a text from Clifford. I'm bringing over your keys. Meet me at Shell Haven.

Well, there was no time for sentimentality. Or further conversation. She pushed the bench out from the table and stood up to leave.

She had a house to move into.

Chapter Three

Olivia Cooperman pushed through the heavy doors of the Tribeca art deco office building just after eight o'clock in the morning. She swiped her ID card in the turnstile and smiled at the security guard.

For the past eight years she'd spent more time at 32 Sixth Avenue than in her own apartment. She still got a thrill out of the commanding lobby with the tiled map of the world, the mosaic ceilings, the bustle of all the people coming from and going to the twenty-seven floors filled with businesses ranging from radio stations to fashion labels to PR firms. Olivia was headed to the twenty-second floor, home to HotFeed, one of the biggest celebrity social media–management companies in the country. Olivia oversaw a team of twenty people running the accounts of movie stars, athletes, reality-TV stars, and musicians.

Last week HotFeed had won the business of a breakout star from a Netflix show. The actress, barely out of her teens, had appeared at the office for one meeting with her army of publicists and agents. Now Olivia and her colleagues were waiting to see which HotFeed account manager would get to take the reins of the plum account.

Olivia wanted the assignment. Badly.

At thirty years old, while many of her friends were planning weddings, moving to the suburbs, and having babies, Olivia devoted herself to work.

"You can have a personal life *and* a professional life, you know," a friend had told her recently over drinks. A friend with a newly acquired diamond on her left ring finger.

"I think the myth that you can have it all has been debunked," Olivia replied. The myth had certainly been disproven in her own life experience. The most recent casualty of her demanding career: her two-year relationship with a banker named Ian Brooks. Just last week, he'd broken up with her in the middle of dinner at Blue Hill.

"I hope you and your phone will be very happy together," he'd said before he walked out.

The impossibility of a work-life balance had been painfully clear to her from the time she was a child. She'd always resented her mother's preoccupation with her business. Ruth Cooperman had spent long days at the office; she'd never made it to any of Olivia's school plays or baked for a single fund-raiser. She hadn't even given a thought to dinner half the time. Her father had managed all that. Olivia had promised herself that if she had an intense career, she wouldn't make the mistake of adding a child to the mix. For Olivia, it wasn't just career *first*. It was career *only*.

She'd thought she'd made that clear to Ian from the start.

"Good morning, Dakota," she said to her assistant, who was already settled in her cubicle outside of Olivia's glass-walled office. Olivia had hired Dakota just over a year ago, fresh out of NYU. Dakota had a communications degree, a tattoo of Dorothy Parker on her left shoulder, and the ability to produce endlessly creative hashtags.

"Hey," Dakota said, biting on the end of a pen. "There's a delivery there for you."

Olivia had already spotted it, a long rectangular vase filled with exotic flowers twisted into a train of petals that seemed to float on the surface. She began humming softly to herself, some pop song she'd listened to during the subway ride to the office. It could only be congratulations from someone. Someone who knew she'd landed the account. Or, more likely, the person who had granted her the account.

It was happening. Her hard work, the sacrifice of her personal life, was paying off. It didn't matter what other people thought.

She closed her office door and smiled as she opened the small white envelope.

No hard feelings, xoxo Jessica

What? She looked through the walls of her glass office to the cubicles just outside. There, next to Dakota, was another assistant, Jessica. Jessica was young, Jessica was cool, Jessica was...getting the new account?

Heart pounding, Olivia texted her assistant. Can you come in here, please?

Dakota scurried in carrying a razor-thin company-issued laptop and her phone.

"Close the door," Olivia said. "What have you heard about Jessica?"

"She got a promotion. And the new account," Dakota said. "I thought you knew."

Olivia shook her head. "This doesn't make any sense," she muttered.

"I mean, it kind of does," said Dakota.

"How do you figure?" Olivia asked, her mouth dry. She'd put eight years into this company; Jessica had been there eighteen months.

"Well," Dakota said casually, as if pointing out the obvious, "she does have the biggest Instagram following in the entire office."

"Right," Olivia said, her mind racing. *It's okay,* she told herself. *You've got this.* The only answer to work problems was to work harder.

* * *

Elise and Fern closed the shop at six and, exhausted, retired upstairs for an early night.

The studio apartment above the tea shop had needed a lot of work. While the storefront had come with beautiful moldings and a filigree ceiling, the living quarters on the second floor had fallen into disrepair. Over the winter, a contractor had updated the electrical wiring and plumbing, plastered the walls, and stripped the floors. But the bedroom furniture had arrived just days ago.

Their first night in their summer accommodations, both Elise and Fern shifted uncomfortably in the unfamiliar bed.

Elise closed the book of essays and placed it on her nightstand alongside the blue candle she had bought to match the walls, which were painted a shade called Sapphireberry. At the shop, she'd been told the candle was for healing, forgiveness, fidelity, happiness, and opening lines of communication.

It's going to take a lot more than a candle tonight, Elise thought.

She lit the candle.

Next to her, Fern paged through a short-story collection. Elise knew neither one of them could absorb a word of any book. They hadn't spoken since midafternoon.

"Do you think this blue is too blue?" Elise said, to break the ice. She had selected the bright color herself, and Fern, who usually had a more conservative eye for interior design, had not protested. In an attempt to overcome Elise's reluctance about renting out the house for the summer, Fern had given Elise a lot of leeway in decorating their new living quarters.

Fern closed her book and looked at her. "Are we going to talk about what happened today?"

Elise sighed. "I'm sorry. I've said I'm sorry a million times. It was a temporary freak-out." She reached for Fern's hand and Fern didn't pull away. That was a good sign.

"We have a contract with our tenant. This is business," Fern said. "What you did today undermined everything we'd agreed on."

Elise nodded. Starting Tea by the Sea was a risk financially, and renting out the house for extra income was insurance. They were already renting the building Tea by the Sea was in and working long hours there. It made perfect business sense to give up the house for the summer.

Except Shell Haven was not business. It was personal. It had never been just a house. It was their first step toward starting a family.

Their decision to move to Provincetown was not based on the natural beauty of the place or the fact that Provincetown was one of the country's oldest artists' colonies. It wasn't that it had two bookstores within a mile of each other and a magnificent library in between. It wasn't that Commercial Street had only one traffic light (if you didn't count the flashing light where Commercial and Bradford merged). It wasn't the literary festival or the film festival or the wildlife sanctuary or the lobster rolls at the Canteen.

It was that they could live their life together without anyone raising an eyebrow. Ever.

But while they succeeded in finding their dream home, one thing had not come easily. Their first attempt at IVF failed. Their second attempt worked but ended in a miscarriage, as did their third.

Their fertility doctor, a specialist in Boston named Dr. Sparrow who was as tiny and birdlike as her name, tried to keep their attitudes positive. Elise clung to her words of encouragement like gospel. Still, it didn't happen for them.

Frayed from the hormonal roller coaster, Elise barely recognized herself. She felt betrayed by her body for failing to carry the pregnancy to term. As for her relationship with Fern, it became less like a love affair and more like a business partnership struggling to get a failing endeavor off the ground. They were miserable.

"Enough," Fern finally said after the second miscarriage.

"We can take a break," Elise agreed.

"No," Fern said. "Not a break. I'm done."

She didn't even want to try anymore. At first, her decisiveness was a relief. Elise was too emotionally exhausted to make rational decisions.

After a few months, when her head cleared a little, Elise thought maybe Fern could try to carry their child.

"Elise, I meant what I said. We can't keep going down this road. Financially, physically—it's not healthy. We gave it a shot, it didn't work, and we need to be happy with what we have. Each other."

"But we always planned to be parents," Elise said.

"It's out of our control."

"You're just giving up! What about what I want?"

But Fern wouldn't hear another word about it. The last conversation had been over Valentine's dinner at Napi's Restaurant; they'd ended the evening with an argument and went to bed without speaking. There was a time when it seemed they might break up over it. But they'd gotten past it. Now there they were, sleeping in their new bedroom above the tea shop. Surrounded by bright blue walls.

"I'm sorry," Elise said again.

Fern hugged her. "For the record, I like the paint color. How can you go wrong with something called Sapphireberry? In fact, if we get a dog, I'm voting for that name."

Getting a dog had also been explored last year. Another consolation prize.

Stay positive, Elise told herself. She leaned over and blew out the candle on her nightstand. "You know what I was thinking we need for this room?" she said. "We should buy a mosaic from Amelia." See? She was invested in the new space. She was contributing ideas. She was on board.

Fern smiled. "I have a better idea. You can take her class and make one of your own. It might be a good hobby for you."

Amelia Cabral taught mosaic-making out of the art studio on the third floor of the Beach Rose Inn, classes she'd started three years earlier, shortly after she'd been widowed.

Yes, Elise would busy herself with the tea shop and maybe take a mosaic class. She would decorate and embrace her new temporary living quarters. She would move forward, not looking at what she'd left behind.

She would do it for Fern.

Chapter Four

For her first night at Shell Haven, Ruth slept with the curtains open. She wanted to greet the day with a view of the water.

At dawn, she pulled on her robe and walked to the window. The sky was cerulean, and the houses across the street appeared to be lit by a pale pink glow. She had long remembered this about Provincetown, the spectacular, almost otherworldly light.

Despite the scenery, Ruth could not stand still for long. Always in motion—her blessing and her curse. She headed down to the kitchen.

Yesterday, following her very bumpy arrival, she'd managed to stock the kitchen with essentials (of which coffee was at the top of the list) and unpack a few of the boxes that she'd sent ahead.

The house was in a prime location with gorgeous views, but the kitchen had sealed the deal for her. It had a French Country feeling, with long shelves of unfinished wood filled with mismatched bowls, white subway tiles on the floor, a white hutch displaying a collection of tin plates, glass-fronted cabinets, and a rustic wood table that could seat six to eight. Clifford Henry told her it had been made by an artisan in Provence. The wide windows overlooking the back patio and the garden were clearly a modern addition.

Ruth made her coffee, then sat at the table and contemplated the day ahead of her. Six months after selling her company, she still felt the occasional moment of panic at the seemingly endless stretch of free time ahead of her. *Think positive,* she told herself. Retirement wasn't an ending. It was a beginning!

And yet, last winter, she'd been reminded that it wasn't that simple. Her newfound leisure time became a minefield when she decided to go for a manicure.

It started out fine. Inside the salon she was greeted by a familiar—and gratifying—sight: a wall of narrow white shelves filled with bottle after bottle of the nail polish she'd created thirty years ago, a brand she'd named Liv, after her daughter, Olivia.

When Olivia was small, she'd happily answered to Ruth's nickname for her. As a teenager, she insisted on Ruth using her full name. Now the only trace that remained of Liv the sweet toddler was the label on the bestselling nail polish in the country.

Ruth had scanned the shelves of Liv bottles meticulously arranged by color and shade. She searched through the deep reds, looking for her signature color—the first she'd put on the market—Cherry Hill. She looked and looked, moving farther into the purple shades, thinking it might have been misplaced. No luck.

She asked a technician for help finding the color and was told, "Oh, that's been discontinued."

Discontinued? Impossible. Cherry Hill was a classic. Ruth insisted there had to be some mistake. The woman told her that she was not the first to request the color, and when they'd called their distributor, they'd been told no more bottles would be shipping.

Cherry Hill was the most perfect red, a true red, not too orange, not too pink. It flattered every skin tone. It was a perennial bestseller. But more significant, it was her sentimental favorite. How could the new owners of the company do such a thing?

This discovery accelerated her growing sense that selling the business had been a colossal mistake. She had signed on the dotted line, believing the buyers' promises about an ongoing consultant role—and then never heard from them again.

She tried not to think about it, tried to accept it, but if the new owners would do something like discontinue Cherry Hill, the day might come when her brand, her baby, was unrecognizable. And there was nothing she could do about it.

This was the realization that had sent her looking for something else to put her energy into. She'd turned her attention to the new phase of her life with fresh vigor. And now, six months later, there she was in Provincetown. And yet...

Ruth got up from the table, leaving her coffee, and walked up to the second floor, where there were a few remaining unpacked boxes. She knew that buried somewhere inside one of them were the last remaining bottles of Cherry Hill. It suddenly felt very important for her to find them and make sure they had weathered the move.

Her approach to packing had been as ordered and methodical as her approach to everything in life, so she easily found the box labeled BEAUTY/SUPPLIES. She sliced through the tape.

On top, protected by bubble wrap, was a cosmetics mirror. It was the type sold at any high-end drugstore, with a metal stand and a rotating mirror that was magnified on one side. But this particular model was nearly fifty years old. It had belonged to her mother.

Ruth had vivid memories of her mother sitting in her bedroom in front of her vanity performing the morning ritual of "putting on my face," as she called it. In the 1960s, this entailed making the eyes as big as possible with heavy, winged black eyeliner, pale blue eyeshadow, and false eyelashes topped with gobs of mascara. Ruth would watch with fascination, certain her mother was the most beautiful woman in the world.

Joan Goldberg had been a loving mother but a very unhappy woman. Her life advice to Ruth? "Don't start cooking dinner every night. Then it will always be expected of you."

Her mother received a weekly allowance of ten dollars from her husband; she had to save up to buy things. Ruth decided early on that she would not live like that. She would be financially independent of her husband—if she bothered to get married at all.

And then, when she was just eighteen years old, she met Ben Cooperman. They were engaged one month after his college graduation.

Ruth placed the mirror to the side and continued digging. As expected, she found a small cardboard box, a six-pack of Cherry Hill. She opened it and shook one bottle into her hand. How painfully ironic that the product that had changed her life was the first thing to go. It was like the universe was telling her: *You're really done. There's no looking back.*

And yet here she was, her life packed up in boxes, sitting alone in a beautiful home that was not hers. It was difficult not to look back. At her age, you were left with the results of decades' worth of decisions, large and small.

The doorbell rang. Ruth looked up, startled. She closed the box, brushed the dust off her hands, and descended the stairs to the front hallway. She peeked out the window. No one was there. She unlatched the door and opened it. An infant car seat had been left on the doorstep.

With a sleeping baby inside.

The string of small bells above the Tea by the Sea front door heralded the arrival of customers; this time, it was a family of tourists. The parents gravitated to the shelf of tea tins while the teenage girls stood in front of the window taking selfies with the backdrop of the bay.

Elise breathed deeply as she watched Fern explain their different blends and open a few tins so the customers could experience their aromas. Elise was filled with gratitude—for her marriage and for the wonderful shop, which really was a dream come true. She had to let the other stuff go.

The big decision they had to make at the moment was whether or not to hire part-time help. Elise and Fern vacillated between feeling they could go it alone and wanting the insurance of a third set of hands.

"I think we should offer the job to that Cynthia Wesson woman," Elise said after the family of tourists left, briefly looking up from the tin she was filling with loose-leaf, custom-blended tea. When two ounces of tea had been measured out and dispensed into a tin, Elise labeled it with three stickers—the name of the blend on the front and top, the brewing time and temperature on the bottom—and finished it off with a navy-blue ribbon. It was a time-consuming but wonderfully meditative task. It reminded her of what she enjoyed about tea in the first place, the way it encouraged you to slow down. "She seems genuinely interested in tea and she's been visiting P'town from Chatham her whole life."

The front door's bells chimed again. This time, the arrival was a petite middle-aged woman. She had thick dark hair with a white stripe on one side and blazing black eyes.

"It's the Wicked Witch of the West End," Fern muttered. "When did she get back to town?"

"Be nice!" Elise whispered. Louder, she said, "Hi, Bianca."

The woman squinted up at them. "My sister-in-law told me about this place. I walk up and down the street and there's so much change. And not for the better!"

"Welcome back. At least you were able to escape the cold by spending the winter in Florida. Where are you staying?" Elise asked pleasantly.

"At the boatyard," the woman said. "Since you two got your hands on my daughter's house, where else would I stay?"

Elise and Fern exchanged a look. "Pilar was happy to sell to us, Bianca," Fern said.

When they'd first moved from Boston to Provincetown, finding a single-family house to buy seemed too much to hope for. Very little real estate was on the market, and most of the living quarters for sale were condominiums made from large houses divided up for multiple owners.

That first summer, they'd sublet the bottom floor of a Victorian just off Conant Street and begun the search for a forever home. How bad could sharing a cottage with a few other couples be?

As it turned out, pretty bad. Their upstairs neighbors rolled in from the A-House or the Crown and Anchor in the earliest hours of the morning, blasting music and treading on the hardwood floors like a herd of elephants. The afternoons weren't much quieter.

Fern and Elise found escape by renting a sailboat and mooring from Barros Boatyard. Marco made it easy for them to get set up on the water. His father, Manny Barros, had run the boatyard for fifty years, and he'd taken it over from his own father. Marco had also started an oyster farm on the two-acre grant of intertidal water that his paternal uncle—and godfather—Tito had given him.

Fern and Elise spent so much time at the boatyard that they struck up a friendship with the Barroses. They were invited to the Fourth of July party at their house, then to a few Sunday-night barbecues. They met Manny's wife, Lidia, and his sister, Bianca. And that summer, Bianca Barros's daughter, Pilar, was looking to sell her home.

Fern made a deal with Pilar over oysters and gin on Manny's deck. That's how things happened in Provincetown real estate—through a friend of a friend of a friend. The right place, the right time.

"You got that place for a steal," Bianca said now, glaring at Fern. "And I do mean *steal*."

Fern shook her head. "Can I offer you an iced tea? On the house, of course." She winked at Elise.

"I heard a disturbing rumor I hope you can put to rest. You didn't rent out the house to a summer person, did you?"

Elise and Fern looked at each other. "Yes, we did," Fern said.

"That is an outrage. An affront to me and my family and everything that house has ever stood for. My great-great-great-grandfather built that house!"

"Bianca, with all due respect, it's our house now and there's nothing wrong with renting it out for the summer."

"You would say that—you're barely more than tourists yourselves." She peered up at the menu and clucked with disapproval. "You think you can get away with charging that for an iced tea?" She stormed out.

"See," Fern said with a pointed look at Elise. "That's what happens when you don't let things go. You turn into a Bianca."

"Very funny," Elise said.

The shop phone rang, and she reached for it. "Tea by the Sea, Elise speaking."

"This is Ruth Cooperman. I don't know what's going on here, but I need Fern to come back to the house right away."

"What's the problem?" The last thing Elise wanted to think about was Ruth Cooperman at Shell Haven. She sighed impatiently. "Is the key not working? Sometimes the back door gets stuck in the heat."

"The doors are not the problem. The problem is that someone left a baby on your front porch."

Chapter Five

Ruth had not held a baby in almost thirty years.

Ruth guessed the infant—a girl, judging from her pink knit cap—was about two weeks old. She was small enough that Ruth would have been nervous handling her, and so she didn't. Swaddled in a standard-issue hospital receiving blanket, the baby appeared to be no longer than Ruth's forearm. Ruth left her in the car seat.

Whoever dropped the baby off at the house had also left a diaper bag filled with Pampers, two bottles, a few cans of Enfamil, and a pink carrying sling. Fortunately, she was asleep, and Ruth did not need to use any of the supplies. Fern Douglas would hopefully arrive before that changed.

Ruth took the car seat into the living room. She turned the air-conditioning on and sat on the edge of the couch. Someone had felt comfortable leaving the baby unattended, but Ruth couldn't, in good conscience, leave her alone in the room. Truly, this town might be more than she had bargained for. It was one thing to leave keys in a mailbox. It was quite another to leave a baby on a front porch.

She stood and paced, looking at her phone. Shouldn't Fern be here by now?

The baby stirred. *Oh no—sleep. Sleep!*

Her tiny rosebud mouth was puckering even though her eyes were still closed. And just like that, Ruth recalled her own newborn baby's phantom sucking from long ago, how, even half asleep, her daughter would root around for her breast. It was all so primal, so different from the way everything else could be scheduled and tamed. Ruth had been shocked by it. She'd thought she could manage motherhood the way she'd planned her career; with enough discipline and hard work, things would run smoothly. She could keep it all under control. What no one told her, what perhaps she should have guessed ahead of time, was that becoming a mother was all about letting go of control.

She heard the back door open, then footsteps in the kitchen. Finally!

But it was not Fern Douglas. It was the unpleasant strawberry blonde from yesterday. She rushed into the room, her hair clinging to her forehead and neck in damp tendrils. "I got here as fast as I could," she said, barely glancing at Ruth. Her eyes locked on the car seat. She approached it slowly, almost reverently, and knelt down, peering at the baby.

"And…you are?" Ruth said.

"Elise Douglas. Fern's wife," the woman said. "I'm sorry. We got off to a bad start yesterday."

That was an understatement. But in the spirit of moving things along, Ruth was willing to let bygones be bygones. "Yes, well, there is a more immediate problem at hand. I guess your friend or whoever dropped her off here didn't realize you rented out the house for the summer?" Ruth said. Elise did not respond. It was like Ruth wasn't even in the room.

The baby stirred. Elise reached into the car seat and pulled the small bundle into her arms, murmuring something that Ruth couldn't quite make out.

She shifted impatiently on her feet.

"Okay, well, you should probably...take her back to her house. I don't mean to be rude, but I really would like to get settled," Ruth said.

Elise finally looked at her. "I don't know where to go. I don't know whose baby this is."

What?

The baby began to cry. At first, it was just a squawk, like a bird, but it quickly escalated into a wail. How could such a tiny thing make so much noise? There was something impossible to endure about a baby's cry. As a mother herself, Ruth was hardwired to respond.

"Perhaps you should call Fern and see if she knows. Or, better yet, take her to the tea shop and discuss it there."

Elise shook her head. "I'm sorry, Ms. Cooperman. I have to figure this out, obviously. But I can't take the baby anywhere."

"Well, you can't keep her here."

"What if the person who left her here comes back? Just give me time to sort this out." She looked down at the baby and then back at Ruth. "And please—don't mention this to anyone."

Who would she mention it to? Ruth thought. And why the secrecy? She sighed and looked out the window. It was a gorgeous day.

"I'm going out for a bit," she said. "I expect to return to an empty house."

Olivia could not imagine a worse time to have the flu. She'd never taken a sick day, and now—*bam!* She'd been in bed for three days straight. The optics were bad. It looked like she was sulking over the account she hadn't been awarded.

The truth was, she'd run herself down by working eighteen-hour days to keep her mind off her recent breakup. The irony was that her job was social media, and while doing her best not to think about Ian, she'd stumbled on a photo of one of her very attractive clients at a lavish black-tie fund-raiser—on Ian's arm!

For the past few nights, Olivia had tossed and turned, her body seemingly unable to regulate its temperature. Hot and then cold, she opened and closed her bedroom window as her mind ran around in circles wondering if she'd made a terrible mistake letting her relationship languish. Digging deep, she had to admit that she probably was not in love—had never been in love with anyone. Maybe she was meant to be alone.

That left the worry about work. Now that she had so much time to think, the significance of being passed over for the new account really hit her. If she wasn't getting the big clients, it was only a matter of time before she was phased out.

It was time to leave, to go out on her own.

She'd been preparing for this day, debating whether she should stay with HotFeed and take her chances or start her own company. She would be leaving the security of her steady paycheck and her roster of clients, but she'd put out feelers and knew at least one client would leave with her. April Hollis was a thirty-something reality-TV star turned shoe designer whose every move, purchase, and thought was followed by eighteen million people on social media. When Olivia had met her six years earlier, she'd been a real estate broker in Hoboken spending her days off going to casting calls.

Olivia had already reached out to her.

"Whatever you need, doll," April had said.

Still, the logistics were daunting. At HotFeed, she had a copy writer for the content and a person who created and managed a calendar of posts and made sure the posts went live and were properly tagged. She had someone who scoured the internet, found mentions of clients, and replied to the commenters. And the company had an analytics team to see what content was getting the best results. She would not have all this support as a one-woman operation. It would take time to build her staff. But she would manage in the meantime.

Her doorman buzzed up on the house phone.

"Hello?" The single word triggered a coughing fit.

"Ms. Cooperman? Your father is here."

She should have known he'd show up even though she'd spent the past two days assuring him she was fine. When she was growing up, it had been her father who bandaged a skinned knee, who ministered to summertime bug bites, who counseled her over teenage heartbreak. Her mother was always traveling for work.

She opened her front door and found her father holding two bags from the Second Avenue Deli.

"Dad, really, you didn't have to," she said, overwhelmed by how happy she was not only to see him but to have company. Sure, she had friends in town. But they were people she went out with, networked with, had fun with; they were not people to sit on her couch and watch Netflix with.

"I wish you would find a lasting relationship," he said a few minutes later over their matzo ball soup. "I don't want you to spend your life alone."

"Dad, I wish *you* would meet someone. I don't want you to spend *your* life alone."

Her parents had divorced when she was in middle school. The divorce had been difficult on them both—*both* meaning Olivia and her father. Ruth hadn't seemed to miss a beat. Unlike most of her friends whose parents split up, Olivia ended up living primarily with her father, who kept the house in Cherry Hill, New Jersey, while her mother moved to a condo in Center City, Philadelphia, just across the Ben Franklin Bridge.

Over the years her dad had had a few girlfriends, but nothing stuck. Olivia was afraid that the divorce had left him wary of investing in someone emotionally. How else to explain his persistent single status? Her dad was—her own bias aside—a catch. He was a respected anesthesiologist, had a remarkably full head of silver hair, and kept in shape by playing tennis year-round; his only vice was rich food.

Once again, she tried to push him on this, and once again, he turned it around on her.

"I had my time being married and I have you. What's your excuse?"

"Did you ever consider that I like my freedom?" she said. It was partially true; she liked the excitement of meeting someone, the thrill of the chase or of being chased, that first-night discovery of a man's touch. As far as Olivia was concerned, it was all downhill from there. Clearly, judging from the tenor of her breakups, she wasn't able to give enough. Maybe she never would be.

At a conversational impasse over their personal lives, they finished dinner in easy, companionable silence. Afterward, her father stuffed the empty soup containers and corned beef sandwich wrappers into the empty takeout bags and carried them to the hallway garbage room.

Olivia retrieved a pint of Emack & Bolio's raspberry chip ice cream from the freezer. The two of them curled up on the couch, Olivia on one end, a blanket over her outstretched legs and remote in hand, her father on the other.

"A fine pair we are," she said, smiling at him.

"I'm just happy to see you're on the mend."

She nodded. "I think I'm finally kicking this thing. Definitely going back to work on Monday."

"Getting the flu in May might be a sign you should slow down a little."

"Yeah, that's not going to happen. In fact, I'm planning on leaving the company and starting my own."

As she'd anticipated, her father looked dubious. A physician, Ben Cooperman didn't understand the vagaries of the corporate world. Yes, medicine had its own politics. But her mother was the one she really should talk to about this. Olivia simply had no interest in making that phone call. She prided herself on not needing her mother. She was an independent woman—independent financially and emotionally.

"Are you ready for that?"

She nodded. "More than ready." No need to tell him she felt pushed out the door.

"You're young—you should be enjoying yourself a little. You can't be all work and no play."

"It will be fine," she said confidently.

"Olivia," her father said, patting her leg over the blanket, "I admire your ambition. I'm proud of you. But I have perspective that you don't. Life goes fast. Before you know it…well, I worry that you're going to miss out on the things in life that will make you happy. The things in life that are important. I don't want you to…"

"What, end up alone like my mother? Trust me, I'm nothing like her," she said, reaching for the thermometer.

Just one fever-free day, and she would be back in the office.

Chapter Six

Ruth walked along Commercial, simmering with frustration. She'd thought it was too good to be true that a house as perfect as Shell Haven was available for the summer, and now it was clear she'd been right. The owners had a lot of baggage. Or maybe it would be like this with any place in town. The plus side of Provincetown was that it was quirky and unconventional and people welcomed you with open arms and loose boundaries. The downside of Provincetown was that it was quirky and unconventional and people welcomed you with open arms and loose boundaries. "Sure, I'll just take a walk while you figure out whose baby got dropped on your doorstep," Ruth muttered to herself.

She crossed the street and headed to the bookstore. Commercial Street was three miles long and had two bookstores; as far as Ruth was concerned, that was all you needed to know about this area. Provincetown Bookshop, right in the center of the village, had been around since 1932. Ruth had shopped in the store as a teenager, and a bookseller there had introduced her to Mary Heaton Vorse's Provincetown classic *Time and the Town*. More recently, East End Books had opened its doors, and thanks to the passionate efforts of its book- and film-loving owner, it offered a year-round calendar of author events. During her last trip to town, she had seen Pulitzer Prize–winning author Michael Cunningham doing a reading. Ruth made a mental note to attend more book events; she hadn't moved to a lively, artistic town to be a shut-in.

"Ruth! Ruth Cooperman!"

She looked across the street to see her real estate agent, Clifford Henry, waving at her.

"There she is!" he said. "The house huntress."

Clifford was dressed in a pink button-down and white slacks. Beside him was a handsome, slightly younger man with dark olive skin wearing a black T-shirt and jeans. Clifford motioned her over.

"How fun to spot you out in the wild like this," Clifford said with a wink. "Ruth, this is my husband, Santiago."

"Nice to meet you," Ruth said, shaking the man's hand.

"What are you up to? A little shopping? Late brunch?"

"Oh, I'm just…" *Displaced from my house. Again.* "Getting some fresh air."

"You know Liv Cosmetics?" Clifford said to Santiago. "That's Ruth's company. She started it."

"Well, it's not mine anymore," Ruth said.

Still, Santiago looked impressed.

"Have lunch with us," Clifford said. "We're going to Napi's. We did a two-hour bike ride so we're starving."

"Oh, I don't know—"

"I won't take no for an answer. We want to hear all your glamorous stories about the beauty industry."

Well, why not? Ruth thought. All she had left were stories.

* * *

For Elise, time had stopped.

The baby, calm after a bottle and a successful burping, nestled in the crook of her arm. Her eyes, open and surprisingly alert, were gray and seemed to fix on Elise.

"Who are you, little one?" Elise whispered, dipping her head low, inhaling the sweet, unmistakable milky scent particular to babies.

She wished she could stay like this forever. Just holding the baby, not thinking about the reality beyond the walls of Shell Haven. But her phone had been ringing on and off for a while, and she knew she couldn't ignore it much longer. Fern had to be wondering where she'd run off to.

But this baby.

Elise had been imagining the possibilities since the moment Ruth Cooperman called the shop and uttered the magical sentence *Someone left a baby on your front porch.*

The first scenario was that someone had intended Fern or Elise to find the baby—someone who didn't know they had moved out for the summer. The second was that it was a mistake, that someone had left the infant at the wrong house. But who left a baby unattended on a porch no matter whose home it was? So if it was the right house, or even just a random house, the baby had been left on purpose by someone who couldn't care for her. But who? And if that was the case, why not leave her at the firehouse or the police station? Those were safe-haven locations—no questions would be asked. But then the baby would become a ward of the state. Maybe whoever left this child on their porch didn't want that to happen. Which brought Elise back to the idea that whoever had left the baby at Shell Haven had not done it by mistake— she had been left specifically for Elise and Fern.

The only clue to her origins was a beaded elastic bracelet Elise had discovered around the baby's right ankle. The beads were all pink except for four white beads with black print that read MAY 6. Her birth date? Elise slipped the anklet off the baby and placed it in the diaper bag with the rest of her things. She knew the baby couldn't reach down and pull it off herself, that it wasn't truly a choking hazard, and yet it made her nervous.

Her phone rang again. Elise stood slowly, cradling the baby and keeping her eyes on her, smiling, even as she crossed the room for her handbag. She knelt down and rooted around for her phone. Four missed calls, and Fern was calling now.

"Hello?" she said, bracing herself for Fern's irritation.

"Where are you?"

Elise had left the shop after saying she had to run a quick errand. That had been hours ago. "Shell Haven. Ruth called and needed help with something."

She heard Fern sigh. "I've been calling and calling you. When are you coming back to the shop?"

"Actually, I need you to come to the house."

"Is something wrong?"

Elise hesitated. "No. Not exactly. I'm sorry to be cryptic, but I'd rather talk in person."

On the other end of the phone, Fern was silent. Elise knew Fern wanted to ask her if this could wait until later, maybe tell her to just come back to work. Their typical yin and yang—Elise the flighty one, Fern the practical one.

"I'll be right there," Fern finally said.

Their relationship dynamic had, in some ways, been set from the moment they met. It was fate that had brought them together, but it had also been a classic example of Elise being careless and Fern being a caretaker.

They'd met eight years earlier. Elise had been in her twenties and waitressing at a restaurant by the Boston Seaport. It was not a great time. Her mother was pushing and pushing her to "figure out" her life. Translation: Meet a man and get married. Elise had not yet found the nerve to tell her conservative parents that she had no interest in men. That there would be no husband, no country-club wedding, and maybe—though she hoped this wouldn't be the case— no grandchildren.

Losing patience, her mother had quietly begun tapping her friends for introductions to sons and friends of sons. Elise made every excuse she could to get out of the setups, usually claiming work.

"Waiting tables is not a priority," her father said one night. "If money's an issue, we'll help you out. But your mother is right—you need to think about the future. Don't you want a family someday?"

Hoping to placate them for a while, Elise agreed to have dinner with the son of one of her father's law partners one spring evening. He took her to Eastern Standard, and the fact that he was attractive and nice and a good conversationalist made Elise feel that much worse. She spent most of the appetizer course wishing she were someone else, wishing she could be the person her parents wanted or believed her to be. She was so rattled that when their main course was served, she sliced her finger with her steak knife.

She covered it with a cloth napkin and, cheeks burning with embarrassment, hurried to the ladies' room to deal with the bleeding. Standing at the sink, holding her finger under running water, she silently cursed herself for being stupid enough to agree to the date.

"You should wrap something around that," a woman said from the sink next to hers. "Keep pressure on it."

Elise glanced over, and for a minute, her disastrous date, her failure as a daughter, her throbbing bloody finger—all of it receded. The woman looked at her with concerned, beautiful brown eyes. Her face was defined by prominent cheekbones; her long hair was in thin braids.

"Let me take a look at that," the woman said, her voice like velvet. She reached for Elise's hand. "I used to be a paramedic."

"Are you a doctor now?"

"No," the woman said. She smelled like vanilla and honey. "I'm an investment banker. But I have a good memory. And I can tell you, hon, you need stitches."

Elise realized in that moment that her father was right; she did, in fact, need to get her priorities straight.

"Can you give me a ride to the emergency room?" Elise said.

Two months later, she admitted to her parents that she was in love with a woman, an investment banker two years her senior named Fern Douglas. Her parents did not take the news well, and their attitude plummeted further when they found out Fern was Jamaican.

Elise had not spoken to her parents in a few years now.

Being part of a lesbian, biracial couple brought with it a lot of baggage. There had been many external conflicts, but none from within. Not until last year. Still, it seemed, finally, they had gotten back on track, partly thanks to the tea shop, and partly thanks to Elise letting go of the idea of having a baby.

And now this.

The baby squirmed in her arms. Elise stood up and paced the room, rocking her gently. She did not want Fern to walk in to a crying baby. She wanted Fern to experience the baby as she had—like walking into a dream. Like something that had fallen from heaven.

"I need you to work with me here," Elise said, kissing her forehead. "Shhh."

The tiny eyelids fluttered and then closed. Elise considered trying to place her back in the car seat but she didn't dare disturb the moment of calm.

"Hello?" Fern called from the kitchen.

Elise took a deep breath as she walked briskly from the living room to meet her. Fern had a navy-blue and white Tea by the Sea canvas bag over her shoulder—they'd ordered a few dozen of them to give away and sell at the shop—and a plastic cup filled with iced tea in one hand. It dripped with condensation, and Fern put it down and started wiping the floor as Elise walked into the room.

"Hey," Elise said.

Fern glanced up, tossed the paper towel in the garbage, and said, "Is Ruth here?"

"No," Elise said. "She's out."

Fern was looking at her but not really seeing her. It took a few moments before the baby registered. Elise knew the second it happened, because Fern's lips formed a silent O.

"Whose baby is that?" she said, standing up.

"I don't know."

Fern crossed her arms. "Elise, I'm in no mood for games. Does Ruth Cooperman have family in town?"

"This is not Ruth Cooperman's baby. Ruth called the shop to tell me someone had left this baby on the porch. I ran over here to see what was going on."

Fern stepped closer, peered down at the baby. "It's a newborn."

"A few weeks old, yeah."

"Someone left this baby on the porch? Hours ago?"

"That's right," said Elise.

"Did you call the police?"

Elise swallowed hard. "No."

Fern opened her bag and pulled out her phone.

"Please—don't," Elise said. "Someone could get in trouble. Someone we know."

Fern put down the phone. "What are you talking about?"

"Think about it," Elise said. "It's a small town. Chances are, whoever left the baby here knows us and left her here for a reason. We need to at least consider that. It was maybe an impulsive act. The mother might come back for her. We should wait—at least for one night."

Fern seemed to consider this. "We don't know anyone who was about to have a baby. It doesn't make sense."

Elise's mouth felt dry. Of course it didn't make sense. All she knew was that she didn't want to hand over the baby. Not yet. "Well, you've spent the past week interviewing a dozen young women, some barely out of their teens. One of them might have just had a baby, thought you seemed kind…"

Fern shook her head. "I don't know. Even if that's the case, we need to let the authorities know."

"The authorities? What kind of talk is that? This isn't an 'authorities' type of place. We need to honor that. People in this town take care of one another."

"But you just said yourself it's probably not even someone from this town."

"Well, that person is here now."

"I don't like this, Elise. Not one bit."

"Just one night," Elise said. "We can deal with it in the morning. Please."

Fern, who deep down, despite her efficient, practical, and sometimes even unyielding nature, was a softy at heart, looked down at the sleeping baby, then up at her wife's tear-filled eyes.

"We can't take this baby to the tea shop. People will see us. If the baby cries in the morning, customers will hear it. All we need is someone like Bianca to walk in—"

"So we stay here."

"We can't stay here. This isn't our house this summer."

"Ruth is fine with it," Elise lied. "We can stay in the guest room. And of course, there's the spare room down the hall." The room they'd intended to turn into a nursery.

They exchanged a look, and in that look was three years' worth of shared pain.

"One night," Fern said. "But that's it, Elise. Tomorrow we deal with this."

Napi's Restaurant felt like a secret hideout. It was tucked away on Freeman Street between Commercial and Bradford. If it weren't for the large sign lit with a string of Christmas lights and featuring a giant red arrow to direct people, Ruth might have missed it.

Inside, it was dimly lit and cozy. The dining room had a wood-beam ceiling, brick walls, and a long bar festooned with more Christmas lights and backed by large panels of stained glass. The walls were filled with hundreds of paintings collected by the restaurant's owner, eighty-seven-year-old Napi Van Dereck.

"All by local artists," Clifford told Ruth.

The place was clearly an institution; Napi had been in business since 1975, Clifford told her. He was a walking trivia machine. "Norman Mailer once tried to film a movie here," he said.

A waiter greeted Ruth, Clifford, and Santiago, lit votive candles on the table, and handed out menus. Clifford ordered a bottle of wine.

"It's such a romantic space," Ruth said. "I feel a bit like a third wheel."

"Not at all!" Santiago said. "The more the merrier."

"But just out of curiosity," Clifford said, "is there no Mr. Cooperman?"

She told them she was long divorced.

"You're divorced, not dead, sweetheart. I hate to break it to you, but there isn't exactly a surplus of straight single men in this town."

Ruth reached for her water glass. It was true. On some level, this had to be something that had factored into her decision to move to the town.

Her last serious relationship, with a restaurateur she'd met on a Jet-Blue flight to LA, had ended in disappointment. She'd dated regularly since her divorce, with varying degrees of success. With the restaurateur, she'd thought maybe she had a chance to settle down with someone again, to have something real and lasting. To replace what she'd left behind. In the end, it was another failure.

Sitting in that cozy restaurant across from the happy couple, she realized she had given up on ever again finding romantic love.

"So how's the house working out?" Clifford said.

The house. As tempting as it was to vent to Clifford about the disruption, she remembered Elise's plea that she not mention it to anyone. "The house is great," she said.

"It really is fabulous. Santiago built the patio extension."

"Oh? Well, it's lovely," Ruth said.

"Santiago does a lot of the work on additions around here. And I'll tell you something, Ruth—I've never seen houses rent as quickly as they did this season. If you hadn't come to me in February, you'd be living in Truro right now."

The waiter arrived with their bottle of wine. When it was uncorked and poured, Clifford raised his glass. "To summer."

"To summer," Ruth and Santiago repeated.

She took a sip of the red wine. It was earthy and delicious. She downed the glass, and Clifford refilled it.

Chapter Seven

It had rained overnight, storms that left the windows of Shell Haven beaded with water even as the sun came up. Elise had hoped the rain would last all day, that a storm would rage with such ferocity, she would have an excuse to shelter in place and not take the baby to the police station.

No such luck.

"I can trust you to handle this, right?" Fern whispered, pulling her Tea by the Sea tote over her shoulder. She glanced at the car seat on the kitchen table, the baby asleep inside but starting to stir. "I have to get to the shop."

Elise nodded as she poured a mug full of hot water so she could warm the bottle. She wanted to get the baby outside before she awoke hungry and started crying. Upstairs, Ruth Cooperman was still asleep. Elise had heard her stumble in late. She'd knocked over something in the living room, and Elise could only assume she'd been drinking.

Their tenant had no idea they'd spent the night, and it was probably best to keep it that way.

Fern kissed her on the cheek. "Be strong," she said.

Be strong. Wasn't she always? Elise was tired of being strong. Of taking no for an answer from the universe.

Except this time, it wasn't the universe saying no. This time, the universe had dropped a gift right in her lap. It was her partner saying no.

Elise had hardly slept all night. She and Fern had gone around and around in circles, Elise making the case for keeping the baby, at least for a little while, Fern remaining adamant that they go to the authorities.

"It's been hours. The mother is not coming back," Fern had said. "You gave her a window, and that window is closing tomorrow. We have no right to keep this baby, Elise. And you're too emotional to think clearly about it."

Fern was right about one thing—Elise was emotional. She believed the baby had been given to her for a reason. Fate, divine providence, whatever you wanted to call it—the fact was that it could not be a coincidence that she had been praying for a baby for three years and one had literally arrived on her doorstep.

As for thinking clearly, Elise didn't know why everything had to be figured out right away. What was the rush?

"I need you at the shop," Fern said. "We have a business to get off the ground this summer. Keep your eye on the ball, Elise. We have to do the right thing. The baby belongs with the authorities. Let officials take care of this through the proper channels."

Proper channels. Like this was just another business transaction. She'd broken away from the conversation to feed the baby sometime around ten, and when she returned to the guest bedroom, she'd found Fern snoring softly.

How could she sleep at a time like this? Elise crept down the hall to the spare room they used as an office. She sat in an Aeron chair and held the mystery baby, looking at her tuft of dark hair and her eyes like gray marbles. The baby fussed after her bottle, even after being burped and changed and swaddled. It seemed Elise might never get her back to sleep. She didn't care; she paced the floor for over an hour, holding the baby against her chest, close to her heart.

She stayed awake long after the baby had finally drifted off to sleep.

Commercial Street was packed with delivery trucks, and the sidewalks were full of early-morning joggers. Bicyclists weaved in and out of traffic. No one paid much attention to Elise, a woman walking alone with an infant in a sling. She would have attracted more interest if she'd had a cute French bulldog on a leash instead.

The baby stirred, turning her face from side to side. She made a peep, a primitive sound that prompted Elise to wrap her arms around her little body, even though she was secure in the sling. She felt every cell in her body was becoming attuned to the baby. And as she reached the center of town, halfway to the police station, her stomach churned.

How could she hand this child over to strangers who would put her into some kind of statewide foster-care system? Fern had said Elise wasn't thinking straight, that she was being emotional. But this seemed very clear to her, absolutely black-and-white.

Up ahead, the front porch of the Beach Rose Inn came into view.

Elise gravitated toward it. The voice in her head telling her not to go to the police station was also telling her she needed to talk to someone. Elise might not be objective about this, but neither was Fern.

She knew someone who might be.

She climbed the porch steps, walked inside, closed the front door carefully behind her, and patted the head of Molly the dog, hoping she wouldn't bark.

Rachel Duncan was setting up coffee service.

"Hey there," Rachel said. "Is that a baby?"

"Hi—yeah. I'm babysitting."

"Cool. For anyone I know?"

"Just a friend," Elise said, the words solidifying the tenuous strategy she'd been devising the entire sleepless night. "Is your grandmother around?"

"In the kitchen, as always. Go on back."

Amelia's kitchen—with its pale wood floors, bone-colored cabinets, farmhouse sink, and whisks and ladles hanging from copper piping running along one wall—was warm and quirky, just like Amelia.

"Elise! This is a surprise. What brings you here?" Amelia said, whisking eggs. Her eyes, already focused on the baby, seemed to sharpen.

Elise didn't know where or how to start. Her eyes filled with tears. Amelia did not press. "I happen to have some of that Strawberry Meadows tea of yours. How about I brew some right now for us?"

Elise nodded. And just as Amelia's yellow porcelain teakettle began to whistle, the story came pouring out.

Amelia listened without saying a word. When Elise finished, she said, "You were right to come to me." She brought two steaming mugs to the table.

Relief coursed through Elise like a shot of adrenaline. "What should I do?"

"You can't take this baby to the police. As much as I like Gerry and Brian and the whole crew over there, they won't have jurisdiction over this child. It will go to the state. And this is a Provincetown baby. We take care of our own."

Elise nodded. "That's what I said to Fern. But she said no one in town had had a baby. It had to be a summer person's."

"This place has a long history of people showing up under difficult circumstances to start over or to right a wrong. You and Fern might be washashores, but you've been here long enough to honor the Provincetown way of life." Elise knew Amelia was paying her a compliment. People born in Provincetown were townies; people who moved there were washashores. And no matter how long someone had lived there and no matter how esteemed he or she was, a washashore could never become a townie—not technically. But some of them could in spirit. "We look out for one another, and as a community, we will look out for this baby."

Elise felt weak with relief. "I don't know what to say to Fern. She's going to be furious."

Amelia reached over and patted her hand. "Fern loves you. That's all you need to know."

Elise hoped she was right.

"Now," Amelia said. "On to the practical matters. Come upstairs; I have all the baby gear from when my great-grandson was born. You can latch that car seat onto a stroller bottom, and I have the most adorable bassinet."

She smiled and Elise smiled back. She would allow herself to enjoy this moment—however fleeting it might be.

Chapter Eight

Ruth awoke to the sound of a baby crying.

She reached for the water glass on her bedside table, her head throbbing. Lunch at Napi's had turned into drinks at the A-House, and that had turned into midnight.

Oh, what a mistake! And yet the night had been undeniably fun. It was so easy to sit back and let Clifford do most of the talking. Having lived in Provincetown for thirty years, he was an endless font of colorful stories about the past and juicy gossip about the present.

"Transgression," he'd said, "is a grand Provincetown tradition."

He quoted something that Henry David Thoreau had written about the shores of the Cape: "A man may stand there and put all America behind him." Ruth, in her inebriated state, had confessed, "I've come here to put everything behind me too."

Clifford had reached across the table and patted her hand. "Haven't we all, doll."

Again, the loud squawk of an infant. Ruth sat up and peeked out the window, squinting against the sunlight. Where was that coming from?

And then yesterday's encounter with Elise Douglas came rushing back to her.

Was it possible that Elise and the baby were still here? No. That would be beyond the pale. Absolutely crossing a line.

Ruth pulled on a robe, stepped into her Ugg slippers, and opened her bedroom door. Yes, the noise was undeniably coming from inside the house. She padded down the stairs to the kitchen.

Elise sat at the kitchen table with the crying infant on her lap.

"What are you *doing* here?" Ruth said, incredulous.

"I'm sorry. I don't have anywhere else to take her."

Ruth felt her pulse begin to race. "Elise, I understand that there is some degree of unconventionality in this town. And I respect that, I do. But this is going too far. I paid good money for this house for the summer. You can't just walk in here whenever you feel like it. Frankly, I don't want you even ringing the doorbell to visit. For the next three months, you need to pretend this house doesn't exist. Okay?"

Elise shook her head. "I'm sorry, Ruth. I really am. But this is bigger than the house. It's bigger than whatever money we'd make giving up Shell Haven for the summer."

The woman was clearly losing it. "Elise, I'm not sure what's going on here, but I'm calling Fern."

"No! Please. Don't call Fern. Just…can you sit for a minute? Just…oh God, she won't stop crying."

The baby's face was bright red. The sound was unbearable. Ruth remembered sitting in the kitchen at the house in Cherry Hill holding a wailing Olivia and feeling completely helpless. She'd called her own mother on many occasions, looking for guidance in deciphering the needs of her fussy infant. The words of wisdom, the small fixes, were coming back to her in a rush.

"She must have gas," Ruth said. "You need to change her position. Motion helps sometimes. Here—let me have her."

Ruth lifted the baby, surprised by how light she was. It was easy to forget how small babies were, how utterly helpless. She had forgotten too, that unique baby scent that even now, in her state of irritation, elicited a primal caretaker urge. She stood, placed the baby against her shoulder, and rubbed her back in small circles alternating with firm pats. The crying continued; escalated even. Ruth walked into the living room, paced back and forth. Still no relief. She walked back to the kitchen, where Elise sat looking exhausted and panicked. Ruth kept her hands moving against the tiny back, not letting up the rhythm of rubbing and patting.

"Is this normal?" Elise said, raking her hand through her hair.

And then a burp so cartoonishly loud, they both looked at the baby in surprise.

The crying stopped.

"There you go," Ruth murmured. The baby nestled against the base of her neck. Again, that distinct scent played on her senses. The baby was strange, yet utterly familiar. All Ruth's maternal instincts, muscle memory, kicked in. And yet she had not been able to enjoy the times she held her own daughter. She remembered taking conference calls and typing memos with Olivia strapped across her chest in a sling. How eager she had been to hire a nanny and get back to work. She'd prided herself on not missing a beat but later realized she had not appreciated that first year of babyhood. And she could never get it back.

"I should put her down to sleep," Elise said, standing and reaching for the baby.

Ruth handed her over. "Okay, but where are you—"

"I'm just going to put her in the spare room on the second floor. I have a bassinet."

She swept out of the kitchen before Ruth could effectively protest.

Oh, dear. This would not do. This would not do *at all*.

She leaned against the counter, waiting for Elise to return. Her mind

ticked through the various ways she could reason with Elise about staying out of the house without sounding heartless. Elise and Fern would
just have to do their baby caretaking in their own place. There was no
reason why that shouldn't be possible.

Elise walked back into the kitchen, picked up the empty baby bottle,
unscrewed the top, and started rinsing both in the sink. "Thanks for
your help. Maybe that formula isn't the best for her?" she said, reaching
for the Palmolive.

"Elise, I don't know what's going on here, but you need to take the
baby to your own place. Today."

Elise shook her head. "There's no room for her there. The upstairs of
the tea shop—it's a mess. We fixed up our bedroom area, but the quarters are small," she said, sitting down at the table again.

"Aren't you going to report this abandoned baby?"

Elise flinched. "I'd rather not look at her as *abandoned*. I think someone wasn't willing or able to care for her properly and chose a new home
for her."

Ruth took a breath. "Elise, it's not your responsibility. If you want
help, I'll go with you to the police—"

And then, to Ruth's utter shock, Elise burst into tears. "I've been trying to have a baby for years!"

Oh my.

Ruth opened the cabinet and poured herself a glass of water. She was
dehydrated. Last night's indulgence had not left her in good condition
for a morning like this.

"Ruth, you have to promise me you won't tell anyone about the
baby," Elise said.

"Okay," Ruth said slowly. The last thing she wanted was to get involved in other people's dramas. "But I'm living in this house for the
summer. So you and Fern are going to have to work something out on
your own."

Elise nodded. "You're right. I have to go talk to Fern. She's probably wondering where I've been all this time."

She stood up, pushed her chair in neatly under the table, and turned for the door.

"Wait—you're leaving? The baby is upstairs!"

"Can you just watch her for a bit? I can't take her to the shop. Please. You're good with her."

"Elise, I'm sorry. I cannot be stuck in this house all morning with a baby. I have things to do—"

"There's a stroller frame with wheels out back. I borrowed it from Amelia. Take her for a walk. I won't be long. Thanks, Ruth—you're a lifesaver."

Oh no. Ruth hadn't moved out here to be anyone's lifesaver. Clifford Henry was going to get an earful! She'd had enough of this nonsense. She turned around, looking for her phone, her mind already formulating the message she would leave if she got his voice mail—

The back door banged closed.

Elise was gone.

It was not yet officially summer by the calendar, but the town's population had clearly shifted from year-rounders only; the seasonal renters had arrived, and the streets were flooded with day-trippers.

Fern was too busy servicing the line of people at the counter to do more than offer a quick smile when Elise walked in the door. She jumped into action beside Fern, filling plastic cups with ice for the iced tea and using the instant hot taps for the rest of the orders.

"You took care of the baby situation?" Fern said, brushing past her on the way to the fridge. They were already out of their pre-sliced lemon wedges.

"Yes," Elise said. Fern squeezed her hand, and Elise's gut churned with guilt.

The line began to dwindle. A few customers walked in from the bookstore across the street, but then the shop was quiet.

"We need to refill this," Fern called, opening a tin that was down to its last few scoops.

Elise nodded. "I'll take care of it."

"Hey," Fern said, walking over to her. "I know it wasn't easy to hand over the baby. You okay?"

This was it. No more stalling. Elise had to tell her what was going on.

The front bells jingled with the arrival of more customers.

"Wow, wow, wow, you guys—this place is amazing!" Jaci Barros, Lidia and Manny's daughter, walked in with a look of wonderment. "My mom just told me you were open for business. I had no idea!"

Elise exhaled. A momentary respite from the confession she had to make to Fern.

"Hey there, kiddo. How's the Ivy League treating you?" Fern said, hugging her.

Both the Barros kids were blessed with their parents' Portuguese dark good looks and strong work ethic. Marco had the ambition and follow-through to cultivate the oyster farm, and Jaci was the first woman in her family to go to college. And not just any college—Princeton, and on scholarship.

"Let's put it this way—it's hard to be back," Jaci said.

"Oh, you don't mean that," Fern said. "And don't let your mother hear you say it. She missed you so much."

"I didn't feel like I was even gone that long, and now *this* whole amazing situation is up and running. Congratulations—it's beautiful," Jaci said, walking over to the shelves of tea tins. "Can I open one?"

"Sure, hon. Look around. Enjoy."

Jaci unscrewed a lid and peeked inside. "It smells delicious. Like strawberry shortcake." She looked up at them. "Do you guys need any part-time help?"

"Aren't you working with your brother this summer?" Elise said.

Jaci rolled her eyes. "I'd rather not. Seriously—anything but the oyster farm."

Elise and Fern exchanged a look. "Well, you have to talk to your parents about that," Fern said. "I don't think they'd be on board with you leaving Marco in the lurch."

Jaci poked around some more, ordered a green tea that they refused to let her pay for, then left with promises to be in touch about the job situation.

Fern shook her head. "Lidia can't be too happy about her attitude."

Elise barely heard her. Her mind raced as she searched for the words that would bridge the giant chasm that lay between them, a chasm only she knew about at that moment.

"Fern," she said slowly. "I didn't give up the baby."

Chapter Nine

Ruth napped for about as long as the baby did—close to two hours. They both woke up hungry and cranky. There was food in the house for only one of them.

After Ruth fed and changed the baby, she dialed Elise, hoping she'd say she was on her way back. No such luck; her call went straight to voice mail. If Ruth wanted to get out of the house, she'd have to take this baby situation on the road.

She strapped the infant into her car seat and carried her to the back porch where Elise kept the stroller frame. She latched the car seat onto it and headed off.

It had been a long time since she'd pushed a baby stroller, and she'd imagined the next time she was at the helm of one, it would contain her grandchild, not a mystery baby. And this was certainly not how she had envisioned the start to her carefree summer. And yet, the farther she walked, the more she thought about how things might have been different if she had allowed herself to enjoy her own early motherhood a little more. How many leisurely strolls had she taken with baby Olivia without worrying about the business?

The narrow sidewalk was crowded but she was reluctant to move the stroller into the street. Cars crept by carefully, but she didn't want to take any chances. Her progress toward the Canteen was painfully slow. She needed a cold drink and, after last night's gluttony, something healthy to eat, maybe a quinoa salad.

She checked her phone again—still no word from Elise.

Ruth passed the library, one of her favorite buildings in town. The landmark structure, built in 1860, had originally been a Methodist church and was topped by a dramatic spire that rose one hundred feet from the ground. She saw a familiar figure leaving the building; Amelia Cabral spotted her at the same time and gave her a wave and then raised a finger, signaling for her to wait. She held a thick coffee-table book in her arms, the glossy cover featuring New Orleans's Bourbon Street.

"Hi there," Amelia said cheerily when she reached Ruth. She slipped the book into her tote bag. "I'm getting a head start on my planning for Carnival. The theme this year is Mardi Gras by the Sea."

Carnival was P'town's largest summer celebration. For Ruth, the word *Carnival*—pronounced in P'town as "Carni-*vall*"—conjured an instant memory of late summer 1978. Commercial Street had been packed end to end with revelers from morning until—well, the following morning. She remembered standing outside of Spiritus Pizza in a crowd so thick she couldn't see the entrance and could not make her way back to the sidewalk behind her. It was a situation that would make her anxious today, but it had been exhilarating in the moment.

"I see you have company," Amelia said, peering into the car seat with a smile.

Ruth didn't know what to say. Was she supposed to make up some sort of story? Oh, how had she let Elise Douglas put her in this situation? "I really have to get going," Ruth said.

Amelia waved her hand in front of the baby. "They change so fast at this stage. Pretty soon she'll figure out how to get her fingers into her mouth. My son was like that—constantly sucking his thumb. In some ways, it was better than a pacifier because it couldn't fall out or get lost. But the bad part is you can't just take it away when you decide it's time to stop. He was sucking that thumb until third grade." She looked up at Ruth. "I've already met the little one. This morning. Elise brought her by the inn."

"Oh. Well, I'm actually on my way to find Elise at the shop. I have things to do, and, frankly, babysitting is not my forte."

"Why don't you let me take the baby off your hands," Amelia said. "I'll bring her back to the inn. Rachel and I can manage until Elise is free."

"Oh . . . are you sure?"

"Of course," Amelia said. "But it was very generous of you to step in. The world works in mysterious ways, right? Some babies need a mother. Some mothers need a baby. You're a mother—you understand."

Amelia shuffled through a stack of colorful flyers in her tote bag, then offered one to Ruth. "I was just putting these up on the bulletin board. I'm teaching a mosaic class starting tomorrow morning. Please join us. It's a great way to meet people."

Ruth glanced at the sheet and nodded. "Oh, well—thanks. But I'm not very artistic."

"Everyone says that at first," Amelia said. "You'd be surprised."

"I'll think about it," Ruth said, just relieved to be unburdened of the baby. She couldn't think about tomorrow. She needed peace and quiet.

Amelia winked, then reached for the stroller and turned it in the direction of the inn. She looked back once with a wave, calling out, "See you at the class!"

Ruth stood alone on the sidewalk. She felt strangely lost—almost empty. It took a moment for her to remember where she had been going, what she wanted to do. If it weren't for the sudden hunger pangs, she might have turned around and gone home. Instead, she sought out a place to sit, regroup, and have lunch.

The Canteen was busy; Ruth had to wait in line. At the counter, she ordered a warm lobster roll and, in a nod to trying to be healthy after the previous night's indulgence, a side of brussels sprouts. She took the placard with her number and walked out back to sit at one of the communal tables overlooking the bay.

She poured herself a cup of water from a cooler set up at the condiments table. An iPod on a dock played a rotation of classic pop songs. Blondie sang, "The tide is high and I'm moving on..." and Ruth felt nostalgia rolling in again.

Determined to shake it away, she looked out at the water and focused on rooting herself in the moment. Everything was fine. How fortunate to run into Amelia and be relieved of the babysitting obligation.

You're a mother—you understand.

Did she? Thirty years of motherhood, and frankly, Ruth didn't understand a thing. Thirty years of motherhood, and she was sitting alone in a town with no family.

Maybe it was time to do something about that.

She reached into her bag and pulled out her phone.

Olivia's chest was still tight with congestion, her energy level markedly low. But staying home even one more day—one more hour—was unthinkable.

"Good morning," she said to Dakota, already at her desk. Uttering the simple greeting prompted a coughing fit. "Come into my office."

Dakota followed Olivia and closed the door behind them. "Jeez. That doesn't sound too good. You sure you're not coming back too soon?" Dakota said.

Olivia's response was a raised eyebrow. "I'm going to call a team meeting in an hour. I just need to do some catch-up. But fill me in on anything I need to know."

While Dakota rattled off updates on various accounts, Olivia clicked through the photos on her computer screen, image after image of a nearly naked woman standing under a tropical waterfall. A client had recently landed a deal for a coffee-table book of her selfies and she wanted Olivia's "thoughts." Olivia looked at the carefully staged, professional photographs, and her main thought was that the woman didn't know what the word *selfie* meant. Of course, she would keep that to herself.

"Um, Olivia?" Dakota said. "Did you do those Happy National Wine Day posts on purpose?"

Olivia looked up. Dakota was hunched over her phone, scrolling intently.

"Yes. I did a little work on Friday. I set up some posts for Sam." Sam Saphire was a singer-songwriter whose career had taken off when he opened for John Mayer. For National Wine Day, Olivia programmed a day's worth of wine-related images with quotes like "It's always wine o'clock."

"Um, yeah," Dakota said, looking up with wide eyes. "Except you posted it through April's account."

What?

Everyone at HotFeed used a social media–management tool to schedule posts to go out at a certain time. She uploaded all the images and programmed the date they were to be sent out. It was simple; it was routine. And yet...

Heart pounding, Olivia grabbed her phone and tapped open Instagram and Twitter. Sure enough, the wine posts had gone out on April's feed. April, who was famously, loudly sober as of two years ago.

Oh my God!

She must have been so foggy from fever and the lack of sleep and the cough medicine—she had never made a mistake like this! And of course, she wouldn't have gotten sick in the first place if she hadn't been so upset about the breakup with Ian. This was why she shouldn't get involved in relationships. Nothing but problems.

"Damn it." She logged into her laptop; her fingers flew over the keyboard to delete the posts. In a matter of seconds, they were gone.

"Okay, well, it's so early," Dakota said. "I doubt anyone—"

Olivia's cell phone rang.

She was tempted to send it straight to voice mail, but she was experienced and disciplined enough to know she had to deal with a crisis like this head-on.

"It's April," Olivia whispered.

Dakota shook her head.

"Hi, April," Olivia said, swiveling her chair so she faced the window instead of her assistant's horrified expression.

"'Hi, April'?" said the woman on the other end of the line. "That's what you have to say to me? Do you have any idea how many messages I just woke up to? From my friends, my family, advertisers for the shows—my AA sponsor? What the *hell,* Olivia?"

"First, please know the posts are down. I'm so sorry. I must have logged into the wrong account. I was out all week with the flu and—"

"I don't care if you had the bubonic plague! This is a disaster!"

"I will take full responsibility for the posts."

"Oh, great. Why don't I just put out a press release saying I don't do any of my own social media? My fans will be thrilled to learn they're messaging with a bunch of suits!"

She had a point. "Let me just—"

"You're fired!" April hung up.

Olivia felt woozy. She didn't know if it was because of the disaster unfolding like a six-car pileup or the virus still lingering in her system, but coming into the office suddenly seemed like a very big mistake.

Her phone rang again. It was her mother. What on earth could she possibly want? This call, Olivia did send to voice mail.

Ruth couldn't help imagining her daughter seeing the incoming number and pressing a button to exile her to voice mail. But, to be fair, Olivia was probably at work. Ruth left a message; she would just have to wait patiently for a return call.

She was also waiting for a call back from Clifford Henry. Maybe she had not fully conveyed the gravity of the situation with Shell Haven. She would leave another message. Now, what to do with her afternoon?

The beach was an option, but Ruth was already in the middle of town and didn't want to walk back to the house to get her bathing suit and a towel. Still, the water did beckon to her.

One option was a boat tour of Cape Cod Bay. She knew these excursions launched from Barros Boatyard in the West End, just a short walk from the Canteen.

Ruth passed a small restaurant called Joon. Across the street was Provincia, a gift shop where she'd bought hand-painted Portuguese dishes.

She turned left down an alleyway and passed an aluminum-sided building with arrowed signs reading BOAT RENTAL. She kept walking, the sun-dappled bay now in view. The pavement extended all the way to the water, where an American flag was raised high above a wood dock. To the right, a clapboard shed with another BOAT RENTAL sign. Two white bikes were parked in front of it.

Ruth stopped in front of the boat-rental office. A couple stood at the window booking an excursion. She turned to look around, shielding her eyes from the sun with her hand. Behind her was a three-story wood-frame building with a gray-shingled roof. The second and third floors had wraparound decks. To the side of the house, metal rafters held boats in various stages of repair.

When it was her turn at the boat-rental station, a broad-shouldered man perhaps a few years older than herself helped her. He had small dark eyes, and his features were blunt, unrefined, and unremarkable, but he had a thick head of white hair and an air of authority.

"What can I do for you, young lady?" he said.

Ruth knew not to take the "young lady" as anything more than rote, casual flirtation he probably doled out generously to all his female customers. Still, out of habit, she glanced at his left ring finger and saw that it was bare. *This is not why you're out here,* she reminded herself. "I'm looking to do a boat tour. Do you have anything leaving soon?"

"We have a shuttle to Long Point leaving in an hour and a seal-watching boat leaving in twenty minutes."

Seal-watching? She didn't know the bay had enough seals to merit an entire tour based on their presence. The thought made her uneasy. Where there were seals, there were sharks. Ruth had an intense fear of sharks, like a lot of people of her generation, and this fear had a specific onset date: the summer of 1975. At age fifteen, Ruth had sneaked out to see the movie *Jaws.* It was rated PG, but her parents, having heard from their friends that it was terrifying, had forbidden her to see it. She wished she'd listened to them.

"Do you have any issues with sharks?" Ruth said.

The man gave her a bemused smile. "I guarantee, ma'am, that the captains of all our boats are ready, willing, and able to fight off any shark threat to our passengers."

Ruth crossed her arms. "I believe it's a legitimate question."

"With all due respect, sharks are typically found oceanside. Nothing is impossible, but I'd say you're pretty dang safe."

Ruth did not appreciate his tone. "Well, thank you. This has been an enlightening conversation." She turned and headed back to Commercial Street.

Chapter Ten

In the midst of the baby drama, Elise had forgotten about date night.

They had tickets to a Twenty Summers event. Award-winning novelist Julia Glass and others had founded the arts program to honor the legacy of Provincetown's arts colony and restore the historic Hawthorne Barn, where that legacy had begun more than a hundred years ago. The organization hosted concerts and readings and art exhibits at the barn, and tonight, Fern and Elise were going to see Isaac Mizrahi in conversation with Alan Cumming. They had been looking forward to it for weeks, but now the evening had arrived and they were barely speaking.

The only positive development was that Amelia offered to watch the baby. When Elise told Amelia how badly the conversation had gone with Fern, Amelia had insisted that Elise spend the night trying to find some middle ground with her wife. It showed Elise that she wasn't alone in this; she had Amelia's support. Others would pitch in too. She and Fern would find a way to make it work.

But as they walked silently to the barn, all of this remained unsaid. If Elise didn't speak up soon, they would sit grimly through the evening and then go to bed angry, something they both tried to avoid at all costs. There were times when Fern had been the one to reach out and bridge the divide. Elise knew that tonight, it was her turn.

And she had no idea how to go about it.

They reached a tree-lined white-gravel path, and the shingled brown barn came into view. Elise stopped walking and said, "Fern, I'm sorry for not doing what you wanted, but I'm not sorry for the choice I made. In my heart, I know this is right."

Fern looked at her and put her hands on her hips. She glanced up at the building in the distance, as if considering just continuing on without her, but ultimately she turned back to Elise, shaking her head. "Don't start again with what Amelia said about how things are handled in this town. We've been here five years, so it's easy to exist in a bubble. But this goes beyond that."

"Maybe it does, maybe it doesn't."

"What's that supposed to mean?"

"What if someone intended for us to have this baby?"

A small, bubbly group passed them, laughing and quoting one of Alan Cumming's lines from *Cabaret*.

Fern moved to the side, closer to the trees. "I don't want to go around in circles again," she said. "There's no way for us to know."

Elise bit her lip, searching for a counterargument. And then Fern said, "Even if someone did want us to have this baby, we'd still need to go through legal channels."

It was the first sign Fern was even remotely considering keeping the baby. "Fern," she said, her voice quivering. "The whole time we were trying to start a family, you kept saying, 'If it's meant to be, it will be.' Well, it happened. Not in the way we expected, *but it has happened*. The rest is just details."

"Yes, and what about those details? They're not insignificant."

"We'll figure it out."

Fern shook her head. "I don't want you getting attached to this baby. I bet you've already named her."

Elise smiled sheepishly. "I've been calling her Mira. Short for Miracle. Which she is."

Fern sighed. "Elise. What happens when her mother—or father—comes back? Or what if we try to make this official and find that legally we can't?"

"That's a chance I'm willing to take."

Fern continued down the path, joining what was now a steady stream of people. Elise trotted after her.

"That's it? You're done talking?" Elise called out.

Fern turned back to face her. "I think you're playing with fire. But I also know that you feel I took away your chance to have a baby once before, when I refused to keep trying to have a baby of our own. Our relationship barely survived it. I don't want to be the bad guy again."

"Let's just give it a few weeks. That's all I'm asking."

"We never discussed adopting, Elise."

"Maybe now is the time."

"I'm not ready to have that conversation."

"Why not? Why do you get to decide, unilaterally, when the time is right?"

Fern rubbed her brow. When she looked at Elise, she seemed very tired. "I'm giving this another week, long enough for whoever dropped her off to change her mind and not get in trouble. And if she doesn't show up by then, I'm going to report what's going on. If—*if*—we decide we want to try to adopt her, we have to go through the Department of Children and Families."

"That could take months. And they might not let us. I mean, it's a state agency. Who knows what kind of biases they operate under? We're a same-sex couple, there aren't a lot of school options nearby—"

"Elise, one step at a time. No matter what the hurdles are, we need to do things the right way. Can we at least agree on that?"

Elise nodded.

Fern glanced ahead at the barn. "If we're going to this thing, we have to go now."

Elise stood for a moment, then started walking.

A week was enough time for Fern to come around. Elise knew that although her wife was practical and tough-minded, she had a big heart. A little time with the baby, and Fern would fall in love too.

And when they were both in love, anything was possible.

Ruth sat on one of the white benches in the front yard of Shell Haven holding a glass of wine. She had sat down to watch the sunset, but now it was getting late. Still, she felt no desire to move. An identical bench was positioned across from her own, one of the house's many design touches that suggested the home was a place for company, for a life shared.

She turned sideways to face the street. The town offered great people-watching everywhere; she tried to get lost in the parade of happy strangers.

She glanced, for the thousandth time, at her phone. Still no call back from Olivia. Not even a text. This wasn't unusual or surprising, but for the first time in a long while, it was unacceptable. Ruth didn't know if it was the recent long stretches of solitude, the change in scenery, or the baby she'd held in her arms that morning, but she felt an intense, desperate need to hear her daughter's voice. It was as if the baby had had a chemical effect on her, had unleashed some long-dormant maternal longing that she had buried under years of nonstop motion.

Ruth's chilly relationship with her daughter had been the subject of endless analysis with Dr. Bellow, who'd told Ruth that Olivia no doubt felt abandoned by her mother. Ruth knew this, of course, and suffered immense guilt accordingly.

Olivia had taken the divorce very hard. She'd been a preteen, arguably the worst time to experience a parental separation. In the beginning, for the first year or so, Ruth and Ben had tried to maintain fifty-fifty shared custody, with Ruth as the primary custodial parent. Ben moved out of the house and into a nearby apartment. But it quickly became clear that Ruth's long workdays, unpredictable schedule, and frequent traveling made it unfair for her to hold on to primary physical custody. She moved out of the house, Ben moved back in, and life went on.

It took Ruth years with Dr. Bellow to forgive herself and accept that she had done the best she could do, and this self-forgiveness had been a relatively recent breakthrough.

Now all she needed was Olivia's forgiveness.

She dialed again, prepared to leave a much stronger message, something to make certain her daughter returned her call. What that would be, she had no idea. And then:

"Hello, Mother."

The tone of her daughter's voice was markedly cooler than Ruth would have liked, but at least she had answered. "Olivia! How are you?"

"I'm fine. But this isn't a great time."

"Well, I'm sorry to intrude, but…" But what? And then Ruth realized she did not just want to hear her daughter's voice; she wanted to see her. Yes, this…whatever it was between them had gone on long enough. It had taken her a few decades to build a successful business. If she applied the same focus and energy, surely she could rebuild her relationship with her daughter in whatever time she had left on the planet. "But I need to see you."

"Why? Is something wrong?" Olivia said.

"Not exactly."

"Okay, well, I'll e-mail you some dates and we'll get it on the calendar," Olivia said.

"I was thinking next weekend."

"Mother, I can't drive down to Philly on a summer-holiday weekend. Traffic on the Jersey Turnpike is going to be brutal."

"Actually, I'm not in Philadelphia. I'm in Provincetown."

"Where?"

"Provincetown. Cape Cod. I've moved here."

Silence. Then: "Why?" Her voice was thick with irritation, as if she'd felt forced to ask the question but really couldn't care less.

It was then that Ruth realized there was no way Olivia was coming to visit her. Not that weekend. Not ever—at least, not until there was an urgency. Ruth hesitated just a few beats before saying, "I'm getting my affairs in order." Well, it was technically the truth. Looking for a house to buy was part of her affairs, just as selling her business had been part of her affairs. She was getting her life on track for the next phase, whatever that might look like.

More silence. Finally, Olivia spoke.

"Can I call you back?"

Chapter Eleven

Ruth was a morning person, and yet for close to a year, she hadn't had a reason to be up and out of the house. And so when Amelia sent the e-mail saying the mosaic class started at eight a.m. at Herring Cove, Ruth was delighted with her decision to join the group.

She spotted Amelia, Molly the dog, and half a dozen women near the edge of the ocean. An extremely large seagull walked brazenly close and seemed intent on following her to the sand.

"Ruth! Welcome! We were just introducing ourselves."

The group stood clustered around Amelia. Ruth was surprised to see Elise Douglas among them. After they'd all shared their names, Amelia held up a handful of shells.

"The beauty—and challenge—of mosaics is taking a lot of random and disconnected pieces and putting them together to make a visually satisfying design," Amelia said. "You can make a mosaic out of virtually anything. You can take something broken and turn it into something whole. There's a story in my family about a famous argument between my great-grandparents back in Lisbon during which, well, let's just say the dinner plates didn't survive. Two weeks later, there was a new frame around the mirror hanging in the front hallway."

Everyone laughed, and one of the women turned and made a comment to the woman next to her.

"Don't believe me? I have the mirror on display at the inn. Now, fortunately, most mosaics do not require a domestic dispute. When we go to my studio, I'll show you tiles, beads, buttons…the options for color and texture are vast. But I find the most satisfying works include some pieces that have personal meaning. That's why we're here this morning. For the next hour, I want everyone to walk up and down the beach looking for shells, stones, sea glass—anything that catches your eye. In your final mosaic, you might use everything you find or just one symbolic piece."

Amelia handed everyone a mesh bag with narrow netting. Ruth adjusted her sun hat and followed the group as it marched forward. A few of the women, clearly friends to begin with, broke off in pairs and slowed down. Ruth passed the rest of the group and found herself walking alone until Amelia and Molly appeared by her side.

"She likes the beach?" Ruth said.

"Well," Amelia said, patting Molly's head, "she prefers to laze around the living room. But I force her to get moving—just like I force myself."

Ruth nodded. "I have to admit I haven't been out this early in a while. It feels good."

Amelia smiled at her. "Ruth, I know you're stuck in the middle of this situation with the baby and I just wanted to say thank you. It's a complicated issue, and every bit of support helps."

"Well, I'm not exactly in the middle of it," Ruth said. In fact, she considered herself officially *out* of it.

"Rachel is watching her at the moment. But it's nice to know we have another set of hands if we need it." Amelia winked at her.

What? Ruth had no interest in becoming a regular in the baby-watching rotation. One day was fine; it was a small contribution. She would admit that it had even been a little rewarding. But this was not going to be a summer of caretaking. Ruth was not a good caretaker. She didn't even own a houseplant.

"Actually," Ruth said, to change the subject and to make it clear she had her own life, "my daughter might be visiting soon." It felt like a lie, but incredibly, it wasn't. She had invited Olivia, so there was always the chance—the very remote, very unlikely chance—that she would say yes.

"Oh, that's good news. I remember you mentioning her that first morning at the inn but you said she wasn't coming to visit. How wonderful she changed her mind."

"Well, I don't know if it's changed yet. But I'm doing my best." And then, before she could think twice about it, Ruth blurted out, "But I lied to her."

"Oh?"

"It wasn't a lie, exactly. It was more of a . . . half-truth. But I wanted to get her to come out here." This was what happened when you quit therapy cold turkey after twenty years. You started unloading on strangers.

Late last year, upon discovering that her nail polish had been discontinued, Ruth had called her psychiatrist for an emergency session. "I need to make a change," she'd said. "But I don't know where to go."

"Where were you most happy in life?" Dr. Bellow asked.

Ruth ran through a mental catalog: Growing up in suburban Philadelphia. College in Illinois. Her married years in New Jersey. Her business travel to Europe and California.

"Provincetown," she said.

It had been the summer before she started Northwestern. Her father's architecture firm had spent the previous six months working on a big project in Truro, Massachusetts, and he'd rented a cottage in Provincetown and brought Ruth and her mother out for the summer.

Funny that the happiest she'd been in her entire life was before her life really began.

With this revelation, Ruth realized that she had to have a Province-town home of her own. Facing the milestone of retirement, she now had to figure out the rest of her life. And she realized that she wanted to spend it in P'town. The rest was just logistics.

So, yes—she was getting her affairs in order.

"You don't have to explain to me," Amelia said. "I was estranged from my daughter for twenty years. If there was something I could have said to get her to come home—half lie, whole lie, the whole world of lies—I would have said it."

Ruth looked at her. "Did she ever come back?"

Amelia nodded. "She did. Three years ago."

"Is she here now?"

"Not at the moment. She lives in Italy."

"Is this Rachel's mother?"

"No, Rachel is my son's daughter. But my son never knew her. We lost him a long time ago."

"Oh! I'm sorry."

Amelia stopped walking. "Don't feel bad, Ruth. Our relationship with our children is the most precious thing we have. Do whatever it takes to set that right. Oh, look! That's a beauty." She picked up a cloudy blue stone. "Sea glass," she said.

She handed it to Ruth, who marveled over its deep color and smooth surface.

"It takes decades of tumbling around in the sea for glass to reach this texture and frosted appearance. Some sea glass is a hundred years old."

"I guess some things do get better with age," Ruth said.

"Oh, my dear—don't we all? I'm going to show this to the others." She touched Ruth's shoulder. "Think about what I said."

As if she would be able to think about anything else.

She kept her eyes down, scanning the beach for appealing shells. Something lavender poked out of the wet sand, and she reached for it.

"I used to have a bowl of those in the bedroom at Shell Haven," said a voice behind her.

Ruth straightened and turned to find Elise Douglas. "I'm surprised to see you here," Ruth said, dropping the shell in her mesh bag, "given the situation. I guess you and Fern worked everything out. That's great."

Elise bit her lip. "Well, not *everything* is worked out. I was going to talk to you later, but since you're here..."

Whatever calm and relaxation had settled over Ruth while she walked in the sand and breathed in the ocean air instantly dissipated. Elise was clearly gearing up to say something Ruth didn't want to hear.

Elise stepped closer to her. "We need to move back into the house for a few weeks."

Surely the breeze had kept her from hearing that correctly. "I'm sorry—for a second it sounded like you'd said you need to move back into the house."

"We need the extra space. There's no room above the tea shop."

Behind them, Amelia directed the class to keep walking. Elise and Ruth didn't move, allowing the group to pass them.

"Elise, I am trying to be empathetic, I am. But this is going too far. I paid for this house. We have a contract."

"We'll reimburse you for the few weeks we're there."

"Where am I supposed to go?"

"Oh no—you've misunderstood. You can stay. It's just...we need to be there too."

This was unbelievable. "No, *you* misunderstand. I am here to start a new chapter. A chapter that does not include roommates and a crying baby!"

Elise nodded. "I get it. I do. But can the new chapter start in July?"

* * *

Of course Olivia would tell her father about the conversation. Her mother's words needed to be parsed, examined, turned inside out. The only question was whether Olivia should call him or drive out to New Jersey to talk to him in person.

Getting my affairs in order.

She'd talk to him in person.

Six months ago, after three decades at Penn Medicine, the University of Pennsylvania's medical center, her father had retired. Olivia had been relieved to see him slow down. Unlike her mother, her father had worked to live, not the other way around. It was nice that he'd finally have time to enjoy himself, though he hadn't made any dramatic changes to his life yet. No big trips, no plans to move. He seemed content just to wake up every morning and read the paper at the local diner, play cards with friends, and spend way too much time worrying about her.

As for her own schedule, it was not an ideal time to miss work, not after losing a huge client. Olivia's boss, Peter Asgaard, who'd spent twenty years at a big Hollywood talent agency before launching HotFeed, had not been happy. Still, he conceded, "Mistakes happen. This was not good, Olivia, but it was your first mistake in eight years of solid work." Just thinking about the conversation in his office made her stomach churn.

When she finally turned into the driveway of the red-brick Colonial of her childhood, a calm came over her.

The Cherry Hill house never changed. It was a time capsule from the mid-1990s. After her mother left, her father hadn't bothered to redecorate or even change the family photographs on the fireplace mantel. Yes, the old TVs had been replaced with flat-screens, the ficus plant hadn't made it into the new millennium, and the clunky stereo system in the living room had given way to a sleek digital setup. But it felt exactly the way it had growing up. As much as Olivia prided herself on her independent life, on moving on, there was undeniable comfort in this.

And yet, every time she visited, she said, "Maybe if you sold this house, you could move closer to the city. Or even move into the city. And then maybe you would meet someone…"

Her father always gave the same response: "When your mother and I bought this place thirty years ago, I knew I'd never want to leave."

Olivia was thankful her father was so steady, but sometimes, for his own sake, she wished he'd be a little less so.

"I brought your favorite bagels," she said, kissing him on the cheek and handing him the bag from H & H.

"Coffee's on," he said.

Above the stove, there was a crudely carved wooden sign she'd made in camp arts and crafts when she was twelve that read RUTH'S KITCHEN. Why she'd felt compelled to make that, considering her mother never cooked, was beyond her. Why her father still kept it hanging was even more baffling.

"Why do you keep that thing?" she'd asked years ago.

"Because you made it."

So there she stood, in Ruth's Kitchen, agonizing over the phone call from Ruth.

"What, exactly, did she say?" her father asked.

"She asked me to come visit for the weekend, I said I couldn't deal with the Jersey Turnpike traffic over a holiday weekend, and she said she wasn't in Philly, she was in Provincetown."

"Provincetown?" he said. "Are you sure?"

Olivia nodded. "And get this: She's not there for the weekend. She's moved there."

Her father leaned forward, started to say something, then stopped himself.

"What?" Olivia said.

"Do you want me to call her?"

"No! I feel bad enough involving you as it is." Were her parents in touch? she wondered. "I just don't get it, do you? Why Provincetown? I mean, how did she make that decision? Blindfolded and throwing darts at a map?"

Her father turned away and busied himself straightening up the counter. Olivia felt a pang of guilt for involving him in this. It wasn't his job to deal with the vagaries of his ex-wife.

"Did you ask her?" he said.

"Of course. I said, 'What are you doing there?' And she said, 'I'm getting my affairs in order.' Just like that: 'I'm getting my affairs in order.' What do you think that means?"

Her father faced her again, his brow furrowed. "I don't know. But it doesn't sound good."

Olivia knew they were both thinking the same thing. A few years ago, Ruth's older sister, Cece, had battled breast cancer. Her treatment was successful, but it was scary. And yet her mother had somehow found a way to spin even that into gold. By the time Cece finished her last round of chemo, Ruth had launched a new nail-polish line called Liv Free: no formaldehyde, toluene, or dibutyl phthalate. With the rising call for nontoxic products, Liv Free took her mother's company into the stratosphere. That's when Revlon and Estée Lauder and the other big cosmetic conglomerates had come calling. Her mother had held out until just a year ago, then quietly sold the company for what Olivia could only assume was a fortune. Her mother never discussed the sale, not before or after. Olivia had read about it in the *Wall Street Journal*.

"Do you really think Mom is sick?" Olivia said.

"I just don't know. But you have to find out."

"You think I should go to Provincetown?"

"Olivia, she's your mother."

Chapter Twelve

I've got nothing for you, doll," Clifford Henry said from across his small, meticulously arranged desk in the realty office. "I told you at dinner, this town is booked, booked, booked."

Ruth had been waiting for him on the front stoop of Clifford Henry and Associates since nine in the morning. He showed up at eleven with a large cup of coffee from the Wired Puppy, wearing sunglasses and with a newspaper tucked under his arm.

She'd tried to be patient as she'd waited for him to get settled. He booted up his laptop, plugged in his phone, and muttered something about his assistant being late. She wondered why he needed an assistant since, apparently, there was no property available to rent or buy.

"I'm already showing people places for next summer," he said.

Well, that answered that. "Really?" she said.

"God, I'm so hung over."

Ruth too had indulged the night before. Elise and Fern, baby in tow, showed up at the house after dinner and invaded it like a small native army. Elise had been emotional and apologetic while Fern was all business. She'd handed Ruth a check reimbursing her for the month.

"We'll be out by July first," she said.

Ruth, wordless and furious, took the check and retreated to the master bedroom, where she'd remained for the rest of the night, barricaded behind the door with a new book and a bottle of wine.

"But what's the problem?" Clifford said now, removing his sunglasses and looking at her with sudden interest. "Shell Haven is perfection."

As much as Ruth would have loved to download the crazy story of the baby into Clifford's eager ears, she resisted the impulse. She was frustrated with Elise and Fern; angry, even. But she didn't want to cause trouble. "I think Elise and Fern are having second thoughts," she said vaguely.

"Second thoughts? What does that even mean? You've paid them, you've moved in—it's done and *done,* sweetheart."

"Clifford," she said. "I was never thrilled with the idea of renting in the first place. You know that. I want to make sure we're still keeping an eye out for a house for me to buy."

"Ruth, what am I going to do with you?" he said, fanning himself with a Japanese paper fan decorated with a cherry-blossom design. "I *cannot* sell you a house that *does not* exist. As much as I would love to *snap my fingers,* that's simply not how it works. Unless you're willing to look at some of the new construction just a bit farther out…"

Ruth crossed her arms. "No. I want something in town, a true Provincetown beach house, not some prefabricated nonsense."

"Well, you've moved here and that's a good start. People sell to people they know. They sell to people they *like.* Good houses sometimes don't even make it to market. Keep your ears open."

"Keep my ears open? Isn't that what you're here for?"

"If you hear a whisper, I'll turn it into a shout."

Ruth, shaking her head, stood up and walked to the door. Clifford followed her.

"What's really going on here?" he said. "I can smell a good story a mile away, so you might as well just tell me."

Oh no. She wasn't going to be put in the position of outing Elise and Fern's baby drama. All she wanted was some privacy. "Nothing is going on. I'm just impatient. I'd prefer to rent a house with the option to buy. They'll never sell Shell Haven." This much, at least, was true.

"For the record, I think you're assuming too much when you say Fern would never sell Shell Haven. The woman is nothing if not practical. Money talks."

Was he right? Should she approach Fern about this? Her phone rang. Olivia. "Hello?" she said.

"Hi, Mother," Olivia said, her tone noticeably less frosty than it had been during their previous conversation. "I'm calling to say I'll be out there this weekend to see you."

The difference between a perfect brew of tea and a bad one can be a matter of seconds. Elise made sure to label all of their retail tins with exact timing instructions, and she explained it to their customers. At the start of the day in the shop, she informed a woman perusing the tea tins that she had a little more leeway with herbal teas.

"It can steep longer because it's not made from tea leaves," Elise explained, gesturing at the cup the woman was holding. "So you won't get that bitterness if you overheat it."

"What do you mean, it's not made from tea leaves?" The woman looked down at her Juniper Berry iced tea as if she'd just been informed she was drinking Diet Coke.

"The herbal tea is a compilation of herbs, spices, fruit, and flowers. That's why it's caffeine-free."

The woman contemplated this and seemed to accept it. She bought a tin of chamomile. Across the shop, Fern arranged a display of artful bracelets that were also organic mosquito repellents. They were made by a local who'd approached them about making them available at the shop.

"Why not?" Fern had said. "We have the space. Maybe we can expand to other locally made goods. Maybe even art."

Elise thought it was a distraction but wasn't about to debate it. Compromising on this was the least she could do, considering what was going on.

The front door jingled, heralding the arrival of Jaci Barros.

"Hey!" Jaci said, smiling. Her long dark hair was up in a high ponytail, and she was dressed in a white V-neck T-shirt, cutoff denim shorts, and sneakers. "It smells like licorice today."

"Masala chai," Fern and Elise said in unison, then smiled instinctively at each other. It was the first time Fern had smiled at her in twenty-four hours, so that was a good sign.

Rachel was looking after Mira. She seemed happy to do it, maybe testing the waters for a baby of her own soon. But it made Fern uneasy to have to ask for help.

"People have their own work to do, Elise. We can't burden them with this."

But it didn't seem like Amelia and Rachel felt burdened. They were taking it in stride. She wished Fern could share their attitude a little more.

Jaci looked up at the menu. "I guess I don't need to debate what to try today. I have to go with masala chai. What is it, exactly?"

"It's black tea with spices mixed in—lots of anise and fennel," Fern said, moving behind the counter.

"So I was talking to a friend of mine from school about this place—she got a summer job at the Boston Seaport farmers' market. I told her how I wanted to work here instead of the oyster farm—"

"Jaci, you know your family needs your help."

"Yeah, well, I'm dealing with that. I mean, they can't build their whole business model around me. I'm not moving back here after school."

Elise and Fern exchanged a look. Fern spoke first. "Well, you might change your mind. In the meantime, try not to upset your mother."

"It's such a special place," Elise said. "You'll appreciate it when you're older."

"I've been here my whole life. You two already had the chance to live in a city. Fern, you had that big finance career. I mean, this is a great place to settle down. But I want to experience other things. My family is just going to have to get used to that idea. But anyway, I didn't come here to talk about all that. I told my friend about this place and your amazing tea—Mom's been brewing it nonstop—and my friend said you should come sell it at the Boston Seaport farmers' market." Jaci handed Fern a card.

"Well, thanks, Jaci. That's an interesting idea. I've been thinking a lot about how to expand beyond the physical store. We won't have enough foot traffic in the off-season."

This had been a conversation they'd had since the beginning of the tea-shop endeavor—how would they sustain the business during the winter months, when the town's population was a fraction of what it was in the summer? Fern said they would have to branch out into wholesale, getting restaurants to carry their tea blends and other retail shops to sell their brand, or develop a brisk online business. All of the scenarios involved finding a customer base beyond Provincetown.

"I'm happy to help. Just e-mail her." Jaci smiled. "See? I'm a value-add already. Imagine if I worked here every day."

Fern put her hands on her hips, her head tilted to one side. Elise recognized it as her thinking mode.

"I have to clear it with your mother. Maybe just a few hours a week."

"Thank you!" Jaci said, hugging her. "I'm so excited. I could start now if you want! You can show me how the magic happens."

Fern started to suggest another time but Elise jumped in. "That's a good idea," she said. "Why don't you let Jaci help out behind the counter and I can go home to…take care of that other business."

"Yes! It's a plan!" Jaci said.

A few customers trickled in. Fern greeted them and took care of their orders. She hadn't said yes, but she hadn't said no, and Jaci was already behind the counter. Elise headed for the door. She caught Fern's eye and gave her a wink that said, *See? We've got this.*

Fern looked away.

Ruth, on a mission to speak to Fern, climbed the porch steps of the pale yellow, two-story Colonial that housed Tea by the Sea and opened the front door.

Inside, she was met with gentle music, whirring overhead fans, and floor-to-ceiling shelves of silver tea tins. To the left, two armchairs were arranged in front of a large picture window. Fern Douglas, rattling a metal cocktail shaker, noticed her come in and greeted her with a smile.

"Hello there, Ruth," Fern said. She was dressed in mint-green linen with shiny jade beads around her neck. Her dark braids, showing just a hint of silver strands, were piled on top of her head and held there with a mother-of-pearl clip.

"It smells so good in here," Ruth said.

"That's our masala chai. Would you like a cup?"

"Yes, thank you."

"Hot or iced?"

"What do you recommend?"

"I find the flavors of the teas are more potent when they're hot, but considering the weather…" The door opened, tinkling with bells, and a thin, small woman dressed in black and trailed by a

Yorkie on a leash took one of the seats by the window. "Bianca, we can't have the dog in here. The health department. There's a water dish right outside at the base of the stairs. Just tie the leash to one of the chairs."

The woman waved her off. "I'm just catching my breath. It's a hot one today."

Fern shook her head and turned to the business of brewing Ruth's tea. "It will take about five minutes," Fern said. "I like to let new customers know. Sometimes people think it's like a coffee shop where you order and we just pour. But everything we do is custom-prepared. I think that's part of the fun," she said.

"I'm not in a rush," Ruth said. "I actually wanted to speak with you."

"It's about us being in the house," Fern said quietly, glancing at the woman in black.

Ruth took a breath. "I don't mean to be intolerant. I understand that you two are dealing with something…unexpected. But my daughter is coming to visit, and frankly, I need some privacy."

"I understand," Fern whispered. "I'll work on the situation. I apologize, and thank you for your patience. I hope this hasn't completely upset your enjoyment of the house."

"The house is perfection," Ruth said, trying to keep her voice low too. "I adore it. I have to ask: Are you considering selling? Because if you are, I'm very interested. *Very.*"

Fern looked surprised. "Oh. That's interesting, but no, we aren't considering selling."

Ruth nodded. She had not expected Fern to say, *Great, write me a check and let's do this.* She considered even this preliminary conversation to be progress.

Fern turned her back, readying the tea. When she handed Ruth the hot cardboard cup, sweet steam rising from an opening in the lid, she said, "Again, thanks for your patience."

"No problem," Ruth said, although truly, it was. But she didn't want to make too big a fuss. She had her eye on the bigger picture. *People sell to people they like.*

Holding her cup of masala chai, she walked to the shelves and scanned the silver tins, each wrapped in a navy-blue ribbon and labeled.

"Expensive, aren't they?" said the woman in black, appearing beside her and shaking her head.

"Well, quality things often are," said Ruth.

"I guess if you're looking to buy a house around here, money isn't an object."

Ruth turned away, thinking the woman was just one of the town's eccentrics. She selected a blend labeled STRAWBERRY MEADOWS and carried it to the counter. "I'll take this too."

Chapter Thirteen

Elise had heard about the sleepless nights from her friends with newborns, but it was something else entirely to experience them. Waking up every few hours left her mentally fragmented in a way her college all-nighters hadn't. And yet, she had never felt more fulfilled than she did in those bleary-eyed, predawn moments when she pulled Mira from her bassinet, held her little body close, and tried to rock away her tears while she warmed a bottle.

It was the workday that was unbearable. The town's weekend population had ballooned from pleasantly bustling to downright crowded. It was not, perhaps, the best time for Fern to be away from the store. But Jaci's offer to introduce Fern to her friend at the Boston Seaport farmers' market had proved too tempting to resist.

"I have to check it out," Fern said. "This could lead to secondary revenue streams."

Fine, that was hard to argue with, but it also left her to deal with both the shop and Mira alone—the latter of which, she knew, was a situation of her own making.

Elise packed up a diaper bag filled with supplies, strapped Mira into the car seat on wheels, and walked out the front gate toward the Beach Rose Inn. Rachel, that angel, had agreed to babysit for the day.

"Elise, hey—I was just coming to talk to you."

Elise looked up to see Brian Correia. Brian was a Provincetown native, the great-grandson of a fisherman and a second-generation police officer. Brian's wife, Beth, owned a bakery in the center of town. Fern and Elise had met the couple their first summer here at one of the Barroses' many parties.

"Oh, hey, Brian. What's up?"

Preoccupied with the logistics of her day, Elise didn't realize for a moment that Brian was looking at Mira—and that this was not a social call.

When she figured out what was going on, she could barely breathe. But she told herself that it was crucial to act normally, that Brian was law enforcement but he was also a friend.

"Can we go inside and talk?" he said, glancing back at Shell Haven.

"Is everything okay?" she said, her voice an octave too high.

"That's what I'm here to check out. The station got a call about a newborn who doesn't seem to have parents in town." He looked down at Mira. "Is this a relative of yours or Fern's?"

Elise swallowed hard. It was one thing to keep a secret; it was another thing entirely to tell a blatant lie. She wanted to be honest with Brian, but he would have no choice but to take Mira away from her. So instead, she would have to tell a version of the truth.

"No," she said. "She's not ours. But we're in the process of trying to adopt her."

"Oh!" he said. "That's great news. Beth and I know how much you two have wanted to start a family."

Tears came to her eyes, mostly of relief that the conversation was out of treacherous territory.

"We do."

"I didn't mean to upset you," he said.

"No, no. It's fine. And of course it must seem odd that we have a baby all of a sudden. Like I said, it's not official yet. But we're keeping our fingers crossed."

"Well, everyone is rooting for you. Sorry to intrude on your personal life, but people do talk and I just wanted to make sure there wasn't a problem."

"No problem," she said, trying to smile.

"Great. Well, tell Fern I said hi."

"Will do," Elise said.

She would be in no rush to tell Fern anything about the conversation at all.

The third-floor bedroom at Shell Haven was small and quaint with a sloped ceiling, Shaker furniture, and a window with a perfect view of the bay.

With Fern and Elise occupying the second-floor guest room and the baby in the office, the third floor was the only logical place to put Olivia. It was going to be quite the full house.

But for today, at least, Shell Haven was tranquil. Fern was away in Boston, Elise was working at the shop, and Rachel Duncan had the baby at the Beach Rose Inn. And if things got too crowded later in the weekend, Ruth told herself it didn't matter; there was plenty to do around town. The weather was supposed to be sunny with temperatures in the high seventies. Ruth hoped to take Olivia to the beach. They could go on one of the water tours that the Barros family ran from the boatyard. Or, if they really wanted to make a day of it, there were whale-watching boats that left from the wharf. Then there was shopping, restaurants... but she was getting ahead of herself, wasn't she? Just having a meal together would be a huge first step.

All she wanted was for Olivia to feel welcome. She added a few touches to the bedroom—fresh flowers and the book *Land's End* by Michael Cunningham on the night table; on the dresser, rose-and-black-currant candles from Good Scents on Commercial Street. In the kitchen, there was gourmet cheese, fresh fruit, and bread from the Portuguese bakery.

Olivia would be arriving on the one o'clock ferry, and Ruth felt anxious. She looked out the third-floor window at the bay. It was hard not to consider the fact that they'd barely had more than a five-minute conversation in years. There was nothing to worry about, she told herself. Vacations had a way of bonding even the most intimacy-challenged family members. Provincetown would work its magic on their relationship, just as it had worked its charm on her so many years ago.

At ten in the morning, foot traffic on the sidewalk outside the house was light. From her high perch, Ruth watched bicyclists ride by, a couple walking a Weimaraner, a woman with a baby stroller. A woman with a baby stroller stopping in front of Shell Haven.

She realized it was Rachel Duncan pushing the baby stroller. Ruth watched, incredulous, as Rachel unlatched the gate and made her way up the path to the house.

What was she doing there?

Ruth hurried down the two flights of stairs and met Rachel at the front door, trying to head her off at the pass. Before she could tell her this wasn't a good time, Rachel said, "Ruth! I'm so glad you're here. I have a mini-emergency at the inn. Can you watch Mira for just an hour or so? I can't take her to the shop—Elise is working alone today."

"I'm sorry, Rachel. My daughter is visiting and I can't."

"What time is she getting here?"

"Around one. But—"

"I'll be back by one, I promise!" she said, turning back to the street and waving her hand above her head. "Thanks, Ruth, you're a lifesaver."

Oh no—this was not happening *today*.

"Rachel, wait," Ruth called out, following her. "If you're not back here before one, I'm parking this stroller in the middle of the tea shop. I'm serious. I don't care who is working or not working or what's going on. Understood?"

"Understood," Rachel said. "I'll be back before your daughter arrives."

Chapter Fourteen

Olivia was on the road to Provincetown by five in the morning.

Once she'd made the decision to visit her mother, she had to make a second decision: Drive the whole distance or take a train to the ferry? Driving, she would feel less trapped; at any point on the way to Cape Cod, she could change her mind and turn around. And at any point during the weekend, she could leave.

For most of the trip, she kept SiriusXM tuned to talk radio, keeping her mind occupied. But on a narrow stretch of highway framed by lush green fields, wind turbines spinning in the distance, she found herself struck by a mental montage of idyllic beach scenes with her mother. The two of them could have been played by Meryl Streep and Emma Stone, the vignettes directed by Nancy Meyers. This was dangerous thinking.

How many times over the years had she looked forward to spending time with her mother only to be disappointed? The dinners that were interrupted with urgent work calls. The planned shopping excursions (bonding time) that ended up with her mother giving her a credit card number and telling her to order whatever she wanted online. The college visits that were canceled because her mother had to fly to Manhattan or LA for the company. There was always some fire to put out. Olivia had heard the term *rain check* in her life more times than she'd experienced actual rain. On Olivia's twenty-first birthday, Ruth had canceled her planned visit. She told Olivia that one of her friends needed her, but of course she was lying. It was always work. There was nothing her mother wouldn't do to be at work—get divorced. Give up physical custody of her daughter. Lie.

The lowest point had come during Olivia's senior year at Vassar. On one of the worst days of Olivia's life, the day she'd lost her nana—her father's mother, Elaine—Ruth was out of reach, in Milan. Olivia remembered sobbing at the cemetery, watching her father enact the ritual of tossing dirt onto the casket after it was lowered into the ground, feeling not only the loss of her grandmother but the acute, endless absence of her mother.

It was impossible not to fantasize, to imagine something different. The previous winter, in the months leading up to her best friend Julie's wedding, at which she was the maid of honor, she'd spent weekend after weekend with Julie and Julie's mother shopping for dresses, dealing with the registry, picking out flowers. It was agonizing, not because Olivia wanted to get married—she did *not*—but because she knew that if she ever did, it would be yet another milestone in her life when she'd feel a void instead of a guiding hand. Of course, she had friends who had actually lost a parent. Maybe this should have helped Olivia put her relationship in perspective. But it didn't. Having a mother and yet not having her around created its own kind of suffering. Still, she thought as she drove, she had to admit the long weekend had come at a good time.

She'd felt shaky at work ever since that disastrous post for April Hollis. The whole experience rattled her confidence about making her move. She found herself waking up every morning at four or five, gripped with anxiety. Olivia was not one to agonize over things. She prided herself on her decisiveness. But this was a setback.

By the time she turned onto the main street in Provincetown, she had almost accepted the idea of just going where the weekend took her. A few years earlier, during a particularly stressful time at work during which she'd suffered from crippling back pain, Olivia had consulted a "mindfulness coach." The woman, who had an Indian name that belied her WASPy appearance, urged her not to be so focused on outcomes all the time. She thought, too, of her father's words: "Your mother is just not the nurturing kind," he'd said. "But that doesn't mean she doesn't love you." People had their limitations. Olivia was old enough to know that. She certainly had her own. Her mother was a smart businesswoman. She just wasn't a caretaker, and maybe it was time Olivia stopped taking that personally.

Getting my affairs in order.

Her mother was still relatively young, but her sister had already battled cancer. Olivia couldn't take for granted that she had all the time in the world to come to terms with her mother. Her father had been right to give her the push she needed to make the trip.

At least the town was cute. Even with her phone's GPS, she took a wrong turn too far down Commercial Street, overshooting her mother's address. She followed the narrow road, waiting for a place to turn around, and found herself distracted by the colorful shops and restaurants all jammed side by side, the strolling couples, dogs on leashes, and one shirtless man dressed in billowing American-flag-pattern pants with a matching top hat on his head. Interesting.

A pink pedicab wheeled past her. There weren't any traffic lights, or at least none that she could see, and cars moved slowly. She started to grow impatient. But maybe the delay wasn't the worst thing; she was very early. She hadn't told her mother she wasn't taking the ferry, and now she considered for the first time if her mother might be out running errands or walking on the beach or doing whatever it was people did midmorning in this town. Olivia decided that if her mother was not at the house, she'd walk back to this main street and get breakfast.

Olivia followed Bradford to Bangs Street, made a right back onto Commercial, then turned into the white-gravel driveway in front of the house. The driveway had a tall fence and a hedgerow along one side, so she couldn't just walk directly across the lawn. Bag in hand, she backtracked to the sidewalk, unlatched the fence gate, and followed a red-brick path to the house.

She stood on the porch a minute, collecting herself. Somewhere nearby, an owl hooted. In the distance, a foghorn. The house stood silent, indifferent to the reunion about to take place.

Olivia rang the bell. It took maybe half a minute for her mother to open the door.

Ruth was dressed in pale yellow pleated shorts and a white polo shirt. Her ash-blond hair was held back by an Hermès scarf. She appeared overheated, her face shiny, but her trademark matte-red lipstick (named Joan, after her own mother) was flawless.

She looked good. Her mother always looked good. It was difficult to believe anything could be wrong with her, but as Olivia braced herself for their usual awkward greeting, she was reminded of why she had made the trip in the first place. *Getting my affairs in order.*

"Welcome! I wasn't expecting you for a few hours..."

"I changed my mind and drove," Olivia said, stepping inside. The entrance hall was painted a deep eggplant; there were winding stairs directly in front, and, at the far end of the room, a floor-to-ceiling mirror topped with stained glass.

"Oh, well, I'm just delighted you're here, Liv," her mother said.

She had always been Liv to her mother, a nickname that she'd had since her first memory and that had lasted until she was in seventh grade, the year her mother moved to Center City and her father moved back into the Cherry Hill house. The first weekend her mother had visited, she'd rolled up in her Mercedes and said, "I've missed you, Liv," and Olivia said the one thing her wounded heart could think of: "It's Olivia."

Her mother realized her mistake the moment the name slipped from her mouth and promptly apologized. Olivia didn't say anything. She followed her into a spacious, sun-drenched living room. The walls were white, each one featuring a vivid oil painting of either stark color blocks or a beach scene. A fireplace was topped with an antique-looking mirror. The stone-colored couch was accented with purple throw pillows and a purple, orange, and pink crocheted throw. The wicker coffee table held a pile of books and a bowl filled with shells.

"Is this place yours?" Olivia asked.

"I'm just renting, unfortunately. I would love to buy it but I don't think the owners will consider selling."

"I'm sure you'll find a way to convince them, Mother. You always do."

Ruth looked at her and seemed about to reply but did not. Instead, she redirected with "How was the drive?"

"It felt long but I guess I made good time so I can't complain."

"Do you want to see your room and get settled?"

"I'm pretty hungry. Maybe we can go somewhere to eat?"

Her mother hesitated, looked at her watch. "Sure. I need to take care of one thing first."

"All right, then, I might as well put my stuff in the bedroom."

Her mother led the way up two flights of stairs to a narrow hallway with a small bathroom on one end and a bedroom on the other. The ceilings were slanted and the bathroom ceiling low-beamed. It was like inhabiting a space that wasn't quite real, like a stage set. The bedroom was quaint with modest furniture and a blue and yellow color scheme.

The dresser was decorated with a few Diptyque Baies candles; there were fresh flowers on the bedside table.

"I hope you'll be comfortable up here," her mother said.

"Of course," Olivia said. They stood awkwardly for a few seconds until a sharp sound cut through the silence. Was that...a baby crying?

"Excuse me for a minute," her mother said, turning pale.

What on earth? Olivia looked after her, incredulous. Ruth disappeared down the stairs, and Olivia waited just a few seconds before following the sounds of the escalating wailing.

Down one flight of stairs, on the second floor, Olivia found her mother in an office with a bassinet. She held a small baby swaddled in a pink blanket. "Whose is that?" Olivia said.

"It's a long story," Ruth said. "I'm helping out. She was going to be with someone else by the time you got here, but then you arrived early..."

"You're helping out with a *baby?*" Olivia couldn't help feeling irritated by this turn of events—triggered, frankly. Her mother had never had time for anyone but herself, and now suddenly she was Mary Poppins?

"I'm going to drop her off somewhere on our way to lunch," Ruth said. "It's not an issue."

But it was an issue—at least for Olivia. Her mother had moved to a strange town and was taking care of a little girl when for so long she had not taken care of her own.

Chapter Fifteen

As shaken as Elise was by the police visit, there was no time to deal with it on any emotional level. By the time she arrived at Tea by the Sea, the line of customers stretched from the counter to the front door. Again, she was saved by the kindness of others, as Jaci had volunteered to help out in Fern's absence.

Elise had to admit, the girl's excitement over the tea shop had rekindled her own enthusiasm. She felt a renewed sense of gratitude toward Fern for making it all happen and resolved to tell her that as soon as she returned that night.

The question was, should she tell her about Brian Correia's visit? Did she have a choice?

Jaci pulled her aside and told her a customer was asking for instructions on how to brew loose-leaf tea. The woman was deeply tanned, in her midthirties, with blond hair twisted into a knot and an expensive-looking pair of sunglasses perched on top of her head. Her wrists were covered in beaded bracelets, and she was dressed in white denim shorts and a gauzy shirt with a drawstring.

"This place is just so cute! I want everything," the woman said. She held two tins of tea. "So tell me what to do."

Elise explained that one option was to brew the leaves directly in the teapot—a classic method—and then use a metal mesh strainer to catch the leaves as you poured the freshly brewed tea. "Or you can buy a tea infuser, which is a metal ball with mesh coverings or little holes. You can fill the infuser with the leaves and place that inside the teapot to brew. It works just like a—"

The front door opened, and in walked Ruth Cooperman with Mira in her stroller. What was Ruth doing with the baby?

"Excuse me for a moment," Elise said to the customer.

Ruth had the diaper bag over one shoulder, a bottle in her hand, and a very, very irritated expression on her face.

"Ruth, what are you doing with Mira? I left her with Rachel," Elise said, keeping her voice low.

"Rachel had some sort of emergency, and she left her with me. She didn't want to bother you at work. But I have no problem bothering you here because *I did not sign up for this*. This was not part of the deal. Understood?" Ruth said. Elise looked around to see if the customers had noticed the heated words, but no one seemed to be paying any attention to them. Probably because one of the customers in line was a shirtless older gentleman with a cockatoo on his shoulder.

She was just relieved Fern wasn't around to see this disaster of a day. "I'm sorry, Ruth. I'll take it from here."

"Elise, my daughter is visiting for the weekend. It's a small miracle I got her to come out here in the first place. If I could find somewhere else to stay for the weekend, I would, but I can't. So I need you to respect my privacy, maintain boundaries, and make it clear to Rachel and Amelia and whoever else is sharing baby-watching duties that I am out of it. Understood?"

"Understood," Elise said, swallowing hard.

"And by the way, she's fed," Ruth said, handing over the diaper bag. With that, she marched out the door.

Olivia had not known what to expect of Provincetown, but she had imagined something quaint and a little sleepy. Instead, she threaded her way through packed sidewalks, her sagging energy lifted by a raucous, carnival-like atmosphere. People were everywhere; the narrow street was jammed with cafés and stores—a coffee shop painted in lavender, an open-fronted variety shop of some sort that offered an explosion of trinkets, sweatshirts, and summer gear. The second pink pedicab she'd seen that day inched along beside her, stuck in traffic, the driver blasting Madonna's "Lucky Star" from an old radio rigged to the front.

This was where her mother had chosen to retire? Olivia felt that she simply didn't know the woman at all. And what was with that baby at the house? She shook away the image of her mother cradling it protectively against her chest. She could hear her father's words hanging in the air: "Your mother is just not the nurturing kind." Well, maybe her mother just hadn't been interested in nurturing *them*.

Olivia paused under an awning to check her phone. It was a compulsion, she knew. Every five minutes she was scrolling through Instagram, a constant loop of checking her own feed and her clients'. *But it's for work,* she told herself. *This is my job.* She knew the schedule of weekend posts for the ten celebrities on her roster almost by heart. They had been carefully orchestrated by the team well in advance. A few of the clients were posting photos from earlier trips, photos they'd banked for later use. They didn't want to show where they were actually vacationing lest the paparazzi be tipped off.

Satisfied with everyone's feed, she switched over to an app to find the best place for lunch. There were so many restaurants with rave reviews within feet of one another, she simply picked the one closest to where she was standing.

Spindler's had an open-fronted bar on the street level, a deck on the second floor, and an adjacent coffee bar and café. Olivia snapped a photo and posted it to Instagram. The place was packed. "There's a twenty-minute wait for a table," a young man told her. He was blond and great-looking in his black Spindler's T-shirt and tight jeans. "There might be space at the bar." A quick glance told her there was no space at the bar.

The room was elegant and rustic, with a wood-planked ceiling and a wood-backed bar, deep blue walls, and arrangements of sunflowers and lavender tucked into metal pails.

"May I see a menu?" she asked, light-headed with hunger. She was running on four cups of coffee, a protein bar, and a bag of pretzels. But she figured if she left to find someplace else, she would just encounter the same crowds. Again, she felt a surge of irritation at her mother.

She'd better have a damn good reason for summoning her all the way out there.

Chapter Sixteen

Of all the restaurants in town, Ruth thought Olivia would most enjoy The Red Inn for dinner. Situated right on the harbor in the West End, it had water views but also a fine-dining atmosphere that would give Olivia a nice soft landing for her first night in Provincetown. Oh, she so wanted Olivia to love the town as much as she did. As soon as she'd set eyes on her daughter, Ruth had known that the weekend would not be enough. It was unrealistic to think that Olivia might extend her stay, but Ruth would not give up hope that by the end of the weekend, she would agree to return later in the summer.

Ruth had so many questions as they sat down at the table in the restaurant. Did Olivia have a boyfriend? How was work going? Had she seen her father lately? But she held back from asking any of them, still stuck in apology mode for the bumpy start to the weekend.

"I just don't get it," Olivia said. "How could you let those people move back in when you've paid for the house?"

It did sound crazy, now that she'd been forced to articulate it. "I don't know. Maybe part of the reason is that this is such a close-knit town, and I want to feel like I belong. I don't want to displace locals."

Olivia shook her head. "Well, that brings up the question of why you chose this place to begin with."

From her seat, Ruth could see across the water to the Long Point Lighthouse. The sight of it still gave her a deep pang. "Grandpa Lew brought us out here one summer when he was working on a big housing development nearby. I fell in love with it." *And fell in love.*

Olivia scanned the menu. "I mean, there are a lot of closer beach towns."

"This place has a very rich history," Ruth said, as if that had anything to do with her decision to move.

"Yeah?" Olivia didn't look up from the page.

"President Roosevelt and his wife stayed here when they visited to lay the cornerstone of the Pilgrim Monument—you know, that tower you can see from everywhere in town?"

The waitress appeared, and Ruth ordered a bottle of the Kongsgaard. Olivia had closed her menu but was now hunched over her phone.

"Did you know this was the place where the Pilgrims first landed in America? Here, not Plymouth."

Olivia looked up. "Mother, no offense, but I didn't come here for a history lesson. What's going on? Why are you out here?"

She had been dreading this moment of truth, considering she had drawn Olivia out here with an ever-so-slightly misleading comment. She would delay the discussion as long as possible. At least until the wine arrived. "Let's talk about you first. How are things going at work? You must be running that place by now."

At this, Olivia cracked her first smile of the day.

"Well, not quite. Actually, I've been thinking it might be time for me to go out on my own."

"Really?" Ruth said, smiling broadly now herself. "That's exciting." A woman after her own heart.

"How did you know when it was the right time to start your own company?" Olivia said.

The question nearly brought tears to her eyes. Her daughter, asking for advice! "I don't think there's ever an exact right time," Ruth said. "At least, not one that is ever safe or easy. It's just a matter of feeling you need to take the leap."

The waitress arrived with the bottle of wine, and the uncorking and pouring of a tasting glass took far more time than Ruth would have liked. She didn't want anything to break the moment between herself and Olivia. But then there was the ordering and the arrival of bread. And by the time they were left alone again, Olivia said, "Mother, just tell me the truth. Are you sick? What's going on?"

Ruth reached for her wineglass and fortified herself with a large gulp. "Selling the company was a big adjustment for me," she said slowly. "I'm still not sure I did the right thing."

"Okay," Olivia said. "But what does that have to do with—"

"I came out here for the next stage of my life. And at my age, realistically, there aren't that many stages left."

"You *are* sick." Olivia blinked rapidly, and Ruth saw the fear in her eyes. She was touched by the show of emotion, but she wanted to reassure her quickly. "No, I'm fine. I just—"

"You're fine?" Olivia said, her eyes expressing an altogether different emotion. One much less gratifying for Ruth to witness. "Then what the hell am I doing out here?"

"Visiting your mother," Ruth said. "Isn't that enough?"

"You said you were, quote, getting your affairs in order. You always do this! You lie to me all the time."

"Lie to you? When have I ever lied to you? And I *am* getting my affairs in order. I'm looking to buy a permanent home out here. And a burial plot."

"A *burial* plot?"

"Yes. I want my final resting place to be by the sea." She had thought of this just a few days ago.

"By the sea? What about by Grandma Joan?"

"Oh, Olivia. I can't spend all of eternity in New Jersey."

Olivia put her head in her hands. "I can't believe this. Although I should. Why not? Why expect anything different from you?"

The waitress arrived with their salads. This time, the interruption was more than welcome. Ruth needed a moment to find her conversational footing. Okay, so the worst was over. Olivia knew Ruth had misrepresented the truth slightly, but Ruth felt she had made a solid point. Why not visit your mother? Was that so much to ask? And, really, what had Ruth ever done that was so horrible that it required a fatal illness before she got face time with her only child? "I want to spend more time together," Ruth said.

Olivia picked up her fork and stabbed at a lettuce leaf. "Oh, so now that you don't have your company, now that you're bored, you want to spend time with me?"

Ruth sat back in her seat. "That's unfair."

"I'm sorry," Olivia said. "But it's unfair that you were never around for me when I needed a mother, it's unfair that you outsourced all of your parenting to Dad, and it's unfair that you lured me out here under false pretenses."

Ruth, shocked at the anger, could only shake her head. When she was able to speak, she said, "I never meant to let you down, Olivia. I did my best. And there was nothing false about my reasons for asking you here. I want to spend time with you, not because I'm bored or lonely, but because I miss you. Give me a chance to make up for lost time."

Olivia shook her head. "I'm sorry, Mother. I just…can't. I don't want to get my hopes up that somehow it will be different this time."

She once again checked her phone.

It was early evening when Elise finally heard from Fern.

"How's it going? Are you holding down the fort?" Fern asked, the call breaking up as she spoke. Elise walked to the front door in an attempt to get a clearer connection.

"Great," Elise said, hoping her voice didn't falter. "Jaci's been a big help at the shop." At least, she'd been a big help there until Ruth showed up with Mira. Without explanation, with only a frantic plea and a rushed burst of instructions, Elise converted Jaci from tea barista to babysitter. Good sport that she was, Jaci went along with it.

Elise decided not to share that little detail with Fern. Or the other major detail of the day—the visit from the police. That would have to be discussed in person. "The shop was so busy. It was a massive day. If every summer weekend is like this, I think we'll be in solid shape. We might even consider seeing if that woman from Chatham still wants a job. We're that busy."

"Listen, things went really well here too. So well, in fact, I should stay and work the market again tomorrow," she said.

"Oh? Do you have a place to sleep?" It was a reprieve from having to tell Fern about Brian. And yet Elise felt a tremor of discomfort, an internal warning bell.

"I'm just going to get a cheap hotel room by the seaport. I have to set up so early in the morning, it doesn't make sense to come all the way back."

Elise couldn't remember the last time she and Fern had spent the night apart. Of course, it made sense if the farmers' market sales were substantial, if she was building another customer base. And yet a part of her couldn't help but wonder if this was just a way for Fern to escape what was going on at home.

She kept these feelings to herself. At least, until hours later, when Jaci was helping her close up the shop, Mira asleep in the stroller pushed into a quiet corner. There were no more customers, no more distractions. And Elise could no longer avoid Jaci's questioning glances. It was all too much! The truth was, she wanted someone to talk to.

"So I guess you're wondering about why our tenant dropped off a baby for me to take care of today," Elise said carefully.

"The thought did cross my mind."

Elise walked out from behind the counter, made sure the front door was locked, and asked Jaci to join her at the armchairs by the window.

"First of all, I really appreciate your help today—at the store, and with Mira. You were a lifesaver. And I obviously owe you an explanation. But I cannot express strongly enough the need for this to stay confidential. I love your family, but your aunt Bianca is a bit of a gossip."

"She makes us all insane."

"She means well."

"Does she?" Jaci said, an eyebrow raised.

Elise felt a surge of affection for her. "Well, okay, then. Between you, me, and these four walls, a crazy thing happened last week." She hesitated only a second before unloading the whole story of the mysterious baby on the doorstep and the agonizing decision about what to do.

Jaci's eyes widened. "Who else knows about this?"

"Um, Amelia and Rachel. They've been helping out. And Ruth, our tenant. But other than that, we're trying to keep it quiet."

Jaci sighed. "Hmm. Well, you can't hope to keep the baby a secret. I mean, a baby is pretty visible around here."

"I know. The thing is…" Elise hesitated.

Jaci leaned forward, looking her in the eye. "Elise, I'm not a kid anymore. I spent the whole year away, and believe me, I've grown up a lot.

Whatever it is, if you need someone to talk to, I'm totally here for you. You guys were always there for me when my parents were driving me crazy. Which, by the way, they still are."

Elise knew she'd said enough. "It's fine," she said. "It will work out."

"Can I ask you a crazy question?" Jaci said.

"Sure."

"Are you going to keep her?"

"That's not a crazy question. That's *the* question." Elise stood, walked over to the stroller, and peered down at Mira's tranquil face. Her mouth was making a sucking motion, signaling she would soon be awake and hungry. "I want to. More than anything. I just need to figure out the best way to make that happen."

"Well, if there's anything I can do to help, tell me. Seriously."

Elise looked back at her with a smile. "You really will do anything to get out of working on that oyster farm." She reflexively looked around to share the quip with Fern and missed her with a sudden wave of sadness. She picked up her phone and dialed, aching to hear her voice.

The call went straight to voice mail.

Chapter Seventeen

Olivia packed her bag as soon as she woke up. When she'd finished, she sat on the edge of the bed, collecting her thoughts against the background of loudly chirping birds.

Was it wrong to leave without saying goodbye? Probably. But she couldn't endure one more conversation. Last night's excruciating dinner and walk home had depleted her tolerance. Her mother, with her typical determination, just kept on talking as if she hadn't been busted trying yet another self-serving maneuver in a lifelong line of them.

Her phone pinged. Last night she'd texted her father late: Just to let you know, Mother isn't dying. She's just manipulative. Is that fatal? LOL call you tomorrow.

His response had just come in: Try to make the most of your time. Remember, at the very least, it's a much-needed vacation.

She didn't need a vacation that badly.

She wheeled her bag quietly into the hallway, then picked it up to carry it downstairs. To avoid making noise across the hardwood floors, she carried it the rest of the way to the kitchen, where she quickly popped a coffee pod into the machine. Another few minutes wouldn't make a difference. She could still be on the road by ten. She was surprised her mother was still sleeping. But then, she had consumed the better part of two bottles of wine last night. Olivia couldn't blame her for that. She would have indulged in more herself if she hadn't been stopped by the thought of having to make a five-hour drive with a hangover.

Leaning against the counter, she scrolled through her phone.

The plus side to her twenty-four hours in Provincetown was that the place was one big photo op. The waterfront restaurants, the tiny shop that sold only pink-frosted cupcakes, the pier, the Colonial Revival houses with fences draped in hydrangeas, the art galleries. She posted a photo of the view from The Red Inn across all her social platforms, drained her coffee cup and rinsed it, then wheeled her bag to the back door.

Goodbye, Provincetown. Thanks for the memories.

Halfway down the red-brick walkway, past the hydrangea bushes, she spotted a man opening the gate to the white picket fence. He wore jeans and a red T-shirt that hugged his broad shoulders. His hair was dark, thick, and wavy, and his well-defined arms were deeply tanned. When he looked up, he was just as surprised to see Olivia as she was to see him, and she noted that his eyes were nearly black. She could chisel a rock with his cheekbones. He said something but she completely missed it.

"I'm sorry. What did you say?" Her bag toppled to the ground. She hadn't realized she'd let go of the handle.

"I was just asking if Elise is home," he said, bending down to retrieve her suitcase. He handed it to her, and their fingers brushed in the exchange.

"I'm not sure you have the right place," she said. "My mother is staying here. Ruth Cooperman."

He grinned. "I'm pretty sure I have the right place. This is Elise and Fern Douglas's house."

Right. The keepers of the mystery baby. "Sorry—I forgot. I don't know if Elise is here. I haven't met her."

"Marco Barros," he said, holding out his hand.

"Olivia Cooperman. Do you live—"

Then she realized he was looking past her, at the house. She turned around and found her mother waving at them from the front door.

Elise woke, as she did every morning now, to the baby crying.

Fern preferred to have Mira sleep in her bassinet just a few feet down the hall in the office instead of right by their bed. But since Fern had stayed the extra night in Boston, Elise indulged in having a little room-mate. Still, Mira's company was no substitute for having her wife at home.

Elise had to admit, the lonely weekend had helped her put things in perspective. She wanted to be a mother, and now, specifically, she wanted to be a mother to Mira. But not a single mother.

I'm taking the early ferry and going straight to the shop, Fern had texted her last night. See you there.

Fern was avoiding Shell Haven. She didn't want to see Mira—maybe, on some level, she didn't want to see Elise.

Elise was very aware of the fact that they hadn't so much as held hands since the night of their conversation about keeping Mira for a week or so. She didn't want things to continue in that direction. Over the past few years they had weathered a few dry spells when it came to their sex life. Elise had learned the toll that the erosion of physical in-timacy took on their relationship. When Elise had been going through hormone treatments to harvest her eggs, their physical relationship had receded into the background. Fern had been understanding, but they hit more bumps in the road after each failed pregnancy. Elise was heart-broken, and her sexuality took a nosedive.

"I love you and you're my best friend. But I'm scared we're becoming roommates," Fern told her once. Elise hadn't paid attention to this warning, this signal that something had to change. And then one night last summer, Fern said she was going to see Bobby Wetherbee perform at the Central House Piano Bar with friends. An hour after she left, it struck Elise as odd that she hadn't been invited. True, she'd been less than fun to be around after her last miscarriage. She'd been mostly moping, reading, and OCD-level housecleaning. It wasn't that hard to understand why Fern might want a night out by herself.

And yet something nagged at her, enough to motivate her to change out of her sweats, run a comb through her neglected hair, and walk down to the bar.

As Fern had told her, Bobby Wetherbee was playing that night. Unlike what Fern had told her, she was not in the audience.

Elise waited up until two in the morning. When Fern finally climbed the stairs of Shell Haven, Elise had already prepared herself for the worst. Fern was having an affair. Fern was leaving her. All of the stress of trying to start a family had pushed her away. Elise was surprised that her primary emotion wasn't anger; it was fear. In trying to have something she thought was the most important thing to her—a baby—she'd risked losing the most valuable thing in her life.

"I'm not having an affair," Fern told her. "We just decided to go somewhere else."

"I'm sorry. I'm losing my mind."

"No," Fern told her. "You're not. Because I've thought about it. I mean, things have not been great and there's a lot of temptation this time of year. But that's what marriage is about—riding out the not-so-great times."

The admission that she had considered straying but had chosen not to was an even bigger wake-up call than if she'd actually had an affair. Fern was working harder at the relationship than she was. It was also a red flag that summers in Provincetown, with its massive influx of vacationers looking to have a good time and then leave, were dangerous.

Now, this summer was off to a bumpy start. She didn't want to push Fern away again.

She changed Mira's diaper, making clucking noises to distract her from her hunger, kissed her belly, taped the diaper closed, and slipped her into a fresh onesie. "Your bottle is coming, your bottle is coming," she crooned, heading down the stairs.

A surprising number of voices seemed to emanate from the kitchen, one of them male. Elise walked in to find Ruth, her daughter, and Marco Barros sitting around the table. She mumbled good morning, opened the cabinet, and pulled out a can of formula. Mira fussed while Elise held her in one arm and filled a mug with hot water with her free hand.

"Let me help you," Ruth said, taking Mira into her arms. Elise swirled the bottle around in hopes of warming it faster.

"What brings you by, Marco?" Elise said, taking Mira back from Ruth as soon as the formula reached room temperature. She never ceased to be amazed by the way her little mouth latched eagerly onto the silicone nipple.

Marco shifted in his seat, ran his hand through his hair. "I wanted to see you," he said.

"Me?" she said, looking up.

He nodded. "Jaci can't hang around your tea shop all day or spend hours here babysitting. I need her help with the oysters. It's been a rough start to the season—those late storms—and it's been hard holding on to part-time help. I was really counting on her to jump in when she got home. This"—he waved in Mira's direction—"is a distraction."

Elise fought the panic rising in her chest. "Are you talking about today? Because Jaci said she'd watch the baby for a few hours while I'm at the store." If she didn't show up for work, Fern would be furious—not a great way to reunite after a few days apart.

Marco looked at Mira more closely. "Whose baby is that, anyway?"

Elise was only slightly more prepared for this question after the encounter with Brian Correia. "We're fostering her," Elise said, not making eye contact. "We're trying to adopt."

"Oh—congratulations. I had no idea. Look, I know that this is a big undertaking but you're going to have to look for someone else to help. We need Jaci on the water."

Elise nodded, near tears. She was so tired, and Fern hadn't come home last night, and she had to find a way to reset things between them.

"I'm sorry," Marco said, his expression softening. "But I have to do what's best for my family."

Elise nodded again, biting her lip. "It's fine. I was just up all night." She rubbed her eyes. "I have to open the store in a half hour and I'm just—"

"I'll watch the baby," Ruth said.

"You will?" Olivia and Elise said in unison.

"You're clearly leaving anyway," Ruth said to Olivia. "What else do I have to do?"

"Thank you," Elise said, unabashed in her relief. She looked at Ruth as if seeing her for the first time. Maybe having a tenant for the summer wasn't the worst thing in the world after all.

Chapter Eighteen

Olivia walked outside looking for her suitcase. Her bag was right where she'd left it before her mother waved her and Marco Barros into the house. What had possessed her to go back? She should have just kept right on walking to her car.

Her mother followed her now, carrying the baby. "I wish you wouldn't run off," Ruth said. "You're already here. Why shouldn't we have some more time together?"

"You seem to have your hands full," Olivia said pointedly.

"That's just an excuse and we both know it."

"Did you ever consider," Olivia said slowly, "that you're taking care of an abandoned baby because you feel guilty about abandoning me?"

Ruth appeared momentarily stunned. "I didn't abandon you, Olivia. That's absurd."

"Of course you did. Both me and Dad."

"That's unfair. Really, Olivia. You owe me an apology."

"I owe *you* an apology?" Olivia snapped. The baby began to cry.

"Don't raise your voice!" Ruth whispered loudly. "Yes, you owe me an apology. Just because your father and I divorced and I traveled for work does not mean I dropped the ball as a mother. Maybe I wasn't the same type of mother as your friends', or on TV shows, or whatever yardstick you're measuring me against. But I worked hard for myself; I worked hard for you; I set an example of success. Who are you to judge?"

"I'm entitled to my opinion," Olivia said. "I know you spent the past thirty years around yes-people telling you how brilliant and accomplished you are. And I admit, you are successful. You are a great businesswoman. But I can't say you were a great mother."

Ruth shook her head, mumbled goodbye, and walked back inside the house.

Olivia looked after her for a moment, wondering if she'd gone too far with that last remark. But it was true. Oh, it had been a mistake to make the trip. At least it was over.

She walked to the car. People strolled along the sidewalk carrying tall cups of iced coffee. Directly in front of her, two men walked matching black pugs. Their laughter drifted back to Olivia, mocking her bleak mood. She hadn't intended to end the weekend with an argument. But, really, the irony was too much for her. How could Ruth, who'd never had time to be a mother to her, be caring for the child of strangers?

Her stomach grumbled, but she ignored the temptation to stop in town and eat. The sooner she was back in New York, the sooner this misguided trip would be behind her. She knew she should be relieved that her mother was not sick, that there was no reason to worry. But all she felt was the rawness of fresh disappointment. She'd thought that, after all this time, she was beyond hoping for or expecting something different. But deep down, she'd known she was not.

Her phone brightened with a voice-mail alert. Her father had called, no doubt wondering how things were going. She'd call him from the road. She opened her trunk, picked up her suitcase, and immediately dropped it. A muscle spasm gripped her lower back, immobilizing her.

"Fuck!"

All she could do was slowly lower herself to the ground. And wait.

It had been worth a try.

In the office-turned-nursery, Ruth held Mira in her arms as she sat in the wooden rocking chair. Just a few more minutes of motion would hopefully do the trick.

Ruth had reached out to her daughter. She had attempted to connect with her. She apologized for whatever shortcomings she'd had as a mother. But it wasn't enough to change anything.

Mira squirmed, raising her little fists above her head and arching her body. Her eyelids fluttered and then closed.

If only she'd known way back when that infancy was the easy part.

Maybe she had been unrealistic in her expectations about the weekend. Clearly, she'd underestimated Olivia's degree of resentment. As unfair as Ruth thought it was, she knew from her therapy with Dr. Bellow that defending herself was "invalidating" Olivia's feelings. Still, it had been impossible not to push back. How dare she accuse her of abandonment? Ruth had not been running away from her daughter.

She had been running away from her marriage.

Of course, Ruth didn't like to think of it that way. With the wisdom of hindsight, she knew it was just a case of meeting the potential right man too young. Really, it all went back to trying to make her own mother happy. (This understanding was also courtesy of Dr. Bellow.) She adored her mother and took her advice to heart. What was important in life? Marriage. Family. Who could argue with that? And yet, Ruth couldn't help but notice that her mother's financial dependence on her father put her at the mercy of his moods, his money, and, ultimately, his failures.

Her mother had disdain for the "women's libbers," as she called them, even as Ruth grew more and more fascinated by Gloria Steinem, with her big ideas and short skirts. When she finally summoned the nerve to admit this to her mother, Joan Goldberg just smiled and said, "Well, she does have great style." They never got into a philosophical argument, though in later years, Ruth wished she'd taken the time to challenge her mother so that, in turn, her mother might have had the wherewithal to challenge her husband.

Ruth put her energy into a plan for her own life: She would not make the same mistake her mother had made. She would put her career first.

And yet Ruth was already in love with Ben Cooperman. Eighteen years old with a serious boyfriend—this was not the plan. But how could she risk losing Ben just to see what else was out there?

Was it any wonder her marriage failed?

Ruth paced the floor, the past rushing at her, triggering a wave of emotion she did not want to experience. The only antidote was to get moving; Mira, sleeping, could be transferred to her stroller. It was time to walk, to be swept along by the throngs on Commercial Street.

The last thing she wanted was to be alone in her perfect, empty, rented house.

Chapter Nineteen

Elise, carrying a bag of muffins she'd picked up along the way to Tea by the Sea, spotted Fern sitting outside. The sight of her made her heart flutter.

She was still in love.

The first day the temperature crept above seventy degrees, Fern had run out and bought two wooden-plank garden chairs and set them just to the left of the stairs leading up to the shop. The plan had been that they'd wake up each morning and have tea in that spot, watching the early runners and bikers make their way up and down the street. Then Mira arrived, and Elise had spent only one night above the tea shop.

In that moment, looking at Fern, she experienced the events of the past few weeks from her wife's perspective. She just hoped it wasn't too late to convey that and find some common ground. "Hey there," Elise said.

Fern looked up from the book she was reading and smiled, although with less warmth and enthusiasm than Elise would have hoped.

Elise leaned down and kissed her and slipped into the chair beside her. "I picked up some breakfast," she said, passing Fern the bag of muffins.

"Thanks. I didn't expect you this early."

"Are you kidding? I got here as soon as I could. I missed you."

"I missed you too," she said.

"I wish you'd come to Shell Haven last night."

"Well, I'm not comfortable being there. We rented the house to Ruth Cooperman. Enough is enough."

She was right, of course. "I know," Elise said. "But…we gave her the money back for this month. It's not ideal, but I think she's fine with it."

"She's not fine with it. You know how I know that? Because she came here and *told* me she wasn't fine with it. Her daughter is visiting, and she needs privacy. And you know what? So do I."

Elise felt her stomach tighten. This was not how she'd wanted their reunion to go. And she hadn't even told Fern the worst of it—that people were asking questions about the baby. She wondered who had called the police department. None of their friends would do such a thing. "Fern, you're right. You're right about this whole thing. But that doesn't make it easy."

"I know it's not easy," Fern said, her voice gentle. "But let's be realistic, Elise. People are going to start asking questions."

Elise nodded. *They already have.* She shook away the image of Brian Correia at the front gate. Now was certainly not the time to tell Fern about that. "I think," she said slowly, "if anyone asks, we should just say we're in the process of trying to adopt. That's not even a lie."

Fern shook her head. "I can't be a part of this."

"Fern, *please.* I don't want to be childless, and I don't want to lose you. Maybe I'm greedy, but I want what so many other people have. I want a *family*."

Fern's face softened. "Hon, I understand. But this isn't the right way to go about it."

"So we'll find a solution we can both live with. I just don't know what that is yet. But I do know that I love you. You're my life. I don't want to lose you," Elise said.

Fern reached for her hand. "I don't want to lose *us,*" she said. "I feel like we almost did once."

Elise nodded, fighting tears.

"We need to be on the same side. The same team," Fern said. "It's the only way."

"I know," Elise said.

Two men dressed for the beach, one carrying a large cooler, approached the steps. Elise wiped her eyes.

"Is this place open?" one asked.

"It can be," Fern said, standing up. "Follow me."

"Is it your shop?" he asked.

"It's *our* shop," Fern said, smiling down at Elise. She reached for her hand, squeezed it, then headed up the stairs to open for business.

Olivia's phone was out of reach and she couldn't turn her neck to grab it. She didn't know how long she'd been lying on the lawn. It could have been fifteen minutes; it could have been an hour.

The back problems always surfaced during times of stress. Three years ago, she'd wasted a lot of time and money visiting doctors and physical therapists. She went through bottles of Advil. Then her father told her about a book that said most back pain was the result of mental stress. The pain was real, the inflammation was real, but the source was her mind. It was a trick the body pulled; in order to distract you from emotional pain, it created physical pain.

Olivia hadn't believed it. Only in desperation, after hobbling around for a month, weekends spent in bed, did she resort to reading the book. The solution, apparently, was to let your mind know that you were onto its tricks. She was to ignore the pain, not baby it with heating pads and stretching exercises. Because everything else had failed, she tried it. She read the book over and over until it sank in. And the pain stopped.

Now, it had returned.

Olivia heard the back door open. "Mother?" she called from the grass. She heard footsteps on the brick, saw her mother's strappy sandals and the wheels of the stroller appear inches from her face, but she could not look up to see her mother's expression. Maybe it was just as well.

"What on earth are you doing down there?" her mother said, kneeling beside her.

"My back went out," Olivia said. "I can't move."

"Well, you can't stay like this." Her mother slowly helped her to her feet and into the house.

"I'm sorry," Olivia said. "Obviously I can't drive home right now."

"I never asked you to leave," said her mother.

Chapter Twenty

Monday morning, with Olivia sleeping in at the house on her unplanned third day in town, Ruth debated whether or not to go to the mosaic class. She could have run out to get breakfast, then helped Liv hobble down to the table, and they could have tried to talk once again. But she hated to break a commitment, her lifelong motto being something along the lines of "Showing up is half the battle." She was still trying to figure out what the other half was.

As with her first visit to the Beach Rose Inn, she was met by Molly, the chocolate Lab. But unlike the morning of her bumpy landing into town, she was not alone climbing the porch steps. The other mosaic-class students were arriving and patiently waiting for Amelia to show them into the art studio. Ruth looked around but did not see Elise Douglas.

Amelia appeared, dressed in one of her signature flowing dresses, her white hair in a loose bun. Her tanned arms were adorned with heavy bangles. "This way, troops."

They filed up the three flights of stairs to a large, sun-filled room on the top floor of the house. In the middle of the room was a wide rectangular table that could seat the entire class; at each seat, a sketch pad and colored pencils. The center of the table held bowls of pebbles, plates filled with colorful tiles, and a porcelain bowl that appeared to contain shards of shattered china. And everywhere, vibrant bursts of color: end tables tiled in cobalt blue, a full-length mirror framed with hundreds of pieces of china in a pattern of pale pink and moss green and crimson. Ruth understood the power of color; women had been tapping into it with makeup going back to the days of Cleopatra and before. There was a reason the cosmetic industry was a multibillion-dollar juggernaut, one of the few considered recession-proof. It was more than women wanting to look their best; splashes of color on their faces made them happier.

Amelia instructed the women to find seats at the table. Ruth moved to the far side, a habit from her days of conference rooms and seeking out the power position at the end. She couldn't stop looking around the room, an endless visual feast. To her right, a mermaid statue shimmered with opaque green glass and bits of mirror. Beyond that, the walls were covered with floor-to-ceiling shelves, some housing colorful plastic bins, others holding towers of teacups and plates.

"The first step, and in some ways the most difficult, is deciding on your mosaic design. So today, we're going to spend time brainstorming ideas and then sketching them out on paper."

Ruth already knew what she wanted to create. From the first moment she'd walked into the Beach Rose Inn, she'd been awed by the stained-glass starfish mosaic in the center of the common room. She knew she could not replicate something so artful and elaborate, but she could at least use the starfish design as a starting point.

"But first, to give you some inspiration, we'll talk a little about the materials for your mosaic." Amelia indicated bowls brimming with glass, beads, and tiles and three saucers of small squares that looked like a cross between tile and glass. One was filled with dark blue, one with petal pink, one with bright orange. "Remember, anything can be used for a mosaic—buttons, shards of porcelain, glass, broken mirrors. That's what makes it such a personal art form. If you find yourself bumping up against a limit to your piece, we will push through."

Ruth was all for pushing through limits. And she missed working with her hands. In the early days of her company, she'd mixed ingredients in the stockpots, poured them into molds, boxed the final product in its packaging. As the company grew, she had less and less time for that. And there was less need for her to be that involved. Production was outsourced. She became the front person, the big-picture person. Her days were filled with meetings and travel. Her role changed, but she loved the new challenges just as much. Anything was better than her current role: nothing.

Amelia peered over her shoulder. "How's it coming along?"

"Slowly."

"A starfish! My favorite," Amelia said.

"The one you have in the entrance of the house inspired me."

With a wistful look on her face, Amelia said, "My late wife made that. It gives me great comfort. A starfish represents renewal and regeneration."

"Oh," Ruth said. "That's so lovely."

"Did you know a starfish can regrow lost limbs?"

"I did not," Ruth said.

Amelia squatted down so they were eye level. "By the way, Elise told me what a help you've been with the baby. Please know how much it's appreciated."

Ruth felt warmed by the comment. With her own mother gone, she'd forgotten what it was like to feel maternal approval from someone. It was comforting and gave her the sense of being less alone.

"I heard your daughter decided to visit after all."

"Yes." Ruth smiled. "Although she wasn't thrilled with my little white lie."

"You mean your exaggeration," Amelia said with a wink. "Well, however it came to be, I'm happy to hear your nest is full. Rachel and Luke are having a few people over for dinner at their house tonight. We'd love it if you and your daughter could come."

Ruth's impulse was to decline. But the thought of another evening alone with Olivia, the uncomfortable silences and, worse, recrimination, made the invitation very appealing. Olivia could rest in her room if she wanted, but Ruth was going out. "I can't speak for Olivia, but I will be there," she said.

"Oh, tell your daughter I insist," Amelia said. "See you tonight."

Elise maneuvered the baby stroller onto the sidewalk and latched the fence gate behind her. If she hurried, she could still catch the last half of the mosaic class.

"I thought you rented out this house for the summer."

She turned at the sound of the familiar gravelly voice behind her and found Bianca standing on the sidewalk.

"Oh, hi, Bianca. What are you doing here?"

"I keep an eye on my daughter's house." Bianca wrinkled up her face with a glance at the stroller and crossed her arms. "Whose baby is that?"

I keep an eye on my daughter's house. Had Bianca been the one to call the police on them? "This baby is none of your business," Elise said.

"Well, here's something that is my business. It's bad enough that you two rented my daughter's house to that horrid summer person, but to think of you selling it to her—"

Elise was in no mood for this. "First of all, Bianca, it's not your daughter's house. It's Fern's and my house now. Second of all, we are not selling. It's just a summer rental."

Bianca made a noise, an exasperated harrumph sound. "That's not what I heard."

"Well, maybe you should stop listening to rumors."

"No, I mean I literally heard Fern talking to that woman about selling the house. The other day, when I was in the shop. That woman said she was very interested. And Fern said it was an interesting idea. Since it was all so *interesting,* I'm surprised you don't know about it."

In the early-morning heat, Elise felt her body grow cold. But she would not give Bianca the satisfaction of reacting. She was a gossip and a pot-stirrer. She had to keep her eye on the important thing. She pulled the hood lower to cover Mira's face.

"Always a joy chatting with you, Bianca," she said. "Now I need to get going."

Olivia felt like she was eighty years old.

It took her five minutes just to ease out of bed. She walked to the bathroom bent so far over she didn't have to lean any farther down to rinse after brushing her teeth.

After popping two Advil, she sent off a quick e-mail to Dakota. There was no way she was going to make it into the office tomorrow morning. She'd be lucky to be on the road in time to go to sleep in her apartment.

It was tempting to crawl back under the covers, but she knew she couldn't give in to the impulse not to move around. It was probably a good idea to walk to one of the bookstores and try to find a copy of the back-pain book. Just repeating the mantra *I'm fine, I know this isn't real* wasn't helping.

After a ten-minute, snail-paced odyssey to the kitchen, Olivia made coffee and settled at the table with her phone. A white slip of paper was tucked under a bowl of fruit. Her mother had left her a handwritten note. A note! *I mean, ever hear of texting?* She knew her mother was making one of her not-so-subtle points: *Get your head out of your phone.*

Good morning. I hope you're feeling better. I'm at an art class and will be home at around eleven if you want to get brunch together. If not, there's food in the fridge. Love, Mom

Nothing said retirement like a Monday-morning art class, Olivia thought. God, she was so happy that was far in her future. She had decades of her career in front of her. And she couldn't wait to get back to it.

She scrolled through her phone, checking all of her clients' accounts. A voice-mail reminder window popped up on her home screen. She owed her dad a phone call.

"Hey there," he said, answering on the first ring. "Are you on the road?"

"No, I'm not. You won't believe this, but my back totally went out. I can't drive today."

"I do believe it," her father said. "You're stressed."

"Yeah. Stressed and trapped."

"Don't think of it like that. You'll only make things worse. How's your mother?"

"Well, as I told you, she's fine. At an art class right now, apparently."

"An art class?"

"Yeah. It's the new, improved, chilled-out Ruth Cooperman. Just a few decades too late."

Olivia was interrupted by knocking on the back door. "Dad, I have to run." Or walk very slowly and carefully with determination. "I'll call you when I'm back in the city tomorrow night. Love you."

Olivia eased herself out of the chair and inched to the door. She peered out the window and saw a young brunette in a Princeton T-shirt and frayed denim shorts.

"Can I help you?" she said once she'd opened the door.

"Is Elise here?" She seemed more a girl than a woman, though realistically she might have been any age from eighteen to twenty-five. It was tough to tell. Olivia found that the older she got, the more difficult it was to determine the age of other people.

"No, she left for her tea store," Olivia said.

"Really? My brother said she was here."

Her brother? "Marco?"

The girl nodded and walked right past her, into the house, without hesitation. "That's so frustrating," the girl said. "I could have sworn he said he was just here and he saw her."

"I mean, he was here yesterday. If that's what you're thinking of."

The girl shook her head and declared, "I hate this town."

Now she had Olivia's full attention. "You do?"

The girl turned to her. "I'm sorry. I'm Jaci. And this isn't your problem. Are you... what's the deal? You live here for the summer?"

"My mother is renting this house." She introduced herself. "I'm Olivia, Ruth's daughter. I'm just here for the weekend. Well, and today. For what it's worth, Provincetown seems like a nice enough place."

"That's because you didn't grow up here," Jaci said. "Everyone is in everyone's business, and my family is trying to run my entire life."

"Everyone has issues with family," Olivia said.

Oh, things had gone so off the rails yesterday. Olivia didn't think she was at all wrong with her analysis regarding Ruth's odd willingness to take care of that baby. But the expression on her mother's face! Like Olivia had slapped her. It would have been so much easier if she'd been able to just drive off into the proverbial sunset—or midmorning, as it happened—and have the last word, smug in the knowledge that her mother would never change and that she was justified in having no relationship with her. But then her own body betrayed her.

"I try to avoid my mother most of the time, if that's any consolation," Olivia said to the girl.

"It's not," Jaci said.

Olivia decided she liked her. "Well, I was just about to head over to the bookstore. I'd say you could stay and hang out if you're waiting for Elise, but it's really not my place."

"Where do you live?" Jaci asked.

"New York City."

"I love the city! I went for the first time last fall, a day trip with my roommate to see a movie at the Angelika. We ended up having so much fun walking around, we never even saw the film. Seriously, it's my dream to live there after college. What do you do?"

Olivia told her about HotFeed, and Jaci oohed and aahed about the clients and Olivia's job. "So what are you doing *here?*" Jaci said. "If that were my life, I wouldn't leave for a day. Not for a minute."

Olivia felt a compulsion to check her phone. Something nagged at her. It was the fact that her phone was oddly quiet for a Monday. *It just means everything is running smoothly,* she told herself. She shouldn't need a million beeps and buzzes to feel that everything was okay in her universe. That's why people went to places like Provincetown, right? To let go of all that for a few days.

"You must be so bored," Jaci said.

Finally, someone who was on her wavelength. "I'm leaving tomorrow," Olivia said.

"Are you coming to the party tonight? Please say yes. I want to hear all about your job, and New York, and just…everything!"

A party might be a good idea. A party could be just the distraction she needed to feel better. Either way, one more night, that was it; no matter what condition she was in tomorrow, she was back on the road. By Wednesday, she'd be sitting behind her desk.

And everything would be back to normal.

Chapter Twenty-One

To Ruth's great surprise, Olivia agreed to go to the party with her.

Olivia had spent the entire day alone, hobbling around the house, which must have made her mother's company a bit more palatable. Still, Olivia was quiet as they walked west on Commercial to Rachel and Luke's house, not speaking until they reached Big Vin's Liquor, where Ruth bought a few bottles of wine.

"Who are these people again?" Olivia asked.

"Amelia and her granddaughter Rachel run a bed-and-breakfast in town. I met Amelia my first day here—long story. At any rate, she teaches the mosaic class. The house we're going to is Rachel and her husband's. I'm sure the food will be delicious. Rachel is quite the cook, from what I've heard. Amelia taught her everything she knows."

"Must be nice," Olivia said pointedly. Ruth ignored the dig. Fine, so she had never so much as cracked an egg in Olivia's presence. *Sue me,* Ruth thought.

The sidewalk crowds thinned as they reached the far West End.

It quieted enough to hear the call of birds. A fox dashed under a parked car.

The air was heavy with water and salt, and Ruth inhaled it, breathing in the heady scent of freedom, youth, possibility. The beach was her re-set button, always had been. When she was a child, that beach had been the Jersey Shore, the miles of boardwalk and the casinos glittering like jewels at the tip of Atlantic City. As an adult, she'd spent some time in the Hamptons as a guest at some very memorable homes, all glass and sharp edges with expertly designed infinity pools that suggested the ocean was not enough. But the beach closest to her heart was this three-mile stretch of fantasy that declared, with every breathtaking sun-set and every art studio and novelty shop and waterfront café, that she was home.

Ruth glanced over at her daughter, resisting the urge to reach for her hand, to look at her and say, *There's so much I want to tell you if you'd just give me a chance.*

When they reached the address, Ruth realized she had noticed the house—a white-shingled cottage with turquoise shutters—several times before. Like Shell Haven's, the front lawn bloomed with hydrangeas in violet and white and pale pink. On the front porch, a rocking chair painted the same bright blue as the shutters.

On the front door was a pink Post-it note that read *Door is open. We're out back.*

"Can you imagine that in New York?" Olivia said, referring, Ruth assumed, to Provincetown's very literal open-door policy that had so surprised her when Fern offered to leave her house key in the mailbox.

"I think it's nice," Ruth said, turning the doorknob. "People trusting others. Too bad we can't all live that way."

Inside, the décor was spare but elegant with lots of pale wood and splashes of color everywhere. The living room had a skylight and floor-to-ceiling bookshelves. They walked through, traversing a narrow foyer to a bright kitchen with a white marble island, hardwood floors, and a farmhouse sink. Here, too, the bright accents—lime-green Shaker cabinets, a mosaic fruit bowl made of green glass.

Rachel stood at the island tossing a giant salad of yellow and ruby heirloom tomatoes with feta. "So glad you could make it," she said. Ruth handed her the wine, and Rachel said she shouldn't have.

"This is my daughter, Olivia," Ruth said. It struck her for the first time that Rachel and Olivia were around the same age. She still had a strange mental tic of thinking of Olivia as being younger than she actually was, perpetually just out of college. It was some kind of subconscious denial about the passage of time.

"What a lovely house," Olivia said.

"Thank you—I love it, but I can't take any credit. It's Luke's father's; he gave it to us when he moved west. We did make a small addition to the back, sort of a guest suite. In fact, our contractor Santiago is here tonight. You'll meet him outside."

"Meet who outside?" a familiar voice sang from the French doors at the far end of the room. Clifford Henry.

"I was just telling my friend Ruth here about Santiago's work on the house. Ruth, this is—"

"We know each other!" Clifford said with a clap of delight. He air-kissed Ruth on each cheek, then turned to Olivia. "Who is this gorgeous creature?"

"Clifford, this is my daughter, Olivia. She's visiting from New York. Olivia, this is my real estate agent."

"I promised Rachel no shop talk tonight," he said. "But the hors d'oeuvres have not been served yet, so I consider this a grace period."

"Make it quick, Clifford," Rachel said, rolling her eyes.

"I have my nose to the ground like a bloodhound for you, but nothing solid yet," he said, linking his arm through Ruth's. "Do you have any leads?"

Ruth shook her head. "I'm coming to accept the idea that I won't find something like Shell Haven any time soon."

"Never say never," he declared. "The summer rental is *always* a gateway drug. You're in love with the house." Ruth nodded. He squeezed her arm and added, "Maybe we can work on Fern. Money talks, nobody walks. I'll speak to her."

"Not tonight you won't," Rachel said. "Now, outside, all of you. Before I put you to work."

The French doors opened onto a porch framed by a flower garden. Beyond that, a lush green lawn with a long picnic table dressed in white linen. To the right, a swimming pool. Rachel's husband, Luke, and Clifford's husband, Santiago, were seated at the picnic table along with Amelia and two men and two women whom Ruth didn't recognize at first. And then she realized she *did* recognize one of them; it was the man from the boat-rental office. Oh, good Lord. Recalling her shark-phobic questions, she was embarrassed.

"Ruth and Olivia, this is Lidia and Manny Barros—you've met their son, Marco."

Lidia Barros looked to be about Ruth's age, maybe a few years younger. She had thick dark hair threaded with silver, slightly sun-weathered skin, big brown eyes, prominent cheekbones, and a cleft in her chin. Manny, with his wide nose, dark eyes, and olive complexion, reminded her of Pablo Picasso. "And this is Manny's sister, Bianca."

Ruth recognized the woman with the distinctive white stripe in her hair; she had been in the tea shop the day Ruth spoke to Fern about Shell Haven. She started to say hello, but the woman narrowed her eyes at her in a decidedly unfriendly way. Odd.

"Last, but certainly not least, Manny's brother, Tito," Rachel said.

The man from the boat-rental place shook Ruth's hand. "We've actually met," he told Rachel. "We just haven't been formally introduced."

Barros Boatyard. Ruth hadn't made the connection that it was Marco's family. She looked around the table, putting it all together: There were the three siblings, Manny and Tito and Bianca. Manny and his wife, Lidia, were the parents of Marco. Tito and Manny ran the boatyard. The town instantly became more tightly knit to her, and Ruth had the pleasant realization that she was now a small part of it.

Ruth took the seat next to Bianca, and Olivia slid into the one next to Ruth.

"Nice to see you again." Tito smiled, holding up a wine bottle. "Red or white?"

"White, please," said Ruth. He poured her a glass.

"How rude, Tito," said Bianca. "Don't just reach over me. I'm sure she's capable of handling a bottle of wine."

"If you don't want me to reach over you, then why don't you switch seats? Isn't the whole point of these things to talk to new people? I don't need to listen to you yak all night long."

"I'm not moving," Bianca said.

Rachel appeared with the salad and placed it in the center of the table. Amelia excused herself, retreated to the kitchen, and returned with two dishes. "Codfish cakes and roasted sweet peppers," she announced.

"Avó, sit. I can take care of everything," Rachel said. Amelia rubbed her hands, and Ruth wondered if she suffered from arthritis. How old was she? It was easy to forget Amelia was up there in years; she was so active and seemed to have boundless energy.

"Let me help you," Ruth said, following Rachel back into the house.

"Sometimes I wish she'd just take it easy," Rachel said, peeking into a large pot on the stove. She picked up a plate of cooked shrimp and tossed them into the pot, then added peas, lobster meat, and mushrooms.

"What are you making?"

"Seafood rice."

"Smells delicious," Ruth said. "Yes, your grandmother is a dynamo. She's inspiring."

Rachel nodded. She pulled a glass baking dish from the drying rack, wiped it down, then greased it with butter. "She's resilient. She lost her wife, Kelly, three years ago."

"She mentioned her to me at the mosaic class."

"Yeah, it was rough. That's why she teaches the class. Kelly was a great mosaic artist—that's one of her pieces right there—and I think working in the studio, carrying on the tradition by teaching new people, makes her feel connected to Kelly." Rachel smiled and handed Ruth a wicker basket filled with warm rolls. "If you can take this outside, that would be great. I'm just going to get this rice into the casserole dish. I'll meet you out there."

Ruth held the basket against her midsection as she closed the patio doors behind her. The sun was just starting to set; the sky was streaked a dusty pink and gold. Ruth inhaled deeply, feeling blessed in the moment, having the sense that she was in the exact right place at the exact right time in her life.

When she reached the table, she saw that Tito and Bianca had, in fact, exchanged seats. When she sat next to him, he leaned over and said, "No shark sightings yet this season. Just in case you were wondering."

She shook her head but couldn't resist smiling. "I guess I deserved that."

"I'm just teasing. But I hope you change your mind and come out on the water one day. It would be a shame for you to spend time in this town and not experience the best part of it."

"I'll keep that in mind." Ruth felt fluttery with happiness. She didn't know if it was the attention from Tito or the homemade food; most likely, it was the fact that, seated at a table full of other people's family, she had her own by her side.

Amelia stood. "Now that everyone's here, I'd like to make a toast," she said. "To the start of another beautiful summer."

"To the summer," the guests echoed, raising their glasses.

Ruth smiled at Olivia, but her daughter looked away.

How ironic that Olivia had had to travel to Provincetown to find the two best-looking straight guys she'd ever met.

She'd started the evening sitting between Rachel's husband, Luke, and Amelia. Luke was friendly and talkative; he'd asked a lot of questions about her life in New York. "How long are you staying in town?" he said.

"I'm leaving tomorrow," she said. *No matter what.* "So you and Rachel live here year-round?" It was inconceivable. What on earth could you possibly do with your time during the cold in a place like this? She could barely imagine staying here more than a few weeks even during the peak beach season.

"Yes. During the school year I teach at the University of Rhode Island."

"Oh? What do you teach?"

"Urban planning."

She nodded, not exactly sure what that entailed. "This is a great house."

"Thanks. It's my father's. His health isn't great, so he moved out west for the dry climate."

A few more guests arrived, and everyone shifted around the table to accommodate them. Marco ended up on Olivia's other side. He made no acknowledgment of the fact that they'd met the other day at the house. Was it possible he didn't recognize her? Or did he simply not care? It struck her, as she pondered these two options, that *she* cared. That, to be honest, she had agreed to come to the party just in hopes of seeing him again.

It was ridiculous.

Trying to get her head right, she focused on the food in front of her. She clicked back into professional mode and, recognizing the social media moment, snapped a photo of the charred roasted red peppers and posted it.

Marco turned to her with an odd look.

"It's for Instagram," she said.

He shook his head. "I thought that stuff was for teenagers."

Olivia crossed her arms. "My whole job is based on social media. It's an enormous industry."

"Oh, well—that's interesting," he said, though she could tell he thought just the opposite.

It grew dark; candles were lit. The food kept coming: rice baked with lobster and shrimp; stewed green beans; a roasted chicken; shrimp grilled with garlic and cilantro. The wine flowed, but she abstained. She was taking enough ibuprofen to kill a horse, and still her back seized every time she stood up and throbbed when she was sitting down. How was she going to drive in the morning? Twenty-four hours hadn't given her one bit of improvement.

Rachel, her hosting duties on hold during the main course, sat next to Luke. He put his arm around her. While the table buzzed with chatter, they bent their heads together and talked mostly to each other. It was their own private party.

The sight of their easy, profound intimacy in the center of that joyous, crowded table made Olivia feel very, very alone.

Chapter Twenty-Two

Elise hadn't wanted to go to the party. She and Fern didn't have anyone to watch the baby, so they would have to take her along, which would inevitably bring up more questions. But shutting themselves in the house all summer was not an option.

"I don't know why you're suddenly concerned about what people think," Fern said. "You were the one who told me not to worry."

Elise had yet to tell her about the visit from Brian Correia. She also hadn't told her about Bianca spying on Shell Haven.

"Let's just go out and relax with our friends tonight," Fern said. "We need it."

By the time Elise and Fern had closed the tea shop, changed their clothes, and fed Mira, it was late; they didn't get to Rachel and Luke's until the tail end of dinner.

All day, Elise had told herself to forget about the encounter with Bianca. No doubt the woman had been exaggerating about Fern discussing selling the house. And she did forget about it—until she caught Bianca's eye across the table and heard her words afresh: *That woman said she was very interested. And Fern said it was an interesting idea.*

Elise, who'd been chatting amiably with Ruth Cooperman, could not believe the woman was after her house—not when she'd been so helpful and understanding about the baby. No, Elise would not allow herself to be upset. Not on a beautiful night like this. She poured herself another glass of wine, a crisp white from Argentina. They were going down so easily.

"More rice?" Fern asked, passing her the casserole. The baked-seafood dish was one of her favorites, a Portuguese recipe she'd first tasted at the Barroses' house their first summer.

Elise smiled at her. "Thanks. I should stop, but it's so good."

"It's a party! We can show restraint tomorrow."

Yes, it was a party. And things with Fern were good—not perfect, but good enough. The shop was almost as busy today as it had been over the weekend; it was a beautiful night under the stars; and she had a baby on her lap. *Deep breaths,* she told herself.

When the dinner plates were cleared, in the lull before dessert, it was musical chairs as the guests all shifted around to catch up with whomever they'd missed chatting with during the first two courses. Jaci arrived even later than Fern and Elise, separate from the rest of her family, and immediately offered to hold Mira. Elise handed her over, although she felt no need for relief. Despite the intense work of keeping an infant content, she had a sense of loss every time Mira left her arms.

"I'm so sorry about Marco," Jaci said, looking down at Mira. "I'm trying to change his mind, but my parents are on his side."

"Don't make trouble in your family over a summer job," Fern said. "If you want to come over and hang out in your free time, our door is always open. But you need to support your family's business."

"I'm in school getting a degree so I won't *need* to go into the business," she said. "I'm not planning to spend the rest of my life here. They have to accept that sooner or later."

Mira started fussing, and Jaci stood up. "I can take her for a walk in her stroller."

"Oh, I'll do it. Enjoy yourself—it's a party," Elise said.

Jaci gave her a wry look. "This isn't exactly my idea of a good time. I just spent all day with Marco. I don't need to hang out with him and my parents all night. I'm happy to take a walk."

Fern told her the stroller was parked on the back patio. Elise resisted the urge to call out, *Don't go too far!* She didn't want Jaci taking Mira at all but she knew Fern would be happy to have some adult time.

"I didn't even get a chance to say hello to you ladies," Clifford Henry said, swooping in to fill the seat Jaci had vacated. Elise couldn't focus; she was watching Jaci across the lawn with the baby.

"Relax," Fern said, putting her hand on top of hers.

"So who's the new addition?" Clifford said, following Elise's gaze.

"We're trying to adopt," Elise said.

"Fabulous! How did you—"

"Speaking of additions, we just saw Santiago's work on this house for the first time tonight," Fern said quickly.

"Santiago's a genius," Clifford said with a wave. "And so are you two. I'm in love with your divine store. *In love.*"

"Well, thanks, Clifford. We're pretty happy with it ourselves," Fern said, winking at Elise.

"Are you going to hire part-time summer help or just manage with the two of you?"

"We're trying to figure that out," Elise said. "Why? Do you know of someone who's looking for part-time work?"

"No," he said, leaning closer. "But I do know of someone who is looking to buy your house."

Elise's stomach dropped, but a quick glance at Fern reassured her. She was already rolling her eyes. "Shell Haven is not for sale, Clifford," Elise said.

"I know it's not for sale at the moment. But when it is, I hope you'll come to me first. Ruth Cooperman told me she spoke with you, Fern. That woman is signaling that she is willing to *spend*. It's a seller's market, as you know, so just say the word and I will work my magic."

"You're going to have to work your magic elsewhere," Fern said.

"You two are no fun!" Clifford said.

"I'm going to see if Rachel needs help with dessert," Elise said, standing up, hoping to end the conversation.

"Good idea. I'll join you," Fern said.

As they cut across the lawn to the house, Elise said, "That was irritating."

"Oh, you know Clifford."

"It's like, the second you rent out your house, it's suddenly up for grabs. I told you this was opening a can of worms."

Fern stopped walking and took her hand. "Hey, we're on the same side. No one is selling the house."

Elise nodded and smiled. "Okay. I'm sorry. I'm just a little edgy."

"Well, there's a lot going on," Fern said. "But we'll figure it out."

Inside, they found Rachel at the kitchen island, its surface covered with enough dessert for twice as many people as there were at the party: cream puffs, butter cookies, the mixed-berry pie she and Fern had brought from Connie's Bakery, lemon squares, two other pies, and some sort of pudding.

"Oh, hey, you two. Before I forget, I baked extra of these for you to take home." Rachel reached for a cookie tin on the counter. "They're called lavadores, and they traditionally go with tea."

"Rachel, you shouldn't have," Elise said. "Really, you have no idea

how much I—we—appreciate your help with Mira. I should be baking
for you."

The French doors opened and closed behind them. Marco carried in
some empty plates.

"Are you guys heading out?" he said, setting the plates down in the
sink.

"No," Fern said. "Just getting an early peek at dessert. By the way,
again, we're sorry about letting Jaci spend time at the tea shop and
babysitting when you needed her. We didn't realize it was such an issue,
though we probably should have guessed."

Marco shook his head. "It's not your fault. I don't know what's with
her this summer. She's acting like it's a punishment to be here."

"Don't be too hard on her," Elise said. "She's still just a kid."

"I appreciate that. Actually, Jaci aside, I wanted to speak to you both.
Do you have time to talk tomorrow afternoon?"

Fern and Elise glanced at each other. Elise felt a sudden unease. Was
this about Mira? With that simple question, she realized how precarious
her happiness actually was. They had a secret—a big secret. And with
that secret, a lot of hurdles in front of them.

"Sure," Fern said. "Come by the shop anytime."

"Can you meet me at the dock? I want to show you something I've
been working on. I have a business proposition for you two."

In her relief, Elise said loudly, "Oh, that's great!" Fern looked at her
like, *Are you okay?*

He smiled. "All right, then—to be continued tomorrow. Ready to re-
join the festivities?"

They followed him back outside. Fern reached for her hand and
squeezed it gently. Elise told herself to relax. They would figure things
out together the way they always had. There was no point worrying
about what-ifs when this night was perfect.

And yet, as she rejoined the party and took her seat just as Rachel emerged from the kitchen with the first tray of dessert, she couldn't deny the fact that no matter how much she wanted to believe she was on solid ground, she knew it could shift at any moment.

In the flickering candlelight of the backyard table, Ruth hid her disappointment when Olivia abruptly stood up and left with terse goodbyes.

Ruth had been midconversation with Lidia and Manny Barros, one of those couples who somehow managed to make it all work. They'd been married for thirty-five years and had two great kids and what seemed to Ruth a remarkably retro-style division of labor: Lidia was and had always been a homemaker; her husband managed the boatyard.

"Sometimes I help with the bookkeeping," Lidia said. "But, really, my focus has been the children."

"And the kitchen," Manny added, giving her an affectionate pat. From another man, this might have sounded sexist or patronizing. But Ruth could see from the look in his eyes it had been delivered with adoration. He looked across the table at his children, Marco and Jaci, with the same devotion. Ruth experienced, deeply, the fractured nature of her life in a way she hadn't in a very long time.

"Speaking of the kitchen, I'm going to help Rachel with the dishes," Lidia said.

"I'll join you," Ruth said. Movement. Busyness. Motion was the antidote to *emotion*.

They collected empty plates on their way to the kitchen, where Rachel was already piling a bunch in the sink.

"Oh, you don't have to do that," Rachel said, reaching out to relieve them of the dishes. "I'm just leaving these for now."

"Please, Rachel. Go outside and sit. You've been running around all night. Ruth and I need to stretch our legs," Lidia said, sharing a conspiratorial glance with Ruth.

"It's true. And I need to start working off that wine."

Rachel reluctantly left them, giving one last look over her shoulder and an "Are you sure?" before they shooed her outside.

Lidia opened the dishwasher and pulled the top and bottom racks forward. "I'll rinse, you stack them in the dishwasher," she said, and Ruth immediately felt bad about taking the cushier part of dishwashing duty.

"You have a beautiful family," Ruth said, fitting a serving platter along the side of the dishwasher's bottom rack.

"Oh, thank you," Lidia said, then sighed. "Though I have to admit, I was really looking forward to my daughter coming home for the summer, and so far, it hasn't gone well. She doesn't want to spend time with us—at least, not the way she used to. She didn't even come home for Christmas!"

Ruth searched for some words of wisdom, something about the age or the transition from living at home to living away but not fully being an adult. And she was sure those things were true, but she hadn't experienced them herself. By the time Olivia was a freshman in college, they hadn't lived together for years. To say anything in commiseration felt disingenuous. So she said nothing. This was perhaps a mistake, because in the silence, Lidia added, "I know I sound needy."

"No," Ruth said quickly. "Not at all. In fact, I'm having issues with my daughter as well, though it's an entirely different situation. I understand your feeling of disappointment."

Lidia looked at her gratefully. "I appreciate that. My husband thinks I'm taking it too personally. He's annoyed with Jaci for dragging her heels when it comes to doing the job we need her to do, but he's not emotional about it. Frankly, I wish I could be more like him." She passed Ruth some silverware, then asked, "Are you married?"

Ruth shook her head. "Divorced. Long divorced."

"I'm sorry to hear that." The expression on her face was one of deep sympathy, as if Ruth had been dealt a terrible blow. What would Lidia think if Ruth said, *I initiated it. I'm the one who broke up my family?* She was sure the look of sympathy would change to something else entirely.

"Yes, well, these things happen," Ruth said. "My one regret is that Olivia took it very hard, and our relationship hasn't been the same since."

"Well, it's a good sign that she made the trip out to visit you, right?"

Ruth simply nodded. Talking to this earnest and sweet woman was making her feel like a train wreck. And yet, had the impulse to spend time with her daughter been wrong? She refused to see her attempt to mend their relationship as selfish. Yes, she wanted her daughter back. But she also wanted to be a mother, to offer her a relationship. She wasn't just trying to take something—she was trying to give.

"She's leaving tomorrow," Ruth said. "Though I wish she'd stay."

Lidia shook her head. "It's never easy, is it?"

"No. I guess it isn't."

"Would you like to come over for coffee tomorrow morning?"

Ruth looked at her in surprise. "Really?"

Lidia smiled at her reaction. "Yes, really. It's nice to have someone in town who is my age and who's dealing with a grown daughter."

"Well, I'd love to," Ruth said. And she meant it. Standing in that strange kitchen, washing dishes in easy conversation with a woman she'd met only a few hours ago, Ruth felt remarkably at home. Maybe the choices of her past would limit her future with her daughter. Maybe she would always be alone. But at least she had this place and these people, with open doors and open hearts. She'd come to this town for a reason, a reason she couldn't fully explain even to herself. Ruth had never been one to second-guess her instincts. And once she had an idea in mind, she made it happen. *Motion, always motion.* Provincetown was a fresh start.

She could not force her daughter into a relationship with her. And she would not try. Clearly, it was time to let go.

Chapter Twenty-Three

The morning brought no relief. Olivia didn't feel any more capable of the five-hour drive than she had on the day her back went out. Still, she had to get to the office, even if it meant taking the ferry and returning for her car at a later date.

"What's your rush?" her mother said from across the breakfast table.

Um, not everyone around here is retired. "For one thing, the Wi-Fi here is nonexistent," Olivia said, tapping away at her laptop, trying for the umpteenth time to log in to her HotFeed e-mail.

"There's nothing wrong with the Wi-Fi," said Ruth.

"Well, there must be, because I can't get into my work e-mail." But even as she said it, Olivia was checking the settings and saw she had an internet connection. So maybe something was wrong with the server in New York? She'd have to let someone know. Just as soon as she figured out her travel situation.

"If you want to leave your car here, I could drive it to New York one day next week. We could have lunch," Ruth said.

Olivia looked at her. Suddenly, all the conflicting feelings she'd felt for the past few days crystallized. "I don't think you understand how painful it is for me to see the mother you could have been." She closed her laptop and eased to her feet.

"Could have been? It's the mother I am—today. Why do you insist on punishing me for the past?"

"I'm not punishing you, Mother." Olivia felt a surge of anger. She'd worked very hard not to need her mother. It had been painful, but she'd gotten there. She wasn't about to undo all of that now just because her mother was having a midlife crisis. "I just…look, thanks for the offer about the car but I'll be back for it at some point." Was this something she could hire someone to do? She'd figure it out once she got back to civilization.

Her mother stood up. She reached out to hug her and it was awkward but mercifully quick.

"Well, I'm glad you came," Ruth said. "I really am. And even if the only reason you're coming back is for the car, I'm looking forward to it already."

Don't, Olivia thought. *Don't look forward to it. Don't expect anything.* Olivia knew in that moment she had to make a clean break. There would be no leaving the car and coming back for it, no meeting her mother in the city. She would have to just drive off today, even if it meant stopping every half hour to relieve the pain in her back.

"I'm actually feeling okay to drive," she said. "Can you help me get my bag into the car?"

"This is not a good idea. It's not safe. What's your rush?"

"I have to get back to work, Mother! You of all people should understand that."

Her mother followed her outside, dragging her suitcase, protesting even as Olivia eased into the front seat. The angle of her body behind the wheel triggered a fresh round of spasms, but she did her best to hide it. She took deep breaths and asked her mother to close the door for her.

"Call me from the road. Let me know you're okay," Ruth said.

Olivia would have liked to sit there for a few minutes, to acclimate to the position and maybe make a few phone calls. But her mother continued to stand there, and Olivia knew she wouldn't go inside until Olivia drove off.

She backed out of the driveway and drove one block on Commercial. She pulled over to check her phone. To her left, she glimpsed the bay between houses. Three days in this town, and she hadn't even made it to the water.

Still no e-mail connection.

"What the hell?" She dialed Dakota's office line. It went straight to voice mail. Strange. She should be at her desk at ten in the morning. She tried Dakota's cell phone.

"Hello?" Dakota said.

"Oh, good! You're there," Olivia said. "I'm driving back to the city now but I can't get into my e-mail. Can you ask the IT department to see what's going on?"

"Um, you should talk to Peter."

Why would she bother Peter with her e-mail issues? Before she could ask, her assistant hung up.

It was suddenly very hot in the car. Olivia turned up the air-conditioning and dialed Peter Asgaard's assistant.

"Hi, it's Olivia. Is Peter—"

Immediately, she was put on hold. While she waited, two women walked in front of the car, one holding a colorful bodyboard and the other with a large cooler. Olivia looked out the window at the cloudless sky.

"Peter Asgaard here," her boss said on the other end of the line.

"Oh, Peter, hi. It's Olivia. I'm sorry to bother you. I'm on my way back to the office but there's a problem with the e-mail server."

"There's no problem with the e-mail server," he said.

"Well, yes, there is, because I can't log in."

"I'd prefer to discuss this in person. When will you be back in the office?"

"Discuss what in person?" Olivia's heart began to pound.

"Please report to HR first thing tomorrow morning."

What? This couldn't be happening. Olivia unplugged her headphone and held the phone directly to her ear. "I'm sorry—did you just say—"

"I approached April Hollis, hoping to regain her business. She had an interesting theory as to why you botched her Instagram feed. It appears you might be distracted, considering your plans to go out on your own." A pause. And then: "Olivia, you can't log in to your e-mail because you're no longer an employee of HotFeed Media."

Olivia stammered something, a lame murmur of there having been a misunderstanding. Peter repeated the instruction that she meet with the company's human resources department.

Trembling, Olivia tried to restart the car. She had to get back to New York, to fix this somehow. But she could barely lean forward to turn the key in the ignition; pain radiated from the base of her spine up through her shoulder blades.

A pink pedicab passed in front of the car, and the driver waved at her with a smile.

She burst into tears.

Ruth would not sit around the house all day moping about how the visit had turned out. After Olivia had driven off—ill-advised, but her daughter was nothing if not stubborn—Ruth borrowed one of the bikes resting on the back porch and rode to the beach.

She needed inspiration for her mosaic. She had her design, but she didn't yet see how to bring it to life. Working with tile seemed like the easiest way to go, but she suspected the end result would be far from the shimmering glory of the Beach Rose Inn starfish. Frankly, she wasn't sure she had even the slightest aptitude for this particular art form. And yet she liked having something to focus her energy on, so, for now, she would stick with it.

"Go to the beach," Amelia had advised her when she'd confessed her creative impasse.

In general, Ruth found *Go to the beach* to be sound advice. Need to get some reading done? Go to the beach. Looking to clear your head? Go to the beach. Need some exercise? Go to the beach.

Need to forget about the fact that your weekend with your daughter was a huge failure?

Ruth walked along the edge of the ocean, adjusting her wide-brimmed sun hat and scanning the wet sand for sea glass.

Had she made a mistake in inviting Olivia out in the first place? The time she'd spent here had certainly not brought them closer together. If anything, Olivia seemed angrier when she left than when she'd arrived.

I don't think you understand how painful it is for me to see the mother you could have been.

Ruth did understand, because this weekend had given her a glimpse of what her life might have been like if she'd had more of a relationship with her daughter. She saw it in Amelia and Rachel. She certainly saw it in the Barros family. In contrast, she and her daughter might as well have been strangers.

What had she hoped? That Olivia would find herself as transformed by the town as Ruth had been when she first saw it? She had been a teenager. Olivia was a grown woman—again, a fact she sometimes lost sight of. Maybe, if Ruth had first set foot on the shores of P'town at an older age, it wouldn't have made such an impression on her. But as it was, the town had always been synonymous with her youth. Although, in reality, she had spent only one summer in P'town. The reason Provincetown was so indelible, she decided, was that it had been the hinge in her life between youth and adulthood. If pressed, she might say her final moments of true, unencumbered happiness and, yes, innocence had been spent on that spit of land.

She and her mother had had a routine when they were here: They woke up early, took a walk on the beach, bought bread or pastry at the Portuguese bakery, then made eggs for breakfast. There were no bagels to be found but that was a minor culinary sacrifice for the summer. They spent the rest of the day at the beach, her mother coating herself with oil (oil!). Ruth met a few other teenagers, and they reveled in their understanding that there was no better place to spend the precious time between high school and college than in a town that felt separated from reality.

It was the last night of June when a friend invited her to attend a reading for a play at the Fine Arts Work Center. The center had been founded ten years before as a place for emerging artists to live and work together while developing their craft. Ruth, who had never been particularly artistic, was amazed not only by the prevalence of art and artists in Provincetown but by the casual way people pronounced themselves painters, writers, or actors. It was something she never encountered in Philadelphia; there, either you were a famous artist or you had a real job. In P'town, there was no such distinction.

She had little sense of time that summer; the only clues offering structure to her day were hunger pangs reminding her to eat lunch or dinner and the changing light. As a result, she and her friend arrived late to the play reading, missing most of it. The part she did manage to catch barely held her attention; she was distracted by a boy. He stood a few feet away from her, holding a plastic cup of red wine. Unlike Ruth, he was focused completely on the reading, his eyes locked on the actors. (Or were they the writers?) He was tall and lanky with glossy dark hair. He was dressed in a red T-shirt with a Coke logo on the front and jeans.

If Ruth had a type, this guy was it. He was boyishly handsome. Not gorgeous, but solidly good-looking. More than that, she felt a pull toward him that could only be explained as chemical. She felt it even before she saw his big hazel eyes, but when he did finally look at her—after the reading, during the cocktail portion—it sealed the deal.

They were standing in a small group. Ruth had worked her way into the loose circle just to be near him.

"You can't help but think of Lillian Hellman," he said to the small group, talking about the play everyone had just experienced. "And I mean that in a positive way—not to suggest it's derivative."

Ruth had no idea who Lillian Hellman was and didn't really care. "The play probably couldn't exist without Hellman," Ruth said.

"That's so reductive," a woman said, turning to her, her face red with anger. "Just because it's feminist, it's Hellman?"

Ruth, realizing she was most likely being confronted by the writer, said the only thing she could think of in the moment: "He said it first!" She gestured to Coke T-shirt boy. Incredibly, he laughed.

"This is some high-level discourse," he said.

Ruth, embarrassed, slunk away. She walked around in search of her friend, failed to find her, and returned to the room with the bar. She poured herself a cup of wine. No one seemed to care that she was underage.

"Don't feel bad; Shari gets defensive, but we all do." It was Coke T-shirt boy, right behind her.

"You're a playwright too?" She said.

"Guilty as charged," he said, extending his hand. "I'm Ben Cooperman."

"Ruth," she said.

To this day, Ruth could remember the way it felt when Ben Cooperman first touched her. It was an innocent handshake; well, considering what happened a few days later, maybe not entirely innocent. But she felt that handshake more deeply than any of the kisses or fumbling groping she'd experienced with the boys she'd dated in high school. It was a variation on a feeling she would have again and again that summer, the sense of understanding a moment's importance as it was happening, a certainty that she would never feel that way again and that she would remember it for the rest of her life. She had been right.

Her phone rang, and she was relieved to have something to anchor her in the present. The past was the past. The town, because it was in so many ways unchanged, had a way of playing tricks on her mind, of collapsing the years between then and now so that there was no emotional buffer. She had never been one to look back, and she had no interest in starting now.

She wiped her sandy fingers on the outside of her tote before reaching inside to look at her phone. "Olivia?"

"Mom," Olivia said. "I need you."

Chapter Twenty-Four

The rash appeared overnight, marring the baby's sweet face with angry red blotches. Elise could no longer put off taking her to a pediatrician.

Fern and Amelia had been telling her to go since the third day Mira had been in their care. Elise was just afraid to involve any outside authority.

"I have a friend in Truro," Amelia said. "She's one of us and it won't be an issue."

Elise was not sure what "one of us" meant, exactly. From Provincetown? Gay? Generally unconventional?

When she met Dr. Mary Brandt, Elise decided the answer was at least two of the above. She appeared to be in her sixties and had close-cropped white hair, thick glasses in black square frames, and an Australian accent. She wore clogs and a white medical coat over a blouse and a long denim skirt.

Elise did not know what Amelia had told Dr. Brandt about Mira's origins, but the doctor did not ask. She went about weighing her and measuring her in a brisk, businesslike fashion. She asked Elise and Fern about Mira's eating and sleeping habits, suggested adjusting her formula to one that might produce less gas, and pronounced the rash "baby acne."

"It looks ugly, but it's harmless," Dr. Brandt said.

It went so smoothly, felt so natural, that Elise began to relax. And then the doctor said, "Amelia told me you're in the process of adoption."

Elise froze. She had assumed Amelia had said nothing.

"Very early in the process," Fern said quickly.

"Do you know if she had a hep B vaccination at birth?"

Fern and Elise looked at each other. "Would a hospital do that automatically?" Fern said.

"Typically."

Elise did not know for sure if Mira had even been born in a hospital. The white blanket with the pink and blue stripes seemed like a hospital-issue receiving blanket. But the simple fact was she didn't know for sure and therefore couldn't say. "I can try to find out," Elise said lamely.

"She will need her DTaP, Hib, and RV in a month, so on your way out, make an appointment. And in the meantime, don't worry about the rash. She's still a beauty." Dr. Brandt smiled at Mira and gave her a little wave.

Elise realized now the value of that beaded anklet with the birth date on it. If she'd had to guess about Mira's age, she wouldn't have been able to make accurate decisions about her medical care. She felt with renewed certainty that the baby had been loved and that she had not been recklessly abandoned on their doorstep.

Fern was silent as they walked back to the car.

"Well, that went okay," Elise said uneasily. Fern didn't respond.

Elise buckled Mira into the backward-facing infant car seat, then climbed into the front passenger seat. Fern waited until they were on the road before saying, "This is not okay."

"What? You didn't like Dr. Brandt?" Elise knew that wasn't what she meant.

"We have no legal right to be making medical decisions."

"What's the harm? Do you think a state agency wouldn't give her those vaccinations? You're focusing on the wrong thing. We're being responsible and taking care of her. No one would do anything differently. And if her mother had a philosophical objection to vaccinations, I guess she could have written a note."

"That's absurd."

"Is it? She left us clues. She didn't make us guess her age. The blanket she arrived with is clearly a hospital blanket. Mira wasn't born in the wild somewhere. And the more I think about all of these things, the more I know that our doorstep wasn't randomly chosen."

"That's really irrelevant. Amelia lied to the doctor—she said we were in the process of adopting. Why did she lie? Because the truth is unacceptable."

"It wasn't a lie, it was an exaggeration. We *are* in the process—just the very early process, before we alert DCF."

Fern's knuckles were white as she gripped the steering wheel. "You're putting me in a tough position here, Elise. I don't want to betray you, but I don't want to betray myself either."

Elise nodded, turning to look out the window. "I know exactly how you feel."

Olivia wasn't able to climb three flights of stairs to the guest room, so Shell Haven's first-floor den with the foldout couch seemed a perfect solution. Olivia, however, had her doubts about this setup.

"I won't have any privacy."

"Who is going to bother you? Everyone else is staying upstairs; the kitchen is far enough away you won't hear a lot of noise. Please just stop fighting me on everything," Ruth said.

Secretly, she was delighted about this turn of events. She had resigned herself to the visit ending on a bad note, and now she had the chance to turn things around. Of course she didn't want Olivia to be in pain. But Olivia had told her that the back problem was a nuisance, not anything serious.

Fluffing the pillows, Ruth said carefully, "Maybe this is your body's way of telling you not to run off." She smoothed out the extra comforter she'd found in the closet in the master bedroom and patted it. "Come sit."

Olivia seemed on the verge of tears. "Actually, Mother, I was doing just fine. I was all set to leave. I was practically driving away, but then I found out...I found out..."

Ruth moved close to her, concerned. "You found out what?"

"I lost my job," Olivia said, then began sobbing. Ruth reached for her arm, steered her to the bed, and helped her ease down into a supine position.

"Oh, Olivia. I'm sorry. But weren't you thinking of leaving anyway? That first night at dinner, you talked about wanting to start your own company."

Olivia sniffed and nodded. "I did. I do. But I need clients. I was waiting for the right time. And I totally messed things up." And then out came a story about a breakup, the flu, a sober TV star, and an Instagram snafu.

"Have you been in touch with your ex? Now I feel bad calling you to come out here when you have so much going on in your personal life."

"I was upset when we broke up but it's nothing compared to how upset I am about my job. I don't know how I'm going to fix this, but I have to."

Truly, Olivia's passion for this job made little sense to Ruth. By the time social media became a thing, her company had people for everything and she hadn't had to bother with it any more than she'd had to bother with their traditional ad campaigns. Ruth's focus, her talent, had always been in product development. For her, it was about creating something, not selling something, though of course the selling was crucial to the life of the company. She surrounded herself with people who had a knack and a passion for selling. But at the end of the day, she was always thinking about what women really wanted or needed to make themselves feel and look their best. She understood what Olivia did on a technical level, but on a personal level, she couldn't imagine a career based on something so intangible and, frankly, meaningless.

"Are you worried about money?" Ruth said. "I can help you until you figure out your next move."

Olivia shook her head. "No, it's not that. Thank you, though. I just— my career is my life. I can't believe I screwed it up this badly."

"Everyone makes mistakes," Ruth said. "And no path to success is a straight shot upward."

"Yours was." Olivia sniffed.

"Oh no, it certainly was not." Ruth wished she could tell Olivia that when she was her age, she was juggling the jobs of mothering a toddler and running a company, that she had felt panicked and spread too thin much of the time, but she did not want to imply that motherhood had ever been a burden. Instead, she said simply, "There were many, many weeks in the beginning when I was up all night wondering how we were going to make payroll."

"At least you started the company. You did it."

"True," she said. "But it was never easy—not one minute of it. And I hadn't planned to start my own company. It was just an idea that took on a life of its own."

Really, it was amazing how life had snowballed into shape. Looking back on it, she saw the way the many small choices added up to the big picture of how things turned out.

In the fall of his senior year of college, Ben surprised her by announcing he was applying to medical school. What about writing? she asked. He said, unconvincingly, that he could still do it on the side. When he was accepted to Penn Med, they got engaged, and after they were married, they moved to his hometown of Cherry Hill, New Jersey, just across the river from the university.

She searched the want ads in the *Philadelphia Inquirer,* but the options were limited. By the time she saw an ad for a customer-service position at a cosmetics company, she was desperate. She interviewed on a Tuesday in a small gray room with a man who declared she had a "good phone voice." She was at her new desk the following Monday.

The company manufactured cosmetics and skin-care products. Big brands contracted them to create products in their labs, and then the outside companies packaged these with their logos and labels. Ruth was amazed to learn that no matter the brand name, half the time you were buying the same product; the quality was interchangeable. Sometimes there was customization—a Chanel lipstick had the same basic ingredients as any other lipstick, but the level of pigment might be different. Still, chances were, if you were buying a mascara, it made little difference what brand it was.

Ruth's customer-service job evolved into sales, and she was optimistic she might be able to climb the corporate ladder to an executive position. Her dream was to get more involved in product development. But three years after she'd started the job, just before Christmas 1986, the company's manufacturing facility burned down. The owners told the staff they had no intention to rebuild. Ruth was frustrated to find herself back to the newspaper listings. There was nothing. She settled for a job in retail banking, lasted six miserable weeks there, then told Ben: "I miss the cosmetics company. It was a good business. I want to try to start my own."

Ben, to his credit, supported her ambitions. It heartened her, made her feel confident she would not have her parents' marriage. Ben borrowed a few grand from his parents, and she incorporated RC Cosmetic Labs in 1987. It was a big leap; Ruth had no idea what she was doing, but she surrounded herself with six trusted lab technicians, all women, whom she knew from the previous company. They put the colors and formulas together; Ruth sampled and then approved or rejected them. It was all trial and error and Ruth's instinct. The lab techs cooked with stockpots before Ruth could afford more professional equipment. They worked out of a three-thousand-square-foot rental space in the back of a large manufacturing business in Voorhees.

For her birthday, she asked for twenty-five-pound manufacturing kettles and lipstick molds. That first year, they did $250,000 in business and made a $25,000 profit.

"But when you were my age, you created the nail polish," Olivia said. "After that, you were basically set."

Yes, the nail polish. The game-changer. Ruth thought again about the discontinuation of Cherry Hill and what it meant for the company that she'd been forced to leave behind. "You'll find your own version of the nail polish, sweetheart," Ruth said. "I believe in you. But for now, rest." She kissed her on the forehead. "I'm going to pick up lunch."

She needed to call Lidia Barros and postpone their plans for coffee until later in the day. For the first time in a very long while, Ruth had some mothering to do.

Chapter Twenty-Five

Elise and Fern met Marco on the boatyard dock as they'd said they would the previous night. Of course, they hadn't anticipated their day would start at the pediatrician's office and that the visit would create so much tension that they were scarcely speaking to each other when it was time for the meeting. But one thing Elise and Fern both agreed on was that it would be wrong to cancel.

"Besides," Fern said, "we can't let all this paralyze us."

Elise bristled at the sentiment, because it was something Fern had said again and again when their attempts at pregnancy kept failing and Elise had been unable to focus on anything else. She didn't want Fern equating this new baby with the way things had happened with the IVF. She couldn't let her turn something with possibilities into something doomed and then use that as an excuse to reject it.

Marco was crouched down, tying a skiff to the dock. He spotted them and motioned them over. It was a perfect day to be out on the water, sunny but with little wind. The bay was slate-colored and filled with boats of all kinds. The air smelled like the sea.

Even after five years, when Elise walked on the docks and piers of the town, she still marveled that they lived so close to such natural beauty. She particularly romanticized the three-mile-long breakwater just off Pilgrim Park that stretched out into the water like a bridge to infinity. She and Fern used to take a picnic dinner to the park and then walk out onto the rocks, Elise skittish and unsure of her footing, Fern holding out her hand and leading the way. They should do that again sometime soon.

"You ready for a little sightseeing?" Marco said, smiling. Despite the bumpy start to the day, Elise couldn't help but smile back. Marco was a good man. It wasn't surprising that a few years ago, that wealthy young woman from Chatham had fallen for him. Of course, anyone could see from a mile away that the relationship would never last. But how sweet, how absolutely romantic it had been for Marco to propose to her. The Barroses—and everyone else who cared about Marco—had to pack away their doubts and hope for the best. Only Lidia continued to sound the alarm, confiding in Elise and Fern that the woman was all wrong for her son, that she was already trying to change him, and when she realized that would fail, she would leave and break his heart. And that's exactly what happened.

"We're ready. Is this our ride?" Fern said, looking at the skiff.

"No, we're over here." A larger powerboat was tied on the other side of the dock. It had a metal pole topped with a hook-like contraption near the bow. Elise and Fern climbed onto the stern, where there was a long bench and a few scattered egg crates and coils of rope. Two pairs of protective gloves were tucked into the side of the bench.

"I'm taking you out to where I have my bottom cages," Marco said over the loud rumble of the motor.

Elise had questions, as she was sure Fern did. But once they picked up speed, it was too loud for conversation. Now that they were physically out on the water, the color of the bay was a deeper blue tinged with green. White foam kicked up around the perimeter of the boat, and Elise's hair whipped around her face in the wind.

They were ten minutes out when Marco cut the motor. They were in an area of the water marked by white buoys in horizontal rows.

The stillness made Elise feel off balance the way the motion had when they'd left the dock.

"This will just take a few minutes," Marco said. "I'm not trying to be mysterious, it's just easier to show you instead of explaining."

Marco cast the hook-like contraption at the end of a line down into the water, then set to work rotating a lever on the metal pole. It made a loud cranking sound as it slowly raised the line to the surface of the water and then above. When it was a few inches higher, Elise saw it was pulling up a horizontal rope that was covered in something light brown and slimy.

Marco cranked the lever, lifting the rope higher and higher, and Elise realized it was elevating seaweed. The seaweed hung like a sheet, yellow-brown with a ridged texture, glistening in the sun. The fronds had to be twelve to fifteen feet long. Maybe longer.

Marco leaned over with a knife, sliced off a few pieces, and dropped them into a white plastic bucket.

"Marco, what is all this?" Fern said.

He smiled and wiped his brow. "I'm cultivating seaweed," he said. "Specifically kelp."

The long fronds reminded Elise of crimped hair.

"We can see that," Fern said. "But...why?"

"A few reasons. I'm worried about the future of fishing. The past two seasons have been rough. And every year, I know one hurricane could wipe out the oysters and I'm done. But seaweed gets planted after hurricane season. And since I already have the infrastructure for the oysters, it really cost me nothing to get this up and running."

"Is there a big market for seaweed?" Fern said.

"Good question. It's a growth industry. As a cooking ingredient, it's sort of adventurous right now."

"Have you eaten it?"

He nodded. "I have. Kelp noodles have a very mild flavor. Plain, dried kelp has a sea-salt, nutty taste. There's a lot of variety. It's high in protein, low in calories, and a truly sustainable crop. And remember, not many people were eating kale ten years ago."

"True," Elise said.

"But aside from using kelp as a food source—because I admit it could be a little while before it catches on—I think ethically, we need to grow it. You know excess nitrogen in the water is a major problem here on the coast, and the oysters filter it, but so does seaweed. And a bigger problem is the rising acidity of the oceans. The ocean is absorbing all the excess carbon in our environment and the resulting rise in acidity is threatening shellfish—they can't develop their shells. Seaweed and kelp absorb the carbon dioxide."

"It sounds great," Fern said. "But what does this have to do with us?"

"Instead of sitting around and waiting for kelp to catch on, I was thinking about ways I could be proactive in getting it out there. And then I read about this guy in Maine who's doing kelp teas."

Elise and Fern looked at each other. "Really? I can't imagine that flavor would be palatable at all," Fern said.

"I know—it doesn't sound like something that should work. But he mixes the kelp with green teas and some herbals, and somehow, it does work. I know you guys have your own Tea by the Sea blends, and I thought maybe if I gave you some kelp, you could experiment with it. And by the way, I know you're really into the mind, body, spirit of the whole thing, and seaweed is full of antioxidants and vitamins. I just think this could be an interesting offering."

Elise could tell by the look on Fern's face that she thought it was interesting too. Maybe it was. Maybe two weeks ago she would have been excited about trying something new. Now she didn't want to get involved with anything that might require her to take time away from Mira.

"We're willing to give it a shot. Right, Elise?"

"Sure," Elise said.

"Great!" Marco said. Behind him, the sheets of kelp waved in the breeze. The aroma of salt water and something distinctly of the sea wafted over them. If she could capture it, it would be summer in a bottle. She thought, then, about how the scent of the Strawberry Meadows tea blend filled the shop, how every customer commented on it. The kelp blend could do the same thing. Really, it might not be a bad idea.

"I have one more small request—actually, it's not that small. It's about that size," he said, gesturing toward the kelp.

"Shoot," said Fern.

"I need to dry the kelp and the best way to do that is to hang it from a line in the fresh air—like laundry. But I can't do it outside of my apartment and there's too much foot traffic and debris behind my parents' house where my dad works on the boat repair. Can I use your backyard at Shell Haven?"

"I wouldn't mind but you know we have a tenant this summer. You would have to discuss it with Ruth," Fern said.

"I don't know if we should bother Ruth with this. I feel like we've pushed things way too far as it is," said Elise.

Fern looked at her like, *And whose fault is that?*

"Let me just run it by her," Marco said. "If she has any hesitation, that will be the end of it. I'll find someplace else. Either way, I'm very happy you two are on board with trying out the tea. I love how open you are."

"Yeah, well. Maybe we're a little too open sometimes," Fern said.

Marco looked at Elise, and she shook her head with an expression that said, *That was directed at me.*

He lowered the kelp back into the water.

* * *

By late afternoon, Olivia had determined that sitting was worse than standing, and so she paced in the backyard.

It was more rustic than the manicured front lawn. Along with the hydrangeas, Olivia saw bunches of wildflowers and a patch of tall weeds. She found herself gravitating toward the weeds in all their messy abundance. The orderly beauty of the flowerbeds felt like a rebuke when her own life was unraveling.

The light started to shift, the slightest downgrade from bright sun to something gentler. In one corner of the yard, a patch of shade. She stood in front of a stone bench and stared at her phone. It had been buzzing all day with texts and messages from her former coworkers and clients, all of them offering their sympathy while subtly (or, in most cases, not so subtly) asking what had happened and where she was going next, so she was relieved to find it silent.

The one person she had not heard from was her assistant—former assistant—Dakota. She wondered, cynically, how long it would be before Dakota moved into Olivia's office. It was possible Peter had just been looking for an excuse to fire her. At thirty, she was already old for the company. They could pay one of the kids just out of college a fraction of her salary, and those new hires had three times her social media presence.

Yes, she'd given them cause to push her out the door. But that didn't change the fact that she'd been headed out to pasture anyway.

She looked at her Instagram profile, considered editing HotFeed out of her bio, then decided against it. Why rush to downgrade herself to irrelevant? She had to think of her next move. She could still start a company. It would just be that much harder to get it off the ground.

Without thinking, she bent down to sit on the bench. Pain rippled through her lower back.

How could she think of starting a company when she couldn't even sit down? She was stuck in that town and dependent on her mother after swearing to herself she would never ask the woman for a thing. In that moment, Olivia was as far from independent as she could imagine. And there was only one person she wanted to depend on.

She dialed her father, and he answered on the first ring.

"You made it back home?" he said cheerily.

"Not exactly," she said, then felt the tears start again. The circumstances of the afternoon came out in a jumbled, sniffling rush. By the time she was finished talking, she could not have felt any sorrier for herself.

"Just try to stay calm," her father said. "You always push yourself too hard. This happened for a reason, as difficult as it might be to see that in the moment."

"I never should have come out here," she said.

"I don't think that's the real issue. You need to deal with stress better. So take some time to regroup. Is there anything I can do?"

Olivia glanced back at the house and hesitated only a few seconds before saying, "It's just—I don't want to be here, dependent on Mom. It's awkward. And I don't know when I'll be able to make the drive back to New York. Dad, this is asking a lot, but is there any way you can come for a night and I'll go back home with you?"

Chapter Twenty-Six

Lidia Barros didn't give Ruth an address for the house, just vague directions: "Walk toward the water and you'll see it on the left. If you reach the boat-rental office, you've gone too far."

Ruth turned into the alley leading to the dock and passed an aluminum-sided building on her right and a few buildings on her left along with a GMC pickup truck and boats on lifts awaiting repair. The water spread out before her, reflecting the bright sun. She allowed herself a minute to just soak in the view. It struck her that the last time she had visited the dock, it had been for an ill-conceived boat ride that was derailed by her shark phobia. She never would have imagined that just a few short weeks later, she would be back as a guest of the family who owned the place.

Lost in thought, Ruth walked toward the water until she had, in fact, reached the boat-rental office and gone too far. She turned around and spotted a three-story house of unfinished wooden clapboards. The bottom floor seemed to be a workshop, and a wooden staircase led to a second-story deck. A wooden sign in the shape of an anchor announced the address, and the railing was strung with ropes and a few decorative buoys. Ruth climbed the stairs and found a set of sliding glass doors. At her feet, a welcome mat decorated with the image of a red lobster.

Before she could ring the bell, Lidia appeared. "Welcome!" she said, sliding open the doors. Ruth followed her inside to the kitchen, a real cook's kitchen with a butcher-block island, a farmhouse sink, and a ceiling rack filled with pots and pans.

"Oh, I'm sorry. I guess I missed the front door."

"Everyone misses the front," Lidia said breezily. "I can't remember the last time we used it. Besides, we all end up in here anyway." She wore a plain V-neck T-shirt and denim shorts and her thick hair was pulled back in a clip. Ruth marveled at her absolutely makeup-free face—not even a hint of mascara.

Ruth felt overdressed in her linen pants and button-down shirt. She hadn't adjusted to the casualness of the town.

She handed Lidia the loaves of banana and zucchini bread she'd picked up from Connie's Bakery on her way. She'd learned about the place the night of Rachel and Luke's dinner; Elise and Fern had brought an incredible mixed-berry pie and told her it was from Connie's. It took Ruth a few minutes to figure out it was a bakery and not just another friend.

Lidia directed her to take a seat at the wooden kitchen table. It was covered with floral-patterned oilcloth. "I just put the coffee on," Lidia said, setting out cream and a bowl of sugar.

Lidia sliced up the banana bread and they settled in with their coffee just as the glass doors slid open again. Marco, dressed in all-weather rubbery overalls and high boots, poked his head in. "Is Jaci in here?"

"No, I haven't seen her."

"Damn it," he said.

"Marco, please. There's no need for that."

"Really? I think there is. She was supposed to meet me on the dock twenty minutes ago for low tide. I have to get out to the flats. It's going to take me twice as long to finish without her, and I have a meeting at five." He nodded at Ruth. "Oh, hi, Mrs. Cooperman. I didn't know you were here," he said. "I actually need to talk to you about something."

"Talk to *me?*" What could he possibly have to talk to her about? Clearly, Lidia wondered the same thing because she said, "Is everything okay?"

"Yeah, yeah, it's fine. I don't have time to get into it."

"Well, now that you've made us both curious, I suggest you at least get into some of it," Lidia said, hands on her hips, switching from amiable hostess to firm mother mode in the blink of an eye.

Marco glanced at the water behind him as if torn between the low tide and not angering his mother. When he turned back to Ruth, she knew his mother had won out over Mother Nature.

"I want to know if I can borrow your backyard occasionally to hang seaweed out to dry."

"Marco!" Lidia said. "That's an imposition. What are you thinking?" She turned to Ruth. "I'm sorry. Sometimes my children still think that house belongs to their cousin."

"Ma, I don't think that at all. If anything, I was confused about whether or not Elise and Fern had moved back in for the summer. I talked to them about using the yard and they told me to check with Ruth."

Hang seaweed? Ruth had no idea what this meant, but she could hardly say no since she was sitting at her new friend's kitchen table and this was clearly important to her son. "Of course. No problem," Ruth said.

"Great, thanks! More on that later. I have to run." He kissed his mother on the cheek. "See, Ma? No one's upset. Except with Jaci. If you see her, tell her I'm seriously pissed."

"Marco! Your language."

"Okay, tell her I'm very angry." He winked at Ruth and left.

Lidia shook her head. "Thirty years old and he's still this big, unwieldy puppy." The adoration in her voice was unmistakable. "I just hope you're not put out."

"Oh, no. It's fine," Ruth said.

"That house was in the Barros family for generations and for a while after the Douglases moved in, we forgot we couldn't just drop in. My sister-in-law Bianca—you met her the other night at the party—is still furious about her daughter selling it. She didn't learn about the sale until it was too late for her to stop it."

"Well, as we've been saying, there's not much we can do about the attitudes or decisions of our adult children."

"Oh, she's not angry at her daughter. She's angry at Fern and Elise for buying it. It's completely irrational." Lidia sighed. "Enough about my crazy family. How are you adjusting to life here full-time?"

"I love it," Ruth said. "I have to admit, there was something slightly impulsive about my move. But I needed a change, and this was it."

"Had you spent a lot of time here before your move?"

"Just one summer. Years ago." A lifetime ago.

"Sometimes, with P'town, that's all it takes. At least, from what I've heard. I've never had the chance to experience this place as a newcomer, and as much as I love being a townie, a part of me would love to see it through fresh eyes."

Ruth nodded. "When I came here last year, exploring the idea of the move, I wondered if I would still feel as strongly about it or if I'd show up and realize it was just the rosy glow of nostalgia that drew me back. But as soon as I stepped foot on Commercial, I felt happy."

"I do think that for many people, this place is a cure-all."

Ruth nodded, but the truth was, as much happiness as she experienced waking up in Provincetown every morning, she still missed the sense of purpose she'd felt running her own company. She hated the idea of being irrelevant, and more than that, she had a bad feeling in the pit of her stomach at the thought that her legacy was being erased. Two days earlier she'd read in the *Wall Street Journal* that the conglomerate that had bought her out was consolidating some of their holdings, folding major brands into one another. Her company wasn't mentioned specifically, but if that happened, the discontinuation of Cherry Hill nail polish would be just the beginning.

"Do you want to sit outside?" Lidia said. "Manny was working on a boat earlier and it was loud, but it sounds like he's finished."

Ruth grabbed her mug and followed Lidia onto the deck, where two wooden chairs on either side of a small round table offered an expansive view of Provincetown Harbor.

The ground below was a flurry of activity. To their right, Manny stood talking animatedly to a man next to a motorboat elevated on a metal rack. Ahead, half a dozen people were lined up at the office waiting for tours or rentals, and men on the dock were busy launching boats into the water or assisting with arrivals.

"I guess it's never a dull moment around here," Ruth said.

"Yes, this boatyard is quite an operation. It's changed over the years. It started with my father-in-law with boat repair, and he also built fishing boats. Then Manny began renting out moorings to people, and the mooring field has been a big part of the business. And, of course, the boat rentals—kayaks, pontoons. Last year we started seal-watching tours."

She wondered if Lidia ever felt a lack of privacy, but before she could ask, Lidia said, "It can be challenging to live in such a public space, but at the same time, we have parties and it feels like the whole town is sharing in the fun. My favorite day of the year is the Fourth of July. Oh, you should plan on coming, and bring your daughter. You've celebrated the Fourth of July here before, right?"

Ruth nodded. "Just once. A very long time ago."

* * *

In her mind, that first summer was divided into a distinct before and after. Before the night at the Fine Arts Work Center, she had been satisfied
with the simple delights of walking on the pier or eating an ice cream
cone to the sound of a street musician. But after the play at the Fine Arts
Work Center, all Ruth thought about was Ben Cooperman.

She thought about him during her morning beach walks with her
mother. She thought about him while she was standing in line for
a lobster roll at lunch. But mostly, she thought about him when
she was tucked into her twin bed under the sloped ceiling of her
second-floor bedroom at the rental house. Staring into the darkness,
she replayed over and over the moment when he shook her hand.
Then she took it further. In her fantasy, everyone had cleared out of
the building. The room with the makeshift bar was dark. He didn't
stop at holding her hand.

It was the vividness and repetition of this reverie that made her blush
when she ran into him the morning of the Fourth of July on Commercial
Street, just a few feet from the bookstore. He spotted her first, initiated
the conversation. She'd been fantasizing about him so much, she had almost forgotten he was a real person. In just a few days he had taken on a
mythical quality. It hadn't crossed her mind that she might run into him
again or that she could have sought him out if she'd chosen. Looking
back on it now, she decided that that more than anything showed how
young and innocent she had been.

He'd called her by name, and when she remarked on his remember-
ing it, he said, "Hard to forget. Old Testament. Your parents weren't
messing around with that name."

"Neither were yours," she told him. "Benjamin?"

"Please—just Ben."

He was on his way to the pier. A bunch of people were sailing to Long
Point to see the lighthouse. "You should come," he said.

There were two problems with this: one, Ruth was nervous out on the water because of her fear of sharks. Two, Ruth was supposed to meet her parents back at the house by six for dinner and then fireworks. Would a boat trip fit into that time frame? Looking at Ben, she decided it was worth risking being late for dinner. And death by shark.

During the short walk to the wharf, she learned he was from Cherry Hill, New Jersey, not even an hour from where she lived back in Philly. That they should have spent their entire lives so close to each other only to meet on the tip of Cape Cod, seven hours from home, made their connection seem all the more magical to her. In the fall, he would begin his sophomore year at Penn. She told him she was starting Northwestern at the end of August.

She didn't want to think about all of that. She wanted only that day, with the cloudless sky and the temperature hovering somewhere in the high seventies and the harbor filled with boats, one of which—a sailboat that could fit half a dozen people—was waiting to transport their group across the harbor. Ben Cooperman held out his hand to help her climb aboard.

Ruth had never been on a sailboat, didn't realize there was a motor that could also propel them efficiently through the water. She had been on a boat only once before, a small motorboat in the bay at the Jersey Shore. The vista in front of her, where Cape Cod Bay met the Atlantic, made her previous trip on the water seem like wading in a small pond. This felt like they were at the edge of the world.

The motor created a hum that made talking more trouble than it was worth. Still, the captain, a stocky, deeply tanned guy who seemed barely older than herself and Ben, pointed out landmarks and shared trivia. On the ledge beside her, Ben Cooperman moved closer. She leaned over the side, looking at the white spray of water along the boat's edge, acutely aware of the feeling of his body against her and wanting to turn to see him but not trusting herself, because she knew the look on her face would give away every thought she'd had about him in the past four days.

After ten or fifteen minutes, they dropped anchor a few dozen yards away from Long Point, a hundred-and-fifty-acre peninsula that housed only a lighthouse and a mound of earth that marked the spot of a former Civil War battery. The captain and his first mate readied a dinghy to transport them in groups of two onto land. When it was their turn to leave the sailboat, Ben touched her arm.

"How much interest do you have in that lighthouse?"

Her heart began to beat fast. Her nonanswer was her answer.

"I think we're going to stay aboard, if that's okay with you," Ben told the captain. "We're really into the water more than the sightseeing."

"I don't want you trying to move this boat or swimming ashore. You're okay just to hang tight until we get back? It'll be about an hour."

Ben assured him they would be fine. The captain showed them where jugs of water were stored in the cabin belowdecks. That brief conversation left Ruth alone long enough for her to ask herself the fundamental question: Is this what I want? And the answer was intense and deep and resounding: Yes.

The dinghy motored off, leaving her alone with Ben in a way she had never felt alone with anyone before. She could see the slice of land in front of her, and she knew Provincetown was behind her. But she felt very far from solid ground.

She shielded her face with her hand to look at him, and he opened his knapsack and handed her a Phillies baseball hat. "You're going to burn," he said.

"I wasn't exactly planning on a day out at sea when I left the house," she said, putting it on her head.

"I admire your spontaneity," he said, sitting back on the ledge. He patted the space next to him and she sat, feeling jumpy inside.

"So…" she said to fill what felt like awkward silence.

"Ruth, I've been thinking about you since the other night," he said. She looked at him. His eyes were gold and brown and green, more dazzling than the sun-dappled blue water surrounding them.

"Really?" she said as if she hadn't experienced the very same thing. She'd already followed him onto the boat. She'd already stayed behind with him. She was entitled to hold something back.

He nodded. "After you left I realized I didn't know your last name or whether you were here for a day or a week or a month, and I felt stupid. But I knew if you were around I'd see you again because that's the way it is here. And P'town didn't let me down." He reached for her hand. The day really was so hot and bright.

"I think I need water," she said.

"I'll get it." He jumped up. Fetching water required walking down a narrow but short flight of stairs. Ruth hadn't meant for him to leave; she could have gotten it herself. But he was already halfway down the steps when she said, "I can do it."

She followed him, ducking her head and holding on to the narrow metal railing. She felt the boat sway and she wondered if there was any way it could just drift away from shore. Her imagination began to run wild and she imagined herself and Ben Cooperman in some sort of *Gilligan's Island* situation.

"One water, coming right up," he said, pouring from a jug into a clear plastic cup. The name of the boat, *Amphitrite,* was printed on it in blue lettering. She said the name aloud.

"Goddess of the sea, wife of Poseidon," he said, handing her the cup.

She looked up at him, wanting him to kiss her more than anything she'd ever wanted in her life. He didn't. So she did what any self-respecting, crushing-hard teenager would do: she reached her arms around his neck and kissed him.

They kissed and kissed, eventually folding themselves together on a plush, curved bench against one side of the cabin. When their clothes came off, rushed, fumbling, wordlessly, she felt embraced not just by this man but by the bended arm of the Cape. She knew, afloat in the spot that felt like the tip of the world, that she would return to land a changed woman.

Ruth smiled at Lidia Barros, thinking how hard it was to actually make new friends late in life. There was so much that could never be fully explained, whole incarnations of the self that had come and gone. A friend at that stage could know only a two-dimensional version of you, and that's what made old friends—even old husbands—so precious. They knew you in all your dimensions. For a time, Ruth believed that the only version of herself that mattered was the current one. She'd been so willing at times to shed her skin, to become better, better, better. But what if the best version of herself had been behind her all these years?

"I should get home," Ruth said, standing up. "My daughter's back went out and she's housebound."

"Oh, what a shame! In this glorious weather too."

"I've been encouraging her to at least sit in the yard and get some fresh air."

"Please, just leave that mug and plate. I'll take care of it," Lidia said as Ruth tried to clean up.

They both turned at the sound of footsteps on the wooden stairs. Tito appeared, carrying a large cooler. "I'm here to unload some stripers, if you're interested," he said. "Ruth! Surprised to see you this close to the water."

"Very funny." Ruth smiled.

"Thanks, Tito. Just put them on the counter in there. I'll be inside in a minute. Ruth is just leaving."

Tito walked past them and opened the sliding door. Halfway in, halfway out, he turned to Ruth. "I meant what I said the other night about getting out on the boat. You going to take me up on that offer?"

She remembered what he'd said at the party: *It would be a shame for you to spend time in this town and not experience the best part of it.* Well, she had experienced the best part of it. She thought maybe the best, in many ways, was behind her. But that didn't mean she couldn't try to move forward.

"Sure," she said. "Why not?"

Chapter Twenty-Seven

Olivia felt guilty for asking her father to come visit. It had not been a very adult thing to do. But something about living under the same roof as her mother for the first time in twenty years had reduced her to a less-evolved version of herself. She knew this stress was what had originally triggered her back spasms, and losing her job had compounded the problem. This was what the back pain was all about.

And yet this understanding failed to make it go away. She didn't know what to do.

She stared at the ceiling of her makeshift first-floor bedroom. She'd awakened to the sound of Elise and Fern bickering in the kitchen before Amelia arrived to pick up the baby. Just as she was drifting back to sleep, her mother had knocked on the door to announce she was headed out. Olivia had somehow managed to lose a job and gain three roommates. Four, if you counted the baby. This was her life—headed in the wrong direction.

"Anyone home?" The voice, female, seemed to be coming from the kitchen.

What now? Olivia sat up slowly, then swung her legs over the side of the bed and inched into a standing position while holding on to the nightstand. She looked out into the hallway just as someone with a familiar face rounded the corner of the living room. Jaci Barros.

"Jaci," Olivia said, leaning against the doorframe. "What are you doing here?"

"I won't bother you. I'm just going to hang out." She waved a library book she was carrying.

Olivia sighed. "No offense, but ever hear of a coffee shop?"

"Here's the thing—I'm sort of hiding from my mother, but everyone in town knows me and will narc me out if she tries to find me. I swear, if I have to spend one more minute trapped on a sandbar with my brother digging through boxes of oysters, I'll die. Please just let me sit here and read for a few hours. Once the tide goes out again I'm off the hook for another day."

Olivia sighed. "How did you even get in the house?"

"The back door's open."

Olivia walked past her into the kitchen and closed the back door and locked it. When she returned, Jaci was settled on the couch opening her book.

"It's safe here, you know," Jaci said. "My cousin owned this house for a decade and she didn't even have keys."

"Well, I'm from New York, and when I'm alone in a place, I like to remain alone unless I invite someone over. At the very least, I'd appreciate a doorbell ringing."

"Sorry," Jaci said sheepishly. "I didn't think anyone would be home."

And that made it better? "Jaci, if you don't want to work with your brother this summer, why don't you just tell him? I mean, you're, what, nineteen years old? You're in school. You don't really live at home anymore, right? You're basically just visiting for the summer."

"It's complicated," Jaci said. The expression on her face was pure misery.

"Is it a financial issue? Like, they pay for school so you have to work for them or something like that?"

"No, I have pretty much a free ride at school and I make up for the rest working during the winter."

"So just tell them you're doing your own thing." Olivia didn't understand what the problem was.

"I can't let my mother down. It's hard enough on her that I went away to school. No one in the family has ever left. I'm the first woman to go to college. And everyone is really proud of that but they want me to be the girl who goes to Princeton *and* the girl who works on the oyster farm." Her eyes filled with tears.

"Look, mothers get disappointed sometimes," Olivia said. "And they disappoint us. It's just life. Tell her the truth. Tell her what you just told me. When I was your age I told my mother that I didn't want to work with her."

It was the last month of her freshman year at Vassar and her mother called to offer her a job at the cosmetics company for the summer. She told Olivia she could work in any department she wanted. "I know you're interested in PR and we have a lot going on for Liv Free. You could really run with it." Olivia didn't consider it for a minute even though it would have looked great on her résumé. She spent the summer waiting tables.

"Did your mother *need* you to work for her?" Jaci said.

"Well, no. But she wanted me to."

"Yeah, well, Marco *needs* me. My uncle Tito gave him the water grant a few years ago, and Marco started the oyster farm thinking I'd be in it with him someday. My family has made a living off the water for generations and it's not something that works without a group effort or at least a partnership. It's a really big deal for me to walk away."

"Jaci, you're entitled to live your own life. Besides, it's better to just pull the Band-Aid off and say you're not doing it instead of hiding out here. They'll get over it."

"That's easy for you to say."

"Why is it easy for me to say?"

"Because you're not close with your mother. I mean, you don't understand what I have to lose."

"How do you know about my relationship with my mother?"

"You told me before. The day I met you. You said, 'I try to avoid my mother most of the time.'"

That's right. She had said that. "Well, I have a close relationship with my father," Olivia said defensively. She heard her phone ring in the other room. "Excuse me."

She walked back to the foldout couch and saw that the incoming number was her father's. "Hey," she said. "I was just thinking about you."

"Just checking in," her dad said.

"One second, okay?" Still rankled by Jaci's comments about her family ties, or lack thereof, she marched back into the living room and pointed to her phone. *My father,* she mouthed.

Jaci nodded, looking confused.

Olivia returned to her room and closed the door. "Have you thought about maybe coming out here?" Olivia said.

"I have. But it's a long drive so I want to stay over at least one night. Maybe two. I looked into hotel availability and there's really nothing in town this week or next. I get the sense things are booked up far in advance around there."

"You can stay here," she blurted out. "There's an extra room on the third floor because I'm sleeping in the den."

"Stay at your mother's house? Olivia, you know that's not possible."

"Why not? Honestly, it's not even like it's her house. There are other people staying here."

"What other people?"

"The women who own the house. And a baby they're taking care of. It's a long story. Anyway, this place feels like a hotel. Or a weird bed-and-breakfast. Trust me."

He didn't respond, and she knew he was considering it. She wondered if he was lonely, if maybe he wanted to make the trip as much as she wanted him to come. Or maybe she was just trying to justify her own neediness.

"Have you discussed this with your mother?" he said.

"She's fine with it," Olivia said quickly. And she would be—just as soon as Olivia spoke to her.

"Okay," her father said. "I'll come for a day or two and then drive you home. I don't want you stuck out there indefinitely."

"Thank you!" Olivia said, relief coursing through her. "You're the best. Call me or text me when you decide what day you're coming. I love you." When she hung up, she marched back into the living room.

"My dad is coming to see me," she said to Jaci, who looked up from her book. "We're very close."

Elise had been initiated, in a trial by fire, into the distinct club of working mothers. Did other women, she wondered, spend every minute of their nine-to-five jobs thinking more about their children than the task at hand? Maybe her preoccupation was exacerbated by the uncertainty of her situation. Regardless, she could not enjoy—could barely deal with—the robust business at Tea by the Sea. It was keeping her from Mira.

"We need to hire someone," she said to Fern during a brief lull. "Let me reach out to Cynthia Wesson. If it's like this now, in early June, what will we do in July?"

"I'll call her today," Fern said.

This small bit of progress sustained Elise until she was able to duck out in the late afternoon and pick up Mira from the Beach Rose Inn. The sight of Mira, wide-eyed, buckled into her stroller and ready to go home, warmed her heart.

Back at Shell Haven, she poured four ounces of formula into a bottle. She was feeding her every three or four hours around the clock. So far, she was doing all the night feedings. Fern hadn't volunteered, and Elise didn't feel the climate was right for her to ask for help. She was exhausted.

She kicked off her Converse and settled into the couch with Mira nestled in one arm. Elise found a bookmark wedged between the cushions, moved it aside, and set the diaper bag next to her. There were so many supplies involved in baby care, and managing them was, if not half the battle, certainly a good quarter of it.

Mira sucked on the bottle, her hands curled in tight little fists. Elise brushed her finger over one of them and smiled. She felt she could exhale for the first time all day. The only blight on the otherwise perfect moment was the persistence of the rash on Mira's cheeks. She knew now that it was harmless, but it did look terrible and she was frustrated she couldn't do anything to make it go away.

She heard the back door open and close and then the sound of someone in the kitchen putting away groceries, cabinets opening and closing and the distinct click of the refrigerator door. Elise was tempted to call out hello but didn't want to startle Mira with a loud voice. The baby's eyes were closed, and Elise marveled at the delicate translucence of her eyelids.

"Looks like you've got the hang of things now."

Elise looked up to see Ruth smiling from across the room. "Some things, yes. Others are still a work in progress."

"It's always a work in progress," Ruth said, looking pointedly at the room Olivia had moved into.

"Can I ask you something?" Elise said. "Do you remember if Olivia had baby acne?"

"Baby acne?" Ruth said, walking closer. "I don't think so." She peered down at Mira. "Is that itching her?"

"No, it just looks awful," Elise said. "The doctor said it will go away on its own."

"Maybe she has sensitive skin. You know, you really have to watch what products you use. A lot of things are labeled *all natural* but they're not. I'm very aware of that sort of thing because I was in the cosmetics business for years."

"Oh," Elise said.

"I'll make some soap and lotion for you," Ruth said.

"Really?"

"Sure. It's what I do. Or used to do."

Elise knew Ruth had owned a cosmetics company and sold it for a lot of money. Fern had made a big deal about the fact that she'd paid all the rent for the house up front and in cash. "Were the products organic?"

"Not initially. That came later. My sister got breast cancer ten years ago, and I became much more aware about the potential toxicity of everyday beauty products. I created a nail polish that was free of the five major toxic chemicals, then started a line of organic skin-care products."

"That's really impressive, Ruth."

"Oh, well, it sounds more complicated than it was," she said. "Really, it just happened gradually. Ingredient by ingredient. But I do miss it. So I'm happy to whip up something for little Miss Mira here." She reached out and gently stroked the baby's dark hair before heading up the stairs to her room.

Elise felt, for the umpteenth time since the baby's miraculous appearance, that she was incredibly fortunate to be surrounded by women she could count on. She'd never imagined that Ruth—someone she'd tried to push away—would become part of her support system.

She just wished her own wife could become more of a part of it too.

Chapter Twenty-Eight

Ruth woke up at seven, sent off a quick text to tell Amelia that she wouldn't make it to class, and headed down to the kitchen to organize her equipment—a double boiler, a crockpot, measuring cups, and a few resealable tea bags that she'd picked up from Elise's shop.

She felt bad about missing the mosaic class, but she told herself it was for a good reason. And if she didn't finish her starfish, well, the hours she'd spent in Amelia's studio had gotten her back to working with her hands. Now, thanks to Elise and the baby, she was reminded of what else she could be doing.

Her search through the local shops had been surprisingly fruitful, and she'd managed to track down the ingredients she needed to whip up a batch of organic soap: olive pomace oil, shea butter, castor oil, colloidal oatmeal, bentonite clay, and a pack of Egyptian chamomile buds. The hardest thing to find had been silicone cupcake molds, but a quick call to Lidia Barros led to a friend of a friend who had a few to spare.

Ruth had been tempted to start mixing and heating last night, but she didn't want to disturb anyone—she would have been in the kitchen until the earliest hours of the morning—so she'd waited.

Her first task was infusing the olive oil with the chamomile. The olive oil was moisturizing, and the chamomile had calming/anti-inflammatory properties. Chamomile was one of her favorite go-to ingredients. She poured a little over fourteen ounces of the oil into the double boiler, then measured out two tablespoons of the chamomile buds, put them into a tea bag, and sealed it. She put the packed tea bag into the oil, set the heat to medium, and stirred gently.

How long had it been since she'd created a product from scratch? Years. A decade. She would have sworn that she'd been hands-on until the very end at the company, but really, she had become a conference-room chemist. A figurehead. It had happened so gradually, she hadn't even noticed. But wasn't life like that? One minute you're a teenager, the next you're a bride, the next you're an exhausted working mother with a husband you barely have time to smile at over coffee in the morning. And so it was with her career—one minute she was mixing ingredients in her kitchen and the next she was signing off on multimillion-dollar ad campaigns for a company with her name on it.

She shook her head, thinking that she'd never had a road map to the life she wanted. But to be fair, neither had Ben. Four years of college had disabused him of the notion that he might be the next great American playwright. If this was a difficult reality for him to accept, he'd never complained about it. Although, Ruth realized only looking back on it later, he also never again wanted to visit Provincetown and stopped going to see shows. It was like he was trying to forget he'd ever had artistic ambitions.

But they needed an income while he was in medical school, and so she'd ended up with the company, working around the clock even after Olivia was born. Her one indulgence was getting manicures. At the time, a single brand distributed polish to the salons. It held all of that market share, but then they changed the formula and it started chipping sooner. It drove Ruth crazy so of course she had to try to create a better formula—and she did. She launched with a red called Cherry Hill, put it in a unique, square bottle instead of a round one, and labeled it Liv Lacquer. By the end of the year, she had a hundred different colors and her polish was in every nail salon in New Jersey and Philadelphia. The following year, it was in 90 percent of salons across the country. Ben was a year into his residency when she was able to pay off all of his student loans.

"Wow, what's going on in here?" Olivia said, walking into the kitchen in a T-shirt and drawstring pajama bottoms, rubbing her eyes.

"I'm making an oatmeal soap," Ruth said. "From scratch."

"That seems like a lot of work," Olivia said, stepping around her to reach the counter. "Where's the coffee machine?"

"I put it away. Do you mind going to the Wired Puppy or someplace just for this morning? I need this space clear."

"Seriously?" Olivia said, obviously minding very much. She picked up the jar of bentonite clay, read the label.

"Just for today. Sorry."

"Why are you making soap?"

"Elise needs something gentle for Mira. You know half the stuff they sell as natural or organic is full of parabens and all sorts of things."

"Can't she just order something online?"

"Olivia, the internet is not the answer to everything, despite your beliefs to the contrary."

"Jeez. I'm just asking. It seems like an obvious question."

"Well, the answer is that I'm happy to be doing this. Don't you remember when I used to make batches of products in our kitchen when you were little?"

"No."

"Really? Well, how about the time I took you to see how lipstick was made?"

Olivia shook her head.

How could she not remember? "Olivia, come on. The underground tank?"

"Doesn't ring a bell."

"We had an underground tank and we would have fifteen hundred gallons of castor oil in it at a time. You can't take dry pigment and add it to a base, so you take your dry pigment, which is highly concentrated powder, and soak it for hours in castor oil. Then you put it through this three-roller mill that blends it into a highly concentrated paint." She could see Olivia's eyes glazing over. "Well, anyway, I showed you all this when you were little. I can't believe you don't remember. Your father loved that roller mill—he found it fascinating. I can remember him lifting you up so you could look at it more closely."

Olivia put down the jar of clay. "Um, speaking of Dad, I need to ask you something. Can he stay here for a few days?"

Ruth stepped away from the stove. "Your dad is coming to Provincetown?"

"I think so. And he could drive me back to New York."

As ornery as Olivia could be, Ruth didn't want her to leave. Even just this simple conversation about the soap and the old lipstick mill was a start. It was something. Maybe Olivia didn't remember the trip to the factory that day, and maybe she'd forgotten how her mother had mixed batches of moisturizer in the kitchen in big metal bowls with Olivia sitting at the small breakfast table making things out of Play-Doh while she worked. But Ruth had to believe that one of these conversations would offer a point of connection. One morning, Olivia would have her own memory of a shared moment together. But if not, if for some reason Olivia could remember only the difficult times, then at least now she could try to create new memories.

But having Ben stay in the house? That didn't seem like a good idea. It didn't even seem like something Ben would do. "Your father wants to stay here?"

"Well, no. But he said everyplace is booked this week and next. And we have that room upstairs that I'm not using. We'll stay out of your way, I promise. I won't even try to make coffee here." She smiled.

We'll stay out of your way. There it was—the two of them a united front with Ruth as the outsider. It was time for that to change. Ruth was done being the bad guy.

"Okay," she said. "He can stay here."

Somehow, her new life was starting to look an awful lot like one she had left long ago.

The first thing Olivia noticed was the smell.

Stepping outside to call her father in private, she was surprised by a salty, sulfuric odor that was more beach than backyard. The source of this was even more surprising.

Two clotheslines had been strung across the yard, but instead of shirts and socks hanging to dry, the first line was half covered with yellowish-brown plant fronds reaching nearly to the ground. Even more bizarre, the person at the helm of this operation was Marco Barros.

Olivia was thankful she'd taken the time to change out of her pajamas into jean shorts and a tank top. "Hey—what's all this?" Olivia said, standing in front of the stone bench and putting her phone in her back pocket. The call to her father would have to wait a few minutes.

"Seaweed. I'm hanging it here to dry," he said, barely looking at her.

This, of course, led to a few obvious questions: Why here? Why seaweed?

And one less obvious question: *Why am I so attracted to you?*

Olivia forced herself to focus on question number two.

"Oh. Interesting. What's it for?"

"I'm cultivating it for possible commercial use."

She was tempted to take a photo for her Instagram but refrained. Somehow she didn't think that would go over too well with Marco. "Like what?" she said.

He bent over a wide plastic container, a large cooler, and pulled out more of the seaweed, then moved to a fresh spot on the line and clipped it in place. He didn't answer the question, but he said, "If you're just going to stand there, I could actually use an extra set of hands to make this go faster," he said.

"Oh—okay. Sure," she said nervously. "I'm just having some issues with bending down. My back is sort of..."

"You can stand right here and I'll hand you the plants and you just clip it—like this." He held up what appeared to be a regular clothespin, draped one of the fronds over the line, and clipped it in place. "Simple."

She walked closer to him, willing herself to keep a neutral expression on her face, not to give any hint that she was distracted by his rugged good looks. He really had the most divine face, with sharp cheekbones and a lush mouth and mysterious dark eyes.

Looking at Marco, feeling that undeniable pull of animal attraction, she realized she hadn't thought of Ian since she'd arrived in town. As emotionally taxing as it was to deal with her complicated feelings toward her mother, at least she was no longer burdened by her failed relationship. She had no interest in starting something messy in Provincetown.

Marco bent down and sorted through whatever was in the container—the open lid blocked her view. She looked at the back of his neck, deeply tanned, and noted how his thick brown hair curled just above the nape.

He handed her some seaweed. It was less slimy to touch than it appeared, and she lifted it up carefully so that it didn't touch the ground.

"That's it—just drape it over the line and you can even it out as you go," he said. "Don't worry, it's not delicate. If you're worried about the smell and your hands, I have gloves over there somewhere."

"It's fine." His attention and encouragement felt like the sun warming her back. She smiled and he noticed.

"It's not so bad, right?" he said.

"Not bad at all."

They fell into a rhythm, moving more quickly; they filled the first line and started on the one behind it. They worked in silence, and it wasn't until the silence was broken that she realized the task had become meditative; she hadn't been thinking about her mother inside the house or about her back, and she'd forgotten all about the call she needed to make to her father. If Marco hadn't asked her a question, she might even have forgotten he was there.

"I'm sorry—what was that?" she said.

"I asked if my sister has been around here lately."

"Oh," she said, stalling, thinking of Jaci's forlorn expression when she sat on the couch. "Um, no. Not lately."

Marco didn't respond and they went back to working in silence. When both lines were filled to capacity, there was still a little bit of seaweed left over.

"That's enough for now, anyway," he said, packing up the containers and a knapsack.

Olivia felt a pang that he was leaving and wondered how long it would be before she ran into him again. "You never told me what you're going to do with this stuff," she said.

"Different things. One of them is a bit of an experiment. I'm working with Elise and Fern to make seaweed tea." Olivia's expression must have conveyed exactly what she thought of that, because he laughed and said, "It won't be that bad, I promise."

"I'm sorry. This just doesn't smell like something that would taste good."

"That's why we're hanging it in the sun. It's going to dry, and the flavor becomes more complex. And for the tea, they're going to blend it with other ingredients. In fact, we could use help taste-testing."

He could use her help? She felt an undeniable surge in her mood. "Sure. Just let me know."

Why not have a new friend? It was completely innocent. There was no harm in spending more time with Marco Barros.

Chapter Twenty-Nine

The second-floor office had become Elise's least favorite room in the house. The furniture—desk, file cabinet, Eames chair—seemed to mock her. She couldn't even take pleasure in the paintings on the walls, vibrant fields of poppies by a Cape Cod artist named Anne Salas. She and Fern had found such joy in collecting them, but now they seemed like relics from a long-ago time—a time before disappointment and loss.

The room was not supposed to still be an office. It was supposed to have been their nursery.

Now, a baby had finally arrived, and the only infant-friendly item in the room was the bassinet Elise had borrowed from Amelia.

The nesting instinct had kicked in one night when she couldn't sleep. She'd slipped out of bed, brought her laptop downstairs to the couch, sat in the dark, and shopped online until her eyelids finally grew heavy.

Today, the boxes were waiting for her on the doorstep when she arrived home from work. It was like Christmas morning—she couldn't wait to open every one of them.

The only obstacle to getting Mira's room fixed up was, well, Mira. She looked alert after her feeding, with no yawns or the contented coos she'd started to make that suggested a nap might be imminent. Elise needed an extra set of hands to free hers to do some decorating.

She knocked on the door to the den that had become Olivia's bedroom.

"Come in," Olivia called. She was sitting on the couch, tapping on her phone.

"Hey, sorry to bother you. I need help with something and I was wondering if you had a little time."

Olivia looked at the baby, then at Elise, with a deer-in-the-headlights expression. Clearly, she did have time. But she wasn't eager to volunteer it. "Um, sure," she said.

"I just need a half hour or so to get a few things done in her room. Do you think you could take her out for a walk? I'll put her in the stroller—all you need to do is push it up and down the street. She'll probably drift off."

"Okay," Olivia said, looking nervous. "But I can't lift her. My back…"

"You don't have to take her out of the stroller. I'll do everything."

Reluctantly, Olivia followed her into the mudroom behind the kitchen. Elise gave Mira one final burp, then secured her in the stroller and kissed her on the forehead. The baby's small hands fluttered up to her mouth.

"Her eyes are really dark," said Olivia. "I thought all babies had blue eyes."

"They were gray and now they're turning darker," said Elise. "Please keep this hooded part adjusted so the sun is off her. Thanks so much. Oh, let me put my number in your phone in case you need me."

She felt a pang letting Mira go but told herself she would be fine. Olivia was a responsible adult. Still, she watched until the stroller was out of sight.

The boxes.

Elise wondered, looking at the stack on the dining-room table, if she'd gone a little overboard. But, really, it was all necessary. Okay, maybe not the four plush blue dolphins. Or the yellow-and-cornflower-blue blanket with Mira's name hand-stitched in navy-blue Monterey Script lettering. But certainly the marine-themed mobile, with its felt seahorse, whale, octopus, and starfish, was essential. This was a developmental tool as much as decoration. And of course, Mira needed clothes.

Elise opened the box from Baby Gap first and unfolded the onesies in yellow and pink and white, some with cute sayings on them like FUN IN THE SUN and MAMA'S GIRL, and others with hearts and flowers. She'd also bought half a dozen lightweight dresses with little matching bloomers and sun hats.

Elise put the clothes in the laundry and carried the remaining boxes up to the office.

When Elise and Fern had first embarked on their attempt at motherhood, they'd sat in bed planning their dream nursery. The walls would be painted a soft, pale yellow. The crib would be classic white wood with a matching changing table and dresser. In the corner, there'd be a cushioned rocking chair. Their vision was completely a shared one.

They had always been so in sync over everything—their taste in art, architecture, food. Where to live, how to live. Everything—until they had problems conceiving.

Relationships—strong, enduring relationships—were in some ways one long negotiation. Elise and Fern had always found a way to meet in the middle even if they did not agree entirely about a course of action, the distribution of labor, the spending of money, or whatever issue was at hand. They talked directly and honestly. This was the case when they began the process of IVF. Fern was entirely on board for parenthood on the condition that she was not the one to carry the child.

"I have zero interest in experiencing pregnancy," she'd told Elise. "I'm just missing that gene."

This was not a problem for Elise. She wanted to become pregnant, couldn't wait to experience a life growing inside of her. When the time came to sign all the consent forms, they had done so indicating that either mother could carry the baby. Neither one of them believed that the option of Fern trying to conceive would ever be necessary. Until it became clear that Elise was not physically capable of carrying a pregnancy to term, and it was time to renegotiate.

"You won't even consider it?" Elise said. She knew it was a lot to ask, maybe too much. But the alternative—giving up—was just unthinkable to her. They still had two perfectly good embryos.

"I can't. I'm sorry," Fern said. "The technical circumstances have changed, but my feelings haven't."

She had been so maddeningly businesslike about it, as if they'd been debating how much to bid on a house.

Elise tried not to feel resentful. She told herself that if she'd been straight and married to a man, it wouldn't even be an option to ask her partner to become pregnant.

Another road would have been surrogacy. But by the time Elise floated the idea, Fern had had enough. She framed it as an issue of the health of their relationship, and Elise had backed down.

Sometimes, Elise lay awake at night thinking of their two remaining frozen embryos sitting in a tank somewhere in Boston.

Elise shook all of these thoughts away now, not wanting to cloud the moment with negativity. She pulled the stuffed dolphins out of their plastic wrap and set them in a row on the floating shelf above the dresser. The mobile would take a bit more work. When she opened the package, she saw that the sea creatures needed to be attached to the round circular top from which they'd hang. And then, of course, the entire thing had to be attached to the ceiling.

"Elise, you home?" Fern called from downstairs.

Surprised, Elise set down the mini-octopus in her hand. She hadn't been expecting Fern for another hour or two.

"I'm in the office," she called back, suddenly tense.

She heard Fern's footsteps on the stairs. "Hey," Fern said, appearing in the doorway. "I see Marco has the kelp rigged up out back. It looks half dry already. Maybe tomorrow we can find time to start experimenting with blends?"

"Sure," Elise said.

Fern noticed the mobile pieces in Elise's hands. "What are you doing?"

"I ordered some things for Mira," she said.

"Why?" Fern said.

"What do you mean, why? Because she needs some things."

Fern looked around the room, took in the shelf of stuffed dolphins. She shook her head. "See," she said. "This is exactly what I was afraid of."

"What?" Elise said, irritated.

"You're acting like this is a done deal. You're too emotionally invested in this baby *that is not yours*."

"She's not ours. *Ours*. Have you forgotten that a family is something we have been trying to create together? I might be too emotionally invested, but I wish you were a little more invested. I wish you had been all along." Her eyes filled with tears.

"Elise," Fern said, her expression softening. "I wanted a baby too."

Elise shook her head. "As soon as it got hard, something in you just shut down. You didn't want it like I wanted it."

"I didn't want it if it was going to destroy our relationship in the process, no. You're right. I wanted a baby, but I wanted you more. I *am* invested—in you. In us."

Last year, Elise had chosen being a wife over being a mother. A week ago, if anyone had asked, she would have sworn that she'd made the right choice. Now, left to decide between eating dinner with Fern and putting the mobile together, she wasn't so sure.

"I'm invested in us too," Elise said. "But I shouldn't have to choose."

"You need to send some of this stuff back. It's not helping anything to have all of this here."

Elise felt she could choke on her frustration. "I don't understand how you can be so *removed!*"

Fern stepped closer, reaching for her hand. "I'm not being removed. I'm being practical. Frankly, one of us has to be. Come on—don't be angry. Let me take you out to dinner."

"I'm not hungry," Elise said quietly.

The perfume and toiletry shop Good Scents on Commercial was one of the cutest stores on the block, with its red-barn facade, white window frames, and black-and-white awning. The shelves of the small space were filled with lotions, perfumes, candles, and soaps. It was a toy store for people who loved small luxuries. Ruth walked in looking for inspiration, some ideas for what to create next. Now that she'd started with the soap, she had the bug. There was no turning back.

And yet, even as she sampled a citrus-scented lotion, she could not stop thinking about her offer to let her ex-husband stay at the house.

In the moment, it had seemed logical. Now, she wasn't so sure. Although what was the big deal? They had long been on amicable terms. The initial sting of the divorce had mellowed into something much more manageable over the decades, even though at first, it had felt like a tectonic shift that she would never recover from.

One of the benefits of being older was that you could look back and see that every moment that had felt intractable and awful was just temporary. It was impossible to get a young person to believe that "this too shall pass." It was something that had to be experienced. Yes, some of the pain lingered. Yes, regret was an inevitable part of life. Every choice had repercussions. Did she ever think twice about her decision to end her marriage? Of course. Had it been the right thing to do at the time? Absolutely.

Ruth carried her purchases to the counter—some candles, a bar of lemongrass soap, a perfume, and a few bottles of essential oil.

"That will be two hundred and twenty dollars," the man behind the register said. She startled at the price. Even though she had not had to worry about the cost of things for a long time, she still felt a reflexive jolt when something was expensive, a sort of muscle memory from the time when every dollar counted. She had worked hard to never again be in the vulnerable position she was in when her father went bankrupt.

It had happened the first week of her senior year in college. Ruth stood in a long line to register for her classes, but when it was her turn to fill out forms, the student managing the paperwork told her, "You need to report to the bursar's office."

Ruth was in a sweat by the time she reached the administration building, where a secretary told her coldly that her tuition had not been paid for the semester so she was not eligible for registration.

"There must be some mistake," Ruth said.

Ruth called her mother, who had no idea what was going on but also insisted it had to be a mistake. "I'll take care of it," her mother said. Ruth expected her mother to call back within the hour and tell her it had been a mix-up, a check lost in the mail. Instead, it was close to dinner when her mother called back and said, "I think you need to come home for a few days."

Ruth never returned to Northwestern.

Later, while Ben was in med school, she considered taking the classes she needed to complete her BA. But by then she was already working at the cosmetics manufacturing company; it would have been a burden for both of them to be in school at the same time. She knew she would have to figure out an unconventional career path. And she had.

The man behind the shop counter asked if she wanted anything gift-wrapped. She told him just the candles, and he placed them in white paper bags with purple tissue paper and wrapped the twine handles together with a matching ribbon.

The candles were for Amelia. Ruth had been so caught up in trying to get settled in the house and get a foothold in her life in Provincetown, she'd not properly acknowledged the woman's kindness to her from the very first day she arrived. Ruth felt bad about dropping out of the mosaic class, her starfish abandoned in the sketch phase.

Outside, she inhaled the fresh air. The sidewalk and streets were crowded, and a truck rumbling by halted the foot traffic while it passed. Ruth headed toward the Beach Rose Inn, thinking about the soap she'd made and considering mixing up a little something else to go along with it before giving it to Elise. She could make a protective lotion, a diaper-rash cream, with the bentonite clay. And then, she caught sight of something that made her look twice: Olivia pushing a baby carriage.

It was a scenario she had imagined at one time or another, her daughter with a baby of her own; Ruth, the doting grandmother. This reality, of course, was far from that fantasy. Still, the visual stirred her on some primal level. "Hi, hon," Ruth said cheerily, ignoring the rush of sentimentality. "I'm surprised to see you on babysitting duty."

Olivia's light hair was pulled back in a messy knot. She wore a V-neck T-shirt and green cargo pants and flip-flops. Ruth never did understand this generation's willingness to walk around in flimsy shoes.

"Yes, well, no more surprised than I am. Elise needed to unpack boxes or something. But I'm taking Mira home now." She peeked under the car seat's hood. "It looks like she fell asleep."

"I'll walk back with you," Ruth said, figuring her gift delivery could wait one more day.

Olivia didn't seem put out by her company, and Ruth felt encouraged by this. "Did your father confirm he's coming?" she said.

"Yeah. Tomorrow."

Tomorrow? "Oh, that's soon. I didn't realize..."

Olivia turned to Ruth. "Thanks for letting him stay at the house."

"No problem," Ruth said, though again she was not so sure. She didn't mind the idea of him coming, but she anticipated some awkwardness; seeing him in the kitchen first thing in the morning, for example. Although it couldn't be any more awkward than the last time she'd seen him, about a year ago in Philadelphia. She was having dinner at Scarpetta, on a date—maybe her second or third with a guy she could barely remember now—and Ben had walked in with an attractive woman about their own age. He spotted her at the same moment she'd noticed him, and their eye contact had been jolting in its intimacy. But the wall went back up, the polite veil; he stopped by the table to say hello, and cursory introductions were made. The brief encounter had been enough to throw off the rhythm of her entire evening.

The next afternoon, she was surprised to get a phone call from Ben.

"I was taken aback running into you last night," he'd said. "And obviously it wasn't the best time to talk. But I have been thinking of you, hoping you're well."

She couldn't remember the rest of the conversation, but every time she recalled it, she felt the inexplicable happiness that had followed. She had thought about making a similar call over the years but she had never gone through with it. Most recently, she had wanted his counsel about the sale of the business. As per their divorce settlement, he was entitled to a percentage of the profits. He had no say in the management, but still, she would have valued his opinion. It was a huge step that had made her feel very alone.

"Is your father seeing anyone?" Ruth said.

Olivia narrowed her eyes, squinting with a distinct *Why do you care?* expression. "No. Not at the moment."

She was so protective of him! Ruth couldn't understand why Olivia's empathy was for her father only.

They passed the tea shop, and she looked up the stairs and saw the CLOSED sign on the front door. She wondered if Elise and Fern were both back at the house. She was getting used to having people underfoot constantly, but she still craved privacy and didn't want her time with Olivia to be interrupted. Ruth could see Olivia using Elise and Fern as buffers sometimes, avoiding too much conversation alone.

"I'm starving," Olivia said, pausing outside of Spindler's.

"Well, let's eat. Mira's asleep. I'll text Elise we're here—I doubt she'll mind."

The maître d' standing sentry in front of the restaurant consulted a reservation book before seating them outside on the front patio. Olivia eased slowly into her chair, one hand on her lower back, wincing. Sitting was worse than walking.

"Still no improvement?"

"Maybe a little," Olivia said.

A waiter, young and beautiful with dark skin and bright green eyes, handed them menus and asked if they wanted flat or sparkling water.

Olivia situated the stroller so it was out of people's way. She took one more peek at Mira, then pulled the hood over her. The sight of Olivia being even a little maternal warmed Ruth's heart.

"You're good with her," Ruth said.

Olivia shook her head. "Don't get any ideas."

"What? You don't want children someday?"

"No," Olivia said. "What I want is to get my career back on track."

"You can have both."

"Oh, like you did?"

"Yes, like I did." Why did every conversation have to degenerate into an indictment of her?

"I'm sorry. But I don't believe you can have it all."

Ruth wasn't about to get pulled into a feminist debate. "Well, you seem very comfortable with the baby. I hope you won't entirely rule out the idea of motherhood."

They both looked at the stroller. Olivia moved the hood again. Mira's head was turned to one side, her cheeks pink with sleep. One arm was raised with her little hand curled next to her shoulder. "She *is* cute. But I'm still unclear—who does she belong to?"

Ruth hesitated. The mysterious provenance of the baby had nagged at her. She could remember the bewildered expression on Elise's face when she'd admitted, *I don't know whose baby this is.*

Mira had been left on the doorstep intentionally—that much was clear. Ruth had thought that Elise would take a day or two and then hand the baby over to the authorities. When that didn't happen, she thought Elise was maybe trying to figure out who had left the baby, to handle it privately. Now Elise was telling everyone they were in the process of trying to adopt. Clearly, they were dealing with it through some legal channel she wasn't privy to. With all of this in mind, she had kept her word about not mentioning it to anyone, and yet she suddenly felt the weight of the truth. She didn't want to lie to Olivia. She also, selfishly, wanted a way to bond with her.

"If I tell you something, can you promise to keep it to yourself?"

Olivia nodded, looking at Ruth with interest. "Sure."

"No one knows who Mira belongs to. I found her on the doorstep of the house the morning after I moved in."

"What?"

"Yes. I know. Elise swore me to secrecy and I assume they are handling it but I really don't know what's going on."

Olivia sat back in her chair, reached out one arm, and pulled the stroller closer. She looked at Mira. "That's crazy," she said quietly.

"It's odd. But these things do happen."

"I know people abandon babies, but the fact that they're just keeping it—do you think they notified anyone?"

"At first, no. Elise had this we-take-care-of-our-own mind-set and didn't want to get anyone in trouble. But she said they are in the process of trying to adopt."

Olivia seemed to consider this. Then she laughed.

"What's so funny?"

"Just...the irony. You came out here to, what, retire? Be alone? I mean, you chose a pretty remote place. And then someone leaves a *baby* at your house. I mean, you didn't even want to take care of your own—"

"Olivia, please. Let's not turn this conversation into yet another referendum on my parenting. Okay?"

"Okay," Olivia said. "But you have to admit, it is pretty funny. I wish I could have seen the look on your face."

Ruth laughed. "I was not happy, I can tell you that."

She didn't know who'd left Mira or why. But in that moment, she was thankful for the mystery baby that had given her a reason to share a laugh with *her* baby. Still, she feared that this small moment of bonding was coming too late. Tomorrow, her ex-husband would arrive, and his appearance would remind Olivia of her long-held belief that Ruth was the bad guy.

Her phone vibrated with a text.

Tomorrow still good for a sail? Boatyard at 10 a.m.?

It was Tito Barros. Ruth had forgotten about their talk of a boat outing. She felt certain it had just been polite conversation, maybe a mild flirtation, no firm plans. And yet she did not want to be sitting around the house when her ex-husband arrived. It was best to do something to root herself firmly in the present. The past was the past.

Yes, sounds good. See you tomorrow.

When she looked up, Olivia was observing her.

"Everything okay?" she said.

"Great," Ruth replied. "Let's order."

Chapter Thirty

Their new part-timer, Cynthia Wesson, was someone Elise never would have been friends with in high school. Cynthia was too self-assured, too outgoing. Elise wasn't proud of the fact that she had once been intimidated by the popular kids, but she couldn't help but remember it in the face of such a golden girl.

Cynthia was tall and slender with long-lashed brown eyes and shiny straight brown hair cut in a chin-length bob. Fern had learned during her interview that Cynthia was midway through school at Emory, that her family lived in Chatham year-round, and that she was spending the summer in P'town by herself.

"Why by herself?" Elise had asked.

"Probably to get away from her family," Fern said. "I can relate."

Cynthia was eager to learn, and Elise tried to muster up some enthusiasm as she demonstrated how things worked around the shop despite her sleep deprivation. Mira had woken up more than usual during the night.

Elise opened the wide bay windows to let in some fresh air.

"It's amazing you found a location with such a clear view of the water," Cynthia said, tucking her hair behind her ears.

"Yes, but not so clear today." The morning had begun with the type of haze that would burn off quickly. At the moment, the fog and cloud cover matched Elise's mood.

After Fern insisted that she send back most of the nursery furniture, the rest of their evening proved unsalvageable. Ruth texted that she and Olivia were taking Mira with them to a restaurant, and Fern argued that they should take the opportunity to go out to dinner, just the two of them. Elise reluctantly agreed to go to Strangers & Saints, a Mediterranean-style taverna that was one of their favorites.

Over a shared dish of pan-roasted chicken marinated in spiced pomegranate orange molasses, Fern steered the conversation away from any mention of Mira. Elise spent the entire meal pretending to care about plans for the Fourth of July, the logistics of the seaweed-tea venture, and a possible trip to the Boston farmers' market together. Keeping her phone under the table, she periodically texted Olivia to check on Mira.

Later, in bed, when Fern reached for her, she turned away. When Elise awoke to Mira's cries at two in the morning, Fern pretended to be asleep.

"So, we have two instant hot taps, one at a hundred and eighty degrees and one at a hundred and sixty degrees," Elise said, motioning for Cynthia to follow her behind the counter. "This delicate green tea from Japan, for example, needs the lower temperature for brewing or the leaves bruise and get ruined. We have a list right here of the temperatures for each tea and another list for the number of tablespoons and brewing times for each blend."

Cynthia took notes on a small legal pad.

"This time of year, most people ask for iced tea. We start the day with pitchers of four different iced teas, but customers can request any of our blends cold. They just have to be willing to wait a few minutes for them to steep. Do you ever get iced tea from a place and it tastes so weak it's like barely flavored water?" Cynthia nodded. "We never want that to happen, so we double the measurement of tea for iced. But the brewing time and temperature remain the same."

The door opened—a couple with a small child.

"Hi there," Elise said. The woman smiled and studied the chalkboard menu. She eventually ordered the Sail Away blend, iced.

It was one of their most popular teas, but Elise didn't have any iced that morning. She told the woman it would take just a few minutes to brew and motioned for Cynthia to watch her closely. "This is a black tea with bergamot, blue cornflower, and vanilla," she said, opening one of the tins behind the counter.

"It looks so pretty," Cynthia said.

"Yeah, the blue cornflower is mostly decorative," Elise said, putting two scoops into a tea bag and pouring hot water into a metal cocktail shaker she used for quick brewing. "Take one of the plastic cups and fill ice to the top, almost overflowing."

Cynthia filled the cup and placed it on the counter.

"Oh, I want only a *little* ice," the customer said.

"It's all going to melt down," Elise assured her. "Trust me, we'll probably have to add more before we're done."

The woman's husband ordered a type of iced tea they already had prepared, and Elise let Cynthia handle it while she went to prop open the front door. The fog had lifted and the day was going to be beautiful.

When she was alone again with Cynthia, she said, "See? It's all pretty simple." At least, it was simple until they got a big rush. She hoped that wouldn't happen before Fern came in later in the day. She was spending the morning back at the house, experimenting with blending tea with the kelp.

Elise didn't want to think about Fern.

"So, you grew up in Chatham?" she said to make conversation.

"Yes, born and raised."

"But you didn't want to spend the summer there?"

Cynthia shook her head. "My parents are way too in my space and the town is just...it's uptight. I like it out here. The people are so chill, all the artists. It's so free."

Yes, Elise remembered that sense of freedom when she'd first experienced Provincetown. Now, real life had caught up with her, and she felt the walls closing in.

"Plus, I had sort of a rough year. My boyfriend and I broke up. This just felt like a clean slate."

"I'm sorry to hear that," Elise said.

Cynthia shrugged. "The worst is over. But that's why I really wanted to work here with you guys—brew some tea, calm music, a view of the water. It's great."

"Well, thank you," Elise said. "We're happy to have you."

For the next few hours they fell into a rhythm with a steady, manageable flow of customers, a flow that was interrupted when Rachel appeared with Mira.

"Is it that time already?" Elise asked, caught off guard.

"I think so," Rachel said, checking her phone. "You said Fern would be back here by now and you'd be done."

"You're right. I don't know where she is. But it's fine—thank you so much. I've got it from here." She peeked into the stroller and found Mira wide-eyed and alert. She seemed to kick up her legs at the sight of Elise, and Elise's heart flipped.

"I have to run—but I'm around later in the week if you need help," Rachel called from the stairs.

"You're the best," Elise said, then shot off a text to Fern asking about her ETA. She moved the stroller to the far side of the shop and pulled Mira into her arms. "Hey there, little one," she said.

When she glanced behind to offer some explanation about Mira to

Cynthia, the girl quickly looked away. Had she told Cynthia they had a baby? She didn't think so. But Cynthia didn't ask any questions, not even a polite "How old is she?" or the usual comments about how cute she was. In fact, the appearance of the baby seemed to shut Cynthia down completely. It was odd.

More customers came in. Elise tucked Mira back in the stroller and set it in the corner of the room, away from the flow of foot traffic. Cynthia managed the register while Elise prepped all the orders. From the other side of the shop, Mira began to cry.

"I have the timer set on this turmeric ginger—just finish it for me?" Elise said, moving out from behind the counter and rushing over to the stroller. A wailing baby wasn't exactly in sync with the Zen vibes of the store. As soon as Elise picked her up, Mira quieted. Elise walked in circles, patting her back.

The tide of customers slowed until she was once again alone in the store with Cynthia. The girl remained silent, rinsing cups in the sink while Elise paced with Mira.

Was this Cynthia's idea of good manners? Showing a total lack of interest?

Or did she not ask questions because she knew some of the answers?

No, that was crazy thinking. And yet…

Elise turned to examine Cynthia's face, her heart beating fast. She searched for features that matched Mira's, all the while telling herself she was just under stress, sleep-deprived.

She checked her phone. What was keeping Fern?

The kitchen table was covered with small bowls of loose-leaf tea and diced-up kelp. Olivia sat between Fern and Jaci and across the table from Marco, the four of them busy mixing various combinations of tea with the kelp, scooping the leaves into tea bags, and labeling them.

This was not how Olivia had planned to spend the morning, but she'd walked into the kitchen for coffee and found Fern and Marco chopping up the dried seaweed. She was immediately self-conscious in her baggy drawstring pants, her hair in a messy ponytail, her face bare. But Marco hardly glanced up.

"What's going on?" Olivia had said, though it was fairly obvious. She opened a window; the kitchen had the briny, sulfuric smell that she'd experienced in the backyard the other day. Fern told her they were experimenting with tea and kelp mixtures, trying out ratios and flavor combinations. "We're not taste-testing it today, just bagging up the different varieties. Wanna help?"

She glanced at Marco. He was intently measuring leaves with a tablespoon.

"Um, sure. Just let me get dressed."

She changed into a pink T-shirt and white jean shorts, brushed some mascara on her lashes, put a dab of lip gloss on her mouth, and joined the group at the table.

That had been hours ago. The detail-oriented task of measuring the ingredients, folding them into bags, and labeling them kept her mind busy. Every so often, she would steal a glance at Marco, watching his quickly moving hands, his thick wrists, and the way his jaw seemed to tense. At one point their eyes met, and she nearly lost her breath.

By the time the front doorbell rang she'd forgotten all about her father's arrival. "Oh!" she said, jumping up, ignoring the twinge in her back, and rushing out of the kitchen.

"Expecting someone?" Fern called after her.

Olivia kept running, nearly tripping over an area rug in the living room. She swung open the front door, grinning before she even laid eyes on him.

"I can't believe you're here!" she said.

"Hi, sweetheart," he said, hugging her. "Well, you might not feel great, but you look no worse for the wear."

"How was the trip?"

"Loved the ferry. Very relaxing." He followed her into the living room. "Nice place. Your mother always did have great taste in houses."

"I can show you to your room now or . . . you should come meet everyone first."

"Who's everyone? Oh—yes. The residents of the 'weird bed-and-breakfast,' as you described it."

Had she said that? She didn't remember. But it was sort of true. "Wow. And you still came. Brave of you."

He smiled. "You didn't sound so hot on the phone. I've been worried about you."

Olivia felt a pang of guilt. It wasn't fair for her to have dragged her father out here. It was selfish. But now that he was here, she was determined to show him a good time. It wasn't the worst thing in the world to have gotten him out of his comfort zone.

She led the way to the kitchen, where the group around the table looked up in surprise. Olivia made the introductions.

"Nice to meet you, everyone," her father said. "Sorry to interrupt."

"Not at all," Fern said. "You've got a great daughter there. She's been a big help today."

Olivia felt herself beaming. How had things felt so awful just days ago? "He's staying on the third floor," she said to Fern. "Are you guys okay if I . . ."

"Go—enjoy," Fern said.

"Later, alligator," said Jaci.

"Thanks for the help," Marco said. "We're doing the taste-testing on Thursday if you're around. Fern, what time do you think?"

"Eight in the morning. Sharp. In Lidia's kitchen because she has instant hot taps."

"I'll be there," Olivia said happily.

She walked her father back through the living room. At the base of the stairs, he said, "So what's going on with you?"

"What do you mean?"

He glanced back toward the kitchen, then whispered, "I came out here thinking you were on the verge of a nervous breakdown, but now I get the distinct feeling you might actually be having a good time."

Olivia opened her mouth to speak, then closed it, then tried again. "I mean, I was never having a nervous breakdown..."

"Don't get me wrong," her father said. "I'm relieved that it's not the case. Just wondering if anything's happened in the past day or two to lift your spirits."

"No," she said, the sound of Marco's voice reaching her even as she stood in the foyer. "Nothing at all."

Chapter Thirty-One

Ruth climbed aboard Tito Barros's boat in the middle of dense fog. She was uneasy with the fact that she couldn't see any of the landmarks in the distance. Tito, taking her hand to help steady her, assured her the morning fog would clear.

"And even if it doesn't, we'll be fine," he said.

The poor visibility was not the only thing putting her on edge; Tito's sister, Bianca, had been hauling a bag of oysters on the dock when Ruth arrived.

"Hello, Bianca," Ruth said because it was obvious they had seen each other.

"It's early," Bianca said. "The boat tours don't start for another hour."

"Yes, well, I'm actually..."

"Ruth!" Tito called with a wave, walking up the metal gangway bridging the dock to the boatyard. He was dressed in a navy T-shirt, khaki-colored shorts, and a pale blue and gray Long Point baseball cap.

Bianca crossed her arms and waited for him to reach them before saying, "Don't tell me you're spending the morning out joyriding. Doesn't anyone besides me work around here?"

"Bianca, carrying the oysters Marco picked does not constitute work," Tito said.

"Well." She turned to Ruth. "I see you've helped yourself to my daughter's house and now you're helping yourself to my brother."

"That's enough, Bianca," Tito said, motioning for Ruth to follow him. Eager to escape Bianca's rancor, Ruth walked quickly, keeping pace with Tito down the metal gangway to the edge of the dock. What was that woman's problem?

"Don't pay her any mind. She's gotten ornery in her old age."

Ruth bristled. "Old age? I doubt she's any older than I am."

Tito put his hand to his chest. "My apologies. You seem much younger. It's your lightness of spirit."

"Well, your sister does always seem angry."

Tito nodded. "She feels—well, I guess you could say she feels cheated by life. Her husband died when she was in her thirties. It was a blow, and she's been bitter ever since. But her bark is worse than her bite." Tito knelt down to pull on a rope attached to a small skiff tied to the dock. A very small skiff.

"I thought you said we were going on a sailboat," Ruth said, trying not to sound panicked.

"We are. But she's out on the moorings." He pointed into the foggy distance.

A young man in a Barros Boatyard T-shirt and jeans was already on the skiff, and he helped Ruth aboard while Tito untied the rope tethering it to the dock. Ruth steadied herself, sitting on a small bench while Tito jumped on. The boat swayed heavily from side to side, and Ruth thought she was going to pass out from fear. Her shark-phobia anxiety level was at about a ten, cruising quickly to a twelve.

The Barros Boatyard guy started the engine and they sped out into the water. Ruth gripped the side of the bench like her life depended on it. Tito made small talk with the other man about whether or not the fog would burn off quickly and then he turned to Ruth and said, "Having fun yet?"

Ruth could only nod. He moved closer to her and knelt down.

"Don't worry—you're in good hands. I promise."

By the time they reached Tito's sailboat, the *Maria,* Ruth was in a sweat. The boat was outfitted with a dark-wood-paneled lower cabin that could sleep four or five people and had a bookshelf, a table, a sink, and a comfortable wraparound couch. This was where—to Tito's consternation—she spent the first few minutes of the sail. It wasn't until they were halfway between the dock and Long Point that she climbed the narrow stairs to join Tito on the deck.

"How long's it been since you were on a boat?" he asked from his position behind the wheel.

"I took the ferry here from Boston last month," she said.

"That hardly counts."

"Well, aside from that, it's been many, many years since I've been out on the water like this," she said. In those days, she'd been more brave. What had happened to her?

They passed the lighthouse, and Tito cut the motor and raised the sails. Ruth hadn't realized how much noise the engine made until it was stilled. She was able to hear the lapping of the water against the side of the boat, and she settled onto a shallow bench.

"It's so peaceful out here," she said from her perch.

"Isn't it? I'll tell you, when the town gets overrun in the middle of summer, this boat saves my sanity," he said.

"I see the flood of people on the weekends already. I can't imagine it getting any more crowded."

"You haven't seen anything yet. Every year I think, *This has to be the limit.* And yet the crowds keep growing," he said, glancing at her. "But you're welcome aboard anytime you need an escape."

"That's very kind of you." She looked out at the water, uncomfortable with the directness of his interest in her. He was an attractive man— that much was undeniable, as much as she would have liked to pretend otherwise. Something about his smile and his voice reminded her of Jeff Bridges, an actor she'd been infatuated with since seeing him in the film *The Fabulous Baker Boys*. It would make her life simpler if she didn't find Tito attractive, but watching him at the helm of the boat, the way he divided his attention between watching the controls and looking at her, made her feel good.

Ruth hadn't known what to expect of this phase of her life, but part of the motivation for moving had been finding solitude. With a fresh start, she wouldn't have anyone to disappoint or be disappointed by. And then that baby appeared on her doorstep, like the universe extending a long, scolding finger: *You can leave your marriage. You can leave your company. But motherhood must be reckoned with.*

"Is your daughter still in town?" Tito asked as if she had spoken her thoughts aloud, though she was certain she hadn't.

"Yes, she is. But I don't know for how much longer." She tried not to think about—and certainly did not mention—that as of that afternoon, her ex-husband would also be in town.

It had been difficult to sleep the night before, knowing that in twenty-four hours she and Ben would be under the same roof. While it was true that over the decades, their relationship had mellowed into something amicable, she felt certain they both had unresolved feelings about the divorce. She suspected on his end, he believed she was to blame. For herself, it was guilt.

No matter how it happens, the ending of a marriage is like a small death. Ruth couldn't remember a specific moment when she knew her marriage was over. It had been a gradual slide.

Part of the problem, and she could admit this now, was that her work was all-consuming.

Ruth traveled to New York City three times a week and eventually established a second office there. She spent one week a year in Bologna for the annual trade show, her favorite trip of the year. The show always drew the same people—her friends, colleagues, and competitors. In the 1980s and 1990s, the industry had been a close-knit group. It was her second family, one she began to relate to more than the one she had at home.

When Ruth got worn down and stressed, when she was grappling with a production problem or a demanding account, her impulse was to confide in Ben. But her husband didn't want to hear it. She told herself that he had his own aggravations at work—more serious stakes, dealing with life and death—and so she tried talking only about her successes. He didn't want to hear about that either. And she realized that while the company had been necessary and valuable in the early days, now that they didn't need the income anymore, he resented it.

Their sex life dwindled to nothing.

She suggested couples therapy, and Ben agreed. It didn't mend their relationship, but it did help her realize the issue wasn't about her long hours or the fact that she was outearning him even though he was a respected anesthesiologist. It was the simple fact that she had found her passion in life and he had given up his. Ruth had tried talking to him about this, had suggested that he take time off, go to a writing retreat. "Get back to what you love to do," she'd said.

"I'm a doctor," he said.

He was afraid to try. And he resented her for it.

Olivia was ten when Ruth finally couldn't live with the simmering tension any longer. She found herself avoiding coming home just so she didn't have to deal with it, and that was no way to live and no way to be a parent.

When she told Ben she wanted a divorce, he reacted as if it had come out of nowhere.

"This can't be a surprise to you," she said. "And I don't want our relationship to get to the point where we hate each other."

"What do you think divorce is going to do for our relationship? Enhance it? And what about Olivia?"

"It's better for Olivia not to grow up in such a tense environment."

This reasoning was true. It was what a child psychologist had told her—you can't stay in a marriage just for the child. But, looking back on it now, Ruth was eager to end the relationship because she was exhausted from trying to make it work. She hated the sense of failure she felt every day. She had a very difficult time in gray areas; either a relationship was working or it wasn't. She was a fixer and problem-solver. And in her mind, the way to fix the relationship was to end it. To quit while they were ahead, for themselves, and for their daughter.

Over the years, her relationship with her ex-husband had mellowed, but her dynamic with Olivia had just grown more contentious. Until now.

No matter how awkward it would be to have Ben at the house, she would do it for Olivia's sake.

The breeze lifted Ruth's hair, and she patted it back into place. The haze had burned off to reveal the beautiful morning it had been hiding. Behind them, the Long Point Lighthouse. Ahead, water as far as the eye could see, reflecting the bright sunshine and creating the illusion that she and Tito Barros were the only people in the world.

"Do you have children?" she asked Tito, eager to keep the conversation going, not to lapse into longer silence that would allow the past to creep up on her.

"I never married, and I don't have children," he said. "But Manny's two kids—Jaci and Marco—and Bianca's daughter, Pilar, are like children to me. Bianca thinks I favor Marco; that's why she's angry with me.

I gifted him my water grant a few years back and she was furious. So between Pilar selling the house and Marco taking over the water rights, she feels she's gotten short shrift."

Ruth could barely follow the story of his family drama; she was processing the news that he'd never been married. It was unusual, at least in her experience. "So, did you just never want to get married or was it more a matter of not finding the right one? Or is that too personal?"

"Not too personal at all. The truth is, the sea life is a selfish life. But now that I'm older and slowing down a little, I'm making time for other things. I'm in a place where I can think of someone other than myself, and I want to find someone and make that person a priority." He smiled at her, and she smiled back.

Maybe she should allow herself to do the same. In the years following her divorce, she'd thrown herself even more fully into work. But she missed having a romantic partner. The reality was that when she'd met Ben Cooperman, she'd fallen in love the way you saw in movies. Love at first sight, if one believed in such a thing. She'd never experienced that again, and she wondered if that kind of passion was the exclusive territory of the young. It was interesting that Tito had said Ruth seemed much younger at heart than his sister. She hadn't corrected him, hadn't admitted that she felt she had aged ten years in the last one. Running to Provincetown had been an attempt to adjust to a new version of herself by reaching way back to a self of long ago. "Well, I have to say, I really appreciate this excursion. The house I'm staying in has become unexpectedly crowded. It's starting to make Commercial Street look tranquil."

"Too many guests? It's the unavoidable by-product of having a beach house."

She gave a little wave, dismissing her complaint. "It's fine. But like I said, this little escape is just what I needed today."

"And like I said—anytime."

"Well, maybe our next get-together can be on dry land? I've been meaning to try that restaurant Joon. I pass it every time I walk to the boatyard. Care to join me one night later in the week?"

Now it was his turn to look surprised. She wondered if she was being too forward.

"I'm not much of a restaurant person, but seeing you're not much of a boat person and you ventured aboard, the least I can do is meet you for a potentially overpriced meal."

Ruth smiled as the boat rocked gently underneath her.

When Fern finally breezed into the shop three hours later, Elise was on edge.

She'd managed having Mira at the shop as best she could, leaving Cynthia alone behind the counter while she took the baby upstairs to feed and change her. When Mira fell asleep, Elise planted the stroller in an out-of-the-way corner. Now, Cynthia had clocked out. The store was quiet.

"How's it going here?" Fern said. Her long hair was in braids and piled on top of her head, and she was dressed in a gauzy lemon-yellow dress with a matching chunky beaded necklace. She looked relaxed and lovely.

"Good," Elise said, instantly forgiving her for being late. "How'd it go with the seaweed?"

"Lots of varieties. We're taste-testing the day after tomorrow, so hopefully Cynthia can be here again in the morning?"

Elise nodded. "Sure. I'll check with her."

"How'd she do?"

"Cynthia? Great. She memorized a lot of the blends and has this way of talking to customers like she's been doing this forever."

But Fern was no longer listening. She'd spotted the stroller at the far side of the store. "I thought Rachel was babysitting," Fern said.

"Just in the morning," Elise said. "I've been waiting for you to get back here so I can take her home. But she's sleeping now so there's no rush anymore. I'll stay for a bit."

Fern didn't respond. She walked behind the counter, checked the tins they used for retail service, and found a few nearly empty.

"We should always have Cynthia refill these before she leaves," Fern said, her voice markedly cooler. Elise tensed. She didn't want things to go off the rails between them again today.

"Maybe," she said slowly, "on the day you're doing the taste-testing, I can leave Cynthia here by herself for a few hours and join you."

Fern raised an eyebrow. "I didn't think you were that into the whole experiment."

"Well, you're into it. And the more I think about it, the more it seems like a good idea. Why not?"

"Thanks. But between Marco, Jaci, and Olivia, I'll have it covered."

"Oh. Okay." Elise tried not to feel stung by the rejection.

"Speaking of Olivia, did you know her father is staying with her this week?"

"No. She never mentioned it. We really have a full house."

"Yes," Fern said. "A little too full. We need to move back into the upstairs of this place for the summer as we'd originally planned."

Elise had known that was coming. And really, why was she fighting it? Fern was right; they couldn't stay at Shell Haven. But something deep inside of her resisted. Yes, they could live with Mira in the one room above the shop. She was so little. Sometimes she just fell asleep in the car seat—preferred the car seat, actually. Elise could park her next to the bed and create a small changing station in the corner. It was not a feasible long-term solution, but they would have the house back in September. Elise supposed that her reticence, her fear, stemmed from the idea that living with Mira above the tea shop would make it seem like she didn't fit into their lives—literally and figuratively. They would have less help without

Ruth and Olivia under their roof. Elise would have to hustle Mira out the door every day. Fern would become even more impatient with the whole situation. But Shell Haven had room for a baby. Shell Haven had been bought with a baby in mind. Elise felt as long as they were in their own house, they had a reminder of the family they had planned.

She couldn't say any of this, of course. While she searched for some practical reason to defend staying at Shell Haven, Bianca walked in with her dog on a leash. Her hair, with its distinctive white stripe, was pulled back in a tight bun and she wore a black maxi-dress with cap sleeves. With her strong bone structure and the signature big dark eyes of the Barros family, she was really very striking. Sometimes it was easy to overlook that fact when dealing with her personality.

"Bianca, you have to leave the dog outside, please. There's a water dish at the base of the stairs."

"I find it interesting that you're so concerned about every rule—except the rule of common decency," she said, approaching the counter in a huff.

"What's the problem now?" Elise said.

Bianca ignored her; she was laser-focused on Fern.

"I'm not going to dance around this any longer," Bianca said, crossing her arms. "I was blindsided when my daughter sold you the house. I didn't have the foresight or means to prevent it. But I am done being displaced. I want to buy it back."

"Bianca," Fern said, shaking her head. "We aren't selling Shell Haven."

"The house is filled with tourists! You have one foot out the door. Who are you kidding? I know you're negotiating with that Ruth woman, and I can tell you, *over my dead body*."

"It's a summer rental," Elise said. "It's temporary."

"That woman Ruth has her hooks into everything," Bianca said. "I don't like people who come to town and just take, take, take."

And then, from across the room, a sharp cry. Elise tried not to react, to pretend like she hadn't even heard it. *(Crying baby? What crying baby?)* The cry escalated to a wail.

Elise walked over to the stroller, picked Mira up, and ascertained that her diaper was warm and heavy. It was time to take her home, but she needed Fern's help getting the stroller down the stairs.

Bianca walked over to Elise and peered at Mira. Slowly, she shook her head. "I see what's going on at that house," she said. "You've turned my ancestral home into a circus. You know my mother was born in that house?"

"Enough," Fern said, stepping out from behind the counter. "Bianca, I'm sorry you're unhappy with how Pilar handled the sale of the house. But it's done. It's our house now, and if we want to rent it out, that's our prerogative. We are not selling it—to you or anyone else. And the guests that come and go are none of your business. So please, stay out of it."

Bianca narrowed her eyes. "You two are up to no good," she said. "I can smell it."

She tugged on her dog's leash and walked out the door. When she was gone, Fern wheeled around and marched over to Elise.

"You never should have had the baby in the shop," she said.

"Fern, I've been waiting for you to come back all day so I could leave."

Fern shook her head. "This isn't good, Elise. That woman is a ticking time bomb."

Chapter Thirty-Two

Windblown and salty from the boat ride, Ruth walked back to Shell Haven buzzing from Tito's very flattering attention. Although once she was back on dry land, she'd started second-guessing her impulse to invite him to dinner. It had seemed like a good idea at the time, but really, was she moving too fast? Did she want to start dating someone in town? Did she want to date, period?

She stopped by the post office to pick up some packages—ingredients for new products she wanted to make—and this further distracted her, so by the time she walked into the house, she'd all but forgotten about the arrival of her ex-husband.

"Ruth," Ben said, jumping up from the couch. She didn't know if she was seeing things through the distorted lens of her own memory, but he looked unchanged—as if it were that first summer in Provincetown all over again. Yes, the hair was silver, but it was still all there. Yes, there were the creases in his face, but it was still handsome in a distinctly boyish way. And of course, the same hazel eyes smiled at her.

"Hi, Ben," she said as he leaned in and kissed her lightly on the cheek. The contact gave her a small shock, a frisson. A feeling she didn't quite recognize.

Ruth took a step back. It was not their typical protocol to kiss or hug when they saw each other. Had he felt compelled to do it because he was staying under her roof?

Don't freak out, she told herself. She felt off balance because of the unusual circumstances—seeing him here, in this town. Context was everything. Plus, she'd just spent hours on a romantic boat ride. Also— and this was a biggie—the town had been needling her with nostalgia for weeks now. Whatever she'd felt a few seconds ago was not real. "How was your trip in?"

"Great," he said. "I drove to Boston and then took the ferry."

It was unsettling to look into his hazel eyes, familiar and utterly strange at the same time. They fell into silence, and Ruth struggled to fill it. "Is Olivia here or…"

"She's in her room changing her clothes," he said. "We're going for a walk and then an early dinner."

"Sounds great. Well, I'm just going to…" She pointed awkwardly at the stairs. As she walked away he said, "Ruth, thanks for having me here. At the house, I mean."

She turned around and forced herself to smile. "No problem."

Lowering his voice, Ben said, "I've been concerned about Olivia and this made the trip a lot easier."

"Concerned about her?"

"She just sounded bad on the phone. Losing the job was a blow, and I imagine it's complicated for her emotionally to be spending time with you."

Ruth crossed her arms. "It's not complicated. I'm her mother. The fact that we're spending time together is a positive thing, not something you have to rescue her from."

The door to Olivia's bedroom clicked open, announcing her

appearance. She seemed surprised to see Ruth—or perhaps just surprised to see Ruth talking to Ben. "Oh, hey, Mother. I didn't realize you were home."

"I just got here. Dad tells me you two are on your way to dinner."

"Yeah," Olivia said, glancing at Ben.

"You're welcome to join us," Ben said.

She hesitated, certain he was just being polite but at the same time wanting to pretend the invitation was genuine, that the three of them could go out and have a friendly meal together. Or maybe, on some level, she wanted to continue the conversation with Ben. About parenting. About life. About everything that had been left unsaid during that phone call a year and a half ago.

"Oh, no, no. You two have fun," Ruth said, waving them off.

She walked quickly to the stairs, forcing herself not to look back, not to say another word. She told herself the only way to get through the next few days was to just be casual.

But she didn't feel casual. The day had started with a boat ride with a new man and ended with her face to face with her ex-husband. And she couldn't deny that she felt a stronger pull toward her past than her present.

After processing the weirdness of seeing her parents together, Olivia needed a drink. Specifically, she needed the frozen rosé served at the Canteen's waterfront bar. Her father, more interested in food, ordered lobster rolls.

They sat opposite each other at the end of one of the communal tables. The sun was still strong and Ben angled the table's striped umbrella so the light wasn't directly in their faces. "This is a great place," he said.

Olivia put the small placard with their order number in front of her so the waiter would be able to locate them when their lobster rolls were ready. "I love it. I eat here all the time. It's like my cafeteria," she said. "Sometimes the house gets a little crowded."

"So who are those other people again?"

"Elise and Fern own the house. They rented to Mom but then they moved back in because of the baby."

"So she's renting a house, but the owners had a baby and then changed their mind about renting it out? I don't understand. Why didn't your mother just find a new house?"

"No, it's...first of all, I don't think it's easy to find available places. Look at the trouble you had just looking for a hotel room. And the baby was unexpected."

"How 'unexpected' can a baby be?"

Olivia looked at him. "If I tell you something, don't repeat it to anyone. Promise?"

"Who would I repeat it to? I don't know anyone in town aside from you and your mother."

"Okay, well—it's not their baby. She just appeared on the doorstep. She was abandoned."

Her father looked at her incredulously. "Abandoned?"

Olivia nodded.

"Was this reported? I mean, that's a serious thing."

"I think Elise and Fern are trying to adopt her. I don't know—they clearly love the baby. I guess it takes time."

"This seems like an unusual living situation for your mother."

"I'll never understand her," Olivia said.

"She's an interesting woman."

They shared a smile of comradery.

"I'm really glad you came, Dad," Olivia said. "So, what do you think of the town? Is it what you expected?"

"Expected? I've been to Provincetown before."

She looked at him in surprise. "When?"

"The summer before my sophomore year at Penn."

"How did I not know this? What made you come all the way out here?"

Her father hesitated, turning his bottle of Whale's Tale Pale Ale. "I won a spot at the Fine Arts Work Center for my playwriting."

"You wrote plays? You never told me that." She wondered, seeing the sheepish expression on his face, what else she didn't know about her father.

"It was a very long time ago."

"Yeah, but when I said I was coming out here, you never thought to say, *Oh, by the way, I spent a summer there as a playwright?*"

He shook his head. "Your trip out here isn't about me," he said.

Olivia hated that kind of double talk, and it wasn't something she was used to from him. "Wait a minute," she said, something suddenly dawning on her. The realization was like a weird dream intruding on rational thought. "That day at your house—when I told you Mom had moved out here—I asked you if you had any idea why she'd choose this place. I told you it seemed very random. And you never said anything about it."

Her father took a swig of his beer. "Your mother was out here that summer too. It's where we met."

Olivia felt like someone had pulled the bench out from under her. On the surface, there was nothing nefarious about this, nothing odd about it aside from the fact that she'd never heard it before. But somehow, it felt like her father had colluded with her mother in keeping this origin story from her. It was irrational to feel this way—she knew that. But she couldn't help it.

"You said you met at the beach."

"We did."

"I thought you meant at the Jersey Shore," she said.

He shook his head no.

"Why didn't you ever tell me about this place?"

"Why would I talk about it, Olivia?"

"I don't know!" Olivia said, certain there was some reason he should have.

Her father looked out at the water, then back at her. "Olivia, why are you making a big deal out of this?"

"I'm not. I just don't understand how we all ended up out here this summer and somehow I had no idea that you two have a whole history here."

"Two lobster rolls?" a waiter called out. Olivia held up their number and waved at him.

They ate in silence. The song "Wake Me Up Before You Go-Go," by Wham, played loudly on the sound system, infusing the moment with a bouncy cheer that she did not at all feel.

A group of young people, probably college age, took over the rest of the space at their picnic table. Every one of them held a colorful cocktail, and they were dressed in bathing suits. The women had wet hair. The air filled with a rapid-fire conversation Olivia couldn't quite make out over the music, and it was punctuated with a lot of laughter. Listening to them, stealing glances, Olivia thought that her parents had been around that age when they met. Who had she been dating in her early college years? Certainly no one significant. The idea of a relationship beginning when you were that young and lasting a lifetime was unthinkable. Yes, some couples made it work. But she could barely sustain something now, at thirty. Maybe it had been inevitable that her parents would split up. Maybe if they'd met later in life, they would have had more staying power. Or maybe, if they'd met at a different time, they would have known better than to get married in the first place.

What difference did it make that her parents had met right here, in Provincetown? Why did she care? She wasn't sure. Maybe it was because, for as long as she could remember, she'd simply thought of her parents' relationship in terms of its failure. She was detached from it.

Why should it matter how it began? Now she was faced with this new information about where her parents had met and fallen in love. She was walking the same streets, gazing out at the same water. It made it difficult to keep their marriage and divorce in a neat little emotional box. The idea of them as a couple suddenly had a new dimension, and it made her feel the loss all over again.

Or maybe she was letting herself feel the loss for the first time.

"Well, that's ancient history, right?" she said.

"Of course it is," her father said. "Let's just have a good few days and I'll get you back to the city."

Olivia nodded. That was the plan.

Chapter Thirty-Three

Fern's bedtime routine seemed to be taking an extra-long time. Elise tried to ignore the sense that her wife was hiding out in the bathroom, avoiding her.

When Fern finally appeared, her hair was covered with a terrycloth wrap. Elise smelled the coconut oil Fern used occasionally for deep conditioning. It always reminded Elise of their first vacation together to Negril, where the bedside candles had a similar scent. The hotel, the Rockhouse, was breathtaking. It spanned eight acres of tropical gardens, each "room" a private bungalow perched right on the cliffs of Negril's West End, overlooking the water. The bungalows were made of timber, thatch, and stone and blended in with the stunning natural beauty of the environment.

Fern was very proud of the fact that her favorite resort was Green Globe–certified. "It doesn't just look good—it is good," she'd said. They'd considered having their honeymoon there, but Fern decided they could not celebrate their union in a country that had a major human-rights problem for its treatment of the LGBTQ community.

Six months or so into their relationship, Fern experienced a crisis of conscience about her finance job. She'd reached the point in her life when she wanted to spend her days doing something that "put positive energy" into the world. This talk surprised Elise, because she'd felt that Fern was the focused, practical one of the two of them. But Elise also had a deeply altruistic and spiritual side, and she understood that this was what had drawn Fern to her—Elise was all idealism. In Elise, Fern had found a partner who inspired her to explore the latent side of herself, the aspect that Fern considered the best part of who she was and who she wanted to become.

Away from the day-to-day grind of life in Boston, Elise and Fern saw different sides of each other. Swimming in the turquoise water, dining under the clearest night skies Elise had ever seen, reaching for each other in the middle of the night to the deepest silence and the feeling they were alone at the edge of the world, they realized they were more than a couple: they were soul mates.

Finally Fern climbed into her side of the bed, and Elise reached over and kissed her cheek. "You smell like vacation." Elise smiled.

Fern looked at her, not smiling in return. "It's ridiculous to be living in the guest room of this house. I have to go down the hall to use the bathroom."

"It still gives us more space than the room above the shop."

Fern said nothing and settled as far on the edge of the bed as possible. She opened the novel she was reading, and Elise reached over to her nightstand for her own.

"Did you just give up on the mosaic class?" Fern said suddenly.

What? Where was this coming from? "No. I didn't give up. I just don't have time for it right now."

Fern shook her head. "I just feel like you made a commitment. You started something, you should finish it."

Elise sat up straighter and crossed her arms in front of her chest.

"Well, things are busy around here and I have to prioritize. I'm sure Amelia understands."

Fern just stared at the page open in front of her.

"What? I can't believe you're being so judgmental. I mean, do you want to start an argument over this?"

"No," Fern said, turning the page. "I don't."

Elise opened her own book, but the words swam in front of her eyes. Simmering with anger, she wondered why Fern had to ruin a perfectly good moment with needless criticism. And so she asked her. "What's with you? Why'd you have to go and bitch at me like that?"

At first, Fern didn't react. Elise wondered for a second or two if she was just going to ignore her. But then she slowly removed her reading glasses and turned to face her.

"I'm sorry. I just can't do this anymore."

Elise froze. "Do what anymore?"

"That situation with Bianca today was very disturbing. If she's asking questions, other people must be too."

"Fern, when Bianca was goading me about the house, you said I shouldn't let her get to me, remember?"

Fern shook her head. "This is different. This is serious. We've had that baby for weeks. The mother hasn't come back for her. It's time to call the Department of Children and Families."

Elise's heart began to race. "They'll take her away from us."

"Elise, we have to go through the process."

"Getting approved as adoptive parents could take months. There will be background checks, financial—"

"We have nothing to hide. What are you afraid of?"

"Where will they send Mira while we're going through this *process?* Foster care. What if we never get her back?" Her voice was shrill.

"Why wouldn't we?" Fern said.

"I don't know! Once we get a government agency involved, it's out of our hands. There's no turning back."

"Elise, that's life. We can't control everything, and we certainly can't keep on pretending we're in a legitimate adoption process just to avoid the emotional messiness of the real thing. Enough is enough."

Elise shook her head. "I'm not willing to lose another baby."

They locked eyes, neither one blinking. Fern finally looked away. "Well, I can't be a part of this anymore. I want a child as much as you do. But not like this."

"Don't give me that 'I want a child as much as you do' crap," Elise said.

"What's that supposed to mean?"

"It means that when we found out I couldn't carry a child, you could have stepped in and tried. But you refused. You said you'd never wanted to experience pregnancy, that wasn't part of the deal, and it was just over for you."

Fern jumped up, walked to the closet, started throwing clothes into a duffel bag.

"Where are you going?" Elise said.

"I'm moving back into the room above the tea shop."

"You mean for the night?"

Fern shook her head sadly. "I think you know the answer to that, Elise."

Ruth could not sleep.

An hour earlier, she'd heard Ben climbing the stairs to the third floor. She lay in her bed, picturing him in that room, under the sloped ceiling, next to the books and candles she'd bought for Olivia's arrival. Never had she imagined this situation.

She tried not to think about their reunion in the living room, the strong response she'd felt to his touch. She tried to take Dr. Bellow's advice about handling a troubling thought: Accept it but let it drift away and don't give it too much weight. Dr. Bellow attempted to teach her mindfulness, just existing in the moment, not thinking about the past or the future. Ruth was terrible at it. "Remember, you control your thoughts, your thoughts do not control you," she'd said.

Really? Because at the moment, she felt her thoughts had her on a short leash.

You are not still in love with your ex-husband, she told herself. She repeated the mantra again and again, turning restlessly until she gave up on sleep and headed downstairs.

The entire house was quiet. She lingered for a minute outside of Olivia's door, listening for any sign that she was still awake. The room was silent, but she suspected if she opened the door, she would see the glow of her iPhone. Although lately, Olivia seemed to be a little less glued to it.

Ruth drifted into the kitchen and opened the cabinets looking for the tins of Fern and Elise's loose-leaf tea. She found one labeled SLEEP BLEND; the ingredients were chamomile, passionflower, and lavender. Now she just had to locate that metal ball that worked as a reusable tea bag, a device Elise called a tea infuser.

She opened and closed drawers but came up empty.

"Can I help you find something?"

She looked up and saw Elise standing in the doorway, wearing a red-and-white-plaid robe. Her hair was in a messy ponytail, and even though her eyes were hidden behind glasses, Ruth could see they were red and puffy. "Um, the tea infuser."

"I think it's in the dishwasher."

Ruth checked the utensil tray in the dishwasher and found it. "Thanks," she said. "Want some tea?"

"I need something a little stronger," Elise said, opening a cabinet and pulling out a bottle of Maker's Mark. She poured a glass and drank most of it standing at the counter. "Thanks, by the way, for the soap. I used it for Mira's bath tonight."

"My pleasure. I was thinking…"

Elise started to cry. She turned away from Ruth, put both hands on the counter, her shoulders shaking with sobs. Concerned, unsure what to do, Ruth crossed the room to stand behind her. She placed a hand gently on her shoulder.

"Come sit down," Ruth said. After a few ragged breaths, Elise followed her to the kitchen table, carrying her drink. Ruth handed her a paper napkin, and Elise pressed it to her nose.

The tea would have to wait. "What's wrong?"

Elise shook her head, closing her eyes. "Everything," she said.

"Did you get into an argument with Fern?"

"I guess you could call it that," Elise said, gulping her whiskey. "It's this whole situation with Mira." She seemed to hesitate, then said, "I guess you're one of the few people I can talk to about it since you know the truth."

Ruth nodded, feeling a pang of guilt for having confided in Olivia.

"So you know she was left here on the porch. Obviously—you found her. And, as I said that day, I don't know who left her. But what you don't know," she said, "is how desperately I've wanted to be a mother."

The raw emotion in her voice made the specifics of the situation—the unknown origins of the baby—suddenly less important. The urge Elise expressed was so primal and universal, Ruth felt as if Elise's pain were her own.

"Did you try to have a baby? Before this happened, I mean?"

Elise nodded, finished the last bit of amber liquid in her glass, and spoke slowly and quietly of miscarriages and polycystic ovary syndrome.

"We had so many disappointments," Elise said. "I wanted to keep trying but Fern had had enough. I agreed to move on. And then...this happened. A miracle."

Ruth thought back to the day when she discovered the baby on the porch, the expression on Elise's face when she'd taken her into her arms. Now, looking back on it, the moment took on an entirely new dimension. "So I'm assuming Fern doesn't quite see it as a miracle?"

Elise shook her head. "She wants me to call a state agency. To go through the *proper channels*. And I'm just afraid they'll take her away from me. I need more time. But Fern is done. I don't know what to do. I chose my marriage over a baby before, but I can't do it again."

Ruth exhaled. "You're in a tough position."

"An impossible position."

"I know you're not asking me what to do, and I wouldn't presume to tell you. But I do think the important thing here is to keep the lines of communication open with Fern."

Elise shook her head, her eyes filling with fresh tears. "It's too late for that. Fern left."

Ruth, feeling an almost maternal impulse to comfort her, leaned forward and hugged her. Elise cried in her arms like a heartbroken teenager.

"What's going on?"

Ruth turned around at the sound of Olivia's voice. She stood near the stove, dressed in her pajamas, her hair up in a messy ponytail. She looked very young, and Ruth was struck by the sad fact that her daughter had never confided in her or consulted her during a breakup or heartache.

"Just some girl talk," Ruth said. "I hope we didn't wake you."

Next to her, Elise sniffled but covered up the wads of tissues with her hand.

"No, I'm just getting water." Olivia looked at Elise and seemed about to say something, then turned and retreated back to her room.

Elise stood, picked up her glass, and stuffed the tissues in her robe pocket.

"Thanks for listening," she said. "Olivia's lucky to have you as a mom."

Chapter Thirty-Four

There was something warm and energetic about the Barros house. Olivia felt, sitting at the kitchen table while Lidia helped Fern brew batches of the experimental tea, that she had somehow wandered onto the set of a sitcom called *Happy Seaside Family*. Lidia's husband, Manny, made a big show of opening the windows and saying his house now smelled like a cross between the ocean floor and a fruit farm. But even as he said it, he patted his wife lovingly on her rear and told Marco, "Now, this is what I call thinking out of the box. Or, I should say, oyster cage."

"Here," Lidia said, handing her husband a mug of the green-tea-and-kelp blend, one Olivia had found tasted the most like the smell of the sea.

Manny waved it away. "Let me know when you start experimenting with coffee and seaweed."

"That's not going to happen, Dad," Marco said.

"Well, then, you're on your own. I have a bunch of tourists waiting to see some seals, so I'm off." He kissed Lidia on the forehead and wished them luck on his way out the door.

Olivia didn't know if it was the company, the calming task of sitting at the table sipping tea for hours at a time, or the fact that she'd woken up pain-free that morning, but she felt downright buoyant.

"Okay, so now we're moving on to the honeybush and sea lettuce," Fern said. She poured four mugs, for Olivia, Lidia, Marco, and herself. Jaci hadn't emerged from her bedroom to join them.

The tea was fruity and sweet, one of the best Olivia had tasted so far. She marked the flavor profile on the printout Marco had made listing all the teas. So far, there had been only one she didn't like at all and that was a black-tea blend that was too smoky.

While they waited for the next sample, genmaicha and kelp, to steep, Marco refilled the water glasses they were using between teas to cleanse their palates.

"By the way, Olivia and Fern, we're having a Fourth of July party," Lidia said. "Potluck and clambake starting around seven, and of course we have a great view of the fireworks."

"And plan to stay awhile. Last summer, people were still here at breakfast the next morning," Marco said.

"Oh, my all-nighters are far behind me," Fern said. "But if I'm in town, I'd love to come."

"Are you planning a trip?" Lidia said.

"I might. I'm looking at farmers' markets in a few cities to grow our customer base. We'll see."

"Olivia, be sure to tell your mother. I know I'll see her, but if I forget."

Fern poured the next sample into mugs. "So this is a Japanese brown-rice tea and kelp. I've been wanting to experiment with this tea for a while, so I'm hoping this one's a keeper."

Jaci walked into the kitchen.

"Just in time for some genmaicha," Lidia said. "Have a seat, Jace."

"Sorry, Ma. I've got to run. I'm babysitting."

"You are?" Fern and Marco said at the same time.

Interestingly, Fern seemed more vexed by Jaci's announcement than Marco. And Marco seemed pretty darn vexed.

"Jaci, be back here by one thirty so we can head out to the flats," he said.

"I can't," she said.

Marco looked at his mother, then stood up. "A few weeks of this attitude was maybe tolerable because you had to adjust to being back here. But it's time to get with the program. We need you *here*. I need you out on the water with me today. That baby is not your responsibility." He turned to Fern. "Sorry, Fern."

"No, no—I completely agree. I apologize for Elise overstepping. I'll talk to her."

"No!" Jaci said. She glanced at Olivia, then said, "This isn't about the baby. This is about me and *I'm entitled to live my own life*."

Olivia felt the blood drain from her face. Weren't those the exact words she had used when coaching Jaci to stand up for herself? Oh, what had she done?

Jaci stormed out before Marco could say another word to her. He turned to his mother in frustration. "Can't you do something about this?"

"What am I supposed to do? I can't force her onto the skiff with you."

The relaxed, fun vibe of the morning had been completely ruined and it was all Olivia's fault. Desperate to restore harmony, she said, "I'll help you out today. If you need an extra set of hands." Everyone looked at her in surprise.

"It's work," he said, a comment she found more than a little insulting.

"I'm capable," Olivia said. "I helped you hang the seaweed, didn't I?"

"Marco, she's offering the solution to your problem today, so please just accept it so we can move on," Lidia said.

"Fine," Marco said, a few degrees less enthusiastically than Olivia would have liked. He eyed her flip-flops. "You'll need more practical shoes."

Elise tried to keep busy between customers. No matter how soothing the music over the sound system or how many times she walked to the wide-open windows and looked across the street at the placid water or how many scented candles she lit, her stomach was in knots.

She'd been checking her phone every half hour or so, and still nothing from Fern.

When she'd arrived to open the shop, she'd first gone upstairs to see if she could catch Fern, but she was already gone. The bed was made and the only sign that she'd slept there—that Elise hadn't imagined their argument, as much as she would have liked to pretend she had—was the overnight bag on the floor.

"Everything okay?" Cynthia asked from behind the counter.

Elise, again at the window, turned to her. "Yes. Of course. Why?"

Despite her state of distraction, she'd have preferred to manage the shop alone rather than endure Cynthia's company. Or maybe especially because of her distraction. She still could not shake her unease about Cynthia's attitude toward Mira. On the rare occasions when Mira made an appearance at the shop, Cynthia did not interact with her, comment on her, or even look in her direction. It's not that Elise expected everyone to ooh and aah over Mira like Amelia or Lidia, but Cynthia's demeanor was remarkably standoffish. She found herself continuously studying Cynthia's face, finding it impossible to ignore the fact that her dark-eyed beauty was not unlike Mira's. Today, with her relationship with Fern teetering on the brink, she could not stand the uncertainty any longer. Could Cynthia be the biological mother? Did she dare ask her outright?

"May I ask you a question?" Elise said, walking toward the counter, her heart pounding.

"Sure," Cynthia said, smiling in that easygoing, confident way she had.

"Are you...are you..." Elise could not say it. It was as if the words, if spoken aloud, would magically become true. She settled instead for "Are you uncomfortable around the baby?"

Cynthia sighed, tightening the lid of a tin she'd just filled. "Ugh, I'm sorry. Is it that obvious?"

Elise felt the room tilt. "Is what obvious?"

"I just don't like babies."

Elise leaned against the counter. *I just don't like babies.* A momentary reprieve. Breathing room. *I just don't like babies* could mean anything.

She just doesn't like babies and that's why she gave one up? She just doesn't like babies and would never make the mistake of getting pregnant in the first place?

"I know that sounds crazy," Cynthia said. "But we had so many babies in the house when I was growing up. My dad is an adoption attorney and my mother was always fostering babies and small children."

"Fostering babies..." Elise said.

"Yeah," Cynthia said. "My parents are from Georgia. It's that do-gooder Southern stock. Anyway, I got dragged into diaper duty when my friends were out doing things teenagers should be doing, like chasing boys." She smiled. "So I've had enough of babies until I have one of my own someday. If I ever do."

Her father was an adoption attorney.

Elise had gotten it all wrong. Cynthia was not the reason Mira had arrived in her life. But she might be a way to help keep her in it.

The Beach Rose Inn bustled with guests everywhere—people were sitting on the front steps, on the porch rocking chairs, and on the lobby ottomans; they were standing at the desk chatting with Rachel and drinking coffee. It was perhaps not the best time for Ruth to drop in to see Amelia, but she realized that if she waited for a quiet time, she would be waiting until October.

Holding the shopping bags from Good Scents, she followed Rachel's direction to look for Amelia out back and found her sitting at the same table where she'd first met her. That day seemed so long ago, it felt almost like something she'd imagined. Surely she had known Amelia forever.

"Well, hello there," Amelia said, looking up from the book she was reading. It was the Mardi Gras coffee-table book Ruth had once seen her carrying out of the library. "What an unexpected treat." Her hair was piled on top of her head and held there with a plastic clip. Her dress was a particularly vivid green-and-blue-batik pattern, and she was barefoot.

"I've owed you a visit," Ruth said, sitting opposite her and placing the white bags on the table between them. "And an apology. I'm sorry I haven't been to your mosaic class. I should have called to tell you I need to drop out, but every time I think maybe I can make it…"

"No apology necessary," Amelia said. "It's a good thing if you find yourself busy."

"Well, the class did remind me of how much I like working with my hands. I found my way back to making my own products from scratch, something I haven't done in years. So thank you." She slid the bags across the table. Amelia reached through the purple tissue paper and pulled out one of the candles.

"This is lovely. But entirely unnecessary! So tell me, what have you been making?"

"It started with soap for Mira. She had a rash, and you know, so many products that claim to be gentle and all natural are far from it. So I whipped something up for her and haven't been able to stop since."

"How wonderful to feel inspired." Amelia sighed. "I haven't heard from Elise in a few days. How are things going over there?"

Ruth hesitated. It wasn't her place to share what was happening between Elise and Fern. And yet, if anyone could help, it was Amelia.

"In all honesty, things are not going well. Fern wants Elise to hand the baby over to a child welfare agency, and Elise is terrified she'll never get her back. But Fern is so adamant, she left last night."

Amelia sat up straighter, tapping her fingers on the cover of the book. "I was afraid it would come to this."

"I don't know if I should have mentioned it. Please don't say anything to Elise unless she brings it up herself."

"No, no. I won't. But I am going to have a word with Fern." She inhaled deeply, opened the book, and flipped through the pages. Was that Ruth's cue to leave? She stood and Amelia looked up. "Have you started thinking about your Carnival costume?"

"What? Oh, no. I don't even know if I'm—"

"Don't wait until the last minute. It has a way of sneaking up every year. Suddenly, there isn't a sequin to be had in the entire town. I've already started making a replica of this mask." She opened to the middle of the book and pointed to a purple-and-green beaded mask outlined in gold ribbon and topped with extravagant matching feathers.

"That's beautiful. But costumes aren't really my thing."

"Trust me," Amelia said. "By the end of the summer, we all need a little escape."

Chapter Thirty-Five

Olivia owned many pairs of practical shoes—practical for getting around Manhattan.

What she did not own was anything even remotely suitable for jumping on and off a small boat and wading through mucky, seaweed-filled water to reach a sandbar in the middle of Cape Cod Bay.

She showed up at the dock wearing a T-shirt, a pair of Free People denim shorts, a Yankees baseball hat, a mini–Fjällräven Kånken backpack, and a pair of Tory Sport slip-ons.

Marco took one look at her feet and ordered her up to his house, where Lidia helped her find a pair of Jaci's knee-high rubber wading boots.

"And get a sweatshirt too," he'd told her. "It's fifteen degrees cooler out on the water."

She should have remembered that; Olivia was no stranger to the water. In fact, she enjoyed boating. A few summers ago, she'd dated a guy who owned a house in East Hampton and they'd spent weekends sailing on his fifty-foot catamaran. She had not expected Marco to take her out on a similar vessel, but she definitely had not anticipated the bare-bones Carolina Skiff, as he called it.

"See how there's no big V like other boats," he said. "This is made for shallow water. And when we reach the flats, you'll see why."

The skiff had a scuffed-up white deck and a narrow bench next to the controls that could seat one person. A few ropes were scattered at her feet; there were two egg crates and buckets off to one side and an oblong floatation device tethered to a rope. Marco's knapsack rested next to her.

Over the rumble of the motor, he said, "Everything I grow is in cages. When I first started, I used racks but ended up switching." He glanced over at her. "I just want you to have a sense of the operation. And, really, the remarkable thing is that the whole setup out here was sort of a mistake on the part of the Division of Marine Fisheries."

She'd never heard him so animated. She didn't fully grasp what he was talking about, but she felt a thrill that he wanted to share his work with her.

"What kind of mistake?" she asked, holding her hat on against the wind.

"Truro and Provincetown made a joint effort to take fifty acres of open water and turn it into an aquaculture-designated area—a place where people could raise shellfish in deep water. But it never occurred to the Division of Marine Fisheries that we float most of our gear on the top. They somehow thought we would be sinking everything and bringing it up, but we don't—floating cages are a big part of the operation. I'll show you that another time."

Another time? She bit her lip to keep from smiling.

"It's basically two pontoons and underneath is a cage that holds the oysters. At any rate, it turns out we are located in the North Atlantic Right Whale Critical Habitat. They do not want vertical lines in Cape Cod Bay, so from February to May, our gear has to be sunk to the bottom—and this goes for the lobstermen too. Most everyone gets this done by December because no one wants to be out there in February dumping cages."

"This sounds like a lot of work."

"It is. And frankly, when I took it on, I thought Jaci would be a part of it. So it's frustrating."

A stretch of sand came into view. "Is that it?" she asked, looking up at him.

"That's it," he said. "Two hours ago, that was underwater. And it will be underwater again later, so this is our window."

They cruised steadily forward.

"Do you eat oysters?" he asked.

"Um, no, actually. I don't."

He smiled at her. "That's okay. I'm not offended."

"I'm sure yours are great, though."

He laughed. "It's a matter of personal taste. Oysters take on the flavor of where they're grown. Provincetown Harbor is very clean and the water is salty, so my Long Pointers have a briny terroir."

"Don't all oysters come from salty water? I'd imagine they're all briny."

"There are subtleties. For example, Wellfleet oysters are grown in a more brackish environment and they have mudflats, so I'd consider their flavor profile more musky."

They drew closer to the sand and Marco cut the motor. "Okay, you need to get on the bow there and jump."

"Jump?"

"Yeah, and jump long, not just down. The farther out you get, the more shallow the water."

Olivia climbed onto the wide, flat surface at the front of the skiff. She felt self-conscious, certain she would not get very far with her leap. But with no choice, she took a deep breath and bent deeply at the knee, a motion that harked back to long-jump practice in high-school gym class.

She landed in water that was sufficiently shallow. It didn't rise above her boots. She looked behind her and Marco gave her the thumbs-up, and her chest swelled with an absurd sense of accomplishment. While he climbed off the boat and dragged it to shore, she opened her bag to grab her phone to take a photo of the distant Long Point Lighthouse from her unique vantage point. She tried to post it to Instagram but found she had no internet connection.

Marco carried the egg crates, buckets, and his knapsack. She trudged alongside him in water so thick with green seaweed it was like walking through pea soup. She cringed at the thought of how she'd have managed out there in her slip-ons.

"Welcome to the oyster farm," Marco said.

The farm was half a dozen rows of square wire cages just a few inches deep in the middle of the sandbar. They were exposed to the air, but the residual seaweed clinging to the tops made it clear they had recently been submerged.

Marco set the two egg crates in front of the cages, sat on one of them, and motioned for her to do the same. He handed her a pair of thick, textured gloves and she pulled them on as he unhooked the top of the cages. Opened, the cages revealed hundreds of oysters of various shapes and sizes. She'd never seen anything like it.

"So we're looking for oysters that are three inches in diameter. Measure them with this." He handed her a round metal ring. "If it's not three inches, toss it back in the cage. If it's large enough, put it in this bucket."

"Okay," she said. Sounded simple enough. But then she looked around at all the cages. Going through every single one by hand, oyster by oyster, would take hours. No wonder he wanted Jaci's help.

"But also, if it's too thin, toss it back. We want the oyster to have some depth. Think of how it would look on a plate." He pushed the oysters in his cage to one side, and Olivia did the same with her own. A small crab scuttled across the bottom and she gasped.

"All right," Marco said. "Let's get to work."

When Fern walked in the door sometime during the early-afternoon lull, Elise felt a rush of relief. They had not texted or spoken once all day, and Elise couldn't stand the silence for another minute.

"Hey," Fern said, joining her behind the counter to check the register receipts. "I thought Cynthia was coming in today."

"She's on her lunch break."

Fern did not embrace her or offer any conciliatory gesture. Her expression was stony, and for Elise, being in the presence of her overt, simmering anger was almost worse than missing her.

Clearly, this was not the best time to bring up the news that Cynthia's father was an adoption attorney.

Fern poured herself a cup of iced green tea and adjusted the volume of the music just a notch quieter. "I see you enlisted Jaci to babysit."

"She offered," Elise said. "She likes taking care of Mira."

"Yeah, well, I was at the Barroses' when Marco got the news and he didn't handle it very well."

"That's between Jaci and her brother," Elise said, rinsing the metal shakers in the sink. "It's not my fault she has no interest in the family business. You heard her the night of Rachel's party."

Fern turned to her. "What kind of attitude is that? Lidia and Manny are our friends. If we're doing something to contribute to tension in their family, we should minimize it."

Elise slammed one of the shakers on the counter. "All you do is find fault with me!"

Fern made no move to deny it. They locked eyes, and neither blinked until the front door opened and Amelia walked in.

If Amelia noticed the tension in the room, she didn't acknowledge it.

Her smile was warm and her tone breezy when she asked for an iced tea. "Whatever your tea of the day is."

"It's our Mariner's Mint," Fern said.

"Sounds delightful," Amelia said, perusing the display of bracelets for sale at one end of the counter.

"I'll pour it," Elise said, opening the refrigerator. She needed something to do with her hands, a place to focus. An excuse to turn her back on Fern while she blinked away tears. Scooping ice into a plastic cup, she tried to pull herself together.

"Fern, we've barely had a minute to talk in weeks," Amelia said. "I've seen Elise, but you have been such a busy bee. Come to the house after work for a glass of wine."

Fern began protesting, but Amelia cut her off with "There's always time for happy hour. I will not take no for an answer."

Elise realized that Amelia had not shown up at the shop for a cold beverage; somehow, she knew that things were going off the rails. She was there to help. "We'll be there," Elise said, trying to catch Fern's eye but failing.

"Elise, I've barely had a moment with this one here. Surely you can spare your wife if I promise she'll be home for dinner."

"Oh, sure. I just thought that—"

"I'm happy to spend some time with you, Amelia," Fern said. "In fact, we should have dinner."

Elise poured Amelia's tea over ice and garnished it with a mint leaf, her hand shaking. The subtext of Fern's comments could not be more clear: *I won't be in any rush to get home.*

Chapter Thirty-Six

An hour into oyster picking, Olivia realized that sitting on an egg crate and leaning forward to dig through cages should have sent her back into spasms but, incredibly, aside from a slight tension just above her waist, she felt fine. Better than fine.

Every so often, she looked up at the blue sky or out at the water surrounding them and felt the unfamiliar sensation of peace. There was nothing else she needed to be doing, nowhere else she needed to be—or wanted to be.

It struck her at one point that if her life had not taken this strange turn, she would at that very moment be sitting in a Manhattan office eating salad out of a plastic takeout container and worrying about the quality of a celebrity's vacation photo on Instagram. Looking back on it, she had been like the oysters trapped in the cages by her feet.

Beside her, Marco worked silently. They spoke only when she wasn't sure if an oyster made the cut, but she was increasingly confident about assessing them and so even this minimal conversation was rare.

She kept stealing glances at him. The sunlight shining from above and reflecting off the water around them made him seem even more golden. She tried to be professional, tried to limit how often she set her eyes on his face, but it was impossible to resist. Every time she looked his way, she felt a rush. At one point, her gaze lingered just a little too long and he caught her. Mortified, she tried to think of something to say to make it look like she had turned in his direction to talk.

"So, um, you don't have any employees that help you out? It's just you and Jaci?"

"I had a part-timer in the spring, a merchant marine who helps me during his eight weeks off. But I've had more employees who've stayed for only one day than I can count. People think they are up for it—they romanticize being out on the water and all that—but when they experience the reality, they quit. It's one of those things; you either love it or hate it. There's no middle ground."

"Who wouldn't like this?" she said, looking pointedly at the natural beauty surrounding them.

"In the interest of full disclosure, this is the easy part of the job. The fun part. In April, I was spending most of my time dealing with a barnacle bloom and knocking mussels off my bags."

"How do mussels get on the bags?"

"Mussels are predators. Do you eat mussels?"

She shook her head. "I know I already said I don't eat oysters but I'm not anti-seafood or anything."

He smiled. "Just anti-shellfish."

"I eat shrimp."

"Okay, then. Now I know what to cook if you ever come over for dinner."

If you ever come over for dinner. Was he simply making a point about her limited seafood palate or was he truly suggesting that there was some scenario in which he would invite her over?

"Mussels are predators," Marco said again. "There's a beard on them that you remove when cooking. The beard affixes to the place on the oyster that oysters filter water through. Oysters filter between twenty-five and fifty gallons of water a day. So the beard goes into there and it sits in there, stopping the filtering and killing the oyster. And I'm not talking about a few mussels." He reached for the cover of the cage he was working in and latched it closed.

"I get that it's messy and physical work," she said. "But it's impressive. You're doing something real. The idea that these are going to end up on someone's plate is amazing." It was hard not to think about her own career by comparison. How much time and energy had she spent staging fake photos to post on someone's phone to see how many times strangers pressed a heart button? And it had meant so much to her—everything. How absurd it all seemed now.

Marco smiled at her. "Thanks. So what do you do when you're not out here on vacation?"

"Oh," she said, "I'm not on vacation. I came out here because I thought my mother was sick."

"She's sick?"

Olivia shook her head. "No, I *thought* she might be. She sort of implied she was sick. Or maybe it was just a misunderstanding. I don't know. But I rushed out here because it seemed like something was wrong."

"The call of duty," he said.

"Yeah. Basically."

"I think that's admirable. I wish my sister were more considerate when it came to our parents."

"She's young," Olivia said. "And to be honest, I wasn't that generous with my attitude when I got out here. I couldn't wait to leave."

"And yet you're still here."

She sighed. "It's a long story."

He grinned and looked pointedly out at the water surrounding them. "We've got time."

She shook her head. "I don't know. Right now there's no reason to run back to New York. I'm regrouping, I guess you could say."

"What about your job? You mentioned that night at Rachel's house that you do social media stuff."

Incredulous, she leaned back on the crate to see him better. "You remember that?"

"I mean, it wasn't that long ago."

No, it wasn't that long ago. But it had been such a throwaway comment and he'd barely seemed to recognize her that night. Maybe she'd misread the situation. "Well, yes—my career is about social media. *Was* about social media. Now, I don't know. I messed up at work and everything unraveled. One careless mistake, and eight years of nonstop effort was just completely destroyed." She had to stop feeling sorry for herself. She could only imagine what Marco thought of her in that moment. Pathetic.

And yet there was no indication of judgment on his face when he said, "Maybe it wasn't a mistake."

"What do you mean?"

"You might have done something subconsciously to sabotage yourself. Happens all the time."

"Trust me, it was a mistake. My career means everything to me."

And yet, now that she could reflect back on that time from a distance, she had to admit she had not been happy. She had not been happy for a long time.

Maybe not until that very moment.

They settled back into their work rhythm until the tides were ready to turn and once again submerge the cages. Marco transferred oysters from the buckets into mesh bags and she closed the cage she was working on and fastened the latch.

Water had soaked through her gloves, and her hands were uncomfortably moist. Now that she was done handling the oysters, she peeled the gloves off. "Do you need help carrying stuff?" she said, wiping the back of her shorts. At some point her knapsack had fallen to the ground and it was now covered with sand, seaweed, and salt deposits. She felt sweaty; her hair was matted down under her baseball cap. She could only imagine what she looked like—didn't want to imagine.

"Can you grab the crates?"

They walked side by side back to the boat.

"So what happens to the oysters now?" she said.

"The first thing is to get them cooled down quickly. Ever hear of vibrio?"

She shook her head.

"Well, since you don't eat oysters anyway, I know I'm not risking turning you off."

You couldn't turn me off if you tried. "Oh, wait—does it cause food poisoning?" she said.

He nodded. "We gotta get these oysters down to at least forty-five degrees, and we do that by submerging them in a mixture of salt water and ice. It's called a slurry. And then they'll be tagged with all the info, like harvest date, time, harvest area, and time of icing."

"Do you need help with that?" she said.

"Thanks, but I can take it from here." He looked at her. "You really find this interesting?"

"Of course. Who wouldn't?"

He stopped and adjusted the bags in his hands. "A lot of people," he said with a look on his face that seemed almost wistful. But then something in the sand caught his attention. "See that indentation?" he said.

She looked down and nodded. "Yeah, I think so."

"That's from horseshoe crabs mating. It's their season," he said.

She let out a nervous giggle. "I'm sorry," she said. "I just wasn't expecting to hear about crab sex today."

"Too much information? I guess I didn't want to end the day on vibrio."

She swallowed hard, looking at him and thinking she didn't want to end the day at all.

"Not too much information at all," she said. "It's been perfect."

Chapter Thirty-Seven

It was long after dinner and Fern had still not returned from her visit with Amelia. Elise began to wonder if she planned to come back to the house at all.

Maybe she'd gone too far last night in bringing up Fern's refusal to try to carry a child of their own. But how could Fern look at her and say she'd wanted a child as much as Elise? It simply wasn't true and Elise needed Fern to acknowledge it. She needed her wife to acknowledge her pain—a pain that was not equal between them. But now was not the time to press this fine emotional point. It was not worth pushing their relationship to the brink.

Was Fern truly moving back to living above the tea shop, as she'd said last night? Or was that just the heat of anger talking?

Elise wasn't willing to leave it to chance.

She fed Mira one last bottle for the night, burped her, and dressed her in a fresh onesie. She checked her own limp hair in the mirror and decided she didn't want to waste time doing anything with it. Now all she needed was someone to watch Mira for half an hour. Really, she could just bring her along in the stroller. But she felt, given the current tension between them, convincing Fern to come home tonight would be best accomplished without a baby in tow.

The last she'd seen Ruth, she was messing around with those concoctions of hers in the kitchen. Maybe Olivia was free?

She carried Mira down to the living room and found Olivia on the couch staring into space. "Hey, how's it going?" Elise said.

Olivia smiled dreamily but said nothing. Maybe this wasn't the best time to ask her to watch Mira.

"Are you okay?" Elise said.

"What? Oh, yeah. I'm just tired. I went oyster picking today."

"I was going to ask if you could watch Mira for a few minutes while I run to Amelia's, but it seems like you're ready for bed…"

"No, my dad and I are going out to get ice cream. I can take her with us."

"Really? That would be great. I'll be back soon. She'll probably fall asleep in the stroller."

"No problem," Olivia said.

Elise smiled at her gratefully. She could only hope the rest of the night would go as smoothly.

Work had always been Ruth's escape.

Her escape from the fear of being broke, the fear of ending up unhappy like her mother. Her escape from her deteriorating marriage. And now, though it was technically not work, whipping up batches of moisturizers and soaps was once again her outlet.

This summer was supposed to have been the simplest, most uncomplicated time of her life. Now she had her grown daughter and ex-husband under her roof, and it wasn't even her roof.

It was no wonder she couldn't sleep at night.

Her new products—the facial cleanser with white tea and evening primrose, the body lotion with argan and coconut oil, and the oatmeal/ calendula soap—had overtaken the kitchen counter. No one in the house had mentioned the rows and rows of Glasslock containers; everyone was either too busy to use the kitchen or too polite to make a fuss. But truly, it was getting out of control.

She wanted to start giving away the products, but she couldn't bring herself to hand them out in those plain, utilitarian containers. She'd have to order some pretty jars from one of her old packagers. Maybe something in pale blue, like the hydrangeas blooming in the front and backyards.

But even as she considered how to distribute the products, she sat at the table breaking up stalks of lavender flowers and stuffing them in a mason jar to make lavender oil, her project for the next day or two.

This is what happens when I have too much time on my hands. The biting scent of the lavender—more camphor than floral—would cling to her. She hoped Tito Barros didn't mind the smell. They were set for a dinner date the following night.

"I see old habits die hard," Ben said from behind her.

She was getting used to hearing the sound of his voice in the house, and it dawned on her that in all these years, she had never quite gotten used to not hearing it.

She turned around. "I thought you and Olivia were going for ice cream."

"She's bringing the baby, so I'm waiting for them," Ben said, pulling out a chair and sitting across from her pile of flowers. "It didn't take you long to get back to business," he said.

"This isn't business. This is relaxation. A hobby."

"Come on, Ruth. It's me you're talking to."

She smiled. "And this is the *new* me you're talking to. I'm retired."

He leaned back in his seat and crossed his arms. "So I heard. You're young for retirement."

"I'm not young for *anything* anymore."

"Well, for the record, you look great."

She felt, in that moment, like a schoolgirl. "It's just the Provincetown light," she said quietly.

"I was surprised you sold."

"Oh, come on, Ben. You're retired now too. It's not a big deal."

He shook his head. "It's different. We both know that. I imagine it was a difficult decision."

She nodded. "It was. Very. But it was the right thing to do at the time."

"At the time?"

She shrugged.

"Don't tell me you have seller's remorse," he said.

"I don't want to talk about it," she said, pushing away the thought of the discontinued Cherry Hill.

"Is that why you moved out here? So you wouldn't be tempted to jump back in the game?"

"No, that had nothing to do with it," she said quickly. "I moved out here because it's one of my favorite places. I've wanted to come back for years, but you never wanted to vacation here, and life got so busy…"

"It seems an odd choice," he said.

"Well…" She wondered if it was worth it to say what was on her mind, then decided why not? She had never held back and there was no point starting now. "It seems odd to me that you refused, for our entire marriage, to come out here."

"We had the Jersey Shore."

"Ben, let's be real. Geography had nothing to do with it."

When it became clear he was not going to respond, she turned her attention back to her stalks. Ben continued to sit there. His presence was a bit disconcerting, but, well, she'd welcomed him as a guest.

She was acutely aware of him watching her work.

"Fine," he said finally. "I'll admit it would have been difficult for me to come out here."

"Because you stopped writing."

"Yes," he said, an edge to his voice. "Because I stopped writing."

She knew it. "So why did you just walk away from writing? I never asked you to give it up."

"You didn't have to," he said. "It was one thing to spend my time trying to become a playwright when it was just me...out here...living on the arts council's grant. Or even when I was at school, where it seemed a noble pursuit compared to my friends getting wasted at parties. But once I was about to head out into the real world and try to make a life with you, it stopped making sense."

"There was room for both."

"Was there? Ruth, I was with you when your father lost all his money. I saw what it did to you and your mother. I had no desire to spend years, maybe decades, as a starving artist. And I certainly had no intention of asking you to marry one."

The weight of his words felt crushing to her. She shook her head, wanting to go back in time, to have this conversation thirty-five years earlier. "You never said any of this to me. If you'd said this at the time—"

"You would have panicked."

"That's not true!"

"Ruth, it's easy for you to say that now; you're a woman with total financial security. But think back to where we were. You didn't even have a college degree."

It was true.

"No wonder you resented me," she said quietly.

He shook his head. "I never blamed you. But yes, it was hard at times to see you living your dream when I'd given up my own."

"I encouraged you to go back to writing! Olivia couldn't have been older than eight or nine when I suggested that to you. There was plenty of time."

"Ruth, I devoted years and years and spent a small fortune on medical school to establish myself as a physician. You don't just walk away from that to chase a dream you had when you were a teenager."

She didn't agree. But what was the point of debating it now? Still, she felt a terrible, creeping sense of regret. Yes, she'd always known he'd resented her career. But she'd blamed him for his own circumstances, figuring he hadn't had the nerve to go for it as a writer. Now, hearing him articulate exactly why he'd given it up and realizing that so much of it had been because of her, she felt as if someone had just given her the news of a death.

"I wish . . . " She wished what? What would she have done differently?

"Ruth," he said. "It's not worth getting into all this. I've been very blessed in life. I have no complaints."

He's letting me off the hook, she thought. Ben, who still, after all this time, knew her as well as anyone, must have read the distress on her face.

"And again, I appreciate you letting me stay here. But I'll be out of your way by Friday."

Friday? That was only two days away. "Is Olivia leaving too?"

"That's the plan."

"It seems so sudden. You don't have to rush off."

"Rush off? I've been out here almost a week."

"So? What's the point of being retired if you can't spend time at the beach?"

He smiled. "Ruth. You can visit her in New York. I'm sure that window is a little more open now."

Ruth sighed. "I'm just afraid it won't be the same. I shouldn't fuss— I've had some time with her. But of course, it's never enough." *And I won't see you.*

"Come to dinner with us tomorrow night," he said.

Surprised, she looked at him. Somewhere in the back of her mind hummed the understanding that she had other plans. But it was distant, background noise. It was easily ignored.

"Sure," she said. "I'd like that."

At nine that night, the porch of the Beach Rose Inn was filled with guests lounging on deck chairs, plastic cups of wine in hand. Elise, coming to see Fern, patted Molly's head on her way up the front steps, trying not to feel very much like a contrite dog herself, arriving with her tail between her legs.

The lobby was empty except for Rachel behind the front desk. Next to her, a mahogany English serving buffet held half a dozen open bottles of sauvignon blanc and rosé. Around the room, tables were littered with empty or nearly empty plastic cups.

"They're compostable," Rachel said.

"Oh," said Elise. "I wasn't judging."

"Most people don't, but I still feel defensive. You looking for Fern? She's out back." Rachel handed her a plastic cup.

"Oh—thanks." Elise poured herself half a cup of rosé, tossed it back for fortification, and made her way to the rear of the house just as Fern and Amelia were walking inside.

"I know, I know—I promised she'd be home for dinner and now look at the time. It's entirely my fault," Amelia said, linking one arm through Fern's and another through Elise's. "But some conversations just take on a life of their own, don't they?"

"They certainly do," Fern said.

"No problem," Elise said. "I was just thinking I could walk Fern home. I missed her."

"So sweet! Who says marriage kills romance?" Amelia said. Elise looked over and found Fern smiling at her. She felt such a wave of relief it was almost embarrassing. So Amelia had done it—she'd talked Fern into a truce.

Amelia bade them good night at the foot of the stairs, then said to Fern, "Call me if you need anything."

Elise couldn't help but wonder what Fern could need. Help with the shop? With their relationship? What had they been discussing for so many hours? But then, what did it matter? Amelia could only be trying to make things better.

And yet, once they got outside, the warmth between them dissipated in the night air.

"I'm going to Boston for a few days," Fern said.

"When?"

"Tomorrow. Hoping to make some inroads with the farmers' markets and explore the possibility of getting our tea into a few restaurants."

Elise stopped walking. "But . . . what about the shop?"

"I'm confident you can manage with Cynthia."

Elise just nodded, unable to look at her, certain this trip had nothing to do with farmers' markets and everything to do with Fern putting more distance between them.

Chapter Thirty-Eight

In the days since Fern had left the house, Elise carried herself with a muted sadness. Olivia did not know exactly why Elise was so upset, but her unhappiness was impossible to miss, even for Olivia, who generally focused on herself. And so, when faced with Elise's melancholy over morning coffee, Mira yawning in her arms, Olivia impulsively said, "Do you need help with the baby today?"

Several hours and many diaper changes later, Olivia was questioning why she'd made this offer. She didn't know how often most babies cried, but this one seemed to cry a lot—an awful lot. Midmorning, it dawned on Olivia that perhaps this was her fault, that she was misreading the baby's cues. But what were her options aside from feeding, holding, and changing her? She heated a bottle, pacing in the kitchen, holding Mira, and murmuring "Shh, shh," while it was warming up.

Passing the window, she glimpsed movement in the backyard. She stopped to take a closer look and found it was Marco hanging fresh seaweed. It was the first time she'd seen him since the day they'd picked oysters together. She jumped away from the window, not wanting to get caught spying on him.

Mira's crying got louder, if that was even humanly possible. "I have to put you down to get your bottle," she said, marveling at how quickly she had gotten used to talking to someone who had no capacity to understand what she was saying. She tested the temperature of the formula with a few drops on her wrist like she'd seen her mother and Elise do and determined it was good to go.

The baby's dark eyes seemed intently focused on her as she drank the formula, her little hand fluttering aimlessly up toward the bottle and then down again.

Olivia exhaled. There was something deeply satisfying about resolving such a primal need.

"You know what I think?" she said. "I think after this bottle, we're going to take a walk outside in the backyard to get some fresh air." Yeah, that was the reason. For the "fresh air." Fortunately, her fussy little sidekick was in no position to judge.

Olivia fought her impatience while Mira sucked down the bottle and then proceeded to take forever to give up a solid burp. Finally, Mira was content enough to be strapped into the stroller and wheeled out the back door.

Marco was just starting on a fresh line. "Oh, hey," he said. "I didn't know anyone was home. Wait, let me help you." He lifted the front of the stroller and together they eased it down the porch stairs and set it in the grass.

"Yeah, it's just me. Well, just us," she said, adjusting the hood of the stroller against the sunlight.

"Elise has got *you* babysitting now?"

"Well, in all fairness, I volunteered. I mean, everyone else is working around here. I need something to do."

He glanced at her while he adjusted a bunch of particularly long fronds, drawing them back over the line so they didn't touch the ground. "Anytime you want to help out with the oysters, just let me know."

"Really?" she said.

"Yeah. I get literally twice as much done with help. And like I said, you seem interested. That's really half of it right there."

She swallowed hard. "I loved it."

He glanced inside the stroller. "It seems you wore her out."

Olivia looked and saw that Mira's eyes were closed. "Oh, thank God. You can't imagine how nonstop it's been all morning. I mean, she's adorable—but it's work. It makes picking those oysters seem like a rest." She leaned closer to make sure the straps weren't too tight. "Let me just move her to the shade." She looked around. "If I can find any."

"Maybe back on the porch?" Marco said.

"Okay, yeah. Sorry, can you help with the—"

He was already lifting the undercarriage. "I've got it," he said when she tried to help. She followed him up the stairs. The transport didn't seem to affect Mira. She shifted her head to one side, her eyes still shut tight.

"Well, now I'm not only not helping you, I'm officially slowing you down," Olivia said.

He walked around from behind the carriage so he was standing beside her. She looked up at him, her insides jumping like popping corn.

"So you're not helping me work today."

"Well, no," she said. "Unless…"

He leaned forward and kissed her. It lasted only thirty seconds, but there, in the bright light of the afternoon, she saw stars. She took a step back, feeling off balance. He reached forward to steady her.

"Okay," she said, breathless.

"I wanted to do that the other day on the water," he said.

"You did?"

"Yeah. But I was afraid it might count as workplace harassment."

Olivia hesitated only a second. "Well," she said. "I'm officially off the clock."

He kissed her again.

Determined to find a festive place for dinner, Ruth called the one person she could think of who might have an idea.

"Ciro and Sal's," Clifford Henry said immediately. "You can smell the history. It's in the air."

That was the easy phone call to make. The next one, to cancel her plans with Tito, not so much.

"My daughter is leaving tomorrow, so I want to spend time with her," Ruth said. She conveniently left out the part about her ex-husband, but really, what did it matter? People had friendly meals with their exes all the time (didn't they?). Yes, she'd been having some... feelings. But they weren't anything that couldn't be handled with an emergency phone call to Dr. Bellow.

Tito sounded understanding when he said, "Another time." But they didn't pick a night and she wondered if he had lost interest, or if she'd imagined his interest, or if he felt like she was blowing him off (which she was, but truly, for her daughter). This type of stress was exactly why she didn't want to date in the first place.

Ruth made a stop before meeting Olivia and Ben at the restaurant. It took longer than anticipated, so she was running late by the time she turned off Commercial onto Kiley Court.

Ciro and Sal's was nestled in the middle of a red-brick courtyard bordered by a vine-covered white trellis and marked with a chalk-board sign on the ground reading WELCOME TO CIRO & SAL'S— PROVINCETOWN'S HIDDEN GEM. The building was surrounded by plants, flowers, and trees, some with low-hanging branches strewn with tiny lights.

She walked through the shingled front doorway, and as soon as she stepped inside, the vibe changed from enchanted garden to hidden speakeasy. The restaurant was dark and cave-like with low ceilings, brick walls with built-in wine racks, and Chianti bottles hanging everywhere.

A hostess led her to the table where Olivia and Ben were already seated.

"Interesting choice, Mom," Olivia said when Ruth slid into the seat next to her, across from Ben.

"Sorry I'm late," Ruth said. "How's the menu look?"

"Northern Italian," Ben said. "How could it be bad?"

"Did you order anything yet?"

"Just the wine," Olivia said. Ben picked up the bottle of red and filled Ruth's glass.

Dean Martin played over the sound system. The place smelled woodsy and musty, and Ruth could feel the decades that had passed within the walls. She knew exactly what Clifford meant when he had said that history was in the air.

Ben raised his glass. "To Olivia, who has rebounded after a tough start to the summer. Onward and upward."

"Onward and upward," Ruth repeated. All she could think was how strange and yet familiar it was to be sitting at a table with Ben and their daughter. When was the last time they'd done this? Maybe a college-graduation celebration dinner, but there had been other couples then, Olivia's friend's parents. And then she remembered that the day after her sister had had surgery, Ben and Olivia stopped by the hospital. At some point, the three of them had gone to the cafeteria for lunch or coffee. Still, nothing like this. Something about being around Ben and Olivia together made her feel whole. There was an ineffable rightness about it, and it warmed her more intensely than the wine that was already lighting up her bloodstream.

"And to our last night in Provincetown," Ben said.

Olivia lowered her glass. "We're leaving tomorrow?"

"We discussed this," Ben said.

"I thought you meant *next* Friday," Olivia said.

Was Ruth imagining the note of distress in her voice?

"Olivia, I said I'd come out for a night or two. It's been a week. Besides, I know you've been dying to get back to the city."

"I never said that."

Ben looked at Ruth.

"Why don't you stay a bit longer," Ruth said, never one to miss an opening. "Maybe through the Fourth of July? The Barroses are having a party, and the Fourth is always a great weekend in town." She could not bring herself to meet Ben's eyes as she said this. For years, even after they were married, they had informally celebrated the Fourth of July as their anniversary.

"Perfect!" Olivia said.

Ben shook his head. "Thanks, Ruth. That's very generous of you. But I really should get home. Olivia, if you want to stay and feel you can travel back on your own, that's up to you."

Ruth opened her bag and dug around for the papers that she had picked up on her way to the restaurant. "Well, if you don't want to stay until the Fourth, you might want to consider coming back for that week. There's a lot of stuff going on in town." She slid a brochure from the Fine Arts Work Center across the table, opened to the page of July workshops. She'd circled the five days of playwriting intensives.

Ben picked it up and held it close to the candle in the center of the table, then, still unable to read it, he pulled his glasses out of his jacket pocket. When he finally realized what he was looking at, he placed the brochure on the table, removed his glasses, and folded his arms. "Ruth," he said, shaking his head.

"I just thought it might be fun."

"What is it? What's going on?" Olivia said.

"Nothing," Ben said. He reached for his wine.

The waiter appeared and took their orders, but after that, the conversation that had flowed so easily over the wine somehow dried up. The Fine Arts Work Center brochure sat in the middle of the table like untended baggage at an airport terminal—glaring and potentially dangerous.

"So, Dad, what do you say? We'll stay until the Fourth?" Olivia said. "What's the point in being retired if you can't be spontaneous?"

Ben, incredulous, looked at Olivia. "Since when has spontaneity been high on your list of priorities?"

She shrugged. "You're the one who's been telling me to take time off, to slow down."

"Everything in moderation. I'm glad you've slowed down a little, but eventually you have to get back to real life. This town has a way of diverting you from reality. But the reality is there, waiting. You might as well face it sooner rather than later."

Ruth reached across the table, retrieved the brochure, crumpled it up, and shoved it back into her handbag.

The town had diverted *her* from reality. For weeks now, she had been walking around in a fog, a fantasy, imagining that somehow, she could hit the reset button with her daughter. And maybe she had, if just a little. That was a major victory, and she should have been content with that. But then Ben had arrived, and she started having the same feelings of wanting to correct the past.

This isn't about them, a voice in her head told her. *This is your stuff.*

She had avoided the messiness of her marriage and motherhood, choosing instead to channel all of her energy into something more manageable: her company. Now her company was gone, and the dangling threads of her life were unbearably loose. But there was no way to completely tie them back together again. She had to find a way to make peace with the past. She needed to remember her original motivation in moving to Provincetown: to start fresh. To create a new home that was built for this new stage of her life, not a home for raising children, not an apartment that was easy to maintain while she traveled for work. A home that she could grow old in.

Ben was right; Olivia had to get back to her real life and face whatever problems she had in her career. She had to find her own place in the world. It was selfish for Ruth to try to keep her in town just because she wanted the chance to mother her. And of course, Ben had his life.

Ruth had planted the seeds of her new life in Provincetown. Someday they would take root. Until then, she would have to be patient. There were no shortcuts to emotional peace.

"Your father is right," Ruth said. Both Ben and Olivia looked at her in surprise. "You need to get back to the city."

"I'm not avoiding reality," Olivia snapped. "I'm trying to figure it out. There's a difference."

Ruth and Ben instinctively looked at each other, the shared glance of parents. Everything she'd been thinking just moments before—about letting the past go, about starting over—evaporated. She was tired of going it alone. She missed wordless communication. She missed sharing her life with someone. She missed her husband.

"Okay, okay," Ben said. "There's no need for anyone to get upset."

Ruth sensed a slight opening and decided to push. "For the record, I don't think some more vacation time would hurt either one of you. In fact, I think you could both use it."

Ben looked at her in surprise.

"Yeah, Dad," Olivia said. "I mean, it's the *summer*."

Ben signaled for the waiter, ordered another bottle of wine. He did not say yes, but he did not say no. And after all these years, Ruth knew Ben. And she knew that he would stay through the Fourth of July.

Ruth looked around the table at her family. A few more weeks.

Chapter Thirty-Nine

The Fourth of July was Elise's favorite holiday and had been ever since she'd moved to Provincetown. In P'town, for her, the holiday was not just a celebration of the country's independence but a symbol of her own life journey.

At noon, she sat on the steps of Tea by the Sea watching the parade pass by: the floats and music and hordes of people with their faces painted red, white, and blue; the sequined Uncle Sam hats; a sign that read WE HOLD THESE TRUTHS TO BE SELF-EVIDENT, THAT ALL MEN ARE CREATED EQUAL with the MEN crossed out and replaced in red lettering with PEOPLE.

Sometimes, Elise felt that becoming an adult was a process of unlearning much of what she'd been taught as a child. For most people, growing up was about learning more, and she envied them.

Girls grow up to marry men.

Elise had been six years old when she realized this would never be true for her. It was a big *uh-oh* moment. It remained a big uh-oh until her twenties.

Falling in love with Fern had changed that. Her sexual orientation was not a problem to be dealt with. It was not a mistake. It was not something to apologize for, not even to her parents.

Another sign passed by: LIFE. LIBERTY. THE PURSUIT OF HAPPINESS.

Together, she and Fern had certainly pursued happiness. But ultimately, it was not their parents or society that had gotten in the way. It was just life, the stumbling blocks that every couple faced.

The question was, how much damage had been done? Elise had not seen Fern in a week. One thing led to another led to another, and she was busy every day in Boston. Fern was there for work and Elise had no reason to believe otherwise, but she couldn't help thinking back to that night last summer when she went to find her at the piano bar and she was not where she'd said she would be. *I'm not having an affair…I've thought about it. I mean, things have not been great.*

From a purely business standpoint, Fern should be in Provincetown. What could be more important than building up their clientele while they had the summer foot traffic? Fern could spend the fall traveling to expand. It just seemed too convenient that they were arguing over the baby and suddenly Fern felt this urgency to maximize their wholesale opportunities.

Elise pulled her phone out of the pocket of her cargo shorts and dialed Fern. It went straight to voice mail. A few seconds later, a text pinged: Can't talk.

Fern was manning a Tea by the Sea booth at a big corporate-sponsored outdoor festival that she'd gotten into via one of her old contacts from the financial industry. "It will be great exposure for us," she'd said when she broke the news that she would be working on the Fourth.

Elise typed, Do you think you'll make it back in time to catch the tail end of the party?

Elise waited for a response. Dots appeared then disappeared. And then: Doubtful. But have fun!

Have fun? Elise wanted to cry.

Picnic tables had been set up in the area between the Barros house and the dock, and disco music played. In the distance, the water was filled with so many boats it looked like a regatta. One brazen seagull wandered over to Elise.

"I don't have anything for you," she told it, then let out a deep sigh. The day was beautiful and festive. It was a day meant to be shared. Fern knew what this holiday was like in Provincetown, and yet she'd chosen to stay away. Not a good sign.

Elise parked the stroller at the base of the front steps and carried Mira up to the house. Inside, she found Lidia and Jaci busy cooking. "Marco asked me to bring some seaweed tea," she told Lidia. She kissed her on the cheek and pulled two tins out of her tote bag. "But I figured I'd take pity on your guests and bring some Strawberry Meadows too."

"The seaweed is growing on me. No pun intended," Lidia said, scooping Mira out of Elise's arms and cradling her. "Oh, this baby. She's making me impatient for grandchildren." She turned to Jaci. "Will I get grandchildren someday?"

"I don't know, Ma. Ask Marco."

A timer sounded with a shrill ringing.

"That's my rice," Lidia said, passing Mira back to Elise. "As much as I'd love to just stand here fawning over her."

"Can I help with anything?"

"No, no—go outside and relax. I think Marco is out there."

"Can *I* go outside and relax?" Jaci said.

"Jaci Barros, sometimes I just want to—"

"Why isn't Marco in the kitchen? This family is sexist."

Lidia reached for a pot of oysters. "Marco pulled this out of the sea!

You don't mind sexism when he's doing the heavy lifting." She muttered something in Portuguese, shaking her head.

The door slid open and Clifford Henry appeared, his arms laden with wine bottles. "Let the festivities begin!" he said.

"Heavens, Clifford. Did you leave Vin's with any stock?"

"I was having one of those moments. Indecisiveness is my Achilles' heel. So I bought some red, some white, some rosé, some fizz..."

Lidia relieved him of two of the bottles.

"Allow me," Clifford said, setting the bottle of Prosecco on the table and removing the foil from the top. "And hello to you, Ms. Douglas. It's been a while and I have a bone to pick with you." He popped the cork, and wine fizzed over the side. Jaci quickly produced a few glasses.

Elise could not imagine what his issue with her could be, but she did not have any interest in finding out.

"I thought this was going to be an outdoor party," Bianca said, wandering in. She was wearing her usual all-black garb; today, it was a short-sleeved dress and black mules. Her hair was back in a tight bun.

"Did our merrymaking disturb you?" Clifford said, gesturing for Jaci to hand him one more glass. "You need a drink, my dear. As usual."

"I do," Bianca said. "That parade was exhausting."

"Oh? Were you in it?"

"No. But I suffered through hearing it for three hours straight."

"How about you, Elise? Was there a Tea by the Sea float?" Clifford asked.

"Maybe next summer," she said, shifting Mira in her arms. She felt Bianca looking at the baby and wondered how she could gracefully exit.

"Oh! That reminds me," Clifford said. "Speaking of next summer, my dear, if you enlist me to rent out your house for the season, you must not then decide to *move back in*. Frankly, it's bad for business."

Next summer? She couldn't even think about next week. If she and

Fern broke up, what would happen to Shell Haven? She couldn't bear to think about it. She refused to think about it.

"You shouldn't have rented it out to begin with!" Bianca said. "My daughter didn't sell it to you so you could turn it into some sort of boardinghouse for tourists."

"Okay, that's enough, everyone," Lidia said, shooing them toward the door. "Take the bubbly onto the deck. And while you're at it, grab the sangria I have in the fridge."

"Your sangria should come with a warning label," Clifford said. "And I mean that as the highest compliment."

Elise hung back and asked for a place to change Mira.

"You can use my room," Jaci said.

It was a relief to be alone for a minute. She closed the bedroom door and sat at Jaci's small desk. It was built into the wall, a masterpiece of custom woodworking that Manny had done himself. When Elise had first visited the house, Lidia had proudly detailed all of her husband's handiwork.

It was wonderful to have a partner.

"But it might just be you and me, kid," Elise said, resting Mira on her bent knees. She waved at her, and Mira smiled.

She smiled. *At her!*

"Oh my God. Your first smile!"

A knock at the door.

"Come in," Elise said.

Jaci peered inside. "Sorry to interrupt. I was just wondering if you needed any help with her. I can watch her for a while if you want to hang out with people and be, like, an adult for the night."

"Jaci, you won't believe this. She just smiled! And it wasn't, like, just a gassy smile that was a reflex. I said something to her and waved, and she smiled back."

"Aww, that's amazing, Elise."

Elise resisted the urge to pick up her phone and text Fern the news. She would have to be satisfied with sharing the moment with Jaci. Jaci, who had been so empathetic when Elise had admitted her sorrow over her failed attempt to have a baby. She understood why Lidia might be frustrated with Jaci, but she was a good kid.

Elise changed Mira quickly, then turned to Jaci. "Let's go outside and have some fun," she said.

The extra time with Ben had proved to be a frustrating exercise in proximity without closeness. Occasionally, while Ruth worked in the kitchen, he sat at the table for a few minutes and they talked, but the depth of their earlier conversation about the past had not been repeated. And yet, with each interaction, her feelings surfaced more and more, like a plant that had been dormant, the roots still growing belowground, its leaves just now unfolding.

Two days earlier, with the Fourth of July on the horizon and the clock ticking, she had decided she had to say something. It was the "Speak now or forever hold your peace" of their wedding—just more than three decades late. She didn't know exactly what she wanted or what she could possibly expect from expressing her feelings to him. It just felt imperative to share the thought that maybe, somehow, they had gotten it wrong eighteen years ago. That maybe they should have ridden out the storm. Because now, with all of her striving behind her and their daughter grown, she felt like she was looking at clear skies. The only thing they needed was the willingness to try again.

She'd been trying to find the right moment, but that moment somehow hadn't presented itself. And so, while they waited on the back porch for Olivia to finish getting dressed for the party, she said, "I need to talk to you about something."

Ben nodded. "I think I know what you're going to say."

Her heart soared. "You do?"

"Yes. We haven't discussed it since that night at the Italian restaurant, but I appreciate you finding that playwriting class for me. I know you're trying to give me back something that you think I lost. I'll admit, my first thought was that it was a ridiculous idea. But I found myself thinking about it and thinking about it, and, well, I've decided to do it."

Ruth took a moment to recover and process the turn the conversation had taken. No, he hadn't been thinking the same thing she had about their relationship. But he had reconsidered the Fine Arts Work Center class, and that meant he would stay in town longer.

Now it seemed unwise to admit her feelings. What if she scared him off and he changed his mind? Maybe she needed to let the situation breathe a little. Why rush and risk blowing it? Especially with the holiday upon them. How could Ben not think of the good times, the best times, when they were celebrating together on the anniversary of the day they had first made love, in the town where they had fallen in love?

And yet, when they got to the party, it felt all wrong.

Ruth had imagined cocktails and loose mingling by the water; Amelia and Rachel and Luke and everyone else who had known one another forever would be chatting away, and Ben—a newcomer—would gravitate to her, and they would have a moment. Maybe an entire evening of moments.

Instead, Lidia had put out picnic tables, and as the early evening transitioned to twilight, all the guests seemed happy to sit where they were, much as they had the night of Rachel and Luke's backyard party. There was no mingling, and Ruth was left to figure out how to reposition the highly undesirable seating arrangement. She had ended up sandwiched between Tito and Bianca, leaving Ruth with the double whammy of awkwardness with Tito and separation from Ben.

She had run into Tito just one time since the night she'd canceled their dinner. Lidia had invited her over for coffee, and Tito had stopped by, as Ruth had expected he might. She didn't know if he just happened to be there at the same time or if Lidia was playing match-maker, but either way, their small talk had been awkward. Tito finally said, on his way out the door, "Anytime you want to get back out on the water, just let me know."

Tonight, he did not mention the boat or any scenario of getting to-gether. They exchanged pleasantries and chatted amiably enough about the weather, the parade, and Marco's seaweed farming until Ruth, em-boldened by her second or third glass of sangria, finally said, "I owe you an apology."

He turned to face the water. "Well, I don't see that at all."

"That day on the boat, you told me how you never married because the sea life is a selfish life. You were really smart to recognize that, to see your own limitations. Now you're in a position to meet someone with-out having a lot of emotional baggage. But unfortunately, that's not the case for me."

"Most people have baggage, Ruth. It's not fatal."

"I know. But in my case, I'm realizing I have to deal with some of it before I can move forward. I've always been so busy; it was easy to just pack it all away. But now, like you said, life slows down. And now I have to reckon with it. As much as I enjoyed spending time with you, and as much as my impulse was to do more of that, I can't do that in a way that would be fair to you. Does that make any sense?"

"It does," he said. "I don't like hearing it, but it does."

She held out her hand. "Friends?" she said.

Above the table, fireflies blinked their bioluminescence, a reminder that darkness was setting in and the fireworks would begin soon.

Bianca stood up and announced, "I'm heading to the pier to watch the fireworks."

"We're going to watch them from here, Bianca," Tito said.

"It's a better view from the pier."

"It's exactly the same," Lidia said from across the table.

"Well, to each his own," Bianca said. Then, to Ben, "Care to join me?"

To Ruth's horror, Ben stood up. "Sure, why not?"

Why not? Ruth could think of half a dozen reasons why not, starting with the fact that his family was at the party. Why would he leave with a *stranger?* But then she noticed Olivia was no longer at the table. And clearly, Ben did not share her nostalgia for what the night represented. She realized how foolish it would have been to admit her feelings and what a mistake it had been to convince him to stay longer.

Hand shaking, she reached for her wineglass as Clifford Henry slid into Bianca's now-vacant chair.

"I've been meaning to talk to you all night," he said. "I have some good news."

Ruth just nodded, her eyes cast down as she tried to collect herself. Why would Ben leave with Bianca? She was so awful; even her own brother knew she was awful. How could Ben not see that? Did he find her attractive? *Was* she attractive?

"Earth to Ruth," Clifford said, snapping his fingers.

She looked up at him. "I'm sorry. What was that?"

"I think I found you a house. A perfect, glorious, to-die-for house. With the right offer, you could be moving in by Labor Day."

"Really?"

He nodded, grinning and raising his glass to toast.

"I can't wait to see it," she said. What was that saying? One door closes, another door opens. She would be getting her house after all.

Now she just had to figure out a way to repack her baggage so she could move in.

It was like there was no one else in the room. Or, to be more accurate, no one else on the dock.

Olivia increasingly felt this way around Marco, that everything else blurred into the background, like a professionally crafted portrait shot on a camera. On a night like this, she wished Provincetown wasn't so...Provincetown. That everyone wasn't expected to celebrate together. There would be no enjoying the night for just the two of them except for this moment they'd managed to steal behind the house.

For weeks now, they'd been sneaking around like a pair of teenagers, spending their time tucked away at his apartment, never at Shell Haven or a restaurant on Commercial. This strategy was unspoken but obvious to both of them; the last thing they wanted was to feed the town gossip mill. After all, this was just a casual thing. Nothing to get too excited about.

And yet they couldn't keep their hands off each other.

They stepped around Manny Barros's tools, and Marco pulled her close and kissed her. In the near distance, she heard the din of the party. She glanced back toward the water, hoping no one could see them.

Marco, sensing her discomfort, said, "What do you say we cut out of here and have our own private fireworks viewing at my place?"

Um...yes! "You go first. I'll meet you in front of the house," she said.

Marco rented an apartment in the basement of an 1870s Queen Anne cottage on Franklin Street owned by friends of his family. His studio was small, but Marco barely spent any time at home. He didn't even need to use the kitchenette because his mother still cooked dinner for him every night. Olivia teased him about this.

"You're just jealous," he said.

"You might be right."

She'd told him all about her complicated feelings toward Ruth—the feelings she hadn't felt comfortable sharing that first day out on the water—and he'd confided that his feelings of love and loyalty and obligation to his parents were sometimes complicated. "I want my father to be able to retire soon," he'd said. "I feel responsible."

This sense of responsibility drove Marco so completely, it made him seem older than his age. She thought about the men she'd hooked up with in Manhattan and their work-hard, play-hard ethos. Marco apparently hadn't gotten the memo about the "play" part.

But that didn't mean he wasn't fun. He took such joy in the water, in the vital work of growing food, in the deep roots the Barroses had established for themselves in town. He made her feel alive; he made her appreciate the rewards of working with her hands. A day cleaning cages was difficult and exhausting and dirty and unpleasant. But it did not leave her stressed and riddled with anxiety like her previous work used to. She was sleeping better at night. Her concentration seemed sharper. Sometimes she didn't know where her love of this new lifestyle stopped and her love of Marco began. And, yes, she did feel she was falling in love with him. Not that she would admit this. Not that it mattered. Provincetown was her respite from the messy reality of her life back in New York. It wasn't real. So why bother with real feelings?

She knew Marco would not push her for more emotional intimacy. Marco had told her about one summer fling that should have ended with the summer but instead turned into an engagement and then a broken heart. It was difficult to imagine that romantic, vulnerable version of Marco. He was so practical, so levelheaded. She liked that about him.

The house on Franklin was dark; everyone in town was at the wharf or the beach or various other spots to watch the fireworks. Marco took her hand and led her down the stairs to his studio. He put his key in the door but turned to her before opening it. "We should probably go to the roof for the best view," he said.

"Can we get up there?"

He nodded. They backtracked, walking to the front of the house and using the main entrance to a winding stairwell.

She followed him up three flights to the widow's walk. The night had fully settled into darkness. With every star visible above and a nearly panoramic view of the water, she felt like she was standing at the edge of the universe.

The first firework cracked in the distance, red, white, and blue like electric confetti. If Marco wanted to talk, he hadn't picked an optimal time or place for her to focus on conversation. The sky erupted until it was impossible to tell when one firework ended and another began. Marco stood beside her, an arm around her shoulders, their bodies hip to hip as the sparkles in the sky formed shapes heading into the grand finale: a smiley face, a heart, a flag.

When the sky was dark again, lit only by the stars, Marco tugged on her hand. She turned to face him.

"So, what are we doing?" he said.

"Standing on your roof."

"You know what I mean. All this sneaking around."

She took a small step back. So here it was, the Talk. She had been so certain she would avoid this with Marco. There they were, happily engaged in a no-frills, hot fling—and now...

"Marco, I'm having a good time," she said. "Aren't you?"

"Of course. And I'm really happy we're on the same page about not making a big display of things and getting everyone in our business."

The minute the words left his mouth, she realized she actually wanted the Talk. She wanted him to push back on keeping their relationship under wraps.

"Yeah, I mean, what would be the point?" she said, reciting words that just moments before she'd actually believed.

"Exactly. You're leaving town soon. I don't get involved with summer people. But no one else would understand. My mother, your mother … I mean, can you imagine? They'd be planning our wedding."

He smiled, and she forced a laugh. "Totally." *I don't get involved with summer people.*

He kissed her, and she heard the crack and boom of more fireworks. Or maybe she imagined it.

Chapter Forty

The scene in Lidia's kitchen reminded Ruth of parties she'd hosted years ago at the house in Cherry Hill, back when Olivia was little and Ruth still had time to have her family and in-laws over for summer barbecues. Like Lidia, she'd used paper plates under the delusion that somehow this would minimize all the dishes to be cleaned only to find the kitchen counter and sink overflowing at the end of the evening.

"Please, Ruth, go back outside and relax. I'm fine taking care of this," Lidia said, up to her elbows in dishwater.

"I'm happy to help," Ruth said. She was also happy to avoid the spectacle of Ben and Bianca chatting away. They had returned after the fireworks and were engrossed in conversation. How could Ben not have realized by now that the woman was insufferable? She reached for an oily metal baking tray and realized she should cover the dime-size burn on her left hand—her latest soap-making-related injury. "Do you have a Band-Aid? I have a small burn and I don't want to get it wet."

This prompted another flurry of protests about Ruth's assistance, so Ruth finally said, "Lidia, please. I'm happy to have an excuse not to be outside with my ex-husband. It was a mistake to invite him."

"Well, in that case, check the second-floor bathroom. If you don't see any, there's a linen closet in the hallway with toiletries."

Ruth climbed the stairs, thinking that after helping Lidia, she would go home, despite the fact that the party seemed to have enough legs to keep going until all hours. What would be the point in staying? Olivia had disappeared; Ben was otherwise occupied. She enjoyed talking to her friends but fundamentally, the evening had been a disappointment. There had not been a single family moment in the course of the entire party. At least, not for her family.

A woman's voice startled her. It came from one of the bedrooms. For a moment, she thought maybe she was overhearing some sort of tryst because the woman said, "I love you." But then she heard the distinct coo of a baby, the sound Mira had started to make.

Ruth crept toward the bedroom door. It was slightly ajar. She didn't know exactly what she was listening for, but something in her had shifted into high alert.

She angled herself so she could peer into the room; she had just a sliver of a view but it was enough to see Jaci sitting on the edge of the bed cradling Mira. She stroked the side of the baby's face with one finger, staring intently at her with a look of love.

A look of motherly love.

It was the lull after the fireworks, a brief window when everyone at the party was still quietly taking in the moment. Elise stood near the water, slow to drift back toward the house with the others. Lost in thought, she heard Fern's voice before she actually saw her.

"Better late than never," Fern said, perhaps to Manny, maybe to their group of friends in general. Elise was too far away to tell.

Was it possible to think about someone so much you actually conjured her?

Minutes passed as Fern made her way through the crowd, greeting
everyone, churning through small talk, until she finally reached Elise.

"Looks like I missed the fireworks," Fern said, hands in the pockets
of her jeans. She was dressed for work in her Tea by the Sea T-shirt,
which was not the way she would usually arrive at a party.

"I missed *you*," Elise said. She said it instinctively, impulsively, because it was true, not because it was particularly helpful, considering
what they were going through. She had missed her, but that didn't fix
anything. "I thought you weren't coming."

"Let's go somewhere we can talk," Fern said.

They walked to the farthest end of the dock. They did not speak and
did not touch and Elise thought, *This is it. This is how it ends.* She
thought of Mira back in the house with Jaci and told herself that she
had tried it two different ways. First she had chosen Fern, then she had
chosen the baby, and both ways left a hole in the center of her world.
She had imagined when she was young that life was about learning how
to attain things, but now she wondered if it was actually about learning
how to lose them.

Fern reached for her hand. "I really have missed you," she said.

Elise felt such intense relief, it took her breath away. "I've missed you.
I don't want to be apart." And then, because it had to be said, "But I
also want to be a mother."

Fern nodded. "I want it for you too."

She didn't know exactly what that meant. *I want it for you, and I'll be
a partner in making it happen?* Or *I want it for you but only if it doesn't
inconvenience us too much?* Or *I want it for you but I don't want it for
myself anymore?*

Elise put her arms around her wife. "I love you. I don't know how to
do this without you."

"We'll figure it out," Fern said.

There had been many times when Fern had said this to Elise: Dealing with their disapproving parents. Giving up their lives in Boston to start over in P'town. Looking for a house. Trying to become parents, then trying to let go of that dream. For years, those four words from Fern— *We'll figure it out*—had acted like a talisman on Elise. Fern said they'd work it out, and so they would. But life had proved Fern wrong, and the words had lost their magic.

Yes, she wanted Fern to move back home. But even as they held each other's hands, even as they walked back to the party in the spirit of renewal, Elise wondered if, somehow, more than just the words had lost their magic.

Ruth stepped back from the door to Jaci's bedroom and leaned against the hallway wall. Her heart pounded. No, this couldn't be. And yet two things clicked: Jaci's arrival back from school coinciding with the appearance of the baby on the doorstep and Jaci's persistent interest in hanging around Shell Haven and babysitting instead of spending time with her own family. And so that meant she had…what? Gotten pregnant, hidden this fact from her family, returned to Provincetown with the baby, then abandoned her? It was an absurd thought. And, if true, it was terribly reckless. But Jaci was still technically just a teenager herself.

Ruth started doing the math in her head. Mira had been born in early May. So Jaci would have gotten pregnant at the end of last summer before leaving for school or at the very beginning of her freshman year, hidden the pregnancy throughout the winter, and given birth weeks before returning home for the summer.

Mira cooed loudly again.

"Can you give me a smile?" Jaci said softly. "I saw that smile you gave Elise. You did, didn't you? Yes, you did…"

Ruth stepped forward and pushed the door open wider. Jaci looked up, startled, but recovered quickly.

"Oh, hey, Ruth. I thought everyone was outside."

Ruth moved into the room. "May I sit with you for a minute?"

"Um, I was actually going to head back to the party. I was just watching her for Elise during the fireworks because it was too loud for her outside."

"That was generous of you."

"It's no big deal." Jaci shrugged. "I mean, the fireworks are the same every year."

Ruth sat on the bed. She reached out and gently touched Jaci's arm. "Jaci, is this your baby?"

"What? No, of course not."

Ruth looked her in the eye, and Jaci held her gaze. The denial was calm and convincing. It was the denial of someone who had prepared herself for the question. It was the denial of someone who'd thought things through.

Unfortunately, once truth surfaces, evidence is everywhere. Ruth had only to look at Mira to see everything she'd failed to notice until that moment. The baby resembled Lidia. She had the dark Barros eyes and Lidia's cleft chin. How did no one else see this? Do you only see what you want to see, even when reality is literally staring you in the face? "Jaci, I'm not upset with you. But this can't go on. Someone is going to get hurt."

Jaci's eyes filled with tears. Ruth hugged her, careful not to squash Mira.

"It's going to be okay," Ruth said.

"No," Jaci said sharply, pulling back. "It won't be okay if you tell anyone. This was the right thing to do. I'm sorry, but you're an outsider. You don't understand. And it's not your business."

"It became my business the minute you left your daughter on my doorstep."

"I had no idea Elise and Fern had rented out the house! That wasn't part of the plan."

"And what *was* the plan, exactly?"

Jaci sniffled. Ruth reached over to the bedside table, pulled a tissue out of a box, handed it to her.

"Thanks. I mean, it's pretty obvious, isn't it? I can't be a mother—not now. I have three years left at school. I don't want to live here raising a baby in my parents' house. I want to be like Olivia; I want to move to New York and have a real career. And Elise and Fern—they've wanted a baby for years. I was there the afternoon that Elise had her second miscarriage. She wants a baby more than anything. So giving her mine solves both of our problems."

"Jaci, you can't just *give* someone a baby. There are legal repercussions. Emotional repercussions. What about the father? Does he know about this?"

Jaci wiped her eyes with the bottom of her T-shirt, leaving a smudge of mascara on it. "He told me to get an abortion. Which, considering my Catholic family, was just not an option. Not something I could live with."

"Well, he has a responsibility to this child. He can't just—"

"Ruth, please. Stop. I'm literally never going to see him again. This is bad enough. Just let it go."

Ruth sighed. This was Lidia's domain and none of her business. "What about your mother? Don't you think she'd want the chance to care for her own granddaughter? I've only known your mother a short while, but I can say with certainty she would."

Jaci shook her head. "My mother can't find out about this. I didn't know what I was going to do when I realized I was pregnant, but the thing I did know from day one was that I didn't want to burden my parents. They've worked hard their whole lives to be financially stable; my dad is about to retire. I can't do that to them, make them start over with a baby. You can*not* tell my mother—promise me. It would only hurt her. If you say anything to anyone, a lot of people will be hurt."

"People are already getting hurt! Do you know Elise and Fern are at odds over how to handle this situation? They've been living apart."

Jaci blanched, but quickly recovered. "Elise and Fern will work it out. They always do."

Ruth crossed her arms. Jaci stood up from the bed, placed Mira against her shoulder, and paced.

"I'm going back to the party," she said finally, opening the door. She turned to look at Ruth. "Please, please, I'm begging you—stay out of it. If you don't, you'll hurt all of us. I'm doing the right thing. You'll see."

Chapter Forty-One

Maybe it was the exuberance of the holiday, maybe it was Lidia's sangria, or maybe Olivia just wanted to feel what it would be like to wake up next to Marco. Whatever the reason, for the first time, she did not slip away in the middle of the night to return to Shell Haven.

Seeing the room in the bright light of early morning, she felt a heightened appreciation for its spare but elegant functionality; it was a perfect reflection of its inhabitant. The bedroom had an antique chest at the foot of the bed, a large ceiling fan, and wooden bookshelves stuffed with paperbacks spanning an entire wall.

Marco, beside her, stirred slightly and reached for her. She moved closer to him, pressed her lips gently to his cheek. She was eager for him to wake up so they could talk, but at the same time she wanted the moment to last forever. It was easy to pretend there was nothing beyond the walls of that room, their own private hideaway.

Until she heard a knock at the door.

Marco didn't move. She shook him gently. "Someone's knocking at the door," she whispered.

"What time is it?" he mumbled.

"I don't know—early."

He sat up and kissed her.

"What lunatic is coming by at this hour?" he said. He pulled on his boxers and a T-shirt and made his way to the door. She watched him open it.

"Why aren't you answering your phone?" Lidia said from outside, her voice frantic.

Olivia sat up and pulled the sheet around her bare chest.

"I was asleep," he said. "What's going on?"

"Can I come in? I don't need the whole neighborhood hearing our business."

Marco glanced back at Olivia. She widened her eyes. He turned back to the doorway. "Ma, it's not a good time."

"Not a good time? This is a family emergen—oh. *Oh*. You're...not alone?"

Olivia found her discarded clothes on the floor and quickly pulled on her sundress from the night before.

Marco slipped outside and closed the front door behind him.

Olivia sat on the edge of the bed. This was ridiculous. She felt like a teenager who'd been busted sneaking into her boyfriend's bedroom. And maybe she deserved to feel like that. Keeping their relationship a secret suddenly seemed childish.

She took a deep breath and, barefoot and with disheveled hair, walked out into the bright morning sun to stand beside Marco. Lidia, clearly surprised, said, "Oh, good morning, Olivia."

Marco looked uncomfortable.

"I hope everything is okay," Olivia said.

"It's Jaci," Lidia said. "She's packing up and leaving."

"Today?" Olivia said.

"Today! She won't say why, and she won't hear a word about staying the rest of the summer. I don't know what's gotten into her."

"Ma, you have to calm down," Marco said. "I'll talk to her."

"Your father is beside himself. She won't listen to us," Lidia said as if Marco hadn't spoken.

"Maybe I could talk to her?" Olivia said. She still felt guilty for having been so cavalier with her advice, essentially telling Jaci to feel free to disregard her family and just live her life. This, of course, had been before Olivia knew her family. Before she'd fallen in love with Marco. And, yes, before the thaw in her feelings toward her own mother. "I'm just thinking, since I'm sort of an objective outsider, she might at least hear me out. She seems really interested in my, um, life in New York. I have a feeling a lot of this is coming from her confusion about balancing her life here with you guys and wanting to have a career someday."

Lidia closed her eyes and rubbed her forehead. "I'm willing to try anything at this point," she said.

"I don't know if that's a good idea," Marco said.

"It's worth a try," Olivia said. "Trust me."

"Olivia, if you think it would help, then by all means, try. I'll walk you over to the house right now," Lidia said.

"Ma, give us a second, okay?" Marco took her by the hand, pulled her into the studio, and closed the door. "You don't have to get involved in this," he said.

"I want to."

He shook his head. "I appreciate you wanting to help—"

"Marco, what harm can it do? I'll go to the house with your mother, have a few words with Jaci, and see what happens."

A look passed between them, something that had nothing to do with Jaci's threat to flee Provincetown or the debate about who should talk to her. It was, Olivia felt certain, a mutual recognition that, despite their conversation the night before, whatever was going on between them was more than just "having a good time."

"Okay," Marco said. "Talk to my sister."

* * *

What was Ruth going to do about the truth bomb that had been dropped in her lap?

During her restless night, she'd concluded that she would have to talk to someone—and there was no question who that someone would be.

The Beach Rose Inn appeared sleepy; no one was sitting on the porch and there was no sign of Molly the dog. Ruth climbed the front steps and found a handwritten sign on the door: *Mosaic class, come straight to third-floor studio.*

Ruth checked the time on her phone. When did the class usually begin? Certainly not this early. She was hopeful she had a window to catch Amelia.

The inn smelled like fresh coffee. White thermal carafes and Beach Rose Inn mugs were set out on a side table near the sofas. Ruth had been so anxious to talk to Amelia she hadn't wasted time brewing her own at Shell Haven, so now helped herself to a mug and filled it. She carried it back to the kitchen, thinking she would find Amelia or Rachel there, but it was quiet.

Amelia might already be in the studio. Ruth took the back stairs up to the third floor. She felt like a burglar, padding up so quietly. It was the first time she'd gotten so far in the house without seeing another soul. It felt like she was walking in a dream, and she wished this whole situation with Jaci Barros were just a dream.

The studio door was wide open. Amelia sat at the large central table, arranging tiles on top of a sketch. Ruth knocked on the doorframe. "Sorry to interrupt," she said.

Amelia sat back against her seat. "Not at all. Come in. It's nice to see someone else able to rise and shine this early."

"Well, I'm not sure about the shining part," Ruth said, pulling up a chair and setting her mug down carefully to avoid any stray mosaic pieces. "We missed you at the Barroses."

Amelia sighed. "My energy is not what it used to be. Rachel has been insisting I slow down. I hate to admit it, but I'm happiest when I'm in my bedroom by seven p.m. or so. I'm always up before dawn, and at least this way I have a productive day. Did I miss anything?" She smiled.

This was it. Why be coy? There was no avoiding the reason she had come to speak with her. And there was no question this was the right thing to do. Jaci had been correct about one thing—Ruth *was* an outsider. She didn't yet understand all the nuances of this place or these people. She didn't know the rules. But Amelia did.

"Yes, actually," Ruth said. "We've all been missing something. I learned last night that Jaci is Mira's mother."

Amelia nodded. She looked back down at her sketch, swapped out a blue tile for an orange one. There was no gasp, no widened eyes. No alarm or outrage.

"Amelia?" Ruth said. "You don't seem surprised."

"My dear, these mosaics aren't the only pieces I've been putting together all summer."

It took Ruth a beat to realize what she meant. "Wait—you knew?"

Amelia nodded. "Not at first. But it started to come together in my mind fairly quickly."

"But…how?"

"Well, for one thing, Jaci began acting strangely last winter. She refused to come home for Christmas, some story about spending the holiday with her roommate's family. Lidia was heartbroken. And then Lidia offered to visit for Jaci's birthday in February, and Jaci made excuses why that wouldn't work. Lidia was certain that now that Jaci had gone off to a fancy school, she'd become ashamed of them. I couldn't argue with that theory; things like that do happen. But then Jaci finally did come home—and on the same day that baby showed up on your doorstep."

"Well, that could have been a coincidence," Ruth said.

"It could," Amelia said. "If the baby didn't look exactly like Lidia."

"I know! Once I saw it, I wondered how I hadn't noticed it before. How no one else sees it."

"We see what we want to see," Amelia said.

"So...now what?"

"I'm working on it," Amelia said. "I'm trying to find a way to minimize everyone's hurt. And I'm getting close. But I need more time. So please—keep this to yourself for just a little while longer."

It was not what she'd been expecting to hear. It was not what she wanted to hear. But Ruth would, of course, respect Amelia's wishes. And yet, walking back to Shell Haven, she felt the secret burning inside her, settling uncomfortably in the middle of her chest. If she felt this worn out after carrying the secret for less than twenty-four hours, how could she continue like this for days? Or weeks?

Ruth did what she always did when faced with something troubling— she sprang into action. Back at Shell Haven, she set to work wrapping up the products that had piled up in the kitchen, tying them up with ribbons, and attaching small cards with personal notes. A bottle of lavender oil for Amelia; a sea-salt scrub for Rachel; more soaps for Lidia and Manny; and, finally, a lemongrass body wash for Jaci.

This was the most difficult note to write. And yet, while she crafted it, she realized that the desire to reach out with this message was the entire reason for the hour spent wrapping gifts.

She placed all of her packages in a tote bag and headed back out. Her first stop would be the boatyard.

Chapter Forty-Two

For once, chatty Jaci Barros did not want to chat.

Olivia found her sitting on her bed, headphones on, looking at her phone. Her suitcase, packed but still open, sat in the middle of the floor. When she saw Olivia, she removed her headphones. "Hey, what are you doing here?"

"I heard you're leaving town," Olivia said. "So I wanted to say good-bye. May I sit?"

Jaci shrugged.

Olivia perched on the edge of the bed. "So...why the rush?"

"It's just time to go," Jaci said. "You get that, right?"

"Look," Olivia said. "Your mother is really upset and I'm wondering if you could compromise? Stay a week or two longer just to show you're not, I don't know, running away from them?"

Jaci narrowed her eyes. "Aren't you the one who told me I had a right to live my own life? How did you put it? It's better to just pull the Band-Aid off."

Olivia nodded. "I did say that. But—"

"But what? Now that you're hooking up with my brother, it's not true anymore?"

Olivia bit her lip. "How do you know about that?"

"Come on. You two aren't exactly stealthy." She smiled. "For the record, I'm psyched about it. Except for the fact that now you're taking his side."

"I'm not taking anyone's side," Olivia said. "I just realized I gave you the wrong advice."

"So now I *don't* have a right to live my own life?"

"You do. Of course you do. But I think I was telling you to do whatever you wanted without thinking about your mother's feelings, figuring she'd get over it. And I realized that when we have rifts with our mothers, there's no getting over it."

Jaci's eyes filled with tears. "Well, I have to leave. I just have to."

"Okay," Olivia said. "But maybe do it in a less hurtful way."

Something caught her eye across the room, something gold and glittery sticking out of the small wastepaper basket near Jaci's desk. Now that she was looking, she noticed a trail of glitter from the bed to the desk. "What is all that?"

"Oh. I was making some stuff for Carnival. But now I'm not going to need it."

Carnival. She'd seen it listed on the calendar of events posted on the refrigerator at Shell Haven. She'd heard people talking about it as the biggest party of the summer.

Olivia thought of the way her mother had convinced her father to stay a few more weeks, roping him in over July 4. If she'd just asked him to stay longer, he would have refused. But when she said, *Oh, just stay for the holiday,* it seemed more reasonable. Everybody liked parameters.

She stood from the bed, hesitated a few seconds, then retrieved the gold mask from the trash. It was clearly handmade, the glitter shedding under her fingers. She carried it back to the bed; gold dust littered the bedspread. "Why don't you stay for Carnival?"

Jaci shook her head. "I'm leaving today."

Olivia brushed away the glitter and moved closer to Jaci. "Running off just makes your mother feel rejected. It calls so much negative attention to yourself. Just give them a few more weeks. Otherwise they're going to wonder what's wrong. They're worried about you. And I'll be here too. We can talk about New York and what you want to do after school."

Jaci seemed pensive. "I don't want my parents to freak out. Nothing's wrong, okay?"

"Well, if nothing is wrong, maybe you should prove it by staying."

Jaci said something in response but Olivia was distracted. Was that her mother's voice downstairs?

The first season of any business was trial and error, and Elise and Fern were still figuring out the patterns of their regular customers and the flow of tourists. They had debated what time to open that morning, wondering if they should adjust to some sort of late holiday schedule. But since they had been awake since dawn, and Rachel was available to watch Mira, they opened the doors not long after nine and found themselves alone behind the counter.

"You smell good—like lavender," Fern said.

"It's Ruth's body lotion," Elise said. "I'm obsessed with it. And she puts all her stuff in those cute little blue jars."

"I know. They're everywhere at Shell Haven."

Elise walked over to the shelves of tea tins and rearranged a few, thinking. She turned back to Fern. "What if we sold some of her products here?"

"Skin-care products?"

"Why not? Think about why we became interested in tea in the first place. It all comes down to wellness, and if a product falls under that umbrella, we could carry it in the shop."

Fern nodded. "That's true. And she created Liv Free. She knows what she's doing, so I'm not worried about quality."

"I guess it just becomes a question of *our* brand," Elise said. "Are we a tea shop or are we a tea-and-sundries shop—"

The front door's bells chimed, heralding the arrival of Bianca Barros. Elise noticed immediately that Bianca was wearing white, not black.

"Bianca," Elise said. "This is a new look for you."

"It's a new day," Bianca said. "I am turning a corner."

Elise and Fern looked at each other. "Well, that's great," Fern said. "It's nice to hear you so optimistic."

Bianca walked closer to the counter, squinting at the chalkboard menu.

"Can we get you something?" Elise said.

"Yes," Bianca said, leveling her eyes at her. "I want my house back."

Fern, clearly at the end of her patience, let out a loud groan. "Haven't we exhausted this topic, Bianca?"

"No, I don't think we have," she said. "I'm moving back to town. Two winters in Florida were enough. I am done being displaced. I'm prepared to make you a fair offer on the house—I'll pay what you two paid Pilar for it. But not a penny more."

"We are not selling the house," Elise said. "We told you, renting it out is just temporary."

"Why did you move back in if you're renting it out?" Bianca said.

"We didn't move back in," said Fern.

Bianca crossed her arms. "I know the truth about that baby."

Elise's heart began to beat fast. *She's bluffing,* she told herself. *She doesn't know anything.* Fern walked to the door and opened it.

"I want you to leave," Fern said. "You've been provoking us long enough. I'm sorry that you're unhappy with your life, but I'm not going to let you come in here week after week and take it out on us." Elise wanted to throw her arms around her wife.

Bianca didn't move. For what seemed like a very long time but was probably no more than half a minute, no one said a word. Finally, Bianca walked to the door, but before she left, she turned around and said, "That baby was left on your doorstep. It should be reported to the police. Now, I'm willing to stay out of it. But I want my house back."

Olivia was surprised to find her mother in the Barroses' kitchen and even more surprised by how jittery and off she seemed. Her mother apologized to Lidia for stopping by so early. "I really just meant to drop this off. I didn't think anyone would be awake."

Lidia, distracted by the drama with Jaci, accepted the gift bags and mumbled her thanks.

"We should go," Olivia said quickly, and she hustled her mother outside.

"I didn't expect to actually see anyone," Ruth said. They walked along Commercial, just now coming to life, heading back to Shell Haven. "I just needed to clear out the kitchen. And I wanted to go for a walk. So, two birds with one stone."

"Are you okay?"

"Fine," her mother said. She tried to convince Olivia to keep her company while she made her last stop at her real estate agent's office.

"No, I'm going back to the house," Olivia said.

Her mother suggested breakfast, and Olivia's stomach rumbled.

They reached Café Heaven and found a line already out the door. They decided to wait, since every place would be crowded. Ruth gave her name to the host.

"I'm glad you've struck up a friendship with Jaci," her mother said. "I think...I think that girl needs a friend."

Her mother seemed almost misty-eyed, and Olivia thought, for the dozenth time since reaching town, that Ruth was not the distracted, work-obsessed, selfish person she remembered. Could selling the company have really created such a dramatic change? Or had Olivia, due to her own neediness and lack of empathy, simply judged her too harshly?

Either way, all she wanted in that moment was a mother to confide in.

"Mom," she said. "I wasn't at the house because I'm friends with Jaci. I was there because I'm involved with Marco."

"Marco Barros?" Ruth said, as if there were any other Marco. Olivia nodded. Her mother smiled. "He's adorable."

"Yeah, tell me about it," Olivia said, sighing.

"Is there a problem?"

"The problem is that I don't live here. And Marco has never even been to New York. Once I get back to work, how much time can I really spend here?"

"Oh, Olivia. These are just details. These are good problems to have. The important thing is that you met someone you care about. And who cares about you. Life is full of obstacles, and it just takes patience to overcome them. Do you have to get back to New York next week?"

"No."

"Do you have to get back to New York next month?"

"No. But I should. And I don't want to overstay my welcome at the house. Do you want me to—"

"Olivia, this is a dream for me. All I want is time with my daughter." She stepped closer and hugged her, and Olivia felt the primal comfort of being enveloped in her mother's arms.

Olivia thought about Lidia's despair at the thought of Jaci leaving. "The reason I was talking to Jaci this morning was that she plans on leaving today. Her mother is really upset. I feel responsible because I once told Jaci she needed to do what was best for herself and not worry about her mother."

"It's not your fault," Ruth said quickly. Too quickly.

"How do you know?"

Ruth looked uncomfortable. "I just don't think it is. Is she really leaving town? Today?"

"I don't know. I asked her to reconsider. I tried reasoning with her."

Her mother tensed.

"Mom, is something going on?"

"No. No, of course not."

"If there is, I need you to tell me. Marco is concerned about her; Lidia is upset. Is there something I should know?"

Ruth shook her head. "Just keep on being a good friend. That's all you can do."

The host called out her mother's name and waved them inside. Olivia followed her mother to the table, trying to quell the feeling that her mother was lying to her. It was an old, cynical pattern of thinking, one she was trying to move past in the spirit of having a more amicable relationship.

They were seated by the window, and her mother smiled at her. No, of course she wasn't lying to her.

Everything was different now.

Chapter Forty-Three

Ruth invited Ben to join her when she looked at the house for sale.

"You're a very decisive woman, Ruth," he'd said. "I'm sure you don't need my input."

Of course she didn't. But it was a great excuse to spend some time together; she'd barely seen him since the Fourth of July party last week. He took writing classes during the day and at night he was just as scarce. Her real estate opportunities might be opening, but her window to reconnect with Ben seemed to be closing quickly.

"It never hurts to have another opinion," Ruth said. "Olivia might be able to meet me there but only if she's back from the flats in time."

Olivia seemed to be transforming into a full-fledged oyster farmer. Her wardrobe of trendy cutoff shorts, delicately ribbed tank tops, and strappy sandals had been replaced by utilitarian T-shirts, knee-high all-weather boots, a few pairs of rubber overalls, and an omnipresent baseball hat. She appeared at the house covered head to toe in muck.

Ruth had never seen her happier.

Ben agreed to join her, though she had to schedule the house tour within a very specific time frame.

What was he so busy doing? As the two of them walked to the West End, Ruth debated whether or not to bring up the topic of Bianca Barros. It was none of her business. But then, wasn't it? He was living under her roof; he was supposed to be spending time with Olivia and, well, yes, maybe her. Instead, he was consorting with the enemy. Fine, maybe *enemy* was overstating it. But she did not like that woman— not one bit.

"So what's with you and Bianca?" Ruth said as they passed the library. It was midway through their walk, so if she was going to initiate a conversation, there was no time to waste.

"We're friends," he said.

"Just friends?" she said, eyebrows raised.

"Ruth, is this an appropriate conversation?"

"We've known each other for forty years. We have a child together. If you can't be frank with me, who can you be frank with?"

"Fair enough. Yes, at this point, we are just friends."

"Well, I would keep my distance if I were you," she said, glancing at him. "That woman can't be trusted." She knew him well enough to recognize the look of guilt on his face. "Ben, you didn't trust her with anything private, did you? I don't want her knowing my business."

He shook his head. "I haven't told her any of your business."

"So what did you tell her?"

"Nothing about you," he said defensively. "We just talked."

"Well, I have to wonder why you picked the most unpleasant person in this entire town to become friends with."

"She's not unpleasant, Ruth. She's just had a hard life. Did you know she was widowed in her thirties? She raised her daughter alone, working at the boatyard with her brothers."

"That might be the *cause* of her unpleasantness. But I'd argue there are plenty of widowed single mothers who are also nice people."

"Look, not everyone has as much good fortune and self-agency as you have."

"Good fortune and self-agency? What does that even mean?"

"It means you had a successful company—yes, you worked hard, I know that, but you did achieve success and now you have financial security and freedom. Bianca was edged out of the business by her brothers; her father left his house to her daughter—the house you're currently renting—and then the daughter sold the house and moved to Florida. Bianca feels she's lost her place in the world."

"You always did like the lost puppies. Is that what attracted you to me?"

"You're the least lost person I've ever known, Ruth. Even when things were bad, you always knew how to land on your feet."

They passed the boatyard and Provincia. Soon, they would reach the corner of Nickerson Street, where Clifford was meeting them. Now was the time to tell Ben about her feelings for him—let him know that she had not landed on her feet. That eighteen years ago, she had initiated a permanent fix to a possibly temporary problem, and now she regretted it.

"Always early! I love that about you, Ruth," Clifford called out from across the street, waving at them. He was dressed in a baby-blue seersucker suit and a pink bow tie.

"You look very dapper today, Clifford," she said.

"I always dress up when I show houses for sale," he said. "Although I give myself some sartorial leeway when I'm showing rentals. Glad you could join us, Ben." Then, to Ruth: "I asked Santiago to meet us here too in case you have questions about what can be done in terms of renovation or additions."

"Do you think it needs renovation?" she said.

"No. I think it's perfection. But it's your house," he said with a wink.

"Well, we'll see," Ruth said, glancing at Ben.

They followed him half a block to a three-story Greek Revival, white clapboard with green shutters. It had a front portico and another porch to the left; there was a small cupola on the roof. The brick walkway was flanked by pink and blue hydrangeas.

"The house is named Blue Stone," Clifford said, "after the tiles that used to line the walkway. Talk about curb appeal, am I right?"

Inside, the house had been modernized; there were wide entrance-ways between rooms and an open kitchen with granite counters and state-of-the-art appliances, yet it still had an informal, beachy feel to it. Upstairs, the four spacious bedrooms continued the low-maintenance vibe with paneled walls and French Country furniture. Ruth was already imagining her own decorative take on the interior. She would gloss it up just a bit but keep the overall character of the home.

"And the pièce de résistance, the backyard," Clifford said.

A red-brick patio had been added to the house, topped with a vine-laced pergola. The foliage was lush and just a little wild. Behind the plants and flowers, in the very back of the lawn, a classic white gazebo.

Ruth let out a sigh. "It's perfection, Clifford. It really is."

"What's the asking price?" said Ben.

With a flourish, Clifford produced a small notepad, jotted down some numbers, and passed the page to them both. Ben let out a low whistle.

"I'll make a cash offer," Ruth said. Why not? The house was breath-taking. She had the money. And the sooner she could move out of Shell Haven, the better. The truth about Mira's maternity was eating at her more and more with every passing day.

"I like your style, Ruth Cooperman," Clifford said.

Ben reached for her elbow. "May we have a word alone for a minute?"

"Of course! Talk amongst yourselves. I'll go call Santiago to let him know his services will not be needed today."

Ben walked from the porch into the sunlight and crossed the lawn to the gazebo. She followed him, jarred by the intrusive fantasy that this was their home, that they were spending a leisurely afternoon together. "You don't like the house?" she said.

"It's a great house. But that's a lot of money, Ruth."

"Well, what better way to spend it than on a home?"

"So you're really doing this? You're moving here?"

Give me a reason not to, she thought. "Looks that way," she said.

Ben nodded, smiled, and said, "Well, then—congratulations. I'm happy for you, Ruth."

She should have been happy too. Overjoyed. She would finally have what she'd set out looking for last winter: her retirement beach house. She remembered the frustration of arriving on that mid-May morning, not finding the keys in the Shell Haven mailbox, running around town like a lost tourist. But now she belonged. She had friends, she had a renewed relationship with her daughter, and soon she would have a home to call her own.

That would have to be enough.

Olivia was elbow-deep in oyster cages when she remembered she was supposed to try to meet her mother on Nickerson Street. "What time is it?" she asked Marco. He consulted his waterproof watch and informed her of an hour much later than she'd thought.

"You tiring out on me already?" he said, teasing her.

She told him about her mother's house hunt, that she was afraid she would overpay for something because she was so eager to have her own home. "I want to try to make it in time before she does something impulsive."

"That's probably a good idea," Marco said. "Some of the asking prices for these houses are outrageous."

They wrapped up early, leaving a bunch of cages unchecked. To save time, Marco suggested she just shower at his parents' house. "No one's around. They took Jaci to visit friends in Truro."

"I didn't even bring a change of clothes," she said. He told her to borrow something from Jaci.

Olivia left her muddy boots on Lidia's porch and took the stairs to the second floor, texting her mother that she would be there soon. Are you there yet? Don't leave before I get there. I want to see it.

She knocked on Jaci's closed bedroom door out of habit, then opened it. The bed was made and the windows were half open, letting in the warm breeze. Olivia felt bad going through her dresser looking for a T-shirt, but Marco had assured her it was okay. She wanted to find something Jaci wouldn't miss right away, so she passed over the top layer of crew-neck T-shirts and tanks and dug into the bottom of the pile.

She pulled out a Long Point T-shirt and in the process dislodged a notecard that had been buried underneath all of the clothes. She recognized the stationery her mother had been using for her little gift packages.

How sweet that Jaci had saved her mother's note. She couldn't help but wonder what her mother had written. Olivia was still trying to reconcile the selfish, absentee Ruth of her childhood with the caring, present, infinitely giving woman she had been living with all summer.

Accidentally discovering the note was one thing, but Olivia knew that reading it would be crossing the line into officially snooping. Still, she couldn't resist seeking one more clue as she tried to put together the puzzle of who her mother actually was. Maybe she was both the woman Olivia remembered and the woman she had experienced this summer. If so, what did it mean for the future of their relationship?

She unfolded the notecard and sat on the edge of Jaci's bed.

Dear Jaci,

I know this is a difficult time for you. I know the choice you made feels like the best choice today. But please know, mother to mother, that whoever you are today will change. You will not be the same person five years from now, ten years from now, fifteen years from now. You will change, circumstances will change, but motherhood is forever. I am here if you want to talk.

Warmly, Ruth

Olivia read the note until it was burned into her memory, and only then did she let herself acknowledge what the note meant: the mystery baby belonged to Jaci.

And her mother had known all along.

Chapter Forty-Four

Ruth had been disappointed that Olivia didn't show up to see the house on Nickerson, but she told herself there was plenty of time for that later. The more she thought about the house, the more she loved it, and she wanted Olivia to share in the excitement with her. It was something they could bond over: a new home for this new chapter in their lives together. It would be the place Olivia would visit, where she'd bring her own children someday.

But not only did Olivia fail to show up to tour the house with her, she didn't return to Shell Haven that night or for several nights after. She did not answer Ruth's texts or calls. The only reason Ruth didn't panic was that Marco assured her that she was fine, that she was just busy. They were just doing their thing.

But Ruth knew something wasn't right.

After a call to Marco, she located Olivia sorting oysters by size at a metal table inside the shed behind the Barroses' house.

"What are you doing here?" Olivia said with a level of irritation Ruth had not heard in her voice since the beginning of the summer.

"I came to visit," Ruth said. "I haven't seen you in days."

"I'm working, Mother," Olivia said, scribbling information on a white tag and then attaching the tag to a mesh bag.

"Yes, I see. I'm so happy that you found something that—"

"Oh, save it!" Olivia snapped.

Ruth pressed her hand to her chest. Before she could respond, Olivia said, "I know you've been lying all this time about Mira. I know Jaci is her mother."

Ruth leaned against the table. "She told you?"

Olivia shook her head. "No. Of course not. And Marco doesn't know. *But he should know.* I confided in you the other day, not only about my relationship with Marco but about the problems they were having with Jaci. They didn't understand why she wanted to run off so quickly, and you just stood there nodding, knowing this giant secret the whole time! How could you keep this from me? How could you keep this from Lidia?"

Ruth flinched at the mention of Lidia. The thought of her, more than anything, was keeping her up at night. Lidia's granddaughter was right there but living blocks away instead of under her roof. No matter what Jaci said about the baby being a potential burden to her parents, Ruth knew in her heart that was not how the Barroses would feel.

"I promised Jaci…" But that wasn't entirely true. She had actually promised Amelia, although this was not something she could share. It wouldn't do to implicate Amelia.

"You cannot keep this secret. It's wrong. And it's putting me in a terrible position with Marco. If he finds out that I knew about this…"

"So why would you have wanted me to tell you?"

"I want you to do the right thing! You're an adult. A mother! How can you let her pull this crazy stunt with the baby? You *always* do things like this."

"Always do things like *what?*"

"You avoid, avoid, avoid. You check out when a situation gets inconvenient. But I can't let you do that this time."

"Olivia, this isn't our business. I agree, the truth has to come out. But the time and place for that is not ours to decide."

"Not our business? I'm in a relationship with Marco. I'm involved with that family. It *is* my business. But I can't be the one to do this. Jaci will never forgive me, and I need to have a relationship with her. What if Marco and I end up together?"

Ruth bit her lip. "Is it that serious?"

"I don't know! But I don't want this between us. You have to do something. And I'm not coming back to Shell Haven—or talking to you—until you do."

"Ignore Bianca," Amelia said.

After a nonstop afternoon at Tea by the Sea, Elise wanted to hunker down at Shell Haven with Mira, have a glass of wine, and shut out the world. Instead, she was covered in sequins, glitter, and glue in Amelia's art studio, helping to make decorations for Carnival.

Elise looked at Fern.

Fern, a sequin stuck to the side of her face, put down her glue and said, "It's not that simple. She's threatening us."

Amelia waved the words away. "I've known Bianca since she was this high. Her bark is worse than her bite."

Again, Elise turned to her wife, who seemed unmoved by this comment.

Elise didn't know what to make of Fern's behavior in the past few weeks. She had been certain she would use Bianca's threat as an excuse to go right to the Department of Children and Families. Instead, she appeared determined to do just the opposite. She'd been acting strangely in general: Leaving the room to answer phone calls. Taking a midweek trip to Boston that seemed to have little to do with the weekend farmers' markets. But at the same time, she wasn't pulling away from her; if anything, Fern seemed more devoted and acted more loving than she ever had before.

It was unsettling.

Now that Fern wasn't pushing the issue of going through the "proper channels," Elise felt her own urgency to initiate adoption proceedings. She wanted to make things official with Mira. The insecurity and worry about the future was starting to outweigh her fear of getting a government agency involved.

"I think it's time to call a lawyer," Elise had said just before turning out the lights the night before.

"We're not going to let Bianca bully us," Fern had said.

Elise was starting to get a Twilight Zone feeling; apparently, she was the only one who recognized the precariousness of the situation.

Now, faced with Amelia and Fern in agreement, she decided she would have to speak up more firmly. "I don't think we should take any chances," Elise said. "I can't sleep at night wondering if Bianca is going to make the phone call that *we* should be making. This whole process will be messed up if it starts that way. I can't wait any longer."

Fern and Amelia exchanged a look that completely excluded Elise. The glance was so weighted, Elise wondered if she had imagined it. Fern pulled Mira from her car seat and cradled her in her arms.

"What? What's going on?" Elise said.

Amelia smiled at her and reached across the table to place her hand on top of hers. "Don't act out of fear," she said.

Elise sat with that a minute and finally understood she had been acting out of fear of losing Mira all summer—that was what had gotten her into this predicament.

"I'm trying not to," Elise said, looking to Fern for backup. "That's why I want to make this call. There's something I didn't tell you. Either of you. Brian Correia stopped by the house last month. Someone reported the baby. He believed me when I explained that we were in the process of adopting. But I realize now that I should have told him the truth."

Amelia patted her hand. "A little more time," she said.

Fern nodded her agreement.

Elise had never felt more afraid.

Chapter Forty-Five

Olivia sat at the Barroses' kitchen table dicing up dried seaweed for the genmaicha-and-kelp blend while Marco took a meeting on the East End. The morning was turning into afternoon, and she was eager to finish before Lidia showed up. She had been avoiding spending time with Jaci and her mother ever since discovering the note.

"You're still here, love? I would have helped with all this if I'd known Marco was going to be gone so long," Lidia said, breezing into the room. "I'm starting lunch. Don't run off without eating."

"Lunch sounds great," Olivia said. What else *could* she say?

"Ma, what are you making?" Jaci said, wandering in. She wore the Long Point T-shirt Olivia had borrowed the day she discovered the note. Was this some sort of sign from the universe? Should she be the one to put an end to this? Two weeks had passed since she'd confronted her mother about telling the Barros family the truth; clearly, Ruth had no intention of setting things right. And Olivia could not be more furious about it.

"Bifana," Lidia said.

"That's so heavy," Jaci said. "Is there any salad stuff here?"

"You're not worried about your weight, are you? I swear you've lost ten pounds this summer." Lidia was right: Jaci had lost weight since she first met her. Baby weight, she now realized.

"What's *bifana?*" Olivia asked.

"It's like a steak sandwich but with pork," Lidia said. "I just picked up some fresh bread from Connie's."

The three of them sat outside on the porch with the sandwiches and two pitchers of iced tea, one black peach, one green with kelp. Jaci reached for the peach.

"I'm sorry, but I can't drink that seaweed stuff. Marco is out of his mind," Jaci said.

"It's definitely an acquired taste," said Lidia, smiling at her. "But I'm working on it. I'd do anything for you kids, even start drinking seaweed."

"You're nuts."

"When you're a mother, you'll see," Lidia said.

Olivia chewed without tasting her food.

"It's not too spicy, is it?" Lidia said.

Olivia shook her head, reaching for her own glass of iced tea. "It's great."

Her phone rang. She'd forgotten she'd even brought her phone that afternoon. So often, lately, she forgot about it. A glance at the screen told her the incoming call was from…Dakota? "Excuse me for a minute," she said to Lidia. She took the deck stairs down to the street level for privacy.

"I'm so glad you finally answered," Dakota said.

"What do you mean, finally?"

"I've left you two messages."

It was jarring to hear Dakota's voice in the middle of her new life. Lately, it had been hard for her to remember why she'd been so invested

in HotFeed. But Dakota's chatter brought it all back in a rush: her aspi-
rations, her sense of control, her independence.

"So the bottom line is, I'm leaving HotFeed," Dakota said. "I'm taking five accounts with me, and I want you to come on board as my
partner."

"Wait—*what?*" This was unbelievable. Two months ago, she had
been the one planning to leave, to steal accounts, to bring Dakota along
for the ride. How had her twenty-three-year-old assistant managed to
pull off what she had not?

"Unless... you're not already starting your own thing, are you? I
mean, I would have heard about that, right?"

"No, no... I haven't started my own thing." Olivia looked straight
ahead at the boats bobbing on the water.

"Can you meet for drinks tonight?"

Drinks tonight. In New York. She pictured the view from Rooftop
93 and the after-work crowd at Clinton Hall. "I'm out of town,"
Olivia said.

"For how long?"

Olivia turned her back to the water and closed her eyes, trying to connect with her old life. It was calling to her, literally.

"I'm not sure," she said, opening her eyes and focusing on the alley
leading from Commercial to the boatyard. The alley that Marco was,
at that very moment, crossing to reach her. "Let me call you back,"
she said.

Marco smiled at her and she forced herself to smile in return. All she
could think was that she didn't want to go back to that kitchen table, did
not want to deal with the dilemma of her unfortunate knowledge about
his sister. She didn't want to deal with her frustration with her mother.
And she didn't want to continue to live her life in this strange limbo of
suspended reality. The summer was going to end, and she would be leaving all of this behind. Any thoughts to the contrary were just a way to

avoid the messiness of her professional life. Now there was a clear path to fixing that. It was what she'd wanted all along.

"Hey, you leaving?" Marco said. He was holding a shopping bag. He'd been at a meeting, so he was dressed up, by his standards, in jeans and a button-down shirt. And yet when she tried to transpose the image in front of her to the streets of Manhattan, she could not.

"I was having lunch with your mother and sister but I came down here to take a phone call."

"Everything okay?" he said.

She nodded, but the expression of concern on his face made it clear he knew she was distressed.

"It was my former assistant. She's starting her own company and she asked me to be a partner."

"In New York?"

"Yeah. Of course."

Marco reached for her phone, took it from her hand. "Don't run off so fast," he said. He smiled, but his tone was serious.

"I'm not running off. I mean, at some point I have to get back to my life."

His dark eyes were as intense and focused as she'd ever seen them, and his jaw was set in that serious way of his, the way that made her want to lean forward and put her head on his shoulder and hold him tight.

"If New York is your life, then what has this been?" He was no longer smiling.

"Marco, come on. You said yourself you don't get involved with summer people."

His expression changed so fast, it was like a switch had been flipped. With a nod, he said, "You're right. I'm sorry. I don't even know where that came from." He handed her the shopping bag.

"What's this?"

"Your Carnival costume. No pressure, but for what it's worth, I hope you stick around long enough to wear it."

Carnival. It was three weeks away. An awfully long time to carry the secret.

Herring Cove Beach offered a perfect view of Long Point.

At the beginning of the summer, Ruth had been walking along the edge of the ocean when, out of nowhere, she heard the old song "Last Dance," by Donna Summer. She looked around to find the source of the music and saw a tanned man wearing a lime-green Speedo, a scarf around his neck, and nothing else; on his left shoulder he carried one of those boom boxes that she hadn't seen in ages. Standing in that sun-dappled spot, hearing that song and breathing that salt air, transported her to the summer of 1978. She felt the freedom, the excitement, the sense that everything and anything was possible. It hadn't just been her youth; it was the energy of the town—artistic, wild, unpredictable.

It was falling in love with Ben.

When the man passed her by, the music was swallowed by the roar of the ocean, and she was almost shocked to find herself standing alone, a fifty-eight-year-old woman with more of her life behind her than ahead of her.

Today, her mind was planted firmly in the present. Although, the way things were going, that was no picnic either.

So when she spotted Ben a few yards away, she almost thought she was seeing things. She dropped her beach blanket and bag on a stretch of dry sand, adjusted her straw sun hat, and walked over to where he sat facing the water in a folding beach chair. He wore a Philadelphia Eagles baseball cap and was absorbed in a book.

Ruth was standing close enough to his chair to touch it before he noticed her. "This is a surprise," he said.

"No class today?" she said.

"The class ended," he said, closing his book. "I thought you knew that."

She pointed back at her towel and bag. "My stuff is over there. Mind if I join you?" She didn't wait for a reply before retrieving her things and setting up right next to his spot. "So how would I know that your class ended? I've barely seen you."

"I thought Olivia might have mentioned it because I told her I'm leaving in a few days. And she might be leaving soon too."

Ruth felt her spirits plummet; it was like a physical pain. "She didn't mention it. So…you're both leaving. I thought maybe she'd spend the rest of the summer, since she's been having such a nice time with Marco."

"Well, you know about the job offer? Her former assistant wants to partner with her to start their own company. Olivia sees it as the obvious next move."

Ruth nodded noncommittally, not wanting to admit that Olivia had not spoken to her in weeks. July was quickly becoming August and their relationship was worse than when the summer began.

Ben turned his chair around to face her more directly. "Is something going on with you two? She's barely been at the house and I suggested she invite you to dinner with us the other night and she said no."

He wanted her to go to dinner with them? And Olivia had said no? Oh, the news was such a double-edged sword. "We're having a disagreement about something. We'll work it out," she said. And then, to change the subject: "So how was the writing class overall? Worth the extra time out here?"

"I owe you a thank-you for pushing me to do it."

Ruth beamed. "Does this mean you're ready to embark on your second career as a playwright?"

"Actually, it confirmed that I was smart to go to medical school."

"Oh, Ben. I'm sure that's not true. I read your work all those years ago. It was good!"

He smiled warmly at her. "Ruth, I'm content with my life. And I hope you are too. I really do."

A seagull wandered close, nearly stepping on her blanket. Ruth started to say that yes, she was content with her life, of course she was.

"I'm not," she said. "I think we made a big mistake eighteen years ago with the divorce." Looking up at him, the sun in her eyes, she couldn't read his expression.

"Ruth," he said, shaking his head slowly.

"We were both so busy and tired and stressed out. I was spending too much time at work, yes, I'll admit it. But we made a decision based on the misconception that it would always be that way. The way we felt that year or two—it would have passed. It has passed. Look at us now."

"Yes, we've managed to find our way to a friendship. I'm very happy about that. But it doesn't mean we should have been married for the past decade and a half."

"I still have feelings for you," she said.

"Oh, Ruth."

"You don't feel anything?" Decades ago, years ago, she could never have asked such a thing. Her pride would have come first. But she was the older, wiser version of herself. Age did not have many upsides, but maybe, just maybe, wisdom and a little more courage were two of them.

"Ruth, I care about you. I do. But as my co-parent. And as *your* co-parent, I'm asking that you focus your energy on fixing whatever is going on between you and Olivia."

Chapter Forty-Six

Carnival day dawned bright and hot, perfect parade weather. The theme: Mardi Gras by the Sea. Commercial Street was transformed into a wonderland; everywhere you looked, you were met with a flash of tulle, glitter, or feathers. The costumes created a riot of color, and the town was packed end to end with revelers young and old, native and tourist, gay and straight. Perched on the porch steps of Tea by the Sea, Elise and Fern had a front-row seat. They'd draped a big banner in front of the store that read HAPPY FORTIETH CARNIVAL! and handed out free iced tea to the people on the floats.

An hour after the parade ended, the costumes kept coming. A troupe of men dressed in Café Du Monde T-shirts, Speedos, and yellow knee-high socks glided past on roller skates. Behind them were two old women in long black dresses holding black parasols above their heads; their faces were covered in heavy stage makeup, and ropes and ropes of Mardi Gras beads hung around their necks. The beads were everywhere, in fact; even dogs on leashes were sporting a necklace or two.

A small group of police walked by, the only people not in costume.

Brian Correia spotted the two of them and waved. Elise glanced at Fern but saw no indication of discomfort or concern on her face. *Don't worry about anything today,* Elise told herself. *It's a celebration.*

Fern, holding Mira, noticed the baby's eyes fluttering closed and gently placed her in the car seat resting between them.

"All the excitement has her tuckered out," Fern said, smiling tenderly at the infant.

When the parade began, Mira had been alert and excited, kicking up her legs and waving her arms at the sound of the music. In the past few weeks she had become markedly, adorably more interested in the world around her.

Two women strolled past arm in arm, each one in a red bedazzled bikini top, red fishnet stockings anchored with a bedazzled belt, a long red train, and red platform heels. Their heads were topped with lobster hats, their hands covered in claw gloves.

"Wow. I'm loving the lobster costumes. Maybe we should have done that instead?" Fern said. They would be dressed as mermaids for Amelia's party tonight, wearing matching green sequined tube tops and tails Elise had ordered online that fit over their shorts and had an opening at the bottom to facilitate walking. Elise had also made matching green-sequined eye masks and found a mermaid onesie for Mira to wear to the party.

"She's really out," Elise said, adjusting the hood of the car seat. "Do you want to bring her in for a nap and, I don't know, hang out, just the two of us?"

Although she and Fern seemed to be back on track since the holiday last month, they still didn't have enough time alone together. Elise felt Fern's affection; she felt they were in sync and, for the first time in a long time, really working toward the same thing on all fronts, yet their physical intimacy had dropped off. This time, it was not Elise's doing. Fern fell asleep as soon as they climbed into bed every night.

Fern smiled at her, stood up, and brushed off a purple feather that clung to her sundress. Her Mardi Gras beads clinked together. "I'm actually going to head up to catch a quick nap. Need to get my second wind for the party tonight." She kissed Elise on the forehead and walked inside. Elise looked after her, worry settling in the pit of her stomach, and a voice in her head telling her something was off—a voice that could not be drowned out even by the celebratory noise surrounding her.

Ruth was not a big costume person.

Even when Olivia was little and Ruth had been expected to dress up in a festive Halloween costume, she'd phoned it in with a simple witch hat or devil horns. So when Amelia's Carnival invitation arrived at Shell Haven with *No costume, no entry* at the bottom, she hesitated to accept.

"I might sit this one out," she'd said to Ben, using a Tea by the Sea magnet to stick the invite on the Shell Haven refrigerator.

"Oh, no, you won't," Ben said. "If I'm going, you're going."

"Why are *you* going?" Ruth said, already bristling; she assumed it was because of Bianca.

"Olivia insisted I make it my last hurrah. So if I'm roped into this thing, you're going too."

Ruth pondered her costume options for days, searching online for inspiration. Since the theme was Mardi Gras by the Sea, she decided to focus on the "sea" aspect of the event and ordered a 1940s-style double-breasted sailor dress. It was navy blue with big white buttons, a white hem, and a flared skirt. She topped it off with a white sailor hat. By the time the party rolled around, after seeing how everyone in town went all out for the parade, she felt silly for ever having balked at the idea of a costume. Ben had also opted for a nautical-themed costume: he was dressed as a pirate.

Nearly every storefront that day posted a sign or banner recognizing the fortieth anniversary of Carnival; Ruth calculated that her first

summer in town had marked the debut of the festival. How full circle, how impossible to consider a coincidence. She would embrace
Carnival, she would get into the spirit. She felt certain it would somehow be a momentous night. Life had drawn her back here, and for
one final night, her family would be together. She had to make the
most of it.

The door of the Beach Rose Inn was marked with a fleur-de-lis and
an elaborate wreath of gold tulle. Inside, Molly rested by the ottoman,
a purple, green, and gold scarf around her neck. Rachel greeted guests
and handed out masks and instructed everyone to head outside to the
backyard.

The house was festooned with streamers, balloons, and hundreds
upon hundreds of beads hanging from the ceiling, the stairs, and the
doorways. Out back, jazz music played over the sound system. Ruth was
on the early side but there were already a few dozen guests mingling
against the backdrop of the bay, the water shimmering in the light of the
early-evening sun.

With all the guests in costumes and masks, it took some work to recognize people. She spotted Elise and Fern in mermaid costumes—hard
to miss with the baby stroller next to them.

Ruth's stomach tightened. Every time she saw Mira, she felt the clock
ticking on her decision to keep silent. Ben had been right when he'd
told her that her priority had to be mending the rift with Olivia. She'd
been honoring Amelia's wishes—and Jaci's secret—long enough. Still,
Jaci needed to be the one to tell her own truth. Ruth had been thinking
and thinking about how to make this easier for her.

"Ruth!" Lidia Barros waved to her. She wore a starfish-pattern dress
with a foam starfish hat and starfish glasses. "I feel like I haven't seen
you in weeks."

Yes, that's because I've been avoiding you. "I know, I know—I've been
busy."

"I love the hand lotion and the lavender oil. You're amazing. You should be selling this stuff."

Ruth nodded, distracted, and looked around for Olivia. "Have you seen Olivia?" she asked Lidia.

"Yes—she's over there with Marco. The two of them are joined at the hip, as usual." She leaned toward Ruth and winked conspiratorially. "I could not be more thrilled."

Ruth smiled. "I feel the same way. I just need to talk to her for one minute. I'll be right back."

"Ruth! How adorable. I love your *ensemble*." Amelia, wearing a foam costume that seemed to be some sort of square pastry—a beignet?— intercepted her midway across the sand. How fitting that Amelia was dressed as a comfort food. She was such a comfort to them all.

"Thank you," Ruth said, feeling a rush of affection for the woman. It was Amelia, after all, who had given her the ultimate piece of wisdom that summer, the first day at her mosaic class on the beach: *You can take something broken and turn it into something whole.*

Amelia might not approve of the conversation Ruth was about to have with her daughter. And yet, Ruth knew that if Amelia were in her position, she would do the same thing. Amelia was a mother, a grand-mother, and a great-grandmother.

Ultimately, Amelia would understand.

Ruth kept moving, passing two men dressed in pink shorts and pink T-shirts holding clear parasols with big googly eyes in front and rib-bons hanging around the edges. It took her a moment to realize it was Clifford and Santiago costumed as jellyfish.

"Ruth Cooperman!" Clifford called, waving her over.

"I almost didn't recognize you," she said.

"Then we've done a good job," Santiago said, lowering his parasol. "I just don't think we factored in what a hassle it would be to carry these all night."

"Everyone suffers for their art," Clifford said. "Now, Ruth, I know it's a party and I shouldn't be doing business but…" He reached into his shorts pocket, took out a set of keys, and handed them to her.

"What's this?" she said.

"The keys to Blue Stone. Congratulations!"

Ruth looked at the keys for a moment before slipping them into her purse. She knew they had closed on the house, but it still felt unreal. "Thanks, Clifford," she said.

"Thank *you*. I have to say, Ruth, that you were a bit of a handful when we first met. But now it feels like you've always been here, like it was meant to be. Don't you think?"

She smiled. "I do, Clifford."

How easy it would be to just talk amiably with Clifford and Santiago, to ignore the serious conversation she had to have in favor of the playful one she was engaged in. But she couldn't.

"Can you excuse me for a minute? I have to talk to my daughter."

"Go forth and mingle," Clifford said, then headed off to the buffet table.

Ruth looked ahead, trying to locate Olivia in the growing crowd near the bar. She saw her standing near the far end of the backyard, where the short stretch of grass gave way to sand. The bar had been set up in this waterfront section, and the guests migrated toward it. Olivia was deep in conversation with Marco, who was dressed as some sort of nautical king. Poseidon? He held a three-pronged trident in one hand.

They were eye-locked with each other, engaged in the type of intimacy that made it clear they were a party unto themselves. Ruth walked toward them. *Here it goes,* she thought.

This was the right thing to do. It was a conversation she had to have. It had seemed, when she awoke in the middle of the night, so obvious. At four in the morning, still foggy and operating on dream logic, she had complete faith in her idea to set things right. Now, in the bright light of reality, she wasn't so sure. Still, even one more day of inaction was unthinkable.

Olivia noticed her approach but pretended she didn't. Marco was the one who greeted her, welcoming her into their tight twosome.

"Poseidon?" Ruth said to him.

"Yes, you got it," he said. "Love the sailor dress."

"Thanks. And Olivia, you make a beautiful…" What was she dressed as? Her long hair hung loose, and she wore a sea-green gown with a fitted bodice and a full skirt that was decorated with what appeared to be real seashells. She carried the same trident as Marco. "Mermaid?"

"I'm Amphitrite," Olivia said.

Amphitrite. The name of the boat on which she had lost her virginity to Ben.

It was suddenly so hot. Ruth swayed, just enough to catch Marco's attention. He reached for her arm. "Are you okay?"

"Fine, fine," she said, trying to collect herself, to focus on the task at hand. "Marco, I need to borrow Olivia for a few minutes."

Olivia protested, made some excuse about how they were just about to go inside to the buffet, but Marco offered to check out the spread and bring her some hors d'oeuvres.

When they were alone, Olivia turned to her in a huff. "What is it, Mother?"

Chapter Forty-Seven

Ruth led Olivia away from the bar to the opposite end of the sandy stretch, closer to the water.

"I know you've been upset with me for keeping Jaci's secret. And I know it can't go on, but *she* needs to be the one to break the news—not me, not you, not Amelia."

"Amelia? She knows about this?"

Oops. "Never mind. The point is, Jaci needs to see that there's a good alternative to the choice she made. She doesn't want to jeopardize her college education and future career, but she also doesn't want to burden her retirement-age parents with a baby, forcing them to start over."

"It's Lidia's granddaughter. I don't believe she'd see it as a burden."

"Not emotionally, no. But there are practical issues. There are things you can't understand if you've never been a mother."

Olivia crossed her arms. Her eyelashes were thick with blue mascara, her eyebrows lined with turquoise sequins. It was distracting to have such a serious conversation dressed as a 1940s sailor girl talking to a mythological queen. And yet she had the feeling many an important conversation had occurred in Provincetown under even more outlandish circumstances. Wasn't this in part why she'd fallen in love with the place? The sense that anything can happen, that anything goes?

Hadn't she returned to recapture that very feeling?

"What's your point, Mother?" Olivia asked.

Ruth shrugged. "Well, you're here, and you're involved with Jaci's brother. The two of you could help out..."

"Mother, I'm sorry. This is some absurd fantasy of yours, some idealized life you think I should be living. You've asked me to understand and respect the choices you made, and you need to respect my plans."

"What plans?"

"I have a job opportunity in the city, a chance to start my own company—just like you."

An alarm sounded deep inside Ruth. She reached out and touched Olivia's arm. "Don't let your life revolve around work, around a company. Not even if it's your own."

"Isn't that ironic advice, coming from you?"

"It's not irony. Olivia, until this summer, I thought that getting married too young was my mistake. Now I realize my mistake was putting so much time into my career. I can't do things over. But you can do things differently."

Olivia's expression softened. Nothing was said for a moment. Ruth, if she was being honest with herself, wanted to hear something from Olivia, some sort of absolution. Something like *It's okay. I know you did the best you could.* Short of that, she would settle for Olivia not dismissing her advice out of hand.

Across the yard, they saw Marco making his way to them carrying two paper plates. He dodged would-be conversationalists as he cut a clear path to Olivia, his eyes completely focused on her.

Ruth turned back to Olivia. "That man's in love with you," she said.

"That's more important than any career. Please, at least think about what I'm saying."

Cynthia Wesson wore the most elaborate costume of the evening, a purple corset top and a floor-length peacock-feather skirt. Her mask extended half a foot above her head with feathers and draped below her chin with beads. Elise recognized her only because of her height, especially in her purple platform heels.

She was also notable because she was accompanied by the only person at the party who wore no costume—not even an eye mask. He was an older gentleman with a bald head wearing a bow tie and linen pants.

Cynthia waved at Elise and threaded her way through the crowd toward her, her bow-tied guest close behind. Elise shifted Mira in her arms, wiping perspiration from the baby's brow and wondering if she'd be cooler resting in the stroller instead of pressed against Elise's body. Maybe she should take her inside.

"Elise, I'm so glad you're here. I stopped by the shop earlier, but you'd already closed for the day. I want you to meet my dad, Mitt Wesson."

Elise stopped fussing with Mira, virtually freezing in the presence of the adoption attorney. She'd thought many times over the past few weeks of reaching out to him, hesitating only because of Fern's odd change of attitude. Elise had told herself that she would know when the time was right. And now here he was, right in front of her. "A pleasure to meet you, Mr. Wesson. Your daughter has been a big help to us this summer."

"The pleasure is all mine, Ms. Douglas," he boomed with a Southern drawl. Elise remembered now that Cynthia said he was from Georgia. *It's that do-gooder Southern stock.*

"And who is this pretty little lady?" he said, peering at Mira.

"This is Mira," Elise said. "Actually, I know this isn't the best time

or place, but Cynthia told me about your work and I have some professional questions for you. Maybe I could make an appointment for
sometime next week?"

"You looking to adopt?" he said.

Elise swallowed hard, nodding.

"I'd be happy to talk to you."

"My circumstances are a little out of the ordinary," she said.

"Young lady, if there's one thing I've learned in forty years of practice,
there's no such thing as ordinary." He pulled out his wallet and handed
her a business card.

Elise slipped it into her diaper bag, her hand shaking ever so slightly.
She had taken the first step toward truly making Mira her own.

The buffet table stretched the length of the Beach Rose Inn's front
room. Ruth remembered that on her first bumpy afternoon of the summer, Clifford had declared Amelia the best cook in town. Tonight, she
had expanded her typical Portuguese culinary repertoire to include
Cajun staples like jambalaya, po'boy sandwiches, and gumbo, and from
what Ruth had managed to sample, all were delicious.

Ruth sat on the round central ottoman with her po'boy in one hand
and the cocktail Luke had whipped up for her in the other. It was a
bright red classic Hurricane—fruit juice and two types of rum. She'd
taken just a few sips and it had already gone to her head.

"They should issue a warning with those," Ben said, sitting next to
her with a bowl of gumbo.

"I just realized that." She set the drink down on the floor. There was
enough going on without her getting drunk on top of it. "I should actually put this someplace where it won't get kicked over. Can you hold this
for a second?" She handed him her sandwich, got up, and put her drink
down on a table. When she turned back to the ottoman, Ben was gone.

"I'm here," he said, standing beside her.

From across the room, she saw Bianca glaring at them. "Let's go back outside. It's too crowded," Ruth said.

"Good idea." He handed her the plate with her sandwich and they walked through a beaded curtain toward the back door. There was a logjam of people. When they finally made it outside, Ruth walked to the far side of the yard, looking for a quiet spot. Ben followed her.

"I saw you talking to Olivia earlier," he said. "That's a positive development."

She looked around the crowd for Olivia. At first, she didn't see her anywhere. Then, at the farthest edges of the party, she spied her talking to someone: Jaci Barros.

Could she possibly be taking her advice already?

"Ben, you should know I told Olivia to stay here, not to go back to New York to start that company."

He didn't seem pleased with her announcement. "Ruth, it's understandable that you want to make up for lost time, but the summer can't last forever."

"It has nothing to do with the summer or wanting to spend more time with her. I believe she should give her relationship with Marco a chance. I told her that if I could do it all over again, I'd do it differently."

"Ruth, that's not true," Ben said.

"It is," she said, her voice breaking. "It is true."

They stared at each other for a long moment.

"Do you remember," Ben said, "the night about a year ago when we ran into each other at Scarpetta?"

She nodded, not trusting herself to speak. She'd been lukewarm on her date to begin with, but after seeing Ben it was all over.

"I couldn't stop thinking about you the rest of the night," he said. "I was with a perfectly nice woman, and in that moment, I realized I would never feel about her the way I'd felt about you, so what was the point?"

Ruth's heart began to beat fast. "Why didn't you tell me?" she whispered.

"Why would I?" he said.

"Because maybe I was feeling that exact same way that night."

It had been a mistake to walk away from the marriage.

"Ruth," he said. "You divorced me. I'm no longer angry about that. But at the same time, I don't live in the past. What's done is done."

She stepped forward and, under the setting Provincetown sun, reached her arms around his neck and kissed him. He kissed her back, and for a moment, it was the summer of 1978 and they were on a boat anchored just off Long Point. And then he pulled away.

"What was that?" he said.

"That was history repeating itself," she said.

Chapter Forty-Eight

It felt very important to Elise that Fern meet Cynthia's father tonight, at the party. It would be a seamless, informal way to move this whole process forward. Whatever Fern was waiting for, whatever change of heart had created the dramatic shift in strategy and timeline, Elise was hitting the reset button.

The problem was that she couldn't find Fern anywhere. She walked inside, checked the crowd lingering around the buffet table, and then back to the sandy stretch near the bar. It was hard to maneuver the stroller in the crowded spaces.

Lidia Barros peeked under the hood. "What a face on that child," Lidia said. "Like an angel. And all that dark hair. Jaci was the same way."

"I should just park her upstairs for a while to sleep but I won't hear her if she wakes up," Elise said.

"I'll help you keep an eye on her," Lidia said.

Elise was distracted by the abrupt cessation of the jazz music that had played throughout the evening. She turned to the sound of loud clanging. "Oh, what is my crazy sister-in-law up to now?" Lidia muttered.

Bianca Barros stood on the picnic table, a dark vision in a black waistcoat dress, a top hat, and her face painted with a black, red, and white sugar skull. She was more Day of the Dead than Mardi Gras, but that probably surprised no one. She banged a metal utensil against a glass.

"Attention, everyone—I'd like to make a toast," she said. "This is my fortieth Carnival, and some of you have been here since that first auspicious celebration, a Day in Rio. There have been many inspiring themes over the years. I think a lot of us remember Broadway Musicals, Heroes and Villains—"

"Peace, Love, and Go-Go Boots!" someone shouted.

Bianca nodded. "But I think this year tops them all—Mardi Gras by the Sea. Mardi Gras, as I learned in researching costumes, is also known as Shrove Tuesday, and *shrove* means 'confess.' Confess! What a fitting notion for the end of the summer—especially this summer."

Was Elise imagining things or was Bianca directing her kohl-rimmed, spooky-eyed gaze straight at her?

"In the spirit of unmasking, I'd like to invite confessions right here, right now, tonight. Any volunteers?" The crowd broke into a murmur. A few people clapped. Encouraged, Bianca walked to the edge of the picnic table. She pointed her finger, and now Elise knew she was not imagining it. Bianca was pointing at her.

"Elise Douglas, why don't you come up here and tell us where your mystery baby came from. Please—share the news! You're so open with your house; surely you can be open with the truth about the new addition to our community."

This could not be happening. Elise's first impulse was to run, to get the hell out of there. But she was boxed in by the crowd that had moved together more densely to hear Bianca's toast. There was no way she could flee with the stroller. She looked around for Fern, panic rising in her chest.

Amelia made her way to the table, looked up at Bianca, and shouted, "That's enough!"

"I'm just asking a simple question," Bianca said from her elevated perch. "Who's the mother?"

Elise knew Amelia would put a stop to this if she could. But at her advanced age, she couldn't climb up on the table. Someone needed to drag Bianca down from there.

"This is outrageous." Lidia Barros appeared beside Elise and put her arm around her. "I'm so sorry."

Elise couldn't speak. Where was Fern? She craned her neck and saw Jaci breaking through the crowd, heading for the table. Fern was just a few feet behind her, but she turned and moved toward Elise. "See—Jaci is going to put a stop to this," Lidia said, then she cupped her hands around her mouth and yelled, "Get her down from there, Jaci!"

Jaci climbed up on the table, almost tripping over her costume. Marco and Manny were not far behind, and they each took one of Bianca's arms to usher her off the table.

"This can't be happening," Elise said to Fern.

"I need to talk to you," Fern said. "Let's go inside."

Bianca had been removed but Jaci remained on the tabletop. The music resumed, but she yelled for Amelia to turn it off. She removed her wig and her mask and tossed them aside while every guest stood still and hushed, aware that the show was not yet over.

"My aunt Bianca is right," Jaci said. "It is time to confess, and since everyone is here, I can do this once instead of a dozen times over. You can hear it from me: I'm the mother of the baby."

Lidia let out a shriek. Fern reached for Elise.

Elise felt the earth disappear from under her.

Chapter Forty-Nine

Olivia woke up to an empty bed.

She checked the time; it was eight in the morning. That meant she'd gotten about five hours of sleep. Even that slumber had been broken; she'd woken up intermittently due to Marco's tossing and turning. They'd both had too much to drink.

After the spectacle at Amelia's party, the entire Barros family dispersed. Lidia and Manny ushered Jaci home while Marco fled to Old Colony Tap. Olivia followed him to the bar, trying to talk to him, but he said he needed a few shots of vodka first.

By one in the morning, they were huddled in a booth at Spiritus Pizza, and still he didn't want to deal with Jaci's bombshell. Actually, Olivia was in no rush to push the issue. Any in-depth discussion would require her to admit she'd known the truth for weeks. She couldn't have a lie between them.

But now it was a new day, a new reality. Olivia pulled on sweatpants, Marco's Long Point hoodie, and a pair of flip-flops. She headed out back, where she found him sitting on the deck with a cup of takeout coffee.

"Hey," she said. "You went *out* for coffee?"

"I didn't want to wake you," he said, reaching down for another cup by his feet. He handed it to her. "It might be cold by now."

"How long have you been awake?"

"A couple of hours," he said, gesturing for her to grab one of the other chairs. She pulled it up next to him. "You feeling okay?"

"I really should know better than to try to keep up with you at a bar," she said.

"Sorry about that," he said. "That was a lot even for me."

"It's understandable." She reached for his hand.

"I just can't believe Jaci would get herself into this situation and then handle it in such an outrageous way." He shook his head. "I'm shocked. I'm just...really disappointed in her."

"Oh, Marco. She's still a kid. And this whole thing with Elise and Fern...I think she meant well."

"She made such a big deal about not wanting to work on the oyster farm and about wanting a career. She was the first woman in our family to go to college. Did you know that? Princeton, no less. And now what?"

Olivia took a deep breath. "Now she goes back to school, like she planned."

"With a baby?"

Olivia shook her head. "Not necessarily."

"Yeah, right. The only way around that is if my parents—who have already worked so hard and should be slowing down—step in to take care of an infant full-time. It's not fair."

"Or..." Olivia said. This was it, the point of no return. "Or I could stay in town for a while and help you take care of Mira."

He took off his sunglasses.

"Olivia," he finally said. "That's a really generous thought. A really selfless offer. But I don't know if it's realistic, given, well, given how little time we've actually had together. The last we spoke about things, you were seriously considering heading back to New York to start that company. I don't think you could have changed your mind so drastically overnight."

"I didn't change my mind overnight," she said. "I've been caught between my feelings for you and my belief that my real life is in New York City. If I have to pick one over the other...I'm saying I pick you."

Marco stood up and pulled her into his arms. Holding her tight, he said, "I love you. I do. But we can't make a major decision based on my sister's crisis." He stepped back, took both of her hands in his. Looking into her eyes, he said, "I think we need to sit with this for a few days."

Olivia nodded, not trusting herself to speak. She knew that everything he was saying was reasonable. And that maybe she had been overly influenced by her mother's impassioned speech last night and the dramatic events that followed it. Still, it felt like a rejection.

It felt like he was saying goodbye.

Elise could not go to sleep. Sleeping meant time away from Mira. Time, she now knew, that was borrowed. Had been borrowed from the very beginning.

She sat awake until dawn in the office that would never truly be transformed into a nursery. She watched Mira curled up in her bassinet, fed her a bottle at three in the morning, and held her in her arms long after Mira had fallen back to sleep.

In her mind, she replayed the events of the past few months. It was like a foreign film that suddenly had subtitles. Jaci had had an unwanted baby and she knew Elise had been trying desperately to get pregnant, so in her childish logic, this solved everyone's problem.

It explained her interest in hanging around the house all the time, her offers to babysit, and her insistence that she didn't want to spend her days out on the water. Jaci might not have been ready to be a mother, but she felt a mother's pull toward her infant.

Was there any way Elise could have seen this? Had she been willfully blind to the reality? She didn't think so. She remembered the day she thought Cynthia might be the mother. But it had never crossed her mind that Jaci Barros—Jaci, whom she'd known since she was in middle school—would be in that predicament.

In the end, what difference did it make? Once again, she was losing her chance at motherhood.

"Elise," Fern said from the office doorway. "Don't cry. Don't do this to yourself."

Fern was dressed in a lavender tunic, her hair already done. What time was it?

She pried Mira from Elise's arms, returned her to the bassinet, and knelt in front of the rocking chair. "It's going to be okay."

Elise sobbed, covering her face with her hands. "It's not," she said.

"I know it seems like it won't," said Fern. "But trust me—it will. You need to hold it together."

The doorbell rang. Neither one of them was expecting anyone.

"I'll get it," Fern said. "Will you be okay here for a few minutes by yourself?"

Elise was relieved to have the privacy. She didn't want to "hold it together." She was done holding it together. This was the final loss, the one from which she would never recover.

She heard Fern talking to someone, a female. She probably could have figured out who it was if she'd opened the office door and listened, but she didn't bother. She didn't care.

Mira let out a small sigh. Elise stood and peered into the bassinet, watched her hand find its way to her mouth. She'd been sucking her thumb lately, a new development. Mira would change so much in the next few weeks and months, and Elise wouldn't witness it.

A knock on the office door.

"Elise, we have a visitor," Fern said from the hallway. A visitor? Why on earth would Fern let someone come inside at a time like this? Elise pulled her robe more tightly closed and opened the door.

Lidia Barros.

Of course Lidia would come over. Lidia, Mira's grandmother.

Elise felt a surge of anger, then reminded herself Lidia had not asked for this to happen. She was just as much a victim of circumstance as Elise. Still, Lidia would leave with Mira. She had a new granddaughter, and once again, Elise's arms would be empty.

"I don't mean to intrude," Lidia said, stepping into the room. Fern followed behind her.

"Of course. I...we should have called you this morning. I'm sorry," Elise said, looking at Fern, who nodded.

Lidia shook her head. "I actually came by to apologize. Jaci explained to me what she did and why, and although it might have been well intentioned, I can't imagine the pain it must be causing you. So there's no rush to bring Mira to our house."

And yet, her eyes darted to the bassinet.

Elise stood there, woozy from sleep deprivation. Her eyes, bleary from crying, could barely focus. She walked over to the bassinet and found Mira awake and staring at the mobile they'd recently installed. Elise picked her up and cradled her against her shoulder. She stood still for a minute, her eyes closed, cementing the moment in her mind for all time.

She turned to Lidia and handed Mira to her. Lidia, surprised, took the baby with a reflexive ease.

Mira looked up at Lidia and smiled, the smile that had been so rare that Fourth of July weekend but that now delighted everyone who came in contact with her.

Elise turned away from grandmother and grandchild, choked back her sobs, and walked into Fern's waiting arms.

Chapter Fifty

The doorbell woke her. Ruth's first thought was *Who would show up at Shell Haven this early?* The second was *I'm not in my own bedroom.* The third was *My body feels different.*

It had been a very long time since she'd had sex.

She sat up, taking in the details of the third-floor room, the space she'd prepared so carefully for Olivia's arrival at the start of the summer. On the bedside table, one of the rose-and-black-currant candles she'd purchased at Good Scents and the copy of *Land's End*. And next to her, Ben.

The events of the night before came rushing back to her, the good, the bad, and the outrageous. The backyard kiss with Ben that had made her feel like the teenager on that boat forty years ago, feelings she barely had a moment to process before Bianca's theatrics and Jaci Barros's public confession. After that, there was no time to think about Ben. The place was in an uproar, and she joined Amelia and Rachel and a circle of other women who were helping Lidia deal with the news. Olivia left with a distraught Marco, and Manny Barros took it upon himself to escort Bianca out of the party.

"I have my own confession to make," Ben said later that night as they shared a bottle of wine in the Shell Haven living room. Outside, Carnival still raged. Ruth knew they would be hearing music and fireworks possibly until the sun came up. "This disaster is all my fault."

Ruth refilled his glass. "What? Tonight? I don't see how that's possible."

Ben took the bottle from her hand and set it down. His expression was miserable. "On my first day in town, Olivia told me about the baby being abandoned. I let it slip to Bianca."

"Why would you do that?"

Ben shook his head. "She had a theory that it was Olivia's. I was telling her no way, it wasn't my daughter's baby. That the baby had been left on the porch."

"Bianca knew the baby wasn't Olivia's! The baby appeared before Olivia got to town. Bianca was just trying to push your buttons. She was fishing. And she got what she wanted."

"I'm sorry."

Ruth couldn't find it in herself to be angry at him when there was so much blame to go around. "Still, that doesn't explain how she knew Mira belonged to Jaci."

"If you have one piece of the puzzle, it's probably not that hard to put the rest together. I mean, the baby does look like their family. And you figured it out, so it stands to reason that someone else might discover the truth too."

She pressed her fingers to her forehead. "I told you Bianca was a menace."

"I'm sorry," Ben said. "I feel terrible. I don't know what to do."

Ruth was suddenly exhausted. It had to be close to one in the morning. "There's nothing to do," Ruth said. "Jaci had to come forward eventually. It's out of our hands now. Let's just...keep this to ourselves."

"Can you forgive me?" he said.

She looked at him. Despite the lateness of the hour, despite all the cocktails and wine, he was focused on her with steely clarity. Were they still talking about the baby?

"Can you forgive *me?*" she said, and it came out as a whisper.

He did not answer; instead, he leaned forward and kissed her. It soon became clear they needed to take their little party of two upstairs.

"Hey," Ben said now, sitting up. His hair was slightly mussed, and without his glasses and just wearing a gray T-shirt in bed, he looked exactly the same to her as he had as a college boy.

"Hey," she said. How was it possible that so much time had passed and yet they could wake up in bed like it was forty years ago, like nothing at all had happened?

That had to mean something.

"That was some night," he said, smiling.

What if she suggested they pick up where they had left off? Or, rather, that they pick up from where they had been the most happy. Ruth had once been asked the question: If you could choose any age to be forever, what would it be? This felt similar. Did an ideal version of themselves as a couple exist, one they could try to find their way back to? Or would they have to push forward, become something new entirely? Did they have it in themselves to do that?

"Don't go back to Cherry Hill," she said.

"Ruth," he said. "You always have to push."

"Is that a bad thing?"

Ben put his arm around her, and she leaned against him. "No. It's not. But Ruth, we're too old not to be realistic. I have my life there."

"And I just bought a house here," she said quietly. Blue Stone. Her forever home. Then there was the fact that Elise and Fern were starting to sell her handmade products in the shop. She was on her way to launching a new small business—nothing on the scale of what Liv had become, but something. She would not mention this to Ben, would not remind him of the career-obsessed woman she had once been. Things were different now. At least, she wanted them to be different.

Ben tightened his arm around her. "I think we need to see the past few weeks—and last night—for what it was."

"And what's that?"

"A beautiful ending to our story."

It was beautiful, that was for sure. "It doesn't have to be an ending."

He kissed the top of her head.

"Ruth, I'll always love you. And I'm grateful we had this summer together. But let's not be irrational."

Why wasn't it rational to think that now, at an entirely different stage of their lives, they might be in a place to appreciate each other and be together again? It wasn't about rationality. He simply didn't trust her. And why should he?

He was the one who'd made sacrifices for their life together. She never had.

Somehow, she had to show him that she was capable of that.

Elise sat hunched over in their bedroom while Fern packed up Mira's clothes and bottles and diapers and brought them downstairs.

Manny came over to pick everything up, and when Elise heard the front door close and the sound of Fern's footsteps climbing the stairs, she burrowed under the covers and pulled the comforter over her head. She did not want to talk to Fern—or anyone. She didn't want to be a part of the world.

Fern sat on the edge of the bed. "Elise, I need to talk to you."

Elise shook her head, then, realizing Fern couldn't see it, let out a muffled "No."

"It's important. Just listen to what I have to say and then I'll leave you alone. I promise." Fern pulled back the covers and rubbed Elise's shoulder gently.

"I'm going to sleep," Elise said. *For the rest of the year.*

"This is sooner than I wanted to tell you about this, but everything that's happened is sort of forcing my hand." Fern paused, then said, "Amelia told me about Jaci last month."

Elise sat up. "What?"

"She figured it out."

"I don't understand. When did she tell you?"

"Remember when Amelia came to the shop and insisted I stop by the inn for a drink?"

Of course Elise remembered. And she also remembered that Fern left the next morning for Boston.

"That's when she said she was certain the baby belonged to Jaci. She wanted me to help break the news to you gently—she knew you were hoping to keep her. And I didn't want you to lose another baby, so I asked her to give me some time."

"I don't understand. Why did you keep this from me? All along, you said I was getting too emotionally invested in Mira, and then you made it worse!"

"I didn't want to make it worse. I wanted to make it better. I wanted to figure out a way to fix this so that you weren't heartbroken yet again. And so, once I realized that we would never be able to keep Mira—that she belonged to Jaci—I went to see Dr. Sparrow."

Dr. Sparrow. In Boston. Elise didn't dare breathe. "Why?"

"I had our remaining embryos implanted. Like I said, it's earlier than I wanted to tell you about it, but...we're having a baby."

Chapter Fifty-One

Low tide arrived just before six thirty a.m. The sun had barely been up for twenty minutes when Olivia and Marco climbed onto the skiff.

Their hours on the water had become a welcome respite from Marco's family drama. His father had unceremoniously kicked Bianca out of the house for publicly shaming his daughter, prompting Bianca to fly back to Florida. Manny had also not spoken a word to Jaci since the night of Carnival, but Lidia insisted he just needed time. As for Lidia, no one was surprised to see her hands-on with the baby, but Marco was not prepared to see the ongoing chill between his sister and mother.

"It's not ideal; she made some bad choices," he said to Lidia. "But it's going to be okay. She's a good kid. We'll get through this."

"What keeps me awake at night is the lying," Lidia said. "For months and months, never once confiding in me. Going through this alone. And then trying to give her baby away without even letting me have the chance to help. Is this how I raised her? It's a betrayal. There's no way around it."

Marco and Olivia took care of Mira as much as possible, trying to give Jaci and her parents breathing room to heal their relationship. And time was running out—later that day, Jaci was leaving for school.

Marco's bachelor pad was less than ideal for caring for Mira, so they ended up spending more and more nights at his parents' house.

"Sorry about this," he'd said to her just that morning. Both of them were in Lidia's kitchen getting ready for a few hours on the flats while also trying to feed Mira and get her back to sleep before they left. "I know this isn't what you signed on for."

Wasn't it, though? Wasn't it exactly what she had offered the morning after Carnival, the day he'd told her it was premature for them to undertake something so serious together?

Now, walking behind Marco through the shallow seaweed-dense water and across the sand to the cages, she noted that the morning was chillier than it had been in weeks. It was a reminder that September was right around the corner—that summer would not last forever.

For days, ever since she'd declined Dakota's offer to join her in the new company, she'd been thinking about what would come next. All she knew was that no matter what happened between her and Marco, no matter how short or long a time she remained in Provincetown, she could not devote her life to something as ephemeral and meaningless as social media. Her mother, for all her faults, had at least created products that made women feel pretty. Even now, she was making things to help people feel good. Marco spent his time harvesting food, sustaining people in the most primal way. Surely there must be something worthwhile for her to do with her life.

They sat side by side, pulled on gloves, and unlatched their cages. Olivia pushed the oysters to one side to make room for her methodical inspection of each one. She held the first up to measure it, a motion she would repeat a hundred times in the coming hour.

Picking oysters had become one of her favorite ways to spend time with Marco. Sometimes they passed the hours chatting away about everything, from her life in New York to books and movies to Marco's memories of P'town growing up; other days, they sat in comfortable silence and just focused on the task before them. That day seemed like one of their quiet sessions; Marco was deep in thought. She looked over once or twice to say something, but then, noting his look of concentration, refrained.

When he finally spoke, she was zoned out, completely in her own little world. The sound of his voice surprised her.

"What do you think of this one?" he asked, passing her an oyster. He was asking *her* advice?

"You must really be distracted today," she said, taking it from him. It was too light. It didn't feel like more than a shell.

"Just look at it," he said. "Tell me what you think."

"There's no oyster in there."

"I think you're right," he said. "But something is."

She opened the shell wider and found a large pearl. No, a pearl *ring.*

What was going on? Marco took the shell from her, removed the ring, and reached for her hand.

"Olivia, I don't know…maybe you'd prefer a diamond. But I thought something from the sea would be a more fitting way for me to ask you to become my wife."

"Your wife?"

"Olivia," he said, "will you marry me?"

And there, on that wet sandbar in the middle of nowhere, surrounded by water and kissed by the sun, she saw what her life was supposed to be.

"Yes," she said. "Yes, I'll marry you."

He slipped the ring on her finger. In her heart, she'd never be back on dry land.

* * *

Elise agreed to Ruth's suggestion that they walk over to the Barroses' together to say goodbye to Jaci.

She knew that if she and Fern had not had their precious secret, she would not have been able to face Jaci. She still missed Mira every minute of the day. She woke at night, expecting to hear her hungry cry. The emptiness felt unbearable, but at least she had hope.

She and Fern had agreed not to tell anyone else about her pregnancy. It was too early; Fern would have waited another few weeks even to tell Elise if circumstances had not forced her hand. For now, they would keep the news to themselves, praying every day for the tiny life inside Fern to thrive.

In the meantime, Elise found great strength and solace in the lengths her wife had gone to in order to make her happy. Every small chip of resentment Elise had been harboring for the past year disappeared; there was no denying or mistaking the fact that she had a truly unselfish partner. Whatever happened with their quest to become mothers, Elise vowed to herself that her new understanding of the true depth of her marriage would sustain her.

"She's upstairs in her room," Lidia told them after she greeted them at the back door. Her olive skin showed even darker circles under her eyes than usual.

"How's Mira doing?" Elise asked—could not help asking. She'd wondered if the Barroses would change her name. So far, they seemed to be sticking with Mira, so maybe Elise's small contribution to the life of that child would be an enduring one.

"She's an angel. And as you know, she's really got an appetite," Lidia said. "But to be honest, Olivia and Marco have been taking care of her the most."

Elise nodded, ignoring the tightness in her chest. Why was it still so difficult?

"Is Jaci here? We just wanted to say goodbye," Ruth said, then held up the paper shopping bag. "I brought her a little care package to start her year."

"That's so sweet. She's in her room. Go right on up."

Elise headed up; Ruth lingered to make plans with Lidia to meet for coffee. "You need to take an hour for yourself," she heard Ruth saying. Clearly, she too had noticed the exhaustion in Lidia's face.

Jaci's bedroom door was open; packed suitcases stood at the foot of her bed. She was on her phone, music playing quietly. Elise rapped on the doorframe to announce herself.

"Oh, hey," Jaci said, sitting up straight and putting down her phone. "Come in."

"I just wanted to say goodbye," Elise said, coming over to the bed.

"Please, sit," Jaci said.

Elise perched uncomfortably on the edge. "I can't stay long," she said. "And Ruth is on her way up too."

"Elise, I'm so sorry for any upset I caused. I really had this idea that it would be win-win. I didn't think it through. It was an emotional decision, not a smart one, and you got caught in the middle of it. Can you ever forgive me?" Her big dark eyes teared up. Her eyes were so much like Mira's, Elise once again wondered how she could have missed the clues. But there was no sense in going over all of that again. It was time to let it go.

In the spirit of letting go, of moving forward, Elise reached into her pocket and pulled out the tiny beaded anklet Mira had worn the day she appeared on the doorstep.

"Of course I forgive you," Elise said. "And I wanted you to have this."

Jaci held the plastic beads and closed her hand around them.

"I made this myself," Jaci said. "I wanted you to know her birthday, and I wanted you to know that she was loved."

Elise leaned forward and squeezed her hand. "I realize now all the time you spent hanging around our house, offering to babysit, wasn't just about avoiding the oyster farm."

Jaci nodded, sniffling. "It's been so much harder than I thought."

"Motherhood always is," Ruth said from the doorway.

She walked into the room and set her care package on Jaci's nightstand. Jaci sniffled again and pulled her knees up to her chest. Elise scooted over to make room for Ruth. The three of them sat in silence for a minute.

"Jaci," Ruth finally said. "I just want you to know that there's no such thing as a perfect mother. We all make mistakes, big and small, along the way."

"I can't *be* her mother," Jaci said. "That's what all of this has been about."

"Well, your feelings—and circumstances—might change in time. And take it from me, it's never too late."

It's never too late, Elise thought. *I hope that's true.*

Two floors below, Lidia let out a squeal. Ruth jumped up and ran into the hallway. "Everything okay?" she called out.

"Ruth, you need to come down here," Lidia yelled.

Ruth rushed down the stairs. Elise and Jaci looked at each other and ran down after her.

They found Marco and Olivia standing in the kitchen, covered in mud. Olivia was holding out her left hand.

"What's going on?" Ruth said.

"Mom." Olivia beamed. "We're engaged."

Chapter Fifty-Two

There was no better place to prepare the dried seaweed than Lidia's long kitchen table. Somehow, Marco's mother had found a way to accommodate their complete takeover on the days when they had to do their chopping and sorting. It had become one of Olivia's favorite parts of the workweek because, unlike when she was sitting with Marco out on the flats or working on the dock, here she could keep the baby nearby. Today, Mira amused herself with a row of rings on a new bouncer Lidia had bought her. Olivia and Marco worked in comfortable silence, the only sound the distant grind of Manny's power drill outside.

"Your phone's ringing," Marco said.

"Is it?" Only then did she hear the faint tri-tone of an incoming call. She looked around for her tote bag and retrieved the phone; her mother's face filled the screen. "Hey, we're just chopping seaweed. Can I call you back?" Olivia said.

"I'm at the new house on Nickerson," Ruth said. "I need you and Marco to stop by for a few minutes."

Oh, the house. Olivia still had not checked out the place her mother would be moving into in just a few weeks. It was amazing how her sense of time had changed now that she had a baby to care for. An errand or visit that might have been spontaneous or happen easily just weeks ago now took military-style planning.

"Okay. Maybe before dinner? Mira's dinner, I mean. So around—"

"I need you to come by now," her mother said. Olivia glanced at Marco; he was completely absorbed in the work in front of him.

"Let me talk to Marco and call you back," Olivia said. When she relayed the odd summons, Marco sighed, looked at the clock, and said, "We should just go and see what's going on. Maybe she needs help with something."

Nickerson was a two-minute walk from the house. They put Mira in the stroller and decided to just call this their lunch break.

Marco was good-humored about the interruption; now that he felt more confident about the business, it was like a weight had been lifted from his shoulders. Spindler's had just added the seaweed tea to its menu. He felt he had successfully created a category instead of just trying to compete in a market that was already competitive. It was a big step for his business.

Still, it would be a while before they could afford to move into a place of their own. Considering they'd outgrown his current living quarters, their next move was a question mark. Lidia was happy to have them under her roof, but Olivia didn't see that as a long-term solution. She'd had enough of communal living during her months at Shell Haven.

"I think my mother is just trying to distract herself from the fact that my father is leaving tonight," Olivia said.

Days after Carnival, Olivia's parents had invited her to dinner and announced they were "spending time together" again. Olivia didn't know who was more surprised by this development, herself or her father, who, frankly, seemed a little shell-shocked. Still, it had to mean something to him because he delayed his departure yet again. But tomorrow it was back to Cherry Hill. Olivia knew it was probably rough on her mother, who had acted like a googly-eyed teenager at that dinner. But a summer fling was a summer fling—even if it happened with your ex-husband.

"She'll find a way to keep busy," Marco said. "This town has a way of keeping everyone busy long after the summer ends. You'll see."

They followed the house numbers until they reached a three-story Greek Revival.

"I know this house," Marco said.

"You do?"

"Of course. How can anyone miss it? It's a beauty."

Ruth waved at them from the front porch. Olivia turned to Marco. "We'll make this quick," she said, maneuvering the stroller onto the stone walkway.

"I'm so glad you two could come," Ruth said.

"Well, Mom, it seemed very important to you. But we don't have a lot of time."

"Neither do I," Ruth said, handing her a set of keys.

"What's this for?"

Ruth spread her arms wide. "It's the keys to your new house."

Olivia looked at Marco. Marco looked at Ruth.

"I'm not sure I follow," he said.

"I bought this house but now I don't need it. But you two do. I mean, you *three*. So please—accept it as an early wedding gift."

"Mom, it's a lovely thought, but you need a place to live," Olivia said, bending over to retrieve the pacifier Mira had dropped on the ground. Honestly, sometimes her mother was just absurd. It was as if she needed melodrama to breathe.

"No, I don't," Ruth said. "I'm leaving with your father tonight."

Olivia straightened up. Her mother was beaming.

"What? So you're giving up this house?"

"That's right," Ruth said. "I'm moving back to Cherry Hill."

* * *

The light still had the ability to take Ruth's breath away even three months into the Provincetown summer.

Ruth and Ben sat on a bench at the water's edge waiting for the ferry. As daytime turned to twilight, the sky became a pale rainbow, blue to yellow to orange to pink and lavender at the horizon. She'd never seen a lavender sky before her summers in Provincetown, and it was one of the many things she would miss.

The hardest thing to leave was her new group of friends, the people gathered beside her at the edge of MacMillan Wharf to see her off: Amelia and Rachel, Elise and Fern, Clifford and Santiago, Lidia and Manny. And, of course, she was saying goodbye to her daughter. She focused on Olivia, taking in the sight of her holding Mira in her arms, Marco by her side. Ruth was leaving Olivia, but she was leaving her smiling. She was leaving her happy.

Amelia appeared beside her, touched her arm. "A little going-away present. It was supposed to be for your new house," she said. She handed Ruth a bubble-wrapped package in a brown paper bag. It was heavy.

"Oh, Amelia. You shouldn't have!" Ruth gingerly pulled at the masking tape at the edge of the bubble wrap. The gift inside was square and flat and she was able to slide it out of the wrapping.

She gasped. It was her starfish drawing, transformed into a tile-and-seashell mosaic. In the center of the starfish, the piece of blue sea glass.

Amelia leaned close and said quietly, "I told you, you can take something broken and turn it into something whole."

Ruth felt her eyes fill with tears.

She had been right to follow her instinct back to this magical place. She'd come searching for a house, looking for a place to belong. She'd believed she had nothing from the past to build on, that she was starting over. Instead, Provincetown brought her back to the beginning and showed her that the building blocks of your life didn't fall away and disappear; it was all there, still solid, waiting to be leaned on.

The ferry pulled up to the dock. Ben grabbed their bags, and they hugged everyone goodbye. Ruth tried not to cry as she boarded the boat and followed Ben to the upper deck.

"I'm going to miss it," Ruth said.

Ben put his arm around her. "Me too."

The whistle sounded. The ferry pulled away from MacMillan Wharf. Ben looked straight ahead, but Ruth turned to watch the Pilgrim Monument fade from view, holding her starfish mosaic to her chest.

Regeneration. Renewal.

I'll be back.

Acknowledgments

When I first visited Provincetown, in the spring of 2015, I didn't know a single person in town. Today, I count some of the residents of this special place among my dearest friends. How did that happen in such a relatively short time? That's the magic of Provincetown.

I met author A. C. Burch while browsing the shelves of the Provincetown Bookshop that first trip, and he has since become a wonderful friend. He's an endlessly fascinating source of Provincetown history and helped immensely with this novel. Thank you, A.C., for giving my early draft a P'town read! (Any errors are entirely my own.) When I was looking to research oyster farming, he introduced me to Lory Santos, a woman who created her own second act with her Provincetown oyster farm and company, Detail Fish. Lory, thank you for taking me out on the water, sharing your stories, and showing this city gal how to get her hands dirty. Thank you to Manny Correia and his husband, Tom Harvey, for opening their magnificent home to me so I always have a place to write. (Manny, you are a rare soul and I'm so fortunate to have you in my life.) I met Manny in East End Books...which leads me to another special person, East End Books owner Jeff Peters. Jeff, you have been an invaluable champion of my books and I appreciate every introduction, every conversation, and every impromptu dinner party. The book world is lucky to have you. Thank you to lead librarian of Provincetown Public Library, Nan Cinnater, and Deborah Karacozian of Provincetown Bookshop for your passionate support of writers and literature, including your work hosting the annual Provincetown Book Festival. This festival brought another great person into my life, Clayton Nottleman. Special thanks to Mary Alice Wells and Cass Benson for hosting me in your glorious home two years in a row.

The tea shop in this book, including the creative names of blends of tea, was inspired by Provincetown's the Captain's Daughters, founded by Meghan O'Conner and Dani Niedzielski. A big thanks to Meghan and Dani for teaching me about the intoxicating world of tea. Your shop is really special.

Thank you again to the Anchor Inn Beach House, a hotel that always feels like home and the inspiration for the Beach Rose Inn featured in both this novel and *The Forever Summer*.

Thank you to Olga Cohen of Grohen Technologies for sharing the story of her remarkable career in the cosmetics industry, and to Robert Rave for giving me insight into the world of social media management.

At Little, Brown, I have been fortunate to have the support of an excellent team, including my editor Judy Clain, Reagan Arthur, Craig Young, Terry Adams, Alexandra Hoopes, Ashley Marudas, Shannon Hennessey, and Lauren Hess. Thank you to my outstanding publicist, Maggie Southard Gladstone.

Lastly and most importantly, thank you to my agent, Adam Chromy. You make every story better.

About the Author

Jamie Brenner's previous novels include *Drawing Home, The Husband Hour, The Forever Summer,* and *The Wedding Sisters.* She lives in New York City and spends her summers visiting the beach towns that inspire her books.

Also by Jamie Brenner

The Forever Summer

"A witty and memorable tale of love lost and found, secrets hidden and revealed, and the family ties that transcend everything."
—Pam Jenoff, author of *The Lost Girls of Paris*

The Husband Hour

"An irresistible must-read about dealing with our pasts, gaining strength from our struggles, and what it really takes to move on."
—Brenda Janowitz, *PopSugar*

Drawing Home

"A captivating novel about mothers and daughters, shifting allegiances, the art world, waterfront real estate, and love. Welcome to the gold standard of summertime escapism."
—Elin Hilderbrand, author of *Golden Girl*